# The LORD of HERRINGS

Antti Hakala is a Finnish actor, comedian and writer. He lives in England.  www.anticomedy.net

Esa Hakala is a Finnish cartoonist, illustrator and game designer. www.esahakala.com

Also by them:

SVEN'S HERRING
SVEN'S BEAR
SVEN'S MOOSE

# The LORD of HERRINGS

## A.K. HAKALA

### Illustrated by E. HAKALA

ISBN 978 0 9931069 9 6

Published in 2017 by Anticomedy Ltd.

*In memory of Väinö*

## Acknowledgements

With warm thanks to Tony Leliw and Lara Eventide for their continuous support and professional input.

My gratitude to my brother, Esa, not only for illustrating the book, but also helping to edit the manuscript along the way.

And finally, to our parents, Helinä and Rauno, for letting us develop an imagination.

Chapter 1

# A BEDTIME STORY

At the age of twelve Sven lost his father, Roar, on a stormy night in the depths of Lake Pihtamo. The last time Sven saw Roar was the night before his disappearance, when he had told Sven a bedtime story about how once upon a time, way before Sven was even born, one shiny coin saved his life from the claws of two ferocious polar bears.

Roar, an undefeatable ice fishing champion at the time, had gone fishing alone somewhere in the Arctic Ocean where his boat, eventually, got shipwrecked on a remote island belonging to the country of Denmark. In total isolation and lacking necessary supplies, he was forced to hide in the safety and warmth of a cave that he shockingly discovered to be a bear's den. Two ginormous, sleeping polar bears occupied most of the den cavity, leaving beside them the only available space: a tiny puddle. He glanced around the den, shook his head in desperation and quietly stepped back outside.

However, once the first freezing gust hit his face, he stopped advancing. He witnessed only the ravaging sea and the moon glimmering thin rays of light through a white snow blizzard on the murky skies. He took a step back towards the den and after a few moments' hesitation, went through his trouser pocket. He felt a small, round and hard object against his palm. He pulled it out, revealing a coin covered in fluff. The wind blew the dust away showing the silver plating. It was a mark coin. He

9

held the coin up and examined it between his woollen mitted fingers. Coincidentally, the moon light reflected off the mark's shiny surface, nearly blinding him. He rubbed his eyes and while doing so, he got an idea.

He leaned over and placed the coin heads up on the snow where the entrance to the den and the end tip of the moon bridge met. Immediately, the coin's illuminating surface reflected moonlight up to the skies like a laser beam, or like a lighthouse that emits a signal to aid and guide fellow sailors.

On tiptoes, he re-entered the den, where he knew he would be between a rock and a hard place. Whether to curl up next to the polar bears or lie in the wet puddle? He chose the former. Exhausted, he fell asleep in their arms.

Every once in a while, he had to sneak outside to revise the position of the coin to keep it aligned with the moon and its bridge.

After some days, the beaming light shining off the coin was spotted by the crew of a local fishing boat sailing past the island. The rescuers discovered hypothermic and malnourished Roar squashed but alive between the two polar bears.

The only item he had with him, a coin, had saved his life. And the lucky coincidence that the moon visibly shone from the skies giving light those few nights he was trapped on the island.

'There is always hope, even when the hope is gone,' Roar wisely summarised the lesson of the story. Conveniently, Sven fell asleep at the end of this true tale Roar proudly named, *Bear's Den Mark*. Roar kissed Sven on the forehead softly enough not to wake him up. Then, he left to face the averse weather. The storm kept ravaging Lake Pihtamo when the night began to turn into early morning hours.

Sven's mother and Roar's wife, Birgget, warned Roar and insisted him not to go, but he didn't listen. What came to fishing, he rarely took advice. He thought he knew what he was doing, always. Nothing or no one could stop him from going fishing, never did. And this day was no different, except that in the end he never returned home, leaving Birgget, together with their only son, Sven, mourning in the November darkness.

After years of uncertainty while search operations extended

to every corner of the town, Lake Pihtamo and the surrounding areas, Roar's body was never discovered. In the end, the family decided to hold a ceremony and funeral with a coffin filled with some of his remaining fishing gear, and championship trophies and medals, and other belongings he had left behind.

Birgget never remarried raising Sven alone, yet each day hoping for Roar to show up on their doorstep telling them that it had all been just a bad dream.

But he didn't return.

Neither did Carl, another top fisherman of the same era, who went missing at the lake around the same time with Roar. Preceding the time Roar and Carl both simultaneously disappeared, Roar had already gained a reputation as the invincible ice fisher. In the recent years, though, Carl had become the biggest threat and contender to Roar, and realistically the only potential candidate, if anyone ever had a chance, to end Roar's winning streak of sixteen years in a row of Lake Pihtamo ice fishing championships. However, Carl's journey to ever become the best ended that same, fatal night. Some believed the incident of losing two greatest in one go was pure coincidence, some thought there was a link, depending on whose side was taken by the doubtful folk, yet any piece of real evidence lacked. The only thing came certain that these two fishermen had left the shores around the same early hours of the morning. The rest of the opinions circulating the little fishing village were only assumptions or accusations which over the years, got slowly buried in the past.

One of the worst rumours about Roar, though, apart from being accused of getting rid of Carl, his most threatening competitor, was that he disappeared in the forests of Pihtamo and secretly became a moose hunter. Shifting one's interest from hunting to fishing or vice versa was gravely frowned upon in the area. It was one of the deadly sins. The two opposite communities had extremely negative opinions about one another. Fishermen believed hunting was for savages, even though the hunters saw themselves as true men, whereas fishing was for good-hearted, even though hunters saw fishermen as lazy gold diggers. The decision which side to choose was to be taken at an early age, and the devotion to one or the other discipline was to be kept eternally. Usually, the family heritage set the direction for the younger generation, and the choice was not taken, but given, by the parents, uncles or grandparents.

'You either have it or not,' Roar always said to Sven, even though there was never any other option given. Their family tree was built on devoted fishermen as far as the genealogy continued. Sven was destined to fish as had been Roar, Roar's father and their ancestors.

Two greatest, fiercest contestants, Roar and Carl, being out of the game had paved way to a new champion, Viljo, Carl's older brother and about twenty years senior to Roar. He had single-handedly dominated the ice fishing circuit in Pihtamo for more than a decade now. There hadn't been any other champion than Viljo since Roar won the title for the last time sixteen years ago. However, Roar was still today hailed as the true champion of the community, even though Viljo had become unbeatable since then. Roar never lost against any fisherman. He only lost against the stormy lake. That was the only time he had met his match, once and for all.

Like many sons, Sven yearned to become like his father: a great fisherman, the best of all, a legend. Roar always wanted to pass all his knowledge to Sven and make him even a better version of him. Whilst still in the cot, little baby Sven joined Roar on his fishing trips, and, gradually, from the age of three, Roar taught Sven everything, or almost, until the time ran out. The rest, a twelve-year old Sven had to self-learn.

The teenage years made Sven grow faster and become somewhat more responsible than many other boys of his peers. Suddenly, he became the only man in the house, and sometimes, the supporter of his own mother. At times, fishing provided the only source of livelihood, together with Birgget's modest knitting business. They only had each other.

Once Sven reached his late twenties, three out of four grandparents had passed on, apart from Roar's old mother, Hilga, who remained demented in a hospital care behind the mountains in Kihlava. She kept forgetting how Roar had been gone for years as Birgget and Sven did in their hearts.

Sven wanted to think that his father's soul still lived and breathed in the water, fish and plants of Lake Pihtamo. He sometimes felt the tranquil presence of his father while strolling along the lake shore or rowing in the middle. His passionate fishing also served as a substitute for all that father-son time he had missed out since his pre-teen years. There was no other place he felt as good and balanced as sitting in solitude in the middle of the ice or in a slightly rocking boat, rather than stomping on a solid ground or rambling through a dense forest.

Being fully self-taught, there was always uncertainty whether he had learned all the best possible fishing techniques or not. He did not continue formal education beyond secondary school, but since then only focused on fishing as a combined career and hobby. He never received any fishing industry education either, but only learned by doing, making mistakes, trying to correct them to his best knowledge at all times, and observing the best at the time, like Viljo.

But there was something he thought his father knew about fishing no one else did. Roar's records seemed unbreakable. He believed that if Roar had never left them, Roar would beat him single-handedly as the majority of town's people thought that he would beat anyone, even the current champion, Viljo. Roar's legacy as the greatest fisherman in the area remained. It was not always easy to grow up in the shadow of a true public's champion, even for Sven as much as he loved his father and cherished his memory.

Today, though, was yet another chance for every fisherman in Pihtamo to prove themselves and potentially rewrite history as the annual ice fishing contest took place.

Chapter 2

# THE COMPETITION

The path was paved for the reigning champion, Viljo, to become hailed as one of the greats of all time. He needed only one more victory to match with Roar's record streak of sixteen titles in a row. Finally, a half century of hard work and dedication could soon pay off and nothing seemed to stop Viljo from chasing his dream even at the age of eighty-four, having arthritis and bad knees. Having survived a war, recessions and Woodstock, made the men of his generation somewhat mentally and physically stronger and more persistent than the younger folk like Sven or Sven's best friend, Jaaku, who also took part in the competition.

Growing up in the shadow of other, more skilled fishermen, like Viljo or Sven, or women, like Irmeli, the top female ice fisher in the region, Jaaku was the wild card. When Sven, in his teenage years, had dominated the junior series, and came fifth in the adult series the previous year, Jaaku hadn't earned any notable success yet.

Earlier this year, Jaaku's self-confidence took another blow when his, now ex-girlfriend of two years, left him and announced she would be moving to more temperate climates of Northern Ireland. She had been attending Erasmoose programme, an international university training for the ones wanting to become elk cultivators and eventually, moose hunters. In the second year of her training, she had met a fellow student, a young Irishman from Londonderry or Derry. The Irishman's striking, ginger looks, abundance of freckles and endearing accent swept the feet off all the young women in the classroom. Unfortunate for Jaaku, she was drawn to the Irish elk hunter.

Jaaku comforted himself with the idea that his and her ambitions didn't meet. He wanted to be a fisherman, she a moose hunter. They simply had no future in Pihtamo. She wanted to be a citizen of the world, whereas he was comfortable where he was: in the cold and silence. Once she was gone, he healed his wounds and drowned his pain by fishing and drinking more Arctic Wodka, a spirit specifically produced in Pihtamo. And trying to remember that the real Irish Elk is long gone, extinct, anyway.

Apart from losing his father, Sven had been much luckier in love. He dated a ski resort entrepreneur's daughter, Ida, who supported him in the audience together with Birgget, her soon-to-become mother-in-law. Their wedding date had been set two weeks after the competition. One day, Sven even wished her to be the mother of his own child, a child that could enjoy the presence of his or her own father longer than himself ever had a chance.

From about thirty overall contestants, Christian, a hunky blond haired thirty-second generation Viking stood out as a man of bold stature. His ancestors used to rummage across the North Sea and further. His appearance lived up to the blood heritage. As a fisherman, he was known of his immense strength, whereas his overtrained physique limited his agility and speed. Known as a fast skater and one of the top scorers on the high school ice hockey team, he was a popular boy. He had been Ida's first boyfriend in high school, yet he still had an eye on Ida, but according to her, they were nowadays "only friends".

Due to a fear of accidents and drownings, the competition this year was held a month later than normally. The most courageous or insane - not a lot of difference there in terms of ice fishing - had a tendency to stay nearest to the edge ignoring the warnings of thinning ice or rising temperatures that can sometimes be life-threatening, or in the worst scenario, fatal. The thin ice on the edges could suddenly break pulling the ice fishers in the freezing cold water. Not having the right tools available, like an ice pick or a knife, the slippery surface can be difficult or almost impossible to climb for a plummeted, heavy man or even a lighter woman wearing wet, winter outfits, furs or sealskin clothes.

The increasing winter temperatures, or global warming, as the scientists have decided to name the phenomenon, deepened concerns amongst the local authorities whether the event should be cancelled for the first time in the history since the year 1876. Not even the world wars or overlapping broadcasts of Eurovision song contests had stopped the ice fishing competitions from being held. Over the years, the event had developed to become like a rite of passage for the men and some women in Pihtamo, despite their social class or background. Everyone from working class to wealthy business owners were able to join free of charge. The latest gear, technology and the most expensive equipment did provide some assistance and ease, but fundamentally the contest was about discovering the best ability to withstand extreme coldness in absolute solitude while exercising persistence, patience and having the largest amount of guts, combined with a great skill set and experience. Understanding the ice movement, lake waters underneath and the behaviour of its underlying fishes, also played an important part on the success of an individual.

This winter, though, the patchy area where the ice was trusted to be strong enough to hold the increasing number of contestants had shrunk to the size smaller than ever before. The concerns were raised, but the aging ice fishing committee with Viljo being one of the most influential members, insisted the competition would get a green light. His personal greed to reach Roar's record bypassed the worries over the safety of the contestants. He was determined that this will be his year of ultimate success; that after his matching record number of championships with Roar's will bring him the respect he thought he deserved as one of greatest fishermen in Pihtamo, if not the greatest, and nothing, not even the global warming was to stop him.

As the competition did go ahead, the anglers of all ages and sizes packed up roughly on the area limited to one square kilometre of ice with a thickness of no more than ten centimetres, at some parts, less. Even the cracking and popping ice under the feet of the fearless contestants didn't stop them from aiming for the most desired prizes for the winner: the annual Pihtamo Ice Fishing Cup, a gold medal, a hundred marks gift voucher to a local supermarket and a free meal for two with a bottle of Arctic Wodka in a local Arctic Bar.

The contestants scattered across the ice, mostly gathering around or in the close proximity of Viljo's chosen hole. Naturally, being the reigning champion and winner for so many consecutive years convinced the others that he knew something they don't; that he knows the best spots where the fish bites.

Viljo moved further away to another hole, but the group kept following like a bunch of fans. He swung his rod up in the air as an attempt to push back the nearest intruders, who only ignored his cry. Or they pretended they couldn't hear or see, but only focused laying out their gear and waited to hear the start whistle. Viljo felt helpless with the crowds circulating him. The situation had developed worse over the years the more popular he had become. There was no ice fishing contest rule he could rely on to keep others away, unless himself as a board member would introduce one. But now it was too late, until next year, perhaps. One hole per each contestant at a time and that was the main rule. The freedom given to follow whoever and wherever you wanted on the ice, was total. Naturally, the majority congregated around Viljo. About a dozen of fishermen and women now circled him and chose their pre-made holes nearest to him where he had laid his seat and gear. Unfortunately, due to the small size of the icy area this year, the holes were also drilled disturbingly near to one another, each participants' shoulders nearly touching.

Avoiding the mainstream and the masses, Sven instead stuck to his solidarity as usual. When he was a child, his father showed him the best fishing spots they believed were at the time. Stubbornly, he relied on those, old trusted areas that were nowhere near Viljo's hole.

Jaaku, being devoted to his best friend and trusting his judgement skills, started near to Sven, even though he kept peering, hesitantly, over his shoulder towards the crowds gathered around the current champion.

As the start whistle echoed, the men dropped their baits in the water and began their vigorous battle. After less than three seconds, Viljo had already caught the first herring. The other top fishermen, like Sven and Christian, were not bothered, yet a few novice anglers around Viljo momentarily halted their tasks to admire in awe the old man's rapid catching technique.

Irmeli caught her first one after about five seconds, Christian after six, Sven after eight. Jaaku dropped his gear in the hole and lost time fishing them up first.

With a constant flow, the buckets kept filling with salmon, pike perch, cod, haddock, all sizes, colours and ages imaginable, but most of all herrings, which the lake was famous for. The competitors completely ignored the ice movement underneath the most crowded part. They only had eyes and ears for their holes.

The breeze got nippier, yet the overall temperature remained above average. The winter in Pihtamo this year had been the warmest ever recorded making the surface of the ice glaring, watery and clear of snow.

The pace of fish biting had slowed down dramatically though and the total numbers of fish caught declined in comparison to the previous years. Halfway through the competition, Viljo was leading with twenty-one fishes in the bucket, whereas the year before he had thirty-two by the halftime. The record was held by the all-time ice fisher, Roar, with forty-six fishes by the halftime and hundred and nine fishes overall after the full time. This record breaking year happened twenty-five years ago, when Sven was only three years old and too young to remember, but he had read about the event from the old ice fishing magazines, record books and publications. Even the papers and journals confirmed that his father was hailed as a hero of the time, a legend that never left the hearts of ice fishing communities. There were still writings and memoirs about him published occasionally.

The fishermen together with the public were somewhat puzzled by the decrementing number of fish caught within the recent years and the numbers only seemed to be dropping. Some explained the phenomenon with global warming which seemingly was causing the increasing temperatures, lack of snow and thinning ice. But the climate change in connection to lack of fish even the scientists struggled to reason, apart from possible lack of oxygen in the water, that however, only occurs when the water temperature changes rapidly, which was not the case in Lake Pihtamo. Only the average temperatures had risen, but over the past years.

Nevertheless, the winner was always a winner and the lack of fish increased the demands of the contestants to push themselves that extra kilometre. Some experts even claimed that winning the contest was tougher nowadays due to the changed environment and the pressure it laid upon the competitors, whereas in the past the fish, literally, *jumped* on the buckets of the contestants.

Going for the second half after a fifteen-minute intermission, Viljo was on the lead, Irmeli the second with nineteen fishes in the bucket and Sven followed on the third place with only one catch less than her. Christian had dropped to the fourth place with sixteen. Jaaku had caught only nine putting him on the eleventh place.

Sven trotted back to the spot his father had showed him long time ago. It hadn't brought him any championships, yet he trusted if he tried and repeated long enough, the perseverance would begin to pay off. A wise man once said: *Insanity is doing the same thing, but expecting different results.* However, Sven wanted to think differently. He always believed the following: *Repeating the same thing persistently will eventually bring your dreams into the daylight.*

Irmeli swore after losing two fishes in a row to Christian by the hole next to him. The mistake cost her the second place that was taken over by Sven. Viljo was still on the lead, despite the disturbing, tampering crowds around him. Irmeli also found a hole nearer to Viljo.

Jaaku kept losing ground. He was not sure what position he was at anymore. In desperation, he looked around and at the competitors gathered around Viljo and then back to Sven, who ignored his friend and only fished for his life and for himself as the best ones should do. A moment of hesitation from Jaaku and a difficult decision followed. He chose to stand up and leave beside Sven.

Out of the corner of his eyes, Sven saw Jaaku walking away. Momentarily, he lost focus and raised his gaze. 'Where are you going!?' Sven yelled. Otherwise, the howling Arctic breeze would have drowned his voice.

Jaaku slowed down and peered over his shoulder. 'I'm sorry.' He didn't stop, though, but kept walking away sheepishly towards the foggy end of the lake to adjoin the other contestants following Viljo's success.

Sven couldn't help but feel disappointed to his friend's choice. The distraction, while he observed Jaaku stepping away, had caused him his second place to Christian.

Viljo still kept the lead as Jaaku approached the group circling the reigning champion. He peered for an empty hole, but all the nearest ones to Viljo had been taken. 'Five minutes remaining!' a voice on the loud speaker from the shore announced, when Jaaku located a desolate, empty hole on the outer edges of the crowd. He slammed his bucket upside-down next to the hole. As he sat on the flat bottom of the bucket, the ice underneath snapped loudly and fractured. The surface moved as if something was broken, permanently. The cracks began to spread starting from where Jaaku sat and advanced all across the fishermen surrounding Viljo. Even Viljo stopped fishing for the first time since the start whistle blow, when a gap in the ice travelled between the soles of his snow boots. Puzzled, he gazed around and saw apologetic Jaaku spreading his arms in the distance. The other anglers around Viljo also froze to listen. The widening crack formed a circle around all the nearest contestants. They all held their breaths.

Less than three minutes left on the clock and the contest got an ending unheard of within its nearly one hundred and fifty years of history. The ice broke plummeting most of the leading contestants into the freezing water: Viljo, defending champion with forty-six fishes in the bucket, Irmeli and six others including Jaaku. The captured fishes from their buckets escaped to freedom. While trying to save themselves, some got tangled in their gear and lines.

Sven's and Christian's score at the time the incident occurred was forty-four, each, and luckily both of them sat far enough on a solid, unbroken ice that kept them in the competition.

The official ice fishing rules of Lake Pihtamo stated clearly that: *In a case of life-threatening danger or an accident, the competition shall be halted and the results ruled void and null, if the incident occurs earlier than ten minutes before the end whistle.*

As the fiercest competitors were out of the way in the most controversial circumstances, the last minutes became the race between Sven and Christian. Although Christian being positioned nearer to the edge of the broken ice, lost valuable time while shifting further away from the danger. Sven surpassed him after having caught two more fishes.

As the rescuers began to pour on the ice, Sven pulled out a big one that seemed to have a few smaller fishes riding on the back. He wasn't sure how many, but he scooped them all into his bucket. Christian also kept catching non-stop, when the final whistle blew. The competition had ended.

Pandemonium followed. Sven and Christian looked at each other breathing heavily, until they were escorted to safety by the officials, where they could follow the rescue mission. The sunken fishermen and women were pulled out of the lake. Some of them genuinely congratulated the ones who made it dry till the end; some showed less enthusiasm or even bitterness, like Viljo. And Jaaku only wanted to hide in shame.

Ida and Birgget observed from the audience their arms raised halfway not knowing whether to celebrate or not. They only stared at Sven who shrugged his shoulders. He didn't know how to react either.

The officials collected the buckets from the remaining contestants and took them to weighing and counting. Two categories were awarded: the total quantity as well as the biggest individual fish.

Most of the anglers who fell into the water lost their buckets and their fish swam away. Viljo was the only exception, who had gone to extra lengths by holding onto his full bucket and keeping it above the surface till the end while himself nearly drowning. The last two fishes had swam inside his overcoat. Once being rescued from the water, he emptied them straight into the bucket before handing it to the officials.

After the weighing and counting was concluded the head

judge stepped near the podium to announce the results.

'The results of the hundredth and thirty-third Lake Pihtamo Ice Fishing Championship contest... The third place with forty-eight fishes in the bucket: Christian Hurmårdu... The second place with fifty fishes caught: Viljo Laaksokala...'

Sven sought eye contact with Ida again. They gave each other a subtle, anticipating smile.

'And the new Pihtamo ice fishing champion, winning both categories, the biggest herring weighing eight and a half kilograms and total of fifty-three fishes: Sven... Ro... Birggetsson!'

In disbelief, Sven dropped his gear to the ice. Ida squealed in joy, waited for the steward to look away, until she jumped over the fence and rushed onto the ice despite the restrictions.

The commentator asked the three medallist to approach the podium, but only two of them did. Sven took the top spot and Christian the third place, whereas Viljo stayed away receiving first aid and warmth from the medics. Assumingly, though, he would have had the strength to collect his medal, but the motivation was gone. He only exchanged grief looks with Jaaku, who he believed was the core sinking element. Jaaku understood the hint, quietly packed his remaining gear and disappeared from the scene.

Sven forced a smile to hide the confusion as he celebrated on the top podium. Finally, the years of hard work combined with persistently relying on his father's fishing spots paid off, however, though, in the most controversial circumstances and with the worst overall results in the history of the championships. He tried to convince himself, though, that this was only the *nature of the sports*. *These things happen*, he justified the victory as the town mayor handed him the prizes. Even though, deep down inside he felt uncertainty who was really the number one at this very moment, and he knew that there will be talks, debates and arguments about this particular competition in Pihtamo for years, decades and centuries to come.

Nevertheless, Sven received his first gold medal and soon he was about to marry, to his opinion and many others, the most beautiful girl in town, who just arrived in front of the podium.

'You did it!' Ida rejoiced.

Sven lightened up to a genuine smile and jumped down in front of her. 'My dad would be so proud!'

'We all are,' she replied.

He took her into his arms and they kissed. *Could life get any better than this?*

Chapter 3

# HER RING

On the day of Winter Solstice, a thin layer of snow had arrived to decorate the outside lawn of the picturesque, old wooden church dating back to the eighteenth century - a unique, historical structure that had stood the test of times through the world wars, the great fires and arsonists. The church spire dominated the flat skyline of Pihtamo town centre. The sound of the bells echoed bouncing off the mountain range and the glacier walls on the north side of the lake, announcing the locals about a wedding ceremony that was soon to begin. The flickering greenish and yellowish Aurora Borealis illuminated the dark afternoon sky. The warmth of the colourful mosaic windows shone dim light to the surrounding church yard. As the bells muted, the sound of the organs became audible through the thick timber walls. The intimate and delicate mood inside the church was boosted with candles flickering throughout the room and with the warmth of the loved ones seated on both sides of the aisle.

Ronja, the bridesmaid and Ida's best friend lead the way spreading pieces of spruce branches on the aisle floor. The familiar-looking crowd stood up and turned to admire as Ida, in Sophia's, her mother's, white wedding gown escorted by her father, Gustav, entered through the wide, wooden double doors. The winter breeze from outside gave Ida and Gustav a good push together with a few snowflakes flying in before the doors closed behind them.

Wearing a three piece charcoal dinner suit, Sven stood in the altar his palms and forehead sweating. Beside him stood the best man, Jaaku. Naturally, the priest was in front of the men facing the audience.

As Ida and Gustav walked arm in arm down the aisle, they passed Jaaku's parents Siimiuut and Aajamaak, the town pie shop owners; Tomas from the Arctic Bar together with a few regular punters; and most of the ice fishing committee board members, apart from Viljo who was invited, but didn't show up.

Ida's older sisters Margherita and Anne had flown nearly thousand kilometres to attend the wedding for mere responsibility. Ida's entire family had somewhat wished more prosperous marriage for her than the fisherman's lifestyle and limited growth opportunities Sven had to offer. Dissatisfaction the family members felt was palpable as Sophia together with Ida's sisters, all forced a smile in the front row.

Birgget across felt the opposite. She struggled to hold back her tears of joy, when her only child was getting married with someone she got along so well and someone she felt she can trust. Perhaps, her tears had a tinge of sadness in them knowing that she wouldn't be the only woman in his son's life anymore as well as the fact that Sven's father wasn't there to witness the moment. His only son getting married would have meant a world to him. A thought of Roar being somewhere above watching and enjoying the ceremony brought her relief.

The wooden planks of the church floor creaked under Ida's high heels and Gustav's shoes as they arrived to the altar. Feeling a slight resistance, Sven had to forcefully yank Ida off her father's arm to his own. Distraught, Gustav gave in, took a step back and sat down beside Sophia.

Sven and Ida stood on the altar facing one another and holding hands. They looked deeply into each other's eyes as the priest begun to deliver his well-rehearsed lines. Four and a half years of dating had finally climaxed into this one, brief, but once-in-a-lifetime moment, to seal the special love between two people in a holy matrimony.

Line by line, they began repeating their wedding vows. So far, everything seemed almost magical, exactly as Ida had always imagined the day to be.

Next, Sven took Ida's left hand while his other hand went into his trouser pocket. 'With this ring, I wed you, and pledge you my love...' Suddenly, though, he felt unrecognisable movement in the pocket, something that wasn't hard like gold or silver or a ring box, but much softer, wetter and slimier. He circled his hand around, felt every corner of the pocket, but always ended up with same results. Now, there was a wet spot on his trousers, near to the crotch. He blushed, embarrassed. The priest gave him an odd, anxious look. The guests began glancing around each other as the tension grew.

*He has lost her ring,* thought Jaaku, his eyes widening. Sven looked over his shoulder and gave Jaaku a desperate look, but Jaaku could only respond with a smile. He had no ring. He had never even seen it. They had agreed together that Sven will take care of her ring himself and himself alone. Jaaku was there next to the altar only to support him in the duties mentally and supposedly to host the party afterwards.

With rosy cheeks and sweat dripping Sven sensed the awkward atmosphere spread till the backbenches of the church hall. Gustav and Sophie shook their heads in the front row as if they had anticipated a disappointment like this to happen, yet not quite as soon though.

Birgget observed tensely folding her hands as if she was praying for her son.

By now, Sven had examined the entire pocket several times always ending up in the same conclusion, same two options: he could just pull out an empty hand and play it as a joke or he could reveal that wet surprise whatever it may be hidden in his pocket. *Perhaps, her ring is somehow attached to... the slimy thing in my pocket*, he thought, turned his head and whispered in Jaaku's ear. 'Psst! Jaaku... Did you plant something inside my pocket? Because if you did... it's not funny at all.'

Jaaku shook his head. 'Sorry, mate. I have no idea what you're talking about. Just do what you gotta do. It's your big moment now. I know you can,' he said, gave Sven an encouraging tap at the back and stepped aside.

Sven sank into deeper despair. He saw no way out, except to

go through all his pockets. He released his other hand from Ida's and went to search the other side, too. Both hands in his trouser pockets in front of God, the priest, his beautiful bride and the loyal family and friends, Sven wanted to disappear. *What have I done to deserve this? Please let there be something, anything made of metal that has a ring shape that I can put on Ida's finger so we can get outta here.*

The other pocket brought him even less success. It was empty.

'Erm...' the priest's patience began to run out. He leaned forward towards Sven and whispered, 'Her ring?'

Ida's anticipating face had turned sour. She was almost in tears, but not of joy anymore.

Sven's only option was to gamble, yet the odds were poor. *Something or nothing.* He could raise his empty hands and arms, give up, admit he had lost her ring and beg for forgiveness. Or, he could reveal the secret lurking inside the other pocket, hoping that the surprise would solve the situation somehow. Seconds felt like hours when the odd fifty people, family, friends and a few villagers stared impatiently. He overheard some general murmur developing within the crowd. Their restlessness had become obvious.

Most of the romantically charged people in the Western world wish to have only one wedding day in a lifetime, though, many end up having two, three or more. Nevertheless, the big day is always supposed to be unforgettably beautiful and things have to run smoothly, almost perfectly. But sometimes plans can go poorly wrong, and in the worst case the big day can make it to *The Funniest Home Videos.*

That was exactly the direction the situation was heading towards: Sven ending up being laughed at by millions and millions of people around the world. Not even the nominal fee paid by the production company that gets their hands on these juicy tapes about unplanned incidents in normal people's lives would be enough of consolation and save him from this trouble.

Despite the fear, his options and time were running short. Some guests stood up and tapped their feet, impatiently, including Gustav in the front row. 'What is he doing?' he snorted towards Sophia and made gestures.

Ida heard his father's cry. She spread her arms. Her graceful posture began to sink. She felt less beautiful and elegant, less special, or just like any normal girl getting disappointed with too high hopes about romance and men.

Sven felt he had no other choice than to hold onto whatever lurked in the left side pocket, the only pocket that had something inside. Optimistically, he hoped, whatever moved in his pocket was better be something really good or funny that could save him from the embarrassment, and perhaps, even make everyone laugh a little. He wished that her ring could somehow be linked to the slimy, moving thing he felt on his hand. He squeezed and pulled the "thing" out.

'Herring!?' Ida screamed and burst into tears. 'Waa!' she covered her watery eyes under her palms as Sven offered her a sloppy, half dead, wet herring. In a split second, her dream wedding had turned into one smelly, fishy nightmare.

'Blasphemy!' the priest furiously pointed his forefinger at Sven and the herring.

The guests let out a condemning gasp as Sven stood dumbfounded on the altar examining the fish whether there was a ring hidden somewhere: inside the gills, mouth, behind the fins. But he saw nothing but the fish.

Jaaku covered his face to hide his mixed emotions. He was embarrassed on behalf of the couple, yet simultaneously struggled to hold back his giggles. He thought, if this was being filmed by anyone as it must have been, how likely the footage would end up in the Funniest Home Videos. His sympathies, though, were on Ida's side. He hoped that she could forgive Sven, if not now, but one day, for spoiling her perfect day. But after all, she had decided to marry a fisherman and this was something one could expect.

'The wedding is ruined,' Ida sobbed.

'I swear to you... I have no idea how this got into my pocket,' Sven mumbled.

'Sorry. I cannot do this...' Ida pulled up her dress, rushed off the altar and ran along the aisle towards the exit.

Her parents on the front row gave Sven a disgusted look and followed their daughter. Two sisters got up too and left their seats.

'Please, Ida! Don't go! I'm sure there's a ring here... somewhere. There has to be!' Sven screamed behind her, but his voice blended with a loud bang of the heavy outdoor. She had left the church, the priest disappeared to sacristy and Jaaku took a step back to join the guests, leaving Sven alone in the altar with the herring. He raised his gaze, saw how the guests slowly left their seats and exited the church. As they did, a few of them gave a final, pitying glance at Sven, whereas some were just too embarrassed on Sven's behalf to look into his eyes. They just walked out. 'Ida!' Sven jumped off the altar and tried to push his way through the crowd blocking the aisle. Soon, people started avoiding him, when he waved the smelly fish up in the air.

Once he stepped outside, he only saw the backlights of Ida's parents' snowmobiles taking her away. The back of her white, long veil flickered in the distance before they disappeared into the dark forest. She didn't look back, never looked back.

The crowd kept exiting the church, totally ignoring Sven. He stared at the empty forest still holding the wet herring that began to gather frost on its scale.

One of the only guests who came to Sven was Jaaku. He grabbed Sven's shoulder. 'What just happened there?' he asked, dumbfounded.

No answer. Sven only stared in the distance where Ida had vanished.

'Was that supposed to be a joke? I never thought Ida would like herring that much... and obviously, she doesn't. I know you do, but...'

'Do you remember last night? My stag do?' Sven interrupted and turned to Jaaku.

'Vaguely. Why?'

'I woke up around two o'clock at night... lying alone in the middle of the lake ice...'

'I told you not to have a stag do the night before the wedding.'

'...wearing a bear onesie costume and under was my wedding

31

tuxedo.'

Jaaku looked at him slightly bemused.

'I think I lost my ice fishing gold medal, too. I still had it around my neck when we started the party.'

'That sounds... terrible,' Jaaku smirked.

'Would you have any idea how all that happened?'

'I... I swear to you I have no idea,' Jaaku said. 'But it sounds kinda funny.'

'It's not funny now,' Sven said, still looking suspiciously at Jaaku. 'The problem is... I have no recollection of last night, except that we went to the Arctic Bar around midnight. Everything after is bit of a blur.'

'I remember, we ran into a hen party. Other guys joined them... but as far as I recall, you and me were mostly downing shots and still talking about the ice fishing competition.'

'Where did you end up then?'

'In... jail,' Jaaku said and scratched his neck.

'Jail!? What did you do?'

'Nothing, apparently. My brother found me passed out face down on the pile of snow next to the Arctic Bar.'

'How nice! Family locking you up.'

'He said he only did me a favour. Saved my life, apparently. He is the town sheriff after all.'

'Glad I have no siblings,' Sven snorted.

'So... the herring?' Jaaku pointed at the fish that had now gone completely frozen stiff on Sven's hand.

'Yes, my son,' Birgget interrupted from the church steps behind them. She was the last one to exit the church. She had been crying. She stepped down and walked to the boys. 'The herring?'

'I'm so sorry, mum,' Sven embraced her.

'You were so happy together,' she whispered to his ear. 'Everything seemed so perfect.'

'We were. It was. We are... still. We will... I don't know.'

'What happened?'

Once they finished the embrace, Sven explained. 'To cut the story short, after my stag do last night, I woke up in the middle of the ice. Don't ask me why. But then, I got this brilliant idea.

I wanted to have my last ice fishing experience before marriage.'

'Sure, you could still go fishing once married, you silly,' Birgget said.

'I can, but it will all be different. Maybe I can't that often. Who knows? Then, eventually, with the kids and everything. I thought there wouldn't be that much time anymore.'

'Of course there will be time. There is always time. Kids you can take fishing with you. That's what your father did, can't you remember?'

'That's what everybody says, but I don't know. Dad's not here with us to say how he really felt. I never really knew my father as a man. I only knew him as a parent. Maybe, us family we were all just slowing him down. Was he fishing enough or could he have done something more in life? Something else he always wanted to do?'

'How he could have done more? He won more championships than anyone ever has. Only thing he could have done more is to stay at home and spend time with his family.'

'That's exactly what I mean. More championships... This morning I felt something magical on the ice. So quiet, peaceful, no one around. It was just me and my thoughts...'

'...and a terrible hangover,' Jaaku added.

'I'm serious. It was something special. Just me, myself and I. I could have stayed there... forever.'

'Is that something you really want?' Birgget intervened. 'I know it's not what Ida wants. Ida wants a family, a man who stands by her side. But also she's not here to take anything away from you, but to support you. In Pihtamo, you can have all the silence, peace and solitude you need if that's what you want. There's always quiet here, everywhere. All Ida needs is you to love her. Apart from that, you can keep all the fish in the world.'

'Okay. You wanna hear the truth! I'm just afraid... afraid of commitment... and losing what I got.'

'What is it you've got? All that fish in the lake is not going anywhere. It's there waiting for you,' Birgget preached. 'Today, because of fish you LOST what you really had.'

'I know...' Sven looked down to the ground.

'So, you thought about proposing to Ida with this herring,

because... you wanted to prove what a great fisherman you are?'

'No. Definitely not! There was a ring, but I must have lost it. The fish in the pocket... I don't understand. I must have put it in there while I was fishing last night. I was catching all sorts of herrings, salmons, perches, you name it. It was the best night ever.'

'Much better than your wedding night will be,' Jaaku smirked.

Sven grunted at him.

'Glad you didn't bring all that fish you caught in the church with you,' Birgget said.

'Actually, I did drop a few in the kitchen for the catering staff to prepare for the wedding reception.'

'Well, there won't be any reception now.'

'I know. You don't have to remind me.'

'You have to learn to let go. Relax. Take a day off from fishing sometimes,' Birgget suggested.

'It's hard. It's so deeply in my blood. I haven't had a day off since I was... twelve years old.'

'Since the day your father went missing.'

'Yes... and that's why I am the champion now. That's the sacrifice I've made to become the best there is.'

'Fair enough. But see what it's doing to your private life. You can't have it all.'

'Really? Who says I can't?'

'Well, I couldn't,' Jaaku intervened. 'I think my devotion, or may I say, obsession for fishing was one of the big reasons that broke my last relationship.'

'We are all different.'

'Yes. You're an idiot,' Jaaku grunted and waved his mitt. He started walking away.

'Where are you going?'

'I'm going home,' Jaaku went to his kicksled and stepped on the runners. 'I have seen enough for today. The show is over.'

'Fine. Just give me a shout if you wanna go ice fishing any day soon.'

'You're hopeless,' Jaaku said and kicked away.

'What did I say?' Sven turned to his mother.

'Could you let go of that herring now?' Birgget said.

'Actually, I was thinking to take it home with me... and have it with some rye bread and dill.'

'But... that fish has just ruined your wedding!'

'Or do you want some?' Sven offered the fish to her.

'I think...' Birgget pushed the herring away, 'I'll go home too, son.'

'Are you alright, mum?' Sven asked.

'Are you?' Birgget replied, concerned.

Sven said nothing.

'Take care of yourself. I will call you in the morning.'

'Did I say something wrong?'

'It's been a long day for all of us. Why don't you go home as well and get some rest?' Birgget said, walked away through the gate and onto the street. Only the pom-pom of her fur hat kept popping above the hedge, until she turned the corner and vanished, leaving Sven with his herring but without his *herring girl* or anyone else to share the fish with. He squeezed the frozen herring back into his pocket and wandered through the graveyard.

Suddenly, all the beauty, vibrant colours of the nature, the Northern Lights, white snow, the deep dark green needles of pine trees, had lost all their colours. Everything in his eyes seemed just grey and black. The clouds covered the sky, the stars and the moon that were all shining so brightly earlier. He walked away and kept walking, not knowing exactly where and why. Not even the catch in his pocket filled the creeping sensation of emptiness.

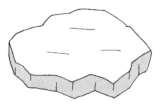

Chapter 4

# A COLD CALL

A striped take-away pizza box shook back and forth on top of an oak chest of drawers. After a few more vibrations, a ringing tone started playing as well, bringing drowsy and disoriented, Sven, back to life. He unveiled himself from under a thick duvet fully dressed in his outdoor clothes. Once he sat up on the bed, the moonlight shining through the window blinded him. His body ached and head felt heavy as if the hangover from the stag do two months ago never left him.

He pushed the duvet aside and looked around trying to locate the noise that woke him up. He got on his feet, and stumbled on the empty bottles and the piles of clothes lying around his bedroom floor. An orange flower vase with dead, white roses on the window sill reminded him of Ida's presence, who was always the one giving love and care, not only to him, but his one bedroom lakeside cottage too.

It had been two months since the catastrophic wedding day; since the last time he saw Ida; and since he touched a vacuum cleaner, a toothbrush, a comb or a razor. As if everything had stopped onto that one single, life-changing moment when he pulled the wet herring out of his pocket. Since losing her, he had taken steps back closer to become a cave man of some sort, who without the presence of a loving woman, was doomed to sink back into the Ice Ages and farther.

Once his eyesight returned back to normal, the moon

bridge lit up the room enough to guide him towards the noisy pizza box. He opened it to discover a half-eaten *Pizza La Pihtamo*, consisting of reindeer kebab meat mixed with *lakefood* and topped with fresh mozzarella, shaved parmesan and green arugula leaves. Next to the leftovers, his mobile phone swam in a lingonberry dipping sauce. As he picked up the sticky phone and placed it about two centimetres away from his ear, the ringing stopped. 'Typical!' he grunted and lowered the phone.

Every missed call, he wished, could have been from Ida desperately needing to tell him how much she had missed him and how she wanted to forgive him. But that day was yet to come, if ever. She didn't return to his calls, messages or voicemails. She had disappeared into void.

While still holding the phone, he started flicking through the missed calls and dialled numbers. Total of twenty-five attempts on the previous night to Ida's number and all of them answered. Neither did he remember making any of those calls nor speaking to Ida. Presumably, all his calls got directed to her voicemail. The phone's log displayed a similar pattern being repeated every single day since the wedding.

Sven had made an attempt to find her about a month ago. He believed she had gone staying at her parents' house in Örebröre, about eight-hour kicksled ride from Pihtamo on the main road. But the short cut route he chose to take through the forest turned into a nightmare of a journey. Halfway through, he had, accidentally, ran into a group of moose hunters, the fishermen's worst enemies. His kicksled front handle and the seat were blown off by a rifle bullet shot, that he wanted to believe, was aimed at a moose standing near to him between two spruces. Although he was well aware of the long-lasting conflicts between hunters and fishermen in the area. The representatives of both disciplines had strong, clashing opinions of which approach is conceived as the righteous one. The moose hunters tried to convince that their activities helped the communities eliminate a large number of pests that moose represented to the forests and people's gardens in the area, whereas the fishermen only saw hunters as savages, bloodthirsty killers and themselves more as environmentalists and patience preservers of the vast forests and numerous mammal species living in them.

The journey to Örebröre was cut short and Sven returned home with a broken kicksled and intensified forest phobia. The experience only confirmed the already known fact that he was, after all, a fisherman to the great extent and the water was his element, not the earth.

The damaged kicksled went into service and he was trapped in Pihtamo for another month.

Until today, when the broken parts of the kicksled were supposedly being replaced and the kicksled was ready for collection.

He sighed and dropped the phone back into the pizza box. He turned to look outside the window. He took a step forward and leaned on the window sill, admired the moon again, the stars and the slowly vanishing Northern Lights that gave space to a brief flash of daylight rising in the horizon. Spring was on its way. *Something to look forward to,* thought Sven. *The sun.*

As much as he cherished solitude, peace and silence, loneliness against his own will was becoming unbearable. At least in the past, the awareness of having someone somewhere waiting and thinking about him, had given him the sense of relief. But now, apart from his mother, he wasn't sure anymore whether there was anyone else really thinking about him and missing him or if there ever will be. He had learned a valuable but painful lesson.

Even his once so precious fishing gear now abandoned in the corner had lost some of that importance. And random pieces of bait and tackle lay scattered on the floor as if being rejected worthless and meaningless. On his night table, a satin box lid open revealed an empty cushion inside where his gold medal used to sit.

He tried to rejoice and relive the glorious moments. But he couldn't feel them, barely remember. Not even the gold medal was there to remind him about his one-time wonder. The glory had evaporated, as if in his memories someone else was winning; another person from the distant past he couldn't recognise anymore; a man also admired and loved by someone important to him.

He always thought: *By the time a dream we once dreamt materialises, we are already looking for the next thing to dream about. It's a continuous cycle. We are the most satisfied whilst dreaming.*

Winning that gold medal and marrying Ida were his dreams. He loved fish and her, equally. Now, though, he had lost the reason to dream again. Medals are reattainable, whereas true love is not. Getting Ida back had to become his next dream. Until that dream becomes reality, he could not see himself moving forward and start living again.

Recently, having more spare time in his hands for pointless activities, like watching daytime television, he had learned how some couples do survive break-ups, or give up and start from the beginning with a someone new. One of his favourite shows had become The Cold and the Passionless, or CP, the longest running soap drama in Pihtamo, where many of the characters married, remarried and re-remarried, sometimes their cousins, sometimes their grandsons ex-partners or neighbours milkmen. Even another television show, Freezer, a sitcom about an Arctic radio talk show host who ran his program from inside an igloo and its main character, Dr. Freezer, moved on after splitting up with his onset wife. He remarried.

But these somewhat twisted images and plots trying to portray human life and relationships at their worse confused Sven emotionally and manipulated his pure sense and mind, who naively wanted to believe in genuine and unconditional love. Watching these programs, had not helped him out of his depression, but the opposite. The power of media spread even as remote locations as Pihtamo, that, otherwise, had remained distant from modern influences of civilization. The way how, especially younger people in Pihtamo spoke and behaved these days, were largely influenced by the spread of media and entertainment. Many members of the youth rather sacrificed their own, true personalities and use of common sense, and rather tried to appear like some, random, vain celebrities they idolised.

Nevertheless, the influence of media never changed Sven's devotion to his true idol: his own father. Roar was the opposite of a glamorous movie star, but a down-to-earth, old-fashioned fisherman. Sven had learned from him how the need for technology is non-existent to become a great fisherman.

The mobile phone rang again, this time in his hand. He jumped. His heart started beating faster. *Ida?* He coughed once to clear the throat and he picked up the phone. 'Hello.'

'Erm... Hello,' said a crackling male voice.

'Hello,' Sven repeated and sighed disappointed it not being Ida.

'It's freezing here...'

'Excuse me?'

'It's freezing cold here, Mr...Sven?' the shivering voice repeated.

'Who is this!? How do you know my name?'

'From the yellow pages, sir,' the man answered. 'It's so cold up here that I cannot feel my toes.'

'Whoever you are, I'm not going to buy any magazines or newspapers, that's for sure!'

'I understand, sir. But are you saying that you're not feeling cold at all, Mr Sven?'

'No, I really don't!'

'Everybody feels cold, sometimes,' the man persuaded.

'Please. What are you calling me for?'

'We're not selling magazines or newspapers. We are just ringing you to tell how cold it is and can be.'

'Right,' said Sven hesitantly under his breath. 'I know very well how cold it is! It's February. Is this one of those cold calls?'

'Of course you do know how cold it is,' the man kept dodging Sven's question. 'You only have to look or step outside to feel the freezing temperatures. It's very cold up here in Greenland, too.'

'You're cold calling me from... Greenland!? How ironic.'

'Yes. In fact, I would dare to say it's even colder up here than in Pihtamo.'

'I don't know about that, but... Hold on! How do you know where I live?'

'Nothing to be worried about, Mr Sven. It's part of our meticulous market research. We scan the area of all the potential customers. According to the yellow pages, you're a professional ice fisher, am I right, Mr. Sven?'

'Erm... Yes, as a matter of fact, I am,' Sven felt momentarily interested and flattered once being recognised. 'But... what's that got to do with this phone call?'

'Very much, indeed. Not always, but sometimes, when you're out on the lake fishing or even worse, ice fishing, you must feel really cold?'

'What!? I really don't have time for this nonsense!'

'Please, please... don't hang up, sir! I didn't mean it like that.'

'What did you mean then exactly?'

'We were just thinking since you live that far up north in this world and the conditions are extremely cold and harsh that... perhaps, you are in a need for a vacation? Is that something you ever thought about?'

'Well... I have never been anywhere else?'

'Never? Interesting.'

'Yes, never. But I am still not interested.'

'You have no idea what you're missing out.'

'What could I be missing out? I have everything I need here in Pihtamo.'

'You do? Really?'

Finally, a question that hit Sven's nerve. For the first time in his life he questioned his adamant belief that Pihtamo had everything he needed. He wasn't certain about that anymore. He sure didn't have someone to love, apart from his mother.

The cold caller gave Sven a moment to ponder in silence, until he continued, 'Because, I have a proposal for you, Mr. Sven.'

'Okay, here we go,' Sven snorted.

'Have you ever been on a beach holiday?'

'I have been by the beach all my life.'

'I know, but we are talking about warmer, pebbly beaches where the drinks come in pints; the sun, when visible, warms you till the dusk; and the fish is even easier to catch.'

'I don't see the point in that. I do get a decent tan here under the Northern Lights.'

'Fair enough. But you can experience more than that. There is a whole world out there waiting to be explored by an adventurous man like you. We organise exotic holidays to destinations in warmer climates for people just like you and me that come from extreme Arctic conditions. When was the last time you saw proper daylight?'

'Daylight? That's been a while.'

'I thought so. In that case, we have a tailor-made package just for you that includes...'

'Hold on,' Sven interrupted. 'I said I wasn't going to buy anything.'

'Are you not interested to see the daylight at all?'

'The daylight will come,' Sven said hesitatingly.

'Yes, sir. It's important for all of us. Energising. Makes us smile more. Soon, the summer will come and we will be having all the daylight in the world. The ice will melt, you can take out your boat again and begin fishing on an open lake.'

With some sadness in his eyes, Sven looked at his dusty fishing gear. 'Yes. I guess I can.'

The salesman on the other end of the line sensed vulnerability in Sven's voice. 'Well, if you decide to change your mind at some point, I want to share with you that we offer special holidays to the destination which has much higher humidity levels, warmer climate and more sunshine per year than Pihtamo. Our all-inclusive holiday package has flights, accommodation by the beach, all meals and transportation.'

'I see. Well, thank you for your call, but I have to turn down your offer this time. Though, it was nice to speak to someone.'

'I understand, Mr. Sven. Was there anything else you wanted to ask me or know about our services?'

'Not really.'

'Fine. Well, I wish a pleasant day and enjoy the cold weather while it lasts.'

'Or... hold on,' Sven hesitated. 'Can you at least tell, what is the destination of this holiday?'

'Great Britain, sir.'

'Right. Sounds glorious.'

'It used to be very glorious place. It still is,' the salesman stuttered, but soon composed himself. 'It has a great history and many people want to visit there or even stay to live there. Millions, in fact.'

'I have heard of Great Britain. My best friend's ex-partner moved to Ireland. Apparently, the weather is very pleasant and warm.'

'Well, that confirms it. I can assure you, it's like a paradise.'

'Just have to be careful not to lose your partner there.'

'I'm certain you and your wife are totally safe there.'

Sven didn't reply. He only felt pain in his chest.

'Our records show that you're married, Mr. Sven? Am I right?'

'I appreciate your... cold call... but perhaps not this time. I'm not really in a holiday mood.'

'But we also do...'

'When I start feeling too cold, I'll give you a call.'

'Fine, sir. As you wish. Before I finish, there's one more thing we do...'

'Good bye.'

'Good bye, Mr Sven.'

Chapter 5

# THE KING OF HERRINGS

The icy decor inside the Arctic Bar developed inadvertently overnight. Two decades ago, Pihtamo Bar had been closed during the Easter break when the owner at the time wanted to go away for a skiing holiday. In the first days of the holiday season, the building's central heating had broken down and the inside began to gather frost on the bar tops, tables, chairs and the walls. Once the owner returned, the interior had been decorated with pure white frost and crystal clear ice throughout.

Later on, the incident inspired an idea: to leave the bar as it was in its natural state, imitating some of the manmade ice bars the owner had come across in some bigger cities. He decided never to fix the central heating again. Thus, Pihtamo Bar became the Arctic Bar.

In no time, the newly opened frozen bar claimed back its usual clients - as there were no alternatives where to drink in Pihtamo anyway - and also the new clientele pilgrimaged from the surrounding regions, once the natural ice bar's reputation began to spread.

The Arctic Bar became a focal meeting point in the town centre. After work drinks, friends' get togethers, stag and hen parties, all started and ended in this same, frosty space.

Jaaku was one of the regulars. He sat by the bar in front of him two shot glasses and a bottle of Arctic Wodka. He kept his seal skin coat and a hood on, but had taken off his scarf and mitts, since the temperature inside the bar was slightly higher than outside. He gulped his first shot.

A handful of fishermen, a few Arctic Wodka factory workers and a couple of moose hunters carried on their slow paced, monotone chattering. Some of them just sat quietly and drank.

In the meantime, outside, Sven plough through a sudden snowstorm towards the town centre on his freshly serviced kicksled. The heavy snowfall reduced the visibility, yet he knew every street and a house even eyes closed. Not that many to be remembered though. A couple of narrow gravel roads winded to log cabins hidden in the deep forest and by the lakeside; a few modern houses and shops spread each side of the paved high street; dominated by the wooden church spire in the middle; canvassed by smoking pipes of the factory producing Arctic Wodka, a spirit popular amongst the local fishermen.

Sven briefly popped into the local supermarket that triggered a flashback from his childhood weekly shopping trips with his mum. On the rare occasion, his dad had joined them, too. Sven was always fascinated by the best before dates of random products, and how some already expired items never seemed to leave the shop shelves, because no one wanted to buy them or the staff kept ignoring them. Every once in a while, when his parents could not see him, as a cheeky youngster he took products that were about to expire soon and as a little prank, hid them behind the shelves or other products in the hope of further expiring them. He remembered specifically one type of Italian tuna in olive oil – a highly exotic ingredient to soak any type of fish at the time on such northern latitudes. Once he located the can, he did his utmost hiding and shifting it, until the tuna reached the sixth year past its expiry date anniversary. Eventually, he lost the sight of the can, long after Roar had already disappeared. He never found out whether the fish was bought by a customer or binned by the staff.

Tuna fish in olive oil was not the first Italian luxury item shipped to Pihtamo in the nineteen seventies. A male singer and a heart throb, Lumbardi Martello found his place, too. Both exotic imports, the tuna and Lumbardi, ended up causing lots of stir and confusion amongst the local population. The tuna fish in the olive oil confused the local fishermen, while in the meantime, Lumbardi wooed their wives.

One of town's longest serving hairdressers, Pirkko, whose salon located opposite to the supermarket, was the first person from Pihtamo to have contact with Lumbardi and somewhat responsible of introducing him to the Arctic environment. Nearly forty years ago, Pirkko on her yearly holiday with her colleagues from the salon travelled to the East Coast of Italy by the Adriatic Sea. The salon staff spent a week in a sea resort town of Rimini, where also Lumbardi at the time supported his stagnated singing career by working as a lifeguard.

One sunny morning on the beach, Pirkko sunbathed alone and needed someone to apply lotion on her pale back. Her two female colleagues still slept in the hotel after partying all night, whereas Pirkko had returned to the hotel earlier, being the sensible one - or so she thought - until her path crossed with Lumbardi's.

Lumbardi spent most of his days on the beach singing, rehearsing lyrics and preparing for evening's gigs, while shifting around sun beds and spotting the most talented women occupying them. Pirkko's immaculate blond hairdo, ice blue eyes and white skin shone gloriously from the distance. Coincidentally, he was the nearest of the beach boys available to help her in need.

Pirkko heard the heavily accented exotic voice approaching her, humming a cover of some popular Beatles song or something similar. She turned to look and there he was: a tanned, slim, dark haired, brown eyed beauty, singing the mating song. *A demigod*, she thought.

'*Ciao bella!*' he greeted cheerfully, oozing confidence.

Transfixed and speechless, Pirkko handed him the sun lotion bottle and let him rub it on her silky skin without any resistance. She was under his spell from that moment onwards.

'Very soft, ' he complimented the quality of her skin.

'It must be the sauna,' she replied with a chuckle. I go three times a week.'

Lumbardi invited her to see his gig the same evening at the local osteria about half an hour drive inland towards Apennine Mountains. Pirkko knew that her friends would oppose the idea for her to join a total stranger she had just met, so she opt out from her friends' dinner invitation that night and instead, stayed in the hotel alone complaining about stomach cramps. Once the other girls had gone dining and the route was clear, she put on her party dress, her highest two inch heels and sneaked out to get a taxi to see Lumbardi's gig. Her "tummy aches" disappeared in that instant.

After a long and winding ride, she discovered the osteria in a rundown old village. The place had only two people apart from Pirkko: one of the two was the owners son, the other was the man working behind the bar.

'Tuesday's are always quiet,' Lumbardi explained.

None of these insignificant details mattered to her, once Lumbardi's powerful interpretation of *'O Sole Mio* brought Pirkko's house down. It was love at first sight for her, yet another conquest for Lumbardi.

Four months after their bittersweet goodbyes, he showed up at the salon door during her evening shift. Shocked, she sliced a corner of the ear of the customer she was giving a haircut. Since then, the man with a deformed ear became known as The Wrestler.

Naively, Pirkko believed that Lumbardi had done the four-thousand-kilometre-long journey through land, seas and mountains only for her. Unfortunately, she was wrong. The real reason was desperation. His singing career in Italy had reached a dead end, and he was financially broke, only being able to afford a one-way ticket to Pihtamo. The rest - he figured - his charm, impetuous passion and exoticism would help him to re-launch his career in the northern latitudes.

He was not completely wrong. He managed to convince Pirkko and numerous other women borrow him money, and local Arctic Bar- or Pihtamo Bar at the time - to give him his first gigs. He went on for ten months not paying the rent, while residing above the hairdressing salon in a small room in the attic.

But, slowly Pirkko began to discover Lumbardi's real intentions as an incurable womaniser.

When Lumbardi's reputation spread, even his exotic tunes didn't save him anymore and he had to disappear for a couple of decades, possibly, it is believed, to conquer other towns in the region and their women. Until a few years ago, once the smoke had faded, he returned again to establish a pizza restaurant on the outskirts of Pihtamo, that also hosted a monthly karaoke night.

Lumbardi had no direct influence on Sven's life, apart from the occasional reindeer kebab takeaway pizza Sven ordered from his restaurant, such as his last night's supper and this morning's breakfast, *Pizza La Pihtamo.*

Sven picked up one of the tuna cans off the shelf and read the expiry date. Today, though, as a responsible adult, he understood the possible consequences his actions of hiding expired products may have caused, and he would never do that again.

A major salmonella outbreak spread across Pihtamo seventeen years ago, that was believed to be linked to old products sold in this, same supermarket. Sven had decided to keep his dark secret to himself, whether he was directly responsible or not. The epidemic claimed no casualties, but for instance, Birgget had to receive hospital treatment after eating expired eggs. Sven still carried the guilt inside him for purposely expiring items and putting the public in danger.

He moved to the fish counter and bought his dinner, a whole giant oarfish, and exited the supermarket.

Seeing the church spire brought back lot of unpleasant memories from his failed wedding, he didn't bother dealing with now. He sped up past it.

The problem of living in such a small, closed community was that the past was always present, anywhere you looked and in anything you touched or smelled. Everything around reminded of something, whether good or bad. There was no escape.

Around the corner appeared the pipes of the factory again that produced Arctic Wodka, the key ingredient for the birth and the prosperity of the town of Pihtamo, together with its heavy fishing industry. Since the war, the demand for alcohol had steadily escalated. Opening the factory brought three hundred jobs in the region. All employees were given houses that formed the basic infrastructure of the town that earlier was a primitive, rural village and farming land developed around the fertile lands of the volcano called Saalamaa. On a clear day, the peak of the volcano shone visibly behind the factory, but today the fog and snow blurred the entire horizon.

The factory, though, introduced notable prosperity to the region. Soon, the high road was sealed and the services and shops developed around it. Home brewing and boiling of alcohol lost its ground as the public began to shop in the licensed liquor store. Around the same time Pihtamo Bar opened its doors, working closely together with the factory and selling their products.

On the opening days, the liquor store and the bar, both, had about hundred-metre-long queue stretching far outside, despite the freezing coldness. Six people ended up in the hospital that day due to hypothermia, while stubbornly queuing for their favourite alcoholic drink. Three of the hospitalised men managed to return later the same day before the closing time.

Today, the factory had passed its haydays, partly, due to younger generation introducing new trends to Pihtamo by asking for ciders, wine or just non-alcoholic beverages. The number of staff in the factory had been halved within the last decade, leaving men and women without work, who mostly, had to seek for more primitive vocations, such as fishing and hunting.

The town's only set of traffic lights and its zebra crossing now separated Sven from the Arctic Bar. The treacherous weather kept all the traffic away. Once he reached the edge of the pedestrian crossing, the light for the pedestrians turned red. He stopped to wait. He looked left and right, but only saw empty streets filling with more snow. The wind blew the trees nearly diagonal on both sides of the pavement.

In theory, he would have had plenty of time to cross the street and walk through the red light - the risk would have been minimal - since the next vehicle passing the town was possibly minutes, hours or days away. But his inner-build sincerity, honesty and fear to break the rules of the society, prevented him, and made him stand and wait there like a model citizen.

After a good few minutes, the traffic light turned green setting him to trot across the street. He pulled his kicksled in front of the Arctic Bar.

The storm had piled snow blocking the entrance. He yanked

the door open, ploughing the snow away with the lower edge of the door. He stepped into the bar wiping the snowflakes off his coat. He took his hat off and shook it, too. Despite the icy conditions, the ambience inside felt warm and cosy - something opposite to his own cottage, since Ida had left.

All the interior light came from the candles flickering on the tables and a few bigger flames on the wall brackets. The icy seats were covered with reindeer skins.

Sven clocked Jaaku sitting by the bar. He walked to him and tapped his shoulder. '*Hei.*'

'*Hei!*' Jaaku replied, surprised. 'Look at that! Haven't seen or heard from you for last... what... two months?'

'I've... been quite busy.'

'Sure,' Jaaku said sarcastically. 'Seriously?'

'Erm... How are you?' asked Sven.

'As usual. But the question really is, how are you... Birggetsson? Where did that come from? I didn't know you've changed your name.'

'Ah. I did that right before the last competition. I thought it's time to leave certain things in the past and pay respect to my mother and for all the things she has done for me.'

'Fair enough.' Jaaku filled the other glass with Wodka and slid it towards Sven. 'And how are things with Ida?'

'*Kippis!*' Sven said and raised the glass.

'Sure. Let's get pissed!' Jaaku jokingly twisted their native way of saying cheers.

They downed the shot, followed by a refill from Jaaku.

'Haven't heard from her... since the wedding,' Sven said and looked down on the ground.

'You have to do something about it.'

'She doesn't answer my calls. I think she has gone to stay at her parents' place.'

'I'm sorry to hear. Why don't you go there and find her?'

'I tried, but I got ambushed by the moose hunters. They blasted my kicksled seat off. Had to get it serviced.'

'Bloody savages! We must do something about it.'

'Or just stay away from the forest.'

'Have you tried to get to Ida by road, yet?'

'It takes three times longer than cut through the forest.'

'Perhaps, it's worth a shot.'

'That reminds me of...' Sven downed the shot, picked up the bottle and poured some more. 'How come you had two shot glasses by the way? Were you expecting someone?'

'I was... but she stood me up.'

'Sorry to hear. How did you two meet?'

'Actually... we haven't. I've been only chatting with her in Pihinder.'

'Pih... what!?'

'It's a new online dating app for the people in Pihtamo.'

'Can't be too many users then?'

'It's a bit limited.'

'Who were you supposed to meet then?'

'Marjukka. She works in the post office.'

'Well, why don't you go and speak to her in person, if you know where she works?'

'Are you crazy!?'

'That's what I would do.'

'How do you know? You haven't dated... anyone... apart from Ida. You have no idea what it's like to start all over again. It's hard enough to talk to any stranger, speaking about women.'

Sven didn't respond. He only downed his shot. Jaaku did the same.

'Last week, I also attended this singles event, Ice Wide Shut,' Jaaku continued.

'Ice Wide... what?' Sven spilled some Wodka on the table while pouring them both some more. 'What a waste...' he muttered to himself.

'Shut. Blind dating, every first Thursday evening of the month here in the Arctic Bar. Maybe, something also for you to consider, in case things don't work out between you and Ida.'

'What did you have to do?'

'They gave us a time slot to speak to each other, men and women, but as you know, it's so cold here inside that you don't wanna waste too much time talking. Especially, that evening the temperature outside dropped below minus forty, which meant inside was nearly as cold. I could barely see anything, since my eye lashes were frozen together. You just get on with it.'

'Did you?'

'No. There was a weird balance: eight men and two women. And I knew both of the women already. There was Irmeli from the ice fishing competition and Ronja from the petrol station.'

'Ronja? Ida's friend?'

'Yes. I gather you wouldn't attend this dating event next time?'

'Too early. I'm still in love with Ida,' Sven said longingly, 'and this whole dating... business sounds confusing anyway.'

'It is.'

'So, what did you do then?'

'By the time I got to the second girl, Ronja, I think I had a few shots too many and I couldn't really form words that made sense anymore. Pity though, as I kinda like her.'

'You still miss your ex?'

'I do. What bothers me the most is that the last time I saw her before she disappeared to Ireland, she still wore her ring - the one I gave her!'

'Speaking of which...' Sven ducked down under the table and put his hand in the supermarket carry bag. He pulled out a gigantic fish and hung it above the bar top. 'Ta daa!'

'What is that?'

'Don't you know?'

'A giant oarfish?'

'Exactly! As known as the King of Herrings,' Sven said cheerfully.

'Why are you showing it to me?'

'I thought you'd appreciate it. It's a big fish.'

Jaaku turned serious. 'This isn't about herring. Life is not all about herring. Do you understand?'

'What are you saying?'

'I am here talking about an engagement ring I had given to my girlfriend, before she decided to leave to another country,' Jaaku gave Sven a vicious look, gulped another shot and wiped his mouth. 'Is there anything else you think besides fish? I thought these last months would have taught you a lesson or two.'

Apologetically, Sven hid the giant oarfish back into the

shopping bag. He finished his shot, too.

'One day you wake up thinking, what's the point?' Jaaku calmed down. 'First, someone loves you and the next day they're gone. Makes me think, whether I could have done something differently. Too many fishing trips, too much drinking, not enough conversation.'

Jaaku's openness shocked Sven. He thought it was *Wodka talking* while observing Jaaku's sudden emotional outburst. He stared at him not knowing what to say or do. Not that he himself wasn't feeling emotions, but the opposite. He only struggled to portray and express them as many men of his like did in these Arctic latitudes. Simply, keeping warm and general survival in life took so much energy distracting the men from futile tasks, such as unnecessary body language or erratic, emotional behaviour. The face muscles were often too frozen anyway to show much of compassion. However, the hearts and souls of these rugged, Arctic men were filled with warm sensations and deep emotions, that only thick layers of clothing and ice cold skin hid underneath. There were many private parties held inside each individual, where no one else was invited, apart from the host.

Another shot warmed Sven inside out, thus helping to release some tension, and hopefully, portray a wider scale of emotions. A few more shots and he knew he would be *on fire*.

A moment of silence followed after Jaaku's explosive reaction. They both just stared in the distance, remaining comfortable in the silence, though.

'So... where did you get that big fish from?' Jaaku broke the silence and pointed at Sven's plastic bag.

'The King?' Sven came back from the peaceful trance and focused conversing again. 'Erm... I picked it from the supermarket along the way.' He blushed, embarrassed to admit that a great fisherman and a reigning ice fishing champion had to rely on retail counter fish.

'Makes perfect sense,' Jaaku nodded.

'What's that supposed to mean?' Sven turned to look at him, slightly upset. The alcohol had clearly kicked in making Sven also more expressive and extroverted. 'Are you saying that I could never catch a fish like the King here? I beat you all, the whole town three months ago, if you remember?'

'Relax! It's nothing to do with the competition. I just have had some problems catching any fish lately.'

'You have?' Sven said with some arrogance in his voice. 'Well, I've never had that problem.'

'When was the last time you went fishing in Lake Pihtamo?' Jaaku turned to Sven.

'Erm... it's been a while,' Sven lowered his voice and looked away.

'When?' Jaaku demanded.

'Three months ago... in the competition.'

'What!?' Jaaku shook his head. 'What have you done since then?'

'Well... this and that.'

'Like what?'

'Another?' Sven avoided the questioning and shook the empty bottle in front of the bar man. The bar man poured them more. 'It's been... hard. Very hard,' Sven said while looking at the filling shot glass.

'You should get her back, get Ida back.'

'But what can I do?'

'It's really not that complicated. Have you ever thought about approaching her with a real engagement ring? Could be easier for you now anyway since you've been away from fishing for quite some time. You've given yourself a... fishing rehab,' Jaaku smirked.

'I don't know if there's anything I can do. I think I've lost her for good.'

'Those are not the words of a champion,' Jaaku said and encouragingly patted Sven on the back, nearly crossing the boundaries of how much physical attention can two fishermen show in public. 'Have you ever tried to lure her with a ring? Have you ever bought her any real jewellery?'

'Well...' Sven concentrated to think, 'I did give her once this reindeer hoof bracelet.'

'Are you serious!?' Jaaku laughed. 'Is that the best you can do?'

'What are you now, a relationship guru? Your own track

record doesn't qualify you.'

'All I'm saying is that I can help you. I know a friend of mine who makes this an amazing jewellery. It's none of that wooden rubbish or reindeer nonsense for tourists, but proper jewellery made of real gold from the mines of Kitsamo.'

'I already had a ring.'

'That you lost... What if the herring swallowed it?'

'The entire ring box? I don't think so. I gutted and ate that herring after the wedding. I couldn't see, feel or taste anything hard or metallic.'

'Well, think about my offer.'

'I guess...we could give it a go. One more gem is not gonna hurt anyone.'

'The opposite. As long as you don't lose it this time.'

'As long as it's not too expensive.'

'Don't worry. My friend is gonna cut you a good deal.'

A round of shots followed by another five-minute silence. Sven drifted to think about Ida and the good times they've had together. How supportive she had been with his ice fishing career. And the guilt he felt of not being as supportive towards her ambitions. Perhaps, she wanted more from life than just to be his herring girl.

'About the lake...' Jaaku said seriously.

'Yes. You said you haven't caught anything recently? Is it polluted?' Sven smiled.

'I don't know. I'm just concerned. And it's not just me. The whole fishing community are worried. No one's catching hardly anything anymore. The numbers have dropped dramatically as well as the size of the individual catch.'

'What about Viljo?'

'Him too. Absolutely nothing,' Jaaku said. 'I want you to come fishing with me. There's something not right.'

'I guess I could give it a go. It's been such a long time. Pull out a few big ones. Remind you all how it's done.'

Jaaku laughed sarcastically. 'How about tomorrow early morning? We can take my new boat, because the lake ice has already completely melted.'

'Sounds odd this early in the year. Usually, there's still some ice left two to three months from here, if not longer.'

'I know. That has been the other concern. The climate change, they say,' Jaaku said. 'So, you are in?'

'Yes.'

'And after you've "shown us" how it's done, we can go and meet my jeweller friend who will make Ida a proper ring.'

'Sounds like a plan, my friend. No more herrings in the finger.'

Jaaku took the bottle and filled up their glasses.

'*Hölöökynkölöökyn!*' they cheered together.

Chapter 6

# NO CATCH

Pihtamo, like the rest of the world, shared the burden of so-called climate change or global warming - a terminology made popular by the scientist within the recent decades. The lake surface had risen about five centimetres during the last century and half of the rise occurred in the last decade. The glaziers on the mountain sides and the ice bergs in the middle of the lake had been melting and shrunk to about a half of the size they used to be. On the other hand, the historical data available of the changes in the nature was somewhat limited, yet still the town elderly had witnessed with their bare eyes that something unusual was happening. The winters were shorter and warmer, the weather conditions overall more unpredictable.

Unusually warm temperatures had melted most of the ice on the lake making boating and regular fishing possible as early as March - the time of the year Jaaku and Sven met at Jaaku's rowing boat, Yolla.

Jaaku had acquired his Yolla boat in a police auction. The boat was a three seated, plastic dinghy, a model that gained popularity in the late seventies and the early eighties, until its retro design fell out of fashion. In these days, though, Yollas had become unique collectibles and rare boats seen on the waters. Their value had gone up tenfold.

Despite the popularity of the boat's vintage exterior design and style, this particular Yolla had much gloomier past. It used to belong to Carl, who had drowned on the same stormy night Roar disappeared. After Carl's boat was discovered drifting empty on the lake, the local police took and kept it as a crime evidence until its expiry a month ago, when it was handed out to the local auction house in Pihtamo.

Unaware of the horror story behind the boat's history, Jaaku made the winning bid for mere fifteen marks.

A few deep lines of scratches at the bottom of the boat first indicated collision with sharp rocks of some sort. More thorough investigations, though, proved that the marks were from Roar's boat.

The boat lay upside down and its bottom had a morning frost cover. Scattered piles of snow surrounded the edges of the boat. The branches of the surrounding spruces and pine trees kept pointing downwards, even though the weight of the snow had eased.

Jaaku waited beside the boat as Sven arrived, hopped off his kicksled and walked near the waterfront to test the thickness of the narrow strip of ice on the shoreline. The ice crackled with hardly any effort as he tapped it with the sole of his boot. He nodded to Jaaku approvingly. Supposedly, the path was clear for them to row through the ice onto the outer lake.

As they wiped the bottom of the boat, the scratch marks became visible. Sven stopped and stroked them with his mitt. 'What happened here?'

'I don't know. My brother tipped me off about this boat. They were selling it at an auction in the police station. Pretty nice, ey?'

Sven said nothing.

They flicked the boat around revealing two wooden oars tucked underneath. Jaaku unlocked the chain off the tree before they pushed the boat onto the fragile ice. Sven jumped at the back seat and Jaaku took the front. Jaaku slammed the oars through the thin ice and stroked.

The boat turned into a miniature ice breaker of some sort as it pushed its way through. A few more pushes freed them rowing on an open lake. The men could ditch their ice fishing gear aside and only focus on using traditional methods.

With the confidence of a reigning champion, Sven navigated them to places he believed the fish bites the best. One of those hidden secrets he had learned from his father which he had managed to keep only to himself for all these years. Although normally, he was reluctant to reveal any of the good fishing spots, even to Jaaku. But today, after hearing Jaaku's negative news, his own egoistic need to prove everyone else incompetent, had grown stronger. He wanted to show there was nothing wrong with the lake but the amateur fishermen themselves.

One of his many secrets had always been to depart that crucial one to two hours earlier in the morning than other fishermen. He also kept distracting others by changing his spot constantly, even if he was catching more at the place he had left behind. He never revealed the best spots to anyone, yet he kept returning to them slightly more often than the other less interesting spots, yet maintaining the whole process as discreet as possible. He was a very quiet fisherman and didn't make a fuss about catching even the big fishes. He didn't want to cause a scene and be noticed as that would again attract other fishermen near the bountiful places he or his father had discovered. Persistence and patience were his best qualities. He kept moving constantly in a search for the best bite. He was on the move all the time, always a little bit more than the others. His equipment were not the latest fashion items or expensive, but all handcrafted - a hobby he got into at the age of five inspired by Roar. When Sven was little, he had built small wooden boats with anchors, nets, rods, buckets, everything imaginable needed on fishing trips. The boats got only bigger as the years went by as himself became more experienced and confident.

'I would suggest we row along the west coast of the lake and then go around Moose Island and come back down,' Jaaku said.

'That sounds feasible. Or we head straight up north east and from there we could come down past the town along the east coast,' Sven said, oozing confidence. 'I know a few really good spots near where the competition was held.'

'Right,' Jaaku snorted and nodded submissively.

As good as the fishing areas suggested by Sven were, the other reason he wasn't keen about Jaaku's idea to travel west was that his father and Carl had disappeared exactly near Moose Island on the west side of the lake. Or so it was believed. He had consciously avoided that part of the lake since an early age. Even to the extent that he would rather choose to reveal some, but not all, of his secret fishing spots to Jaaku.

Even though, Jaaku felt privileged to have befriended an ice fishing champion, at times like this, he wished they were more equal in terms of skills and achievements.

Whilst Jaaku took first strokes, Sven revealed the ancient trolling device inherited from his father that was given to him by his father, Sven's grandfather, Jørgen. He dropped the lure into the water and let the line extend a good length. The lure raced behind the boat as Jaaku increased the speed.

They passed the middle of the lake. The early morning was calm and mild. The temperatures were again warm for the time of the year, close to zero degrees Celsius. Sven loosened up his jacket. Jaaku pulled down his fur hood.

'Are we there yet?' Jaaku took another long stroke and paused rowing. He raised the oar blades out of the water.

'Not yet. But can you see the tip of the peninsula with the formation of six rocks?' Sven pointed past Jaaku.

Jaaku turned his head around and nodded.

'If you just row between the second and third rock from the left and then about ten to fifteen metres behind them, is one great spot', Sven said, sounding knowledgeable.

After hearing the revelation, Jaaku's eyes lightened. He corrected his posture. At first, he had thought he wasn't bothered about Sven's secrets, but once they were openly shared, the curiosity increased. He slammed the oar blades back in the water and rowed like a reborn.

As much as this journey was about helping the entire community and for the greater good, it was also about proving themselves again as great fishermen. As usual, Jaaku feared to be left in the shadow of Sven, if Sven was to discover fish and show that there is nothing wrong with the condition of the lake. On the other hand, *it was better option than no fish at all,* Jaaku thought. But deep down inside him, he wished it to be anyone else than Sven to make any revealing discoveries.

Yolla glided on the shallow water and through the second and the third rock. The bottom touched a rock slightly hidden below the surface. Dangerous environment for fast speed boats and only suitable for rowing slowly.

Before the investigations showed that the marks on the bottom of the Yolla were from Roar's boat, it was believed that rocks like these just barely underwater had caused Carl to lose control. A few weeks before the incident, Carl had installed a four horsepower back engine on his boat. The turbo boost exceeded the recommended top speed by many kilometres per hour. In fact, Yolla's were not supposed to carry any sort of engines. All the advice Carl ignored.

The tuned up boat mixed together with a possible, few dosages of alcohol, that both, Roar and Carl, were believed to have enjoyed, created a fatal combination. The original theory explained that Carl's boat had hit the rocks at a fast speed. His boat flipped upside down throwing him against the rocks. He fell unconscious. Even Yolla's unsinking qualities didn't save him.

'This is it! Stop!' Sven raised his arm.

Jaaku stopped rowing, yet keeping the oars still underwater. He pushed the oars a little against the current, so that the boat would stop sooner.

'Here!' Sven pointed at the dark blue water.

'The best fishing spot?'

'Not quite, but a good one,' Sven said, examining the water. He retrieved the line and put the trolling device aside. Instead, he took a swivel and a sliding egg weight from his pocket. He grabbed the end of the fishing line of his rod and used Palomar knot to tie the sliding egg and swivel before the hook. He went for his bag, took out a plastic jar of crawlers, opened the lid and pinched one between his fingertips. He pulled the crawler in half and placed it on a hook. As the last thing, he used a needle to pump some air into the crawler. The rod was ready and he cast it about ten metres away. The crawler floated a while until it sunk deeper.

Jaaku observed him with curiosity, until he prepared his own. 'What's that... pumping air inside the worm about? I've never seen that done.'

'It's one of those many things my father taught me. It keeps the worm nicely afloat, until it begins to sink and float, back and forth. The movement's supposed to attract more catch.'

'I see,' Jaaku said, grabbed one of Sven's crawlers and put it in the hook. 'May I try as well?'

'Sure. Go for it,' Sven handed him the needle.

Jaaku filled his worm with air nearly to the extent it was about to burst.

'That's enough! You don't need to make a balloon out of it!' Sven said.

Alarmed, Jaaku pulled the needle off the crawlers skin and cast the bait on the opposite side.

The men sat and waited.

After about twenty minutes of no success, they pulled up their baits and moved around the bay according to Sven's orders and understanding.

However, the next spot didn't bring any catch either.

'It must be because of the competition this bay is empty,' Sven said with a tinge of desperation in his voice. 'I know where to go next...' he grabbed the oars and began rowing himself.

Jaaku pulled up all his gear on the boat as Sven propelled the oars vigorously. An orange halo developed on the horizon. The sun was about to rise in the next half an hour or so. A few other fishermen had appeared on the shores to prepare their boats and gear. However, none of them had hit the waters yet, but soon.

Moose Island was getting nearer in the direction they were heading towards.

'I thought you didn't wanna go west?' Jaaku asked.

'I changed my mind,' Sven admitted, face red from all the hard work.

'I can row for a change,' Jaaku suggested.

'We are almost there,' Sven took another few strokes and looked around and at the water. He glanced towards Moose Island. The distance seemed right to all the landmarks. Sven stopped rowing.

'This is a good spot?' Jaaku asked, surprised.

'The best of all spots. Right here,' Sven said, panting, took a deep breath and continued more seriously, '...and where...it all happened...'

'Happened...what?'

'Carl's boat was discovered... and presumably, my father got lost,' Sven said, swallowing.

'Both of them... at the same place?'

'So far, there is no other explanation. The investigators at the time said that back in the shore where the two had departed, they found my father's footsteps on the snow next to Carl's boat. There had been some form of interaction between them already before they left the shore. Their boats were parked not so far from each other. There may have been even a struggle between them two. The snow was left really messy and tampered between the parking lots of their two boats. There was an empty bottle of Wodka found on the tampered snow. The forensics found my father's DNA in Carl's life vest that got washed up on the shore some weeks later. Or what was left of the life vest.'

'Your father was a man of peace.'

'So was Carl as far as I remember. He was opposite to... for example, Viljo, who has a short temper.'

'I found it hard to believe there were any quarrel between them two. Viljo is different, though. He's a bitter old man. Especially now after you beat him in the competition.'

'He won fifteen times, though. I think he had his share of glory.'

'But he never won against your father and now you've beaten him too. It must bother him and make him doubtful, whether he really was the true champion all those years.'

'It doesn't matter. I respect him and his victories. But as you say, it must have bothered Carl as well, the fact that he never beat my father.'

'Sure. But he wouldn't attack your father just two weeks before the competition. That just wouldn't make sense.'

'You think Carl found out my dad's secret fishing spots?'

'What are you suggesting?'

'Nothing.'

'Who really knows?'

'Only God knows, since they're both gone now.'

'I can imagine, though, that Carl must have been really fed

up and jealous.'

'With what?'

'Of losing,' Jaaku said it himself. The words "losing" and "jealous" were like from the story of his life - the position he had had to endure to the great extent. If years of losing drove the situation between Carl and Roar that critical, where his and Sven's relationship would turn into within the years to come? He didn't even want to imagine. Unless, he would start winning. *But how?*

Sven examined the clear surface of the lake. Early morning hours always gave him sense of tranquility; those few magical moments before the nature and people wake up and begin their noisy routines. The trees stood still and the water remained flat and calm. Not a day went by he didn't think about his father. He hadn't returned to this place after his death. The memory of Roar whom he remembered like yesterday made him avoid the ghastly spot. He had often sailed nearby, but never had the courage to face the pain. The presence of Jaaku helped him stay manly and not cry.

'Are you alright?' Jaaku asked.

Sven hid his emotions. 'Yes. Let's move on around that corner,' he said and pointed at the rocky tip of Moose Island. 'As far as I remember, there are some good spots, too.'

Enthusiastically, Jaaku looked to the direction Sven steered the boat. He was looking forward what lay ahead. He felt like he was that kid again in a candy store or a fish enthusiast in his favourite fishmonger. This particular part of the lake was more unfamiliar to him and he was curious to hear more about Sven's expertise that, potentially, would help him in his future career. He would definitely be returning back here, alone.

Light grey clouds lined up at the horizon ready to block the soon-to-be rising sun, whereas in the middle of the lake above Sven and Jaaku the sky was clear and blue. Some fishermen on the shore had just departed their daily journeys.

As Sven steered the boat towards the island, he started to hesitate. He got second thoughts about revealing the best spots, even to his most trustworthy friend, let alone the other fishermen soon filling the lake, who could see their boat's location and recognise him, the champion. His palms began to sweat. His hand slipped over the oar handle.

'Are you sure you're alright?' Jaaku asked, more concerned.

Sven nodded and grabbed the oar.

The best kept fishing secrets were the legacy Roar had passed on to his only son, the knowledge Sven had used well and further developed exploring the lake's unlimited capacity. He had known Jaaku since they were kids. They were like brothers. He felt guilty about the distrust towards Jaaku or anyone else.

During Sven's fishing career, and especially, after his first victory, there were debates within the fishing community, if Roar in his prime and Sven in the shape he was today were both competing in the same era with the same equipment, who would win? Majority of the village people believed Roar would still be unbeatable. Sven had only won one championship so far, which was nothing compared to Roar's sixteen victories. Roar used more primitive and simple equipment which meant the skill set, knowing the environment and just simple toughness played a more important role, whereas the sports had developed so much within the last decades that for Sven's generation the advanced technology and more developed methods assisted hugely with catching the fish.

That all having said, Sven knew most of the things his father knew and the rest he had to explore himself. Whether he had learned more than Roar could never be seen.

Now, though, Sven had to react fast not to let the family secrets spread all across Pihtamo. The other fishermen were filling the lake around them. The feeling of guilt, if he was to pass on the legacy to Jaaku instead of his own future offspring born in the unforeseeable future with unforeseeable partner, wore him out. Now, he was about to share classified information outside his family only for mere egoistic reasons.

'We are running out of time,' Sven said.

In the meantime, Jaaku prepared their fishing rods using new techniques he had just picked up from Sven earlier.

*He's learning fast,* Sven thought and stopped rowing. He put the oars back in the boat. 'I am gonna tell you something now that I promised on my father's grave, that I wouldn't do. But since you have become like a family member to me, I feel like I can share this secret.'

'You can tell me anything,' Jaaku said convincingly and put his rod aside. He listened attentively.

'Can you see that green patch in the middle of the big bush of light brown reed? We are heading there. That is one of the hotspots in the entire lake.'

Jaaku raised his gaze. He couldn't believe what he saw and heard. A secret kept for more than a half a century was about to become revealed, and he had the only front seat ticket.

Sven pulled up about three metres in front of the patch. He kept the boat steady. He took the oars inside the boat and threw the little stone anchor to the bottom of the lake.

'You must promise me not to share these secrets with anyone,' Sven said to Jaaku, looking straight into his eyes.

'I promise,' Jaaku said and handed him the prepared rod. 'Good luck!' he said and smiled.

'This has nothing to do with luck,' Sven grabbed the rod, turned his back to Jaaku and cast the bait. Jaaku took his rod and did the same at his end of the boat.

They only had to wait for a few seconds, when Sven already felt some resistance. 'I think I got one,' he said, smiling. 'A big one!'

*I cannot believe it,* Jaaku thought and shook his head in awe.

The weight bent Sven's rod onto a steep curve as he reeled. 'Behold! This is how it's done,' he said and yanked forcefully. The end of the line flew up in the air revealing a large stack of seaweed and mud.

'Way to go champion!' Jaaku laughed.

Sven grunted, brought the bait closer, shook the dirt off and dropped it back in the water to let it soak. Frustrated, he released the bait even further out.

'How are you doing then? Any better?' Sven asked sarcastically.

'Not better, not worse.'

'We must go soon. The lake will fill up with the others in a matter of minutes.'

'Why don't we just observe them and see if they catch

anything?'

'Observe? We didn't come here to observe. We came here to fish!'

'Keep it down, will you. You're scaring all the fish away.'

'The fact that you haven't caught any fish recently has really...' Sven lowered his voice.

'Has what?' Jaaku glanced over his shoulder to Sven.

'...damaged your confidence as a true fisherman.'

'You think so?' Jaaku snorted and turned away focusing on his stationary, lifeless fishing line.

'I'm sorry,' Sven's voice softened.

'No. I agree with you...' Jaaku paused and took a deep breath, '...if you catch any fish today. Even just one. If you don't, I'll accept your apology.'

Sven said nothing, neither did Jaaku. They both just sat in silence and fished.

Another fifteen minutes went by without any action, not even a nibble. About a dozen of other boats had departed the shores, a few men already tried to fish at different parts of the lake, a couple of them approaching the island. The horizon had taken more red and pink colour as the sun began to rise. The white clouds moved over the lake.

'We should try another spot,' Sven broke the silence.

'I thought you said this is the best spot there is?' Jaaku asked, bewildered.

'One of them... but we cannot reveal this to the others. They are getting too close. We have to make a move.'

'But we haven't caught anything, apart from your muddy discovery earlier.'

'It doesn't matter,' Sven said nervously. 'There are plenty of other good places. Can you see that grassy area in the middle of the peninsula between those two huts with wooden jetties in both of them.'

'The green grass with yellow tips?'

'Yes, that one. About a boat length in front of the grass line there's an amazing spot with two big rocks underwater. I always put my nets there and catch is unbelievable.'

'Let's go there then,' Jaaku muttered, satisfied. He couldn't believe what he was hearing. All the best secrets were revealed just in one morning. *This is better than the Christmas Eve*, he thought and rubbed his palms together.

They pulled out their untouched baits off the water and placed them next to each other on the boat. Jaaku grabbed the oars this time while Sven showed the direction.

Immediately, another boat from the distance approached the spot they had just left.

'See! Those guys found my favourite spot now,' Sven cried. *All my secrets are being revealed!*

'Doubt they'll be any luckier than us.'

'Why you have to be so negative?'

'Aren't you happy, if they catch nothing?'

'I suppose...'

Jaaku shook his head and kept rowing. *Favourite spot, right?* He didn't want any confrontation now, but rather kept it quiet. He just gave Sven a long blank look and rowed.

Momentarily, Sven felt losing his credibility as the master fisherman, but he wished to regain that once they reach the next location. 'Can you see those two white waterlilies in front of the grass?'

Jaaku nodded.

'Just park between them.'

Jaaku rowed towards the flowers wishing this battle of egos was over soon. He stopped caring about who was right or wrong anymore. He began to wish he was wrong and Sven would just catch something, even the tiniest herring, perch or a crab. Anything living underwater. Even a little frog. The show would be over and they could all go home, forget the suspicions and live happily ever after as good friends, fishing and drinking buddies. Sven would keep believing he's the best fisherman in town and so forth. Unless, Jaaku himself could take a real advantage of what he had learned this morning and alter the future for better. He felt the winds of change could finally start blowing for his benefit. The thought made him go on. 'Here?' asked Jaaku as he stopped between two blooming water flowers.

'Exactly! You know you're so good at rowing that you could become my assistant,' Sven grinned.

'Don't push it, champion! Just show me the fish.'

The two men grunted, turned their backs to each other and threw the baits in the water.

Meanwhile, another boat reached the spot they had just been, Sven's number one fishing spot. The boat circled around and in front of the grass, not quite being able to locate the exact coordinates where Sven and Jaaku had left earlier.

For all of his life, Sven had kept these secrets from the others, until now, because of an insane mission to prove his friend that there is still fish in one of the most bountiful lakes in the planet. His heart turned upside down as he felt betraying his father's trust.

The two other fishermen in the distance lowered their tackle in the water. Another spotted Sven. He showed him thumbs up, thanking him for the tip. And then the man waved. He recognised Sven from the ice fishing competition, but Sven couldn't recognise him as back then he was too concentrated on winning.

Sven feared all the fishermen on the lake would now follow them, one by one, and discover his hidden secrets. Thereby, he would lose his secret weapon against the others in any of the future summer competitions. *Was this all worth it?* He promised to himself that these spots revealed today would be the only spots ever seen by anyone else, period.

'It seems pretty quiet again,' Jaaku said.

'Yes, it does,' Sven replied, deadly concerned. The silence was compelling. Something Sven never had to experience in his twenty-five years of fishing.

'I told you,' Jaaku's voice had a bit more confidence now. 'You've seen the other boat? They went to the spot we've just left.'

'I can see them.'

'Sorry, mate. Now they all know your top spots.'

'That's alright. I still have a few up on my sleeve.'

'Unbelievable!' Jaaku said, sounding genuinely respectful. 'So, have these other men... caught anything?'

'No. Not a single thing.'

'What do you think?'

'Very odd. Although they are not quite exactly on the spot

by the millimetre, but close enough.' Sven pulled out his bait and stopped fishing. 'They should definitely catch something. Like us, too, since we have been right on the spot, twice.'

Jaaku turned to look at him, his bait still in the water. 'It is very odd, isn't it?'

'I can't believe it,' Sven muttered. 'Why don't we just row back to the shore and while we go...' he swallowed and felt a lump in his throat, 'observe the others?'

Rather than feeling relief, or sense of victory over Sven's stubbornness and earlier arrogance, to his own surprise, Jaaku felt sadness watching his friend that he so much admired and looked up to, giving up, and not being able to catch anything. *Sven has always caught something. As long as I have known him.*

Jaaku put away his gear and took the oars.

'Don't worry. I can row,' Sven leaned forward and grabbed the oars from Jaaku.

'Are you sure?' Jaaku asked, bewildered.

'Yes, please. You just keep looking what the others are doing. I will do the same as much as I can.'

'Okay. Whatever you say... champion,' Jaaku said, trying to cheer Sven up.

Aggressively, Sven swung both oars splashing the water around. Quickly, the boat picked up speed. He grimaced and looked at the sun that had fully risen. *The champion, ey? Ha!* The bright red semicircle light peaked behind the tips of the dark green pine trees. The rays of light penetrated some of the thinner clouds while the thicker ones kept blocking them. Many parts of the lake were filled with boats now, yet not quite like at heydays of the fishing boom.

Jaaku kept observing them all in turns, Sven too what he was capable of while rowing. 'No one's catching anything,' Jaaku said as he was looking through a little telescope he had pulled out of his breast pocket.

Sven stopped rowing for a moment. Over his shoulder, he peered at the boats behind them. He sensed frustration in the atmosphere, not only within himself, but the whole community of fishermen. 'Let's get outta here. This is way too odd. I don't understand,' Sven said and started rowing. He faced Jaaku again.

'Maybe we should go and meet that friend of yours.'

'The ring maker?'

'Yes. Since there is no herring here. I think now is the right time to get Ida... her ring.'

'I think so, too.'

Chapter 7

# A DECENT PROPOSAL

For the last three hundred years, Ida's family had had control over twenty acres estate on the lowlands of Örebröre, sheltered behind the volcano of Saalamaa and the surrounding mountain ranges. A three-metre-high corrugated iron gate and thick green hedges securely hid a seven bedroom, two dining room, four bathroom countryside mansion with annexed heated indoor swimming pool and a sauna for up to twenty-five people, and two separate guest cottages. In front of the main entrance lay a circle water fountain that in the winter freeze took different shapes of ice sculptures. The main building had thick, timber window frames and a thatched roof. The garden filled with lingonberry and raspberry bushes also had a hedge maze made of cypress trees where Ida often got lost as a child whilst playing hide and seek with her sisters.

A lucrative ski resort business on the mountainside passed on from one generation to another for the last sixty years provided most of the family's current income and wealth. Earlier on, farming on fertile grounds gave Ida's ancestors bountiful crops making them the largest single producer of swede, turnips and barley.

The ski resort established by Ida's grandfather and currently ran by her father, Gustav, had become a monopoly in the region. Only recently, the warm winters and the lack of snow caused problems and shortened the peak season sometimes from one to two months a winter. It was a setback for the business. However, the family's wealth built up and generated within the past centuries was secured for decades to come, no matter the circumstances around them. None of the family members had to work, ever. The function of the current business venture was to pass time; a cure for boredom.

Occasionally, Ida assisted with the company's administrative and secretarial tasks, time permitting. Mostly, though, she kept herself occupied managing her own husky farm that her father arranged for her eighteenth birthday. Örebröre Husky Experience offered sleigh rides for the tourists visiting the ski slopes, and some of the buildings left useless from the decline of the farming business had been converted into agricultural accommodation adjoined by a small farm animal sanctuary and a cafe. She also liked to keep many pets: three cats, a furry rabbit and a white horse called Elma. She loved to spend time in the wild and with her animals.

The interest on the nature and simplicity in life were a few of those characteristics that Ida had in common with Sven, who in his primitiveness was something opposite to the environment and people she had grown up surrounded by: superficial elitists and upper class academics. Almost as if Sven was somewhat of an exotic creature to her; different and raw. He possessed all those rough edges that she had been missing in her life. And yet she was keen to polish those edges, once she got the chance. However, the opportunity went past her with the failing of their relationship.

The two lovers came from a completely different social classes, which however didn't stop them from falling for each other in the first place. Sven's early success in the ice fishing contests made an impression on Ida. She saw the potential in him early on. She had a hunch that one day *he would make it*. Her interest intensified hand in hand with Sven's growing success. As he did *make it*, Ida felt she could take part of the credit being the inspiration and motivator to him. His muse. Until the herring in the altar reminded her that he was just an ordinary man. A fisherman and nothing more.

Unlike Ida's first boyfriend, Christian, who had the looks, wealth and connections, had lost her due to ignorance and neglect. And due to relatively young age and the need to gain more life experience, so to speak. In theory though, Ida and Christian should have been a perfect match. But *something was missing*, Ida had always thought while in a relationship with Christian.

All that time spent together with Sven had also opened Ida's eyes about the imperfection in her own family. She learned from listening to Sven, how Roar, always, besides bringing fish to the table, did his utmost to spend time with his family, unconditionally – type of caring Birgget continued towards their only son to this day. Ida couldn't see the same effort invested by her own parents. Often money and things to buy substituted the time spent together. Mainly, Ida had grown up with her nanny; Sven with his parents. That made a big difference. Sven felt like he really knew his parents, but Ida couldn't say the same. She wasn't sure. She had created an image of them, an understanding and interpretation, which might have been completely an inaccurate portrayal and a product of her imagination. Even though, Sven had lost his father at the age of twelve, he felt he knew him much better than Ida knew her own father. And now, she had grown closer to Birgget than her own mother, Sophia.

Gustav's business and social interests compromised his time spent with the family and children. He worked six, sometimes seven days a week, twelve to fourteen hours a day plus the other responsibilities he felt he had to fulfil, like after-work cocktail parties and the Rotary Club membership duties. Whereas, Sophia was part of the social elite. She co-ordinated the local Tuppervaara and candle house party scenes, and her social network was extensive. Tuppervaara was a local kitchen products line, all made of wood. The brand got its name from a lofty mountain near the volcano.

Gustav and Sophia showed real interest about Ida's errands for the first time, once they found out about her relationship with Sven. Dealing that closely with a lower class fisherman was uncalled for. In any circumstances, they couldn't relate to Sven's working class background. He was the least suitable partner candidate for their blue-blooded daughter.

In an attempt to separate the young couple, Gustav enrolled

Ida to the top university over a thousand kilometres away to start her Erasmoose programme, where her both sisters had ended up, stayed, settled down, found academic jobs and married academic husbands, that both Gustav and Sophie could approve.

Neither did Ida accept his father's effort to force the two lovers apart and she rebelled. She ran away from home to live together with Sven in his lakeside cottage, until the failed marriage attempt broke them apart.

Gustav and Sophia were amongst those very few who actually celebrated quietly the moment the herring appeared from Sven's pocket. Even though, the embarrassment for their daughter was huge, they knew in the long run the wedding being called off would be for her good, and for the best of the family interest and the name.

Gustav's curiosity about his youngest daughter's well-being kept growing, but purely out of his own interest. He wanted to secure that the future and the heritage of the family remains in the hands of the noble. Swiftly, he moved on and spoke to his business associate and a colleague in the Rotary Club, Roger, whose son, Christian, they thought, should be re-introduced to Ida after a few years break. Previously, Ida and Christian had dated in the high school for two semesters.

Now, Christian, at the age of twenty-seven, one year junior to Ida, already managed his own forestry maintenance business set up and funded, naturally, by his father. He was a fresh bronze medallist from the ice fishing competition. And he sat beside Ida on the bed in her bedroom on the top floor of Ida's parents' mansion. Ida glared outside the window in the distant darkness.

'What are you thinking?' Christian took Ida's hand.

'Nothing. I'm just tired,' Ida faced him and forced a little smile.

Ida's father's voice carried upstairs. 'Me and mother are leaving to the party. Don't wait for us. We will be late.'

'Have fun!' Ida yelled, sarcastically.

'Enjoy, you two!' Sophie added. 'You have the house to yourselves now. We've let the security staff go early as well as since Christian is here to protect you.'

'Thank you for letting us know, ma'am!' Christian shouted

politely and turned to Ida. 'Aren't you happy they are leaving?'

'Story of my life,' Ida said. 'They've always been gone. Can't really tell the difference.'

The heavy outdoor slammed shut and soon they heard two snow mobiles skid away. The roars of engines disappeared into the forest.

'So, what would you like to do now?' Christian smiled. 'Watch a film?'

'I'm kinda tired.'

'Would you like to... lie down a little bit?' Christian placed his hands on her shoulders and gave her a little rub.

'I beg your pardon?' Ida pulled away in awe.

'I mean... if you're tired. Or I can leave... if you want to be alone,' Christian mumbled.

'Please don't go. I don't wanna be alone tonight,' Ida said, placed her head on his chest and wrapped her arms around him.

Christian struggled to hide his smile as they embraced. His dimmer success in the ice fishing contest was getting shinier end. He was winning the best price after all. He slid his hand down on Ida's lower back.

'I'm not a toy, though,' Ida whispered suggestively to his ear to slow down.

Politely, Christian brought his hand up on her middle spine. He pressed harder again between her *latissimus dorsi* and *serratus posterior inferior*. As he continued rubbing her, a knock on the door alarmed them.

'Don't stop,' Ida said quietly, but opened her eyes.

'But... there's someone behind the door,' Christian said and stopped the massage.

'It's probably just Jehova's Witnesses,' Ida said and pressed her body closer to Christian's. She shook a little as a hint for him to keep going.

And he did touch her back again, when another, heavier knock on the door followed. 'What do you think?' Christian asked.

'I ain't expecting anyone. Let's wait and see.'

Christian smiled and reached higher on her *rhomboid* minor and major.

No more knocks on the door and they could both relax. Christian reached out for the light switch of the corner lamp. He pulled the string downwards and the room turned dark, apart from the moon and the stars litting them just enough to recognise each other's silhouettes.

As he turned her around, he leaned over to kiss her lips. Subtly, she avoided his lips that ended up landing on her cheek. They both smiled.

Suddenly, though, a loud thumping noise shaking the bedroom window brought them back to reality. 'What was that!?' Ida squealed.

They both turned to look at the window that had a white circle of snow in the middle.

'A snow ball?' Christian said, puzzled. 'Jehova's Witnesses here seem very persistent.'

'They must have seen the light in the window,' Ida suggested.

Christian stood up and took a step towards the window, when a corner of the top of a ladder smashed through breaking the glass in the middle. He jumped back next to Ida and pulled her in the far corner.

'Get the salmon, the frozen salmon!' Ida hushed to Christian. 'The next door, there's a little kitchen corner, where my parents left the salmon on top of a freezer to defrost. Get it, quick! It might come in handy.'

Christian looked at her confused, but did as she told. He got out of the room and as he returned with a gigantic, frozen Atlantic salmon on his hand, a dark shadow appeared behind the broken window.

'Hit the burglar,' Ida instructed, 'with the salmon!'

He gave the salmon a glance before raising it on his shoulder like getting ready to bat a baseball. He sneaked behind the wall beside the window frame when the intruder jumped through and landed on the floor. He gave another quick look at Ida who nodded approvingly. Christian raised the salmon above his head and gave the stranger lying on the floor a good beating.

'*Herregud!*' the man swore in pain and rolled on the floor taking the first hits, but avoiding the rest.

Ida tucked herself in the furthest corner and switched the

light on. Christian kept smacking the floor as the victim kept rolling from side to side. After a few seconds of blindness due to light sensitivity, Ida's vision returned. She recognised the intruder. 'Sven!?'

Christian, though, didn't pay attention, yet took another swing directly on Sven's guts. Sven grimaced in pain. His hands were bleeding as he held his stomach.

'Stop it, Christian! It's Sven!' Ida panicked.

*I know*, he thought and lifted the salmon up above, again, like raising an axe being ready to chop. But he didn't hit anymore, yet he was ready and keen if he had to.

Ida rushed to stop Christian. She pushed him away and kneeled beside injured Sven. She helped him in a seated position against the wall and shook his upper body. 'Wake up, please!' she slapped him on the cheeks.

Sven opened his eyes. He held his jawbone in agony. An object moved inside his mouth. 'Ida... My love. That was some good batting. Have you ever thought about a career in baseball?' Sven spit pieces of one of his back tooth on the floor. Accidentally, he wiped the blood of his palms on the carpet. 'Sorry about that. I will clean up the mess.'

'What on earth you think you were doing!? We thought you were a burglar,' Ida said.

'We...?' Sven looked around and saw a dark shadow standing in the corner.

'Perhaps, he is a burglar of some sort,' Christian added and appeared in the moonlight.

'What is... he doing here!?' Sven jumped on his feet and pointed at Christian with his bleeding hand.

'I believe the question is, why are you breaking into my house in the middle of the night?' Ida asked.

'What do you think, why?' Sven said. 'You've literally disappeared!'

'Do you really understand what you did to me?'

'It was an accident.'

'An accident! How can you mistake a ring for herring?'

'I was...' Sven stuttered. 'It's very difficult to explain. I don't know if I can.'

'I thought you couldn't,' Ida said and turned away.

'Are you alright, darling?' Christian took a step closer to them both, but offered his hand to Ida.

'I'm fine,' she said and ignored Christian's gesture.

'Darling? Did he just call you "darling?"' Sven snorted.

'It's really nothing. This is not what it looks like,' Ida explained and changed the topic. 'We should get you into hospital. You're bleeding.'

'Nothing?' Christian turned to Ida. 'We were just going to bed, until he barged in.'

'Bed!?' Sven squealed. 'You were going to bed with that... loser?'

'Watch your mouth!' Christian puffed his chest and took a step closer to Sven. 'At least I ain't proposing my girlfriend with a smelly fish.'

'Says a man holding a big salmon,' Sven smirked.

'I may have to slap you again if you don't shut your mouth!' Christian raised the fish up in the air again.

'You slap like a woman!' Sven fired back, holding his already bruised chin.

'You two, break it up!' Ida intervened and pushed the men apart. 'You're acting like two children.'

Sven leaned over to her and whispered. 'He's not your new boyfriend, is he?'

'No... Of course not. We're... just friends,' Ida hesitated.

'What are you two whispering?' Christian leaned over, spreading the smell of fish even further.

'I need to speak to her in private, please,' Sven demanded.

'I don't think it's a good idea,' Ida said.

'Of course it's not!' Christian intervened and looked at Ida. 'Don't you think it's time for him to leave now?'

'Please,' Sven said to Ida, ignoring Christian's cry. 'I guess I deserve to be heard. This one time. I have made this eighteen hour journey with my kicksled through the forests that I hate and fear. I have missed a few bullets from moose hunters, avoided your security cameras and guard husky dogs...'

'Hold on. What did you do to my guard dogs?' Ida asked.

'I distracted them with some... herring,' Sven replied.

'Naturally,' Ida snorted.

'They loved it.'

'Go on.'

'And, knowing your parents are not particularly in favour of me either, I have made this journey, only to see you and speak to you. I am begging you, please listen to me, this once, and then I promise, I will never bother you again. Ever. And you can live happily ever after with whoever and however you wish. Please.'

Ida's expression softened a little when he saw Sven's sad, doggy eyes. She turned to Christian, grabbed his shoulders and looked straight into his eyes. 'I'm really sorry. I have to ask you to leave. I hope you understand. I haven't seen him for months and there are certain things we have to discuss through.'

'As you wish...' Christian snorted, 'but please be careful. Don't trust him.'

'I'm so sorry, but I kinda knew this moment would come eventually. I owe this to him.'

'Fine. Call me as soon as you can.'

'Definitely. Speak to you soon,' Ida said and leaned over to hug Christian. He kissed her on the cheek, and while in the embrace, over her shoulder his and Sven's equally nasty looks met.

'Could you do me one last favour?' Ida asked Christian and pulled away to see his eyes again.

'Anything for you,' Christian smiled.

'If you could please put that salmon back into the freezer on your way out? I doubt we need it now.'

'Sure, love,' Christian said, wore his black leather coat, put the salmon in his armpit and exited the room. Once Ida heard the outdoor shut and the snow mobile engine roaring, she stepped in front of the broken window. Christian blew her a kiss that she caught, yet she only responded with a wave. Slightly concerned and jealous, he revved the engine and sped away.

Sven used the opportunity to take a step closer behind Ida. She kept looking outside the window, even though Christian was already out of sight.

'Ida... Let me explain,' Sven started.

'Don't bother. I have moved on. It's all in the past now,' Ida said, determined.

'I don't believe you. It's not in the past and we both know it. We never really talked about what happened. You just walked away and never returned to my calls or my attempts to reach you.'

'What do you expect a girl to do whose been offered...' she sobbed, but soon composed herself, 'a herring on the altar?'

'I know. There is no excuse. The only thing I can say to my defence is that... I am a fisherman and will always be.'

'It's obvious that you were not thinking about me, us. That one day is the most important day for any girl and you were not focused. Your mind was somewhere else.'

'That's not true! There was lot of pressure. And I was focused. I'm always. I had just reached the top by being nothing else but focused, for years, decades, almost all my life as long as I remember. I had just won the most wanted prize in Pihtamo, the ice fishing championship. Many men around here would be willing to lose their arm for the title. I have now what everyone else wants.'

'Are you happy?'

'No.'

'Why not? You just said you have everything you need. People envy you. You can have any girl you want. You're the champion.'

'Things have changed... I have changed. It doesn't feel the same without you. It used to be different, though. Everything was about fish. My life.'

'All about fish?'

'Yes. Until you came along and became important to me.'

'Worth of one disgusting herring?' Ida said sarcastically.

'More than that. Much more.'

Sven tried to touch Ida's shoulder, but she pulled away. 'What do you want from me?'

'I want you back. I cannot fish... or breathe without you,' Sven begged. 'I want us to be back together just like we used to be. We were so happy.'

'Were we, really?'

'I promise. I will change.'

'I don't know if you can.'

'Is it... Christian?'

'Him? No. As I said, we're just... friends.'

'Right,' Sven said doubtfully.

'You understand, things will never be the same.'

'I know. Things can only get better.'

'How?'

Sven reached out for the side pocket of his jacket. 'I have something for you...'

'There's nothing that can make the situation between us two any better,' Ida said and took a step further away from Sven, still her back towards him.

Sven lowered his other knee on the floor and pulled out a blue satin box. He stretched his arm towards Ida. 'Look at me.'

'Give me one reason, why I should look at you?' Ida said proudly, and distant.

'Because I want you to have... this.'

Slowly, Ida turned around revealing her watery eyes. The cold wind blew through the broken window. The curtains sway at her both sides. The full moon shone behind Ida creating a beautiful halo around her aura. She looked like an angel with wings. 'Another herring?' she cried and looked down at wet, bruised and tired Sven kneeling in front of her. He held a box on his bleeding, trembling hand.

'No catch today, I'm afraid.'

'No? You always catch. What happened to you?'

'I told you. Not without you,' Sven pleaded. 'Please open it.'

Hesitatingly, Ida took one step closer, reached out her shaking hand and opened the lid. 'A real ring!?' she burst into tears.

'Yes, my love,' Sven replied, took her left hand into his, picked the ring out of the box and placed it in her ring finger. 'Look. It even fits, too. Perfectly.'

Ida fell speechless. The tears rolled down her cheeks.

'I would like us to try again,' Sven looked into Ida's watery eyes. 'Will you marry me, Ida?'

Ida fell on her knees in front of him and embraced him tight. 'Ah, Sven!'

'Does that mean, yes?'

'Yes, I still want to marry you. I have always wanted to marry you. More than anything else,' Ida said and gave him a kiss. 'The only thing I wanted from you was a wedding ring, not herring.'

'I have missed you so much.'

'Me too.'

Chapter 8

# THE GREAT ESCAPE

The roar of snow mobile engines in the distance halted Sven's and Ida's blissful reunion. Ida wiped her teary face, kissed Sven on the nose and let go of the embrace. She got up and went to look through the broken window. 'It's my parents coming back! They are never home this early. They are never home!'

'I have to get out of here. Sure I'm the last person they want to see here with you,' Sven said and took Ida back into his arms. 'When will I see you again?' he asked, portraying unusual amount of passion for a typical, stoic Arctic man of his like.

Ida's heart nearly jumped off her chest as Sven's strengthened arms pulled her against his body. His hands caressing her waist made her tingle. 'I come with you,' she answered without hesitation.

'When?'

'Right now,' she said, filled with determination. She released herself from Sven's hold and went to open her wardrobe. She searched for something warmer to wear. She caught Sven's attention by dropping her casual wear on the floor and revealing a white, silky underwear set on her. Meticulously, Sven observed every curve and slender and toned muscle in her, yet feminine figure. After months of solitude, seeing her immaculate white skin, strong legs, wide shoulders, and long and curvy back resonated powerfully within his sensitised body and mind. 'What?' she stopped once she caught Sven staring.

'Nothing,' Sven looked away, puzzled. As Ida pulled her thermal layers on, the sound of snow mobiles got louder. Sven approached the broken window and threw his leg through the frame onto the top bar of the ladder. Like a snake, he twisted himself completely outside to stand on the ladder. 'Hurry up! I think I just heard the estate gates opening.'

Fully clothed in her long, blue woollen coat, winter boots, red mitts and a hat, Ida appeared behind the window, 'We have a door as well, you know?' she reminded while spraying a hint of perfume on her.

'Good point,' Sven said, looking stupid.

'Just take the ladder since you started. I'll meet you outside.' Ida rushed out of her room downstairs as simultaneously he descended the ladder. They reunited outside by Sven's kicksled, that made her laugh, 'Total madness to kick all the way here.'

'Well worth it.'

'I can see you've got a new front seat.'

'The old one got blown off the last time I tried to get here. Someone tried to shoot me. The hunters, I gather.'

'You've tried to come here before? How sweet of you,' Ida smiled.

'Yeah. Almost got me killed.'

She embraced him and sealed her lips over his.

Unfortunately, though, their intimate moment couldn't last long. The danger was near. Their lips parted. 'We probably should be going,' Sven said, gesturing at the front seat of his kicksled.

'Yes! But not like this,' Ida said, taking Sven from the wrist. 'Follow me,' she escorted him to the double garage next to the house. She pulled down a moose antler lever attached to the wall that automatically opened the garage door revealing a brand new snow mobile, still wrapped in a red ribbon.

'Wow! Is that yours?' Sven asked.

'Yeah. Nice, isn't it? A present my parents gave me after our wedding disaster. I guess they wanted to make me feel better.'

'How... nice from them,' Sven said, hesitantly.

'Whatever. Or they're just making up the time they never had for their kids by buying us stuff,' Ida said, untied the ribbon and jumped on the driver's seat. 'Hop on.'

'Are you sure this is a good idea?' Sven said, concerned while anxiously climbing on the backseat.

'Got any better ideas? Your kicksled?'

'Probably not,' Sven gave a nervous chuckle. 'You know how to ride this thing?'

'Just relax, but hold on tight.' Ida switched the engine on and revved while her parents' snow mobiles appeared from behind the corner. Gustav came out first. He noticed the open garage and the bright headlights. He sped towards them while Ida twisted the gas handle shooting her snow mobile out of the garage nearly colliding with his approaching father.

'Ida! What do you think you're doing?' Gustav yelled as they passed only a few centimetres away from each other.

'I'm sorry! I will write you both,' Ida glanced over her shoulder after skilfully avoiding the collision with her mother's snow mobile, too.

Both parents brought their snow mobiles to halt and looked dumbstruck behind them as Ida and Sven disappeared around the corner on the driveway leading towards the gates.

'Come back!' Gustav waved his fist. He hopped off the seat and ran towards the driveway. He grabbed a remote control from his pocket and pointed it towards the exit. As he pressed the button on the remote, the old rustic gates began to close in front of Ida and Sven and their speeding snow mobile escaping the estate.

Sven squeezed Ida's waist his knuckles turning pale. 'I don't think we can make it!'

But defying Sven's fearfulness and doubtfulness, Ida only accelerated towards the closing, screeching gates. The snow mobile only picked up more speed while bouncing off the pot holes and bumps on the road leading away from the mansion. Every little jump shot Sven up in the air taking his knees to Ida's armpits, yet he always ended up landing safely back on the seat behind her.

'Are you still there?' Ida glanced behind her.

Sven gave her a silent, nauseous nod.

As they reached the exit, the skis on both sides of the snow mobile scratched the closing gates. The loud screech made Sven cover his ears whereas Ida only hit the gas. Sparks flew as they sped through the narrow gap between the closing corrugated iron. As the snow mobile shot outside in one piece, they understood they had avoided the trap. They had narrowly escaped the slicing guillotine by only a few centimetres.

Frustrated, Gustav smashed the remote into pieces on the icy ground. In fury, he glanced in the distance how the young couple slipped out of their strict control. He hopped back on his snow mobile and put the helmet on. He was ready for a race. Although one of the very few things he knew about his daughter was that she was a skilled driver and that she had a good knowledge of the surrounding areas. He had to react fast. Inside her polite sweetness, there lived a furious petrol head secretly enjoying the adrenaline rush - a side of her even Sven wasn't fully aware about, until now while sitting as her passenger. Although he felt somewhat trusted at the backseat being driven by her. She seemed confident. And he had no other choice. The father-in-law was after them.

As Gustav revved the engine, Sophia, however, put her glove on his on the gas handle. 'Let them go, please,' she said and suffocated the engine.

'But why!? He's no good for her,' Gustav said and re-started the engine.

'She will return, eventually. Trust me. She has to learn her lesson. We all have. He will let her down again.'

'But... we can stop her from doing the same mistake again.'

'We cannot, always. Ida is an adult now. She has to learn, herself.' Sophia stopped the engine again. 'Let go, please.'

He grind his teeth as his daughter's, the black sheep's of the family, snow mobile's sound disappeared into the wild. He wasn't sure if he can ever forgive himself not to go after her. But he didn't go. He listened to his wife. Even though, at this very moment he felt he had failed in his duties as a parent and a father. Yet, if you ask Ida, he had failed all of his life.

Chapter 9

# THE MOOSE HUNTERS

So did Jaaku give in to temptation and soon returned to Sven's secret fishing hotspots. But this time he did it alone. However, the trip brought no further success, apart from the feeling of remorse and guilt of betraying the trust of the best friend.

Once again beaten by Lake Pihtamo, Jaaku dragged himself away from the shore on his kicksled. He pushed up the hill feeling demotivated. As he reached the peak and got to the edge, he sunk into his thoughts. *Where have all the fish gone?* Halfway through the slope, he let the gravity take him deeper into the forest.

Though, he wasn't alone with his doubts and fears. The other fishermen's pride had deteriorated as well and the critical situation began to threaten livelihoods. Fishing as the main industry in the area provided hundreds of fishermen and their families substantial, if not all, income and food on the table. Apart from shifting from fishing to hunting, which no man in Pihtamo has ever done and every one of them deeply contested, the alternatives for survival were minimal and the jobs scarce that required often hundreds of kilometres migration.

Once he hit the bottom of the hill, he started kicking again, sluggishly. He moved like a snail along the forest path leading up on the glacier and eventually, his igloo. He lacked all the motivation and energy. The fish was gone. An empty, cold home waited for him. No hopes for a better future. The spring snow falling off the tree branches blurred the visibility, but he didn't care. He moved on like a slow freight train over the peat, little rocks and cut branches.

Despite the failures and insecurities he had had to deal with, he tried to hold his head up high. He was a thick-skinned and rigid man. His Inuit heritage had helped him to survive in the most extreme conditions. He was known for his ability to withstand hours of freezing gusts of wind on an open ice. Although how equipped he was to survive through the challenges of life, only time would tell.

As he entered the deepest part of the forest, a loud, rippling gunshot slicing through the air caught his attention. He stopped to listen. The howling noise repeated twice. He heard footsteps behind the bushes and vegetation. 'Who is it!?' he called out to the forest. No response. Until the bristling sound of the ground got louder. Two men with rifles appeared from behind a thick spruce tree. One of them had a brown coat, the other green coat, and both wore black wellies. One man showed his teeth, the other didn't have any. The toothless man pulled a sleigh behind.

'Why are you here?' the man with teeth grunted.

'I... I was just passing by,' Jaaku stammered.

'You know, you shouldn't be here,' grimaced the toothless man.

'I was on my way home,' Jaaku said tensely and looked at the men's smoking rifles. 'So... you two are hunters, I gather?'

'Moose hunters, to be precise,' the man with teeth said. 'I am Börje. He's Kalle.' Börje tapped the shoulder of the toothless man who responded with a smile that displayed his glittering gums decorated with two brown stumps of teeth. 'I think you shouldn't be in the forest, when there are bullets flying across. Too dangerous for your kinds,' said Börje.

'My kinds? What's that supposed to mean?' Jaaku asked, agitated.

'You are a fisherman?' Börje concluded, spotting Jaaku's rod sticking out of his bag on the front seat of the kicksled.

'Yes, I am,' Jaaku said proudly.

'Then, tell us one thing. Did you catch any fish today?'

'Yeah. Did you, fisherman?' Kalle added, letting out a

portion of bad breath in the air.

'Erm. Not today,' Jaaku replied.

'And why is that?' Börje inquired.

'Just... didn't feel like it today.'

'I thought so,' Börje said and pointed at the full sleigh behind them covered with a tarpaulin. 'Well, we have caught four moose, six rabbits and one squirrel.'

'Hold on! I thought you guys only hunt moose!?' Jaaku said, raising his voice.

'Why do you care?'

'You shouldn't hunt other animals like squirrels and rabbits. They are...'

'What are they?' Börje interrupted. 'What makes them so different?'

'They are just... nice and cute.'

'Ah! And that's why we shouldn't kill them?' Börje glanced at Kalle and back to Jaaku.

Jaaku nodded.

'But, you kill fish?' Börje said.

'That's different,' Jaaku replied.

'How?' Börje asked, 'Only the fact that most of the fishes are ugly; that they lack furry coats and big cute brown eyes, doesn't justify you to kill them any more than us hunting other mammals and animals. From inside they are all exactly the same, which makes us the same. You and us are not so different after all.'

Kalle nodded, grinning his gums out.

'Not true,' Jaaku said hesitantly.

'We are all, fishermen and hunters... natural born killers,' Börje said. 'Admit it.'

'No! I think both of our choices are... a matter of taste.'

'Please! We all know we don't hunt or fish because of our sense of taste. We do it for the excitement or because we have no other choice. We are men. We were built this way. The nature meant us to be savage, to hunt and conquer,' Börje explained.

'...and stay away from the wife and the kids,' added Kalle.

'You can't change what we are,' Börje continued. 'Sure, it helps if you also like the taste of what you're hunting, but c'mon.

Ultimately, we do this only for survival.'

Jaaku couldn't but agree with what Börje had just said, but didn't want to let it show. Instead, he looked to the ground, speechless. The moose hunters were not completely wrong, but he was too proud to admit it. 'But... how come you are already here in the spring time?' Jaaku remembered. 'It's not the moose hunting season yet. That's in the autumn, right?'

'That's the way it used to be, but the new leader of Pihtamo Hunting Association has become more flexible about the hunting seasons,' Börje said convincingly. 'Since they are pest and rapidly spreading across the area, the hunters must do more to eliminate them. The limited hunting season was not enough to keep them under control. We are doing our society and nature a good deed. We are the embodiment of the true power over our flora and fauna. Us, humans are the only species able to keep this world in right balance.'

'Yeah. Why don't you give it a go?' Kalle said and offered Jaaku his lever-action rifle.

'Yes. Do it,' Börje encouraged. 'First time always hurts and then, gradually, you get the sense what it feels like to be... a real man.'

'A real man, yeah,' Kalle grunted and pushed the rifle right under Jaaku's nose. Jaaku raised his gaze and revealed his discomfort near firearms by taking a step back. He smelled the smoky gun barrel and lead.

'Think about it. We need more recruits to fight the expanding moose habitation,' Börje said.

'I don't need a weapon. I am a fisherman,' Jaaku hesitated.

Börje smirked and took a step closer to Jaaku. 'Let me tell you something. Hunting an animal as big as a moose together with manly men gives us an enormous amount of pleasure. Seeing the wounded animal fall makes the testosterone flow. Probably something you have never had a chance to experience in your life. Much better I believe than sitting morning after morning in the freezing cold boat or on a bucket on the ice, not being able to see your target, ever. Moose hunting gives you the chance to stalk, follow, observe and wait for the right moment to attack. They are our enemies. You're in control. You're in power as the man should be of its nature. We rule the nature and animals, not them us.'

'Like the fish, you can't control. They do as they wish... fish,' Kalle giggled.

'Not true! We lure!' poetically, Jaaku defended his choice.

'That's pure fishers luck, I tell you,' Börje said, annoyed. 'You have no idea what's really going on underwater. No one does, unless you're a diver or you have a submarine. I assume you are or have neither of those. If the fish bites it bites, but you have no control over that. I know you've learned all those best spots that you fishermen talk about, but fundamentally, your fishing is all about coincidence.'

'You have to know the right equipment, the gear, the spots, have years of experience,' Jaaku explained.

'Really? A worm can be enough to lure a fish. That's no rocket science. It's just a stupid crawler. A crawler wouldn't put down a large animal.'

'Well, actually, worms do... sometimes,' Kalle intervened.

'Shut up, idiot!' Börje shouted and turned back to Jaaku. 'Admit it. Sometimes the fish swims into your trap, sometimes doesn't. Who knows? Sure, you can find out the best spots, but that's like finding a bird's nest or bear's den and shooting the poor animal on their home porch. That's not what hunters do, but cowards. Tell me one thing. What sort of skills you really need to catch fish apart from patience and good luck?'

Jaaku listened attentively yet confused. 'Well, sometimes... you can feel them,' he muttered.

'Don't give me that crap!' Börje shouted.

'He's giving you the... crab,' Kalle smirked.

Börje slapped Kalle on the back of his head to shut him down. Then, he focused on Jaaku again. 'I know you fishermen can't feel a thing. Take this rifle now and I will show you true emotions, how it really feels to be a man. A hunter amongst other hunters. Savages with a common purpose. To track, entrap and eliminate.'

This time, Jaaku didn't pull his gaze off the rifle, but kept staring at the smoking barrel with an increasing interest. 'Fine!' he jerked the gun off Kalle's hand. 'I guess one shot won't hurt anyone.'

'That's a man talking,' Börje said, pleased. 'It may only hurt a moose, but that's what we were made of. Remember, we are above them, above all. We, hunters, are the Gods of the nature. We can do anything.'

As a man of peace and a conscientious objector, though, he faced a new challenge whilst holding the warm firearm in his hand. He felt a unique sensation, a mixture of excitement and guilt. Some years ago, he avoided the national military service by claiming his family run pie shop needed someone to manage it due to his father's illness who was the manager at the time. His army recruitment got postponed over and over again after a series of appeals, until the system gave up on him. After a while, his recruitment calls were just simply forgotten by the state and they stopped chasing him. Flawless system in Pihtamo turned out to be imperfect after all. The masters of bureaucracy had been beaten by a simple fisherman. There was hope.

But today Jaaku was taken a step further away from promoting peace. The cold metal parts of the rifle, the weight of the gun, compared to anything that resembled a weapon he had held before, mainly, those plastic toy guns he played with as a child, took him by surprise. He had to correct his stance to get a better grip of the weapon. There was no way of holding it loosely as sometimes he did with fishing rods, but a firm grip was required reminding Jaaku how physically mediocre and comfortable he had become compared to the hunters. All of his life he had only fished repeating the same movements over and over again. However, as versatile different types of fishing techniques can be from netting to hooking and trawling, the use of body and arms are always more or less the same. Unless you are pulling out the big ones on the Pacific or fighting against Atlantic bluefin tuna fish weighing four hundred kilograms. But Jaaku had never been on the outer ocean. In fact, his fishing experience limited on a few fresh water lakes within the Pihtamo region.

The biggest catch he personally ever recorded was a pike weighing about eleven kilograms. He managed to pull it right next to the boat, but the line snapped and the poor, old fish dived back in the depths of the lake with a tackle in its mouth, and the fish was never seen again. Apart from that, his normal catch size averaged to about two to four kilograms with an occasional individual weighing up to six kilograms. He was not a man of size, but quantity. Despite his sturdy appearance and short limbs, he was fast and agile at short stints, until his poor endurance often failed him.

He had all the capacity and skills to move into the outer sea after a bigger catch, but his lack of confidence never allowed him. He had always been in the shadow of other fishermen, either more well-known or experienced ones. He envied Sven, but did his utmost to hide the jealousy and not let it show. First, he tried to consider them as equals, even though Sven always beat him in the competitions. Gradually, though, he started to accept the fact he was no winning material. He couldn't see the opportunities lying ahead and around him. Looking at the combination of his skills and experience, he could have been one of the best, yet he had begun to convince himself that he can never win, but the others were somehow *built that way*. He didn't have those special qualities and the ability to withstand immerse pressure of major competitions. He did well on a local scale and small contests, when superstars like Viljo, Irmeli or Sven didn't participate. He felt stronger, more relaxed and confident, when the worst rivals, the top fishermen, were not distracting him and making him lose focus. The disturbance to his work was imminent, when he was competing against someone he believed was better than him. His poor success was mostly caused by psychological factors that he hadn't learned to deal with. He was trapped by his own insecurities. And the fish disappearing in Lake Pihtamo, even at Sven's favourite spots, deepened the despair.

After giving Jaaku a reasonable amount of time to admire and get familiar with the most common firearm in the world, Börje asked, 'How do you feel?'

The question caught Jaaku's attention, who was being like hypnotised by the feel of a cold trigger and still warm steel barrel. 'I have to admit that I feel... good,' he said and gave the hunters a little, devilish smile. Suddenly, he remembered when his father gave him the first fishing rod at the age of seven. The sensation he felt now was something similar to that special moment from the childhood.

'Now, please. Follow us,' said Börje determined. He grabbed Jaaku's shoulder in a manly manner.

Jaaku abandoned his kicksled and his fishing gear beside the track, and followed the two moose hunters into the deep forest only carrying for the first time in his life, a loaded firearm.

As they rambled through the density of pine trees to search for target practice, Jaaku caressed the rifle. *The new beginning?*

Chapter 10

# RYE'N'AIR

*Not quite as tropical as advertised*, Sven thought as he peered through the tiny round window of Rye'n'Air budget airline flying above South East England. Heavy rain whipped against the glass and grey mist covered the skies as the once-every-three-months flight from Kihlava airport waited for the permission to land in its final destination, London Heathrow. The famous landmarks and buildings were covered under the low lying clouds, apart from the tip of steep pyramid shaped glass structure that protruded through the grey smog.

As comfortably as Sven stayed on a dangerously thin ice for hours or days in a complete solitude, sitting belted and crammed on a narrow economy class seat surrounded by other heavily clothed Arctic tourists was way out of his comfort zone. His elements were down on the ground and near the water, not ten thousand kilometres up in the air.

Unselfishly, though, Sven was willing to go to any length to strengthen his and Ida's relationship. Even the fear of flying didn't stop him from using the offer he had received over the phone from the mysterious telemarketer. Sven managed to reach the cold caller and book their honeymoon after a successful, second wedding attempt.

While escaping Ida's parents on a snow mobile, somewhere between Örebröre and Pihtamo in the deep forest, they had passed a miniscule chapel organising private ceremonies for

96

couples who wanted to get married instantly and secretly. The dimly lit, glass-roofed chapel attracted Ida to pull over, first, only out of curiosity, but once they walked inside and took their first steps on the aisle together, they looked at each other and thought, *why not?* No words were needed, only telepathy. Both knew exactly what they were thinking. Since they had already let down so many relatives and friends at their first wedding, they wanted to avoid any problems what-so-ever the second time. Ida had her doubts whether her parents would attempt another wedding anyway, if the groom was Sven or anyone else from a similar background.

Caught up in the moment, they decided to elope right here, right now. They even had the ring. The conditions were perfect.

The priest on the altar offered them a Chapel of Lasi Vekasi Ceremonial Package that included everything a spontaneous couple would need to get married: herself as the priest, two witnesses, a hire tuxedo, a hire white wedding gown, a flower bouquet that the couple can keep, and once famous Italian folk star, heartbreaker and pizza restaurant entrepreneur Lumbardi Martello finishing the ceremony by singing accented Elvis classics as the newly-wed couple leaves the building.

Sven and Ida seized the day and married on the spot. An old saying circulating in Pihtamo perfectly applied to their wedding day: *He who has happiness, should hide it.*

As a last surprise, the priest came outside and tied some old winter wellies together with 'Just Married' sign at the back of Ida's snow mobile. As they left the chapel as a fresh husband and a wife, Sven rung the cold caller immediately, and the next day they were already on the plane to the warmer climates. *Everything just clicked*, reminisced Sven the wedding day as the plane took another turn in the air. The pilot announced they will be landing in twenty minutes.

Sven finished the remaining crumbs of his cold snack lunch. The familiar taste of overly expensive dark bread served on the plane had given him some comfort and distraction from the winding flight path, yet the airy consistency of the dough together with long, tense sitting began to fill his stomach with some unnecessary gas. *Thus, the airline name, Rye'n'Air*, he thought.

When they boarded the plane a few hours ago, Sven had squashed himself in the middle seat letting Ida sit by the window and admire the clouded views. Soon after being seated and the take off, he learned the positioning was a mistake. The aisle seat next to him was occupied by a slightly oversized man with an Anglo Saxon heritage of some sort. Since the departure, Sven did his utmost to avoid physical and eye contact with a man next to him. Such a close distance to another human being, another stranger, disturbed him largely and again, took him even further away from his comfort zone. Growing up in a culture that glorified solitude and silence had taught him to keep several metres, if not kilometres, safety distance to strangers - like two moving vehicles are supposed to do. He even thought there should be a bill proposed to prevent the distance between two human beings unknown to each from becoming unacceptably narrow. *The penalties should be imposed and the worst offenders should get prosecuted. Every citizen must have the civil right for solitude,* he had reasoned. Most of the flight, he ended up leaning half of his body on top of Ida who got squashed against the window and the wall.

However, departing his first flight ever, encountering so many strangers to him and having to speak foreign languages were a few of the many sacrifices he was willing take for the sake of his and Ida's happiness.

He gathered the man sitting next to him was foreign, and the possibility and fear the man may want to converse or chit-chat using some language unfamiliar to him, like English, German or Latin, existed, when small talk in Pihtamo was non-existent or being kept to a minimum. He had only heard it being used again in the daytime television dramas broadcasted from more flamboyant cultures.

Sven was determined not to have a conversation with the man next to him and only keep quiet for another fifteen to twenty minutes until they have safely landed. He had done so well most of the journey and he didn't want to ruin the silence.

Although he was aware of a similar problem waiting for them on the ground once they've landed, where most of the people are foreign and a conversation with a stranger may be unavoidable.

A few times during the flight, the man on the aisle seat composed himself, making his and Sven's elbows touch each other. Luckily, it was only the sleeves of their thick winter coats rubbing without real physical contact between them what-so-ever. Sven relaxed and took a deep breath.

Eventually, the air his stomach had produced rumbled and the crumbs of dark bread began pushing aggressively towards his bowel system. The urge to visit the toilet had arrived only moments before the landing, which meant he was forced to interact with the man next to him. There was no other route to escape the middle seat. All the seats in front and behind him were occupied as well, if he was to consider climbing over them.

Discreetly, he unbuckled his seatbelt and prepared himself for a giant leap over the half dozing foreigner. But once the belt buckle snapped open, the man composed himself, opened his eyes and turned to look directly into Sven's. The man opened his mouth and a sound came out that vaguely resembled of the English language, a language Sven had been taught the basic grammar and vocabulary at secondary school by a highly accented, old teacher lady who owned seven cats.

The man wanted to know if Sven needed the loo.

Instead of leaping over the man, Sven froze on a half-seated position. The worst had happened. The stranger had spoken the first foreign words to him, directly, and he wasn't prepared. There was no script, no dress rehearsal. The class room situations were long gone. This was all about spontaneity that Sven poorly lacked. This was real life.

The man continued harassing Sven again by questioning whether he wants to go or not.

Sven's brain processed the second sentence that, again, was reasonably easy to understand, but to be able to shoot an immediate reply was harder, almost impossible. A good twenty seconds he pondered in silence and then began to construct some sensible answer, first, in his mind.

However, the man's attention span was much shorter. He began to feel discomfort with Sven's slowness to respond whether vocally or even emotionally. Sven, still leaning on the arm rests, was completely blanked out. The man wasn't able to interpret any of Sven's intentions. The man mumbled a sentence and looked away, puzzled.

'*Vessa...*' Sven muttered.

The man's eyes lightened. He called out for the stewardess and asked her to give Sven some vodka, because he knew how men from the Arctic's like to drink.

'Would you like a shot or a bottle, sir?' the stewardess asked Sven in a language he could finally understand. 'We are landing soon, so we need your orders quick.'

'Not now,' Sven mumbled, still being confused from all the attention he was getting. '*VC?*'

'Ah, toilet. Just down this corridor,' the air hostess pointed. 'Have you got a booking?'

'A booking? For what?' Sven asked.

'From this year, on our Rye'n'Air flights you need to book your toilet access in advance, unless you fly in upper business class, where the toilet access is included. If you haven't booked, you can try and fill a cancelled spot during the flight. There are always some peasantry class passengers who in the end don't need to use the toilet. That will cost ten marks per entry. You can pay the fee for any of us, the flight crew.'

'Unheard of...' Ida snorted.

The Anglo-Saxon or Briton as Sven had concluded, intervened and offered Sven his boarding pass that indicated he had a one, un-used and pre-booked toilet entry.

Ida thanked the man in clear English on behalf of Sven.

The man said he was happy to help his "Danish friend under pressure".

Sven gave the man a grateful, but shy nod.

'Wonderful,' the stewardess said, gestured towards the toilet in front of the plane and walked away to prepare herself for the landing.

The Briton fired another question again to Sven about his possible origin as he handed over his boarding pass.

*Is he never gonna stop?* Sven suffered in silence as he felt the knife of sociability turning in his open wound of shyness. *Just let me go to the toilet and leave me alone, nothing personal, but I am not really in a mood for a long conversation in English. Not yet, not today, perhaps, never. It's not that I'm rude. I just have nothing to say. I don't know what to say. And how? What's the point? I don't know him. I don't know you.*

The man kept guessing if Sven is from Iceland.

Sven didn't react. He only took the boarding pass from him.

The man explained how he travelled to Iceland once about ten years ago with his wife. He thought it was beautiful, but really expensive. He saw the geysirs, hot springs. It was cold and dark February, minus twenty degrees Celsius and cold winds. The sun barely rose above the horizon. They saw the Northern Lights. People drank so much, too. They paid ten pounds for a pint. He found it ridiculous. He wanted to know if it was that expensive in where Sven was from.

Sven nodded in agony. Too many listening ears to hear and correct his grammar and pronunciation mistakes, or laugh at his weird accent, if he was to try reply in English. He shut down completely. Nodding was enough for him.

The man kept explaining how London is expensive too and the rents keep on soaring. He talked about renting a two bedroom house outside M-twenty-five with his wife for sixteen hundred pounds, which to his opinion was a rip-off and way too expensive for a place called Essex.

Sven shook his head. He had no idea what the man was on about.

The man said the public transportation costs have doubled within last five years and a weekly travel card costs more than thirty quid. He found that a disgrace. Apparently, the trains are not even running that frequently and there's more and more cancellations and engineering works all the time. He blamed the new Conservative government who cut on spending and welfare while increasing taxes. He believed it used to be different, there were more jobs and people were just happier.

Sven observed the green light blinking in the distance. The toilet had just become available.

The man told how he went to Norway a few years back. He absolutely loved it.

Impatiently, Sven leaned his hand on the back rest in front of him as if to demonstrate he had to go now.

The man revealed he had bought a cheese slicer from Norway, where apparently the cheese slicer was invented in the first place. The man or his wife hadn't used the slicer yet, though. It was still in the kitchen drawer. Norway to his opinion was even more expensive than Iceland. But he was impressed about the beauty of women, their silky blonde hair and striking blue eyes.

Despite trying to speak more quietly about women, Ida heard the man rambling on about the opposite sex. She gave him a judgemental glance.

Sven kept nodding, even though he started to lose the plot and couldn't understand anymore half the man was saying. As if the man's accent was getting thicker and unclearer the more he spoke.

Apologetically, the man understood holding Sven back. He stood up and stepped aside on the aisle.

Barely touching the Briton, Sven brushed past him onto the aisle and towards the lavatory. He felt an instant relief as he trotted along the narrow corridor between the Arctic holidaymakers getting ready for their dream beach holiday in Great Britain. Being freed from the discomfort of physical closeness with a total stranger he had to withstand the entire flight, left its mark. Now, though, he could stretch his arms and shake off the nasty experience, yet knowing there was still landing ahead which meant being strapped and squashed back onto the seat next to the sociable stranger for another brief moment of anxiety.

Some travellers on the plane examined their snorkel sets and swimming goggles, some spread sun lotion on their pale faces. Sven couldn't wait to hit the beach either, even though the weather didn't seem promising at the moment. But the hopes were high. They had travelled nearly three thousand kilometres further down south. The climate in the destination was expected to be at least subtropical.

Once he reached the end of the aisle, the toilet was still available. Most of the passengers had already strapped themselves onto their seats.

The toilet's grey plastic interior matched well with the

plane's modest décor. Once Sven locked the door, he relaxed seated on the warm rim. He tried to think of something clever to say to the man once he will return to his seat. He remembered the English language he had learned at school. He felt so much more fluent inside his head than outside. The problem was that asking questions often generate more conversation and increase the demand for spontaneity, which Sven did not want to achieve.

While beginning to construct English sentences in his mind, a heavy knock on the door interrupted his thought process. He ignored the knock and tried to remain focused, when another, more aggressive knock drew his attention away. He was forced to finish his business. As he flushed the toilet, a lid opened at the bottom of the bowl together with a suction, he feared, powerful enough to vacuum his privates off. He jumped up quickly. He turned to face the sink to wash his hands. The hot water and soap box were both coin operated services that were neither included nor mentioned in the toilet access booking sheet. A sign on the wall indicated that a tinge of soap costs three marks and for another two marks you get ten seconds flow of hot water. He settled for the plain, cold water that was free, no soap.

Outside queuing, a slightly frustrated upper business class and another pre-booked peasantry class passenger greeted Sven with agonizing gestures waving their free toilet access passes. Sven sneaked past them back towards his seat.

Once back on his row, the Briton stepped away again politely giving Sven space to leap back on his seat. The man informed Sven that they have been circling over an area called The Surrey now for the last twenty minutes due to runway congestion.

This time, though, Sven was determined to take part in the conversation and also to impress Ida with his linguistic skills. On his mind, he began to construct the first words of the sentence he had started in the toilet. As he opened his mouth to begin to speak, the man interrupted him.

The man expressed his gratitude that someone had used his otherwise wasted toilet access. Even though, limiting such a privilege, to his opinion, was cruel. He joked that Rye'n'Air flights are famously known as flying cattle trucks or night buses travelling overseas.

Again, Sven couldn't quite catch everything the man said. The man, instead, was gradually losing his superficial friendliness. He glanced at emotionless and unresponsive Sven. He had overestimated Sven's ability to respond to his banter, bounce off from it or just say anything, even the most simplest thing. He felt as if he was talking by himself, wasting good material. Exhausted, the man turned to stare directly onto the seat in front of him. He couldn't hide his feeling of awkwardness anymore.

Yet, Sven remained determined to say something, despite the man's sudden hostile behaviour. *The question.* He lifted his gaze up and opened his mouth. A primitive, yet unrecognisable sound came out.

Nevertheless, the man's eyes lightened. The man guessed Sven wanted to know where he is from.

Sven bit his teeth together. He had forgotten the sentence. Too much pressure. He froze again. He turned to look at the man. Their eyes met. Sven, although deadpan, but deep down inside him a spark of passion wanted to open his introverted soul.

Excited, the man told how he was born and bred in Hertfordshire, his wife was from Wiltshire, they met in Lincolnshire, he also studied there, and while growing up his family lived in Berkshire, Buckinghamshire and Yorkshire.

*Lots of shires,* Sven thought, looking pleased, even though his rehearsed line had backfired. And the sizable answer was again too much for him to comprehend.

The man enquired Sven if this was his first time in England.

Sven nodded again, seemingly relieved after the toilet visit. The flight was turning into a sociable overload for his kinds. Somehow, though, he felt his ears were getting adjusted by the minute to the sound of the foreign tongue. The people from Pihtamo were generally known to be good listeners.

The man warned about the inclement weather. Jokingly, he concluded, they must be used to the cold and love it.

Sven let out an awkward chuckle, and turned to look at Ida and outside the window as the plane descended in the midst of the clouds. He had managed to strike a conversation with the foreign man. That was enough of achievement from him for one day. *Baby steps*, he thought proudly. Ultimately, he didn't come to England to chat anyway, but to enjoy a private honeymoon with his new wife. He feared if he was to continue chatting with a stranger sitting beside him, *the journey may turn into an extroverted salsa party of some sort*. That was something he avoided to the last straw.

The pilot announced the outdoor temperature on the ground in the destination was twelve degrees Celsius, about fourteen degrees warmer than in Pihtamo the morning of departure.

Since Pihtamo had been warmer than normally around this time of the year, Sven had promised once the temperature increases above minus five degrees Celsius, he will take out the garden furniture set and the barbecue. So he did, and before leaving to the airport Sven and Ida had enjoyed their morning coffee and porridge outside in the garden under the Arctic moon shine. The early start of spring and the barbecue season at home made them almost reconsider their honeymoon trip. But since they felt the need for some quality time together as well as privacy and distance from everything, especially from Ida's parents, or from the critical situation at the lake, going on a break like this did really hit the spot.

Sven decided it's now or never, a trip of a lifetime with the woman he had married and vowed to stay for the rest of his life. The beach holiday surprise to Great Britain was the least he could offer his beautiful bride and money should not be an obstacle. The cold call was made by an angel.

Sven and Ida held each other's hands tight as the plane touched the ground. Ida let out a sweet squeal as Sven squashed her ring finger between the other four.

'Relax, honey. We made it,' Ida comforted Sven on his virgin flight, whereas she had flown a few times to see her twin sisters. 'The first time is always the hardest.'

The seat belt lights switched off. The man offered to shake Sven's hand and wished them a pleasant stay in London. He introduced himself as Ian.

Sven responded giving the man a firm hand shake that was easier without words involved. He also nodded.

The man asked Sven his name where Ida responded on behalf of both of them, because her patience was running short, too.

'What a nice man,' Sven said to Ida.

'What were you two talking about?'

'This and that. About England... Pihtamo. About life.'

'Ah, you're making friends already. You're so... cosmopolitan,' Ida tapped his shoulder encouragingly.

Sven wasn't quite sure what cosmopolitan means, but how flatteringly Ida said the word he had only seen printed on the cover of a glamorous magazine she sometimes read, he thought it must be something positive. He felt genuinely proud of himself.

Chapter 11

# SCAT, MAN!

The last remaining patches of the spring snow covered the forest floor under the feet of three men on their way to the target practice. To the amusement of Börje and Kalle, Jaaku had already tripped over three times whilst trudging down an unfamiliar surface consisting of tree roots, loose branches and sticks, soggy soil and slippery leaves. The fourth time he fell, he hazardously misfired a shot up at the pine tree tops. A few cones came down and landed on his head. Yet, he didn't let the pain and embarrassment show nor did he complain.

'Let us show you our best hunting spots,' Börje waved at Jaaku.

*Why's everyone revealing their secrets to me?*, Jaaku pondered. *What have I done? Everyone's suddenly trusting me.*

Kalle stopped to examine the soiled ground. 'Ski-bi dibby dib yo da dub dub...'

'What are you doing, you idiot!?' Börje said and smacked Kalle at the back of his head. 'You're scaring all the moose away.'

'Scat, man,' Kalle said, whining. He held his painful neck while his other hand pointed to the ground. 'Look!'

'I see. They are near,' Börje noticed a fresh pile of scat on the ground next to Kalle's feet. 'Well spotted.'

'Who's near?' Jaaku asked.

'The moose.'

'Is this thing loaded?' nervously, Jaaku looked at the rifle.

'Ah, dear!' Börje grunted. 'You're hopeless.'

'Deer...' Kalle smirked.

'Of course it's loaded,' Börje said. 'You've already fired one shot up in the air, remember?'

'I shouldn't have cocked it before I gave it to him,' Kalle shook his head.

Jaaku stopped for a moment to examine the rifle. *Cock it?* He tried to remember how the movie stars or cowboys handled their weapons in films, but he could only think of heroes spinning their hand guns before a fast draw. He tried to imitate them by tossing and turning the rifle in circles, ending up only swinging the barrel right in front of Börje's and Kalle's faces.

Maddened, Börje pushed the rifle aside. 'Lesson number one! Don't ever point a weapon to someone else's face. Are you trying to get rid of us?'

'Sorry. I was only checking... the label at the back,' Jaaku gave a clumsy explanation.

'Yes. It is original,' Börje said and inhaled. 'You know, that rifle has never let us down. I have carried it for twenty-odd years. Before that my father had it and before my grandfather. It would take more than a decade for the entire population of Pihtamo to consume the amount of wildlife this weapon has killed,' he explained, yanked the rifle away from Jaaku and demonstrated. 'You cock it... like this!'

Jaaku followed nervously. 'I think... we should probably call it a day. I've been up since five in the morning. It's been a long day. I guess for all of us. Why don't we meet up here at the same place... next week? The same time?'

'Next time?' Börje grunted and fired a shot up in the air. A flock of willow tits escaped the trees. He continued firmly, 'No! This is the moment.'

'You don't get a second chance,' Kalle quoted religiously.

'There's one! I can see it.' Börje got distracted by moose antlers popping above the lingonberry bushes under a tall spruce tree. A dark brown bull moose stuck its head out of the dark and began chewing the berries totally unaware of the threat. 'This is your moment, rookie.' Börje pushed the rifle back on Jaaku's lap and gave him an approving nod like sending the new gang member to go and prove himself.

Jaaku hesitatingly took a step forward, looked down at the warm weapon and then glanced ahead at the innocent moose. There wasn't only just the bull moose anymore, but assumingly its partner and their three little ones. His pulse pumped and heartbeat raced. Being in the presence of such a large, impressive animal made him feel small and vulnerable. He almost felt threatened, even though the moose family completely ignored the men. Hands shaking, he pulled the lever down and up as instructed by Börje. He glanced at the hunters who nodded approvingly. Jaaku assumed he had just correctly *cocked the rifle*. Next, he figured he should *pull the trigger*. He placed his forefinger on it as he had seen done in the movies. But when he looked up and through the front sight, the moose family was already on the move. They had spotted the three hunters. Or the noise cocking the rifle made had caught their attention. Either way. The bull moose stretched its neck long and looked Jaaku straight into his eyes as he held the frightened and defenceless animal at gunpoint. Jaaku stopped breathing. He felt a lump in his throat. He thought closing eyes would help and make the experience less traumatising for him. *No pain, no gain.* He knew there was no return. This was his chance to prove himself, change his life, become something to be remembered from, come out of the shadow of many great fishermen, become a great hunter, instead of remaining mediocre for the rest of his life.

'What are you waiting for?' yelled Kalle. 'Shoot the bloody moose!' His impatient scream freaked out the moose family. The bull moose dropped the berries from its mouth, looked at the cow and they both looked at their calves. They all nodded to each other, and in a split second, galloped back into the depths of the dark forest.

'They're running away...' Jaaku aimed with his trembling hands, his finger still wrapped around the trigger. But by the time he fired, the moose family were long gone and the shot missed poorly hitting a tree trunk. 'They're so fast!'

'They can be... and that's why, we have to be even faster!' Börje screamed.

'I will get the next one,' Jaaku said quietly and lowered his head together with the barrel.

Börje pulled Kalle aside and whispered to him, 'And you have to be quieter or I'll smack you again.'

Kalle nodded apologetically.

'So, what should we do with him?' Börje whispered to Kalle.

Kalle shrugged his shoulders. 'Just dump him in the lake where he belongs.'

'I agree. He's hopeless... but let's give him a second chance. We have to keep recruiting more hunters whether good or bad. We cannot let him go back to fishing. We have to make sure the community of moose hunters does get bigger. That is our mission, don't forget that. This land needs more hunters and less fishermen.'

'Yes, sir,' Kalle nodded.

Meanwhile, Jaaku had gone to examine the area the moose family had been dining. 'We can trace the moose family. There's more snow in their path. They had left hoof prints we can follow,' he suggested the two hunters chattering in the distance.

'See. He's not completely hopeless,' Börje said to Kalle, and then, cheerfully turned to Jaaku. 'Good idea! You lead the way and we follow.'

Once Börje finished the sentence, Jaaku disappeared in the track the moose family had taken. The snowy surface helped him pick up speed. He tread through the forest faster than ever before. The two hunting specialists struggled to keep up with him while he started to develop a new kind of sense: a thirst for blood.

Chapter 12

# THE FAMOUS UNDERWEAR

Martello's Arctic Pizza Buffet was the first and so far the only restaurant to introduce kebab meat to the residents of Pihtamo with its reindeer kebab pizza - possibly the only one of its kind in the world. The exotic delicacy mixed with ingredients from different parts of the globe divided opinions amongst the consumers from sparking controversy to gaining devoted supporters. The pizza grew popular especially as a takeaway and home delivery food after a night out of heavy drinking.

As the spacious black taxi cab drove Sven and Ida from the airport through the outskirts of London, the kebab shops on both sides of the streets as far as the eye could see formed a bittersweet stench that reminded Sven of the controversial delicacy from back home. Despite the familiarity of the startling odours, the sudden kebab overload of a large metropolitan city pushed both of their tolerance to the brink. It was like a savoury punch in the face. Neither had they ever seen so many people roaming the streets nor so much traffic, apart from the news broadcasts that showed, mostly war-torn, images of more populated parts of the world.

In a blink of an eye, the take away shops and ninety-five pence stores gave way to more exclusive pet groomers and organic health stores. Dented, old BMW's and Ford Focuses disappeared and almost consistently congested roads were taken over by golden Lamborghinis and purple Maseratis. The fast sports cars seemed to scream in agony while roaming the streets, not being able to release their full potential in the heavy traffic. Unless they were there only for the looks, which some of them were.

The black cab crossed a bridge over a wide, brown river and, soon, on the south side, they passed a large green grassy area. They circled around the winding, busy streets lined up with rows of red brick houses attached to one another. Every now and then, there was a busy high street with more discount and kebab shops.

Pihtamo municipality had only a handful of wooden houses and cottages, scattered in their own privacy, no one being able to see their neighbour. Neither did anyone really want to see each other, unless they had to. Privacy and solitude were virtues. Just looking at the busy streets of London got Sven and Ida exhausted.

Most awkwardly, some parts of south London reminded Sven about Christmas traditions at home, and how his mother used to cook delicious ham every single year, always the night before the Christmas eve. While trying to spell out the road signs they were passing, he figured, that English ways of treating ham seemed somewhat peculiar. Feltham, the nearest sign to the airport, had the most positive connotation. Him and his parents also had *felt ham* in various, happy occasions. But only for a little while, in their sweaty palms savouring the first, fresh cuts sliced off the juicy pork leg taken straight out of the hot oven. The rest of the Christmas ham was enjoyed from the plate with a knife and fork, and only *felt* with their tongues, in their mouths and stomachs. To Sven's opinion, though, it was a little early to start feeling the ham only in the midst of summer.

But to *clap* or *peck ham* would have been considered a disgrace in Sven's family traditions, but at parts of south of the river Thames people were encouraged to do so using signs, like Clapham and Peckham. These odd phrases reminded Sven of something his father used to teach him: *You should never play with food.*

After a head-spinning two-hour journey through many parts: wealthy and poor; industrial and residential; busy and busier; the driver dropped them to the area called Pimlico in their pre-booked two star hotel. The lobby was like walking to an antique shop. Fitted, worn out carpets decorated the floors, an old chandelier hung from the ceiling and a few old portraits of supposedly important men and women from the recent past filled the walls. The interior had a historical, musky scent to it, like at grandparents' place.

Once they had completed the check-in with a receptionist squashed behind a tiny hole on the wall, they located a lift that may have been out-of-service, indefinitely. They were forced to drag their luggage along the narrow staircase up on the fifth floor. *Sometimes "historical" has its ups and downs*, thought Sven while ascending the carpeted steps on his winter coat and long underpants under his thick woollen trousers.

Sweating and panting, they arrived outside their room. The door was narrow and short. Sven put the large copper key into the hole and turned it. The door slowly opened itself caressing the tilted floor and revealing a tiny room with a small desk on one side and a wooden framed double bed on the other.

'What do you think?' Sven said on a positive note. 'Quite nice, ey?'

'Hmm...' Ida failed to hide her disappointment. 'I guess...it doesn't matter.'

'What doesn't matter? You don't like it?'

'As long as we're together, that's all that matters,' she forced a smile.

'I think it's pretty awesome. Or, I wouldn't know. I've never been in a hotel before and straight away in two stars.'

'Yeah. It's better than one star, I guess,' she said sarcastically.

'Wait 'til you see the view,' he took a couple of steps inside finding himself already at the opposite end of the room against the window. He pulled the curtain to the side. Behind the small, steamy glass, a brick wall of another building stood only about half a metre away. 'What is this!? The travel agency promised a view overlooking the city. I must complain about this.'

'To whom?'

'The reception,' he said and returned to the corridor.

'Maybe it's better we go together,' she followed her.

'Don't worry. I can take care of this myself.'

'I know you can, but it's a different world out here. You have to speak up to get what you want. It's better there's two of us explaining and listening.'

Sven sighed. He wanted to be the tour leader, organiser, a strong character in front of his wife, but already on the first steps of the journey, he felt like the role was slipping away from him. Ida portrayed a great deal of strength and independence that in situations like this almost emasculated him. He still romanticised about the traditional differences between men and women, even though he was aware of the negative connotations of inequality in the world and the difficult history between men and women, and how easily being old-fashioned in today's world was considered the same as being misogynist. The gender differences in and around Pihtamo for instance had been blurred already within last decades. Gender equality had reached the point where everybody, a man or a woman was trying to do bit of everything. There were lesser unwritten rules about what was considered as men's or women's tasks. Although under the surface and at times, men and women even in Pihtamo, missed those old-fashioned roles, and occasionally, played along with those roles to get what they wanted. No matter how strong and independent women wanted to be, they appeared feminine and weak if it was to open certain doors, and vice versa, men often pretended to be more successful, wealthier and stronger than they really were. The biology and the nature were sometimes more difficult to manipulate even with the most rational and equal thinking.

As expected, with a relatively fluent, yet accented and monotone English, Ida explained their situation to the receptionist while Sven stood quiet next to her. Every time he thought he understood something, he only nodded. Otherwise, he just stared at the wall.

The white colour and the square patterns of the wallpaper reminded Sven of the snow-covered ice from his last, catastrophic fishing trip with Jaaku. No matter how far away he travelled, the critical situation in Lake Pihtamo seemed to haunt him. Yet, he was master in hiding his emotions, even from Ida. He crossed fingers that the lake was back to normal once the honeymoon was over and there would be plenty of fish waiting for him.

Ida thanked the receptionist behind the little desk as she

received a key to a new room. She turned to Sven, swung the room key in front of his nose and with her two fingers gave his cheek a squeeze further denting his already shrunken male ego.

They climbed the stairs again, opened the room door right next to the room they had been given before, and walked to the window to discover that the brick wall was still there. Frustrated, Ida snorted and stomped her foot.

'You wanna go downstairs again and complain?' Sven said, opened the window completely and pushed his head out. He looked to the left and looked to the right. 'I think I've discovered the... so-called city view.'

Ida came beside him and looked outside. 'That's it?'

'I think that's it...' Sven smelled her perfume as she leaned over. 'I can settle with this... if the lady is happy?'

'Fine,' she stretched her neck further to admire the partly restricted, yet eye-opening view. 'So many lights, buildings.'

He took a step back inside to examine her curvy figure from behind. *The conditions are perfect*, he thought and softly touched her waist and pushed himself against her body. 'You know, honey... We haven't had a proper wedding night yet.'

'What are you trying to say? I thought you wanna go out and see the old London town first?'

'Later, darling...' he flicked her around, took her hand and laid her on the squeaky double bed next to them.

'Ah, Sven,' she grunted and pulled him closer.

'Wait. I have a surprise for you,' he said, unbuckled his belt, opened his zip and pulled down his trousers.

*He's moving fast, faster than normally*, she thought in awe.

'What do you think?' he asked.

'New... underwear?'

'Exactly. Bought them from Pihtamo fish market... not so long time ago.'

'I didn't know they sell underwear there.'

'In the past it was only fish, but lately, they've been having other stalls as well than just food. There's also this one lady selling little crafted snowmen and angels. I think they're made of clay of some sort. The other stall is filled with some amazing crochet items. You should come and have a look one day. I was thinking my mum should start trading her knitted wear there.'

'How lovely,' she admired and stroked the soft fabric of his new, flashy underpants. 'You know... I've always liked Beckham.'

'I know you do. That's why I wanted to buy exactly this pair of trunks,' he said proudly, but then, got more serious. 'But promise me one thing?'

'What?'

'This will be the closest you ever get to him? Please. As much as you like football.'

'Well... we'll see,' she smirked. 'You never know what can happen or who we run into since we are here... in England.'

'You cheeky...' he laughed, took her in his arms and kissed her.

She wrapped her arm around him. The other arm reached out for the lamp and she switched off the light. They were back in the darkness, where they felt the most comfortable in. Only the city lights of London skyline dimly lit the room - as the shining moon did back home.

Chapter 13

# VILJO'S WAR

The austerities of life and simplicity had kept Viljo alive and reasonably healthy to this date. No one knew for sure, not even himself, how old he really was. *Eighty-something,* he claimed, but people thought at least *two hundred years old.* No birth certificates or any proof of his origins existed. His first memories of the early childhood were mostly fishing related, the only passion that never left him.

He had married young, as his generation tended to do, even to a younger bride, Aune. The marriage ceremony was as short-lived as Sven's and Ida's, but for different reasons. Viljo did not pull herring or any other type of fish out of his pocket on the altar, even though the same risk existed being a devoted fisherman himself as well, but an aerial bomb landed nearby to the church where the wedding was held destroying a large part of slowly developing rural Pihtamo. A large chandelier fell on the floor at the back of the church hall, while Viljo and Aune read their vows at front on the altar. No casualties were recorded, but the damages to the village infrastructure were devastating - the worst in the known history to this date. Luckily, though, most of the population in the area attended the wedding and were saved by the solid engineering of the church building. The event was warmly remembered and remained in the hearts of the generation that lived through the wartime cruelty as *the day when Viljo's and Aune's wedding saved Pihtamo.*

According to Viljo's doctor, though, the marriage may have been one of the secrets to his longevity and what had saved his life. 'Married men live longer,' the doctor had told him.

Aune's presence, caring and sometimes control over Viljo's actions kept him out of many trouble. Not always, though. He was a stubborn and a strong character. When he needed to go fishing, he went. Sometimes, the "fishing" meant something else, like meeting up with his war veteran buddies and getting dangerously intoxicated from drinking moonshine, a homebrew whiskey-like spirit popular in Pihtamo before, during and right after the war, when there were no bars or hardly any alcohol available publicly. Hypocritically, seeing a person drunk was frowned upon at the time, even though almost everyone was drinking their homemade compounds.

Nevertheless, the times were different and more peculiar when Viljo and Aune married. The world was at war and this affected their honeymoon and their wedding night, unlike the younger generation like Sven and Ida who could fly in peace to another country without any problems. This was not possible during those difficult years. Viljo was called back to the front line before the sunrise the next day and didn't return to Aune until two years later. Gladly, though, he did return and she loyally, waited. Many of the men did not return, nor did the women wait, but they moved on.

The enemies attempts to invade Pihtamo failed one time after another. The surrounding superpowers and kingdoms despite their latest technologies, vast materials and capacities ran out of steam against the persistence of united Pihtamo and Kihlava regions rational leaders, hard-boiled troops and men like Viljo and his kinds. The harsh terrain, freezing temperatures and deep snow turned out to be insurmountable for unprepared and poorly equipped opponents who were forced to retrieve.

After years of fighting, the war ended and Pihtamo was in peace and began to prosper. The next forty years and something, Viljo and Aune spent cherishing that simple life, building a typical tall, white wooden house next to Lake Pihtamo. They were never blessed with children, though, as much as there were times they wanted to have them. They developed other ways to occupy their time: Viljo fishing and Aune gardening.

Neither did Viljo and Aune ever become interest about travelling. Pihtamo offered everything they needed. Six years of fighting on the front line of the most violent war in the human history had provided Viljo enough excitement and adventure as well as emotional pain and suffering that he had to carry inside him for the rest of his life. He settled to appreciate basic things in life, like their apple trees.

Twenty years from now, though, Aune had left him. She had passed on. No one knew for sure why or how. She went to bed one evening at nine o'clock, as usual, and the next morning never opened her eyes again. 'A marriage may shorten woman's life,' the same doctor had also told him.

For the first time in his life, Viljo felt true loneliness. Apart from being one of the few remaining of his age group, the surviving veterans, he had lost his best friend for life, the only friend, a companion, who for half a century bore the brunt of his faults, misbehaviour and heavy drinking. All those unsaid kind words and forgotten compliments he never said to Aune weighed as a burden, until they meet again on the other side. If they were to meet. As much as he was raised Christian and vaguely believed in the existence of heaven and hell, he was always uncertain about his own final destination. He believed Aune was in heaven, definitely. And for the first time in his life, though, he actually prayed for forgiveness, not from God, but from her on her grave, simultaneously, trying to convince himself that *he did the best he could*, yet feeling a pinch of guilt crawling inside him.

As a widow, Viljo had dedicated his spare time into fishing like every day was his last and sunken the feeling of emptiness into drinking alcohol like every bottle was his last, yet never mixing those two together. He never missed a day on the lake due to drunkenness or hangover. Every morning before the sunset he had sobered up enough to make it to the fishing boat. The devil took charge only in the evenings, when the darkness and loneliness laid upon him. As much as he enjoyed silence and tranquility, after Aune's passing there was just simply too much of it. Not being able to hear the cracking sound of the wooden floor planks under Aune's feet as she worked in the kitchen or in the laundry room, at times drove him near to insanity. He had developed a daily routine of half a day of fishing and half a day of drinking. Once he returned from the lake, he hit the arm chair, removed the bottle top that stayed open until the midnight, or in the weekends, until the early hours of the morning. That was his way of dealing with the pain. And it must have worked. He was still alive.

His undoubtedly good genes, toughness and persistence made him the oldest reigning ice fishing champion Pihtamo ever witnessed. The first championship he only achieved after he had already announced his retirement. A late bloomer in its extreme. Unfortunately, though, Aune never saw any of the victories. However, he devoted them all to her memory. The loss had given him more time to focus on fishing and perhaps that was, sadly though, the final push his career needed. The level of fishermen had risen so dramatically in the recent years that for many, it was the choice between career or family. Viljo had peaked once his only family, Aune, wasn't there anymore. Suddenly, he had all the time in the world and he used it well. Unlike Sven's story to fame, where the support and the presence of a loving partner brought him the ultimate success. Nevertheless, Aune always remained present in Viljo's heart even after her death. The mixed feelings of anger, sorrow and passion long gone drove him to the top.

Yet, today, was like any other day within last two decades without the presence of Aune. After previous night's binge, Viljo had slept a few hours to clear his head, got up before dawn, drank some black coffee, ate some dark bread with a thick layer of salty butter and a slice of raw herring on top. Once he finished the breakfast, he headed to Lake Pihtamo to check his fishing net. He always had a long net set at different parts of the lake. A few days earlier, he had spread it across one of the lake's deepest points.

Neither was Viljo saved from the rumours spreading across the town about Lake Pihtamo running completely empty of fish. In his seventy years of fishing in the area, the waters had always been one of the most bountiful he had ever laid his rod upon. Like Sven, he believed the rumours were complete nonsense spread by inexperienced, untalented and immature fisherman who were not able to catch a thing, even on a fish farm. He wanted to prove them all wrong and incompetent.

Chapter 14

# THE FISHING HONEYMOON

The purple sunrays penetrating through the thin cotton curtains woke Sven up after the night of heated passion. He rubbed his tired but happy eyes. He turned to the side on the firm mattress. Ida lay asleep beside him on her stomach. The early morning light gave her bare back a tanned complexion as if she had already been sunbathing on the famous beaches of Britain.

Sven reached out for his new underwear bundled on the carpeted floor. He pulled them on, stood up and walked to part the curtains. The narrow gap between the hotel and the brick wall of the building right opposite was barely wide enough to let the light follow through. He enjoyed the moment while it lasted.

Ida turned around on the bed and covered her full frontal under the corner of the duvet. She raised her head, looked at Sven and yawned smiling.

'Today, we could go...' Sven started.

'...on a river cruise? To see West End musical? Visit Tower of London?' Full of enthusiasm, Ida sat up and leaned back against the bed frame. Suddenly, her eyes lit up glistening of joy. She collected a stack of travel brochures from the night table and began browsing them through.

'I was thinking about going... fishing?' he said shyly and pulled out from the side pocket of his trolley two tickets to The Lucky Fish Farm.

'Fishing!?' she said perplexed. 'But... it's our honeymoon.'

He looked away apologetically. 'I know... but this fishing day is actually part of our holiday package.'

'Where would you go fishing here? In that brown river?'

He examined the piece of paper. 'The ticket says... Lake District.'

'Are you serious? We have just arrived and...'

'It would be just...' he flicked the ticket around, 'one day and two nights. Apparently, it's very lovely up there. Many lakes. Plenty of fish.'

'That sounds exactly like... Pihtamo! Aren't you fishing enough at home!?' she snorted, crossed her arms and looked away.

'Of course, but...'

'But what?'

'The last time, I went fishing with Jaaku and...' Sven took a deep breath. He felt embarrassed to admit. 'We didn't catch... anything.'

'Really? Nothing at all?' Her voice got a softer tone. She looked at him again.

'Not just us, but apparently most of the fishermen in Pihtamo have had the same problem already for weeks or months.'

'Sounds very odd. Maybe, it's just a phase you're all going through. You can't all be so lucky all the time.'

'First of all, it's nothing to do with luck! How can you say that!?'

'Of course it's not, my love,' she said, got up and walked to the bathroom. She left the door open. She turned on the tap and began washing her face while Sven peered outside as the sun disappeared behind the corner. She turned off the tap, took a towel and dried her face. She pushed her head through the door frame and asked, 'So, you wanna find out, if you still got it? That's why you wanna go to this Lake District place?'

Sven saw the grey clouds invading the sky and London seemed again more what they had observed from the plane. He didn't answer.

'You don't need to prove anything to me,' Ida said. 'I love you and respect you just the way you are whether you catch fish or not.'

'But... this is about something else,' Sven said thoughtfully, while staring at two pigeons trotting on the opposite roof top. 'I am a fisherman and if there's any doubt that I have lost the edge, I must get it back one way or the other.'

'Can't it wait until we get back home?' she pleaded.

Sven pulled away from the window and sat on the edge of the bed. 'But you see, if I can prove that I catch fish here, then I can catch everywhere. Fishing in Lake Pihtamo is easy. The fish there, literally, swims to your bait. Here... I don't know. I don't know the waters of Great Britain. I have to prove myself... to myself.'

'Why did you take us to London then?' Ida exited the bathroom and sat beside him on the bed. 'Please be honest.'

'I thought you wouldn't understand.' he turned to face her. 'Just one day of fishing and then, I'll promise, we come back here and do all those things you said and more.'

'I should have known,' Ida looked away and sighed under her breath. 'A honeymoon with a fisherman!'

'I'm begging you. I need to find out.' Sven crossed his hands on his lap.

'I thought you were not so bothered about fishing in other places than Lake Pihtamo. Or even travelling anywhere in the first place.'

'Trust me. I'm doing this trip for us.'

'Not the fishing trip, though. That one you're doing for yourself.'

'Please. Just this once.'

'Okay then. But I really do hope our marriage is more important to you than... fish. We've talked about this.'

'Hmm. Depends. What type of fish?' Sven smiled, seemingly more relaxed now. He winked his eye to her.

'Don't play with me.'

Sven's face grew serious. 'Just kidding... I need you more, much more,' and then he smiled a little again and kissed her on the cheek. 'Thank you. It'll be fun. I promise.'

Somehow, she wasn't convinced about the fun part.

Chapter 15

# SOMETHING FISHY

A tattered, white polystyrene cube floated on the surface of the lake to mark one end of Viljo's fishing net. The sinkers on the leadline kept the net near the bottom rather than floating on the surface. It created a fence in the water blocking the route and supposedly catching the fish by their gills, hence the name of the device: bottom-set gillnet.

As Viljo reached the spot, he raised the oars into the boat, rolled up his sleeves and picked up the cube. He took a plastic hook into his other hand. He began folding the rope and the first metres of the floatline around the pointy tip of the hook. Once the first meshes surfaced, one herring revealed itself tangled in the net from its gills, still breathing and alive. Viljo smirked proudly as if he had never caught any fish before. It felt like a small victory. 'I knew there's fish in here,' he chatted to himself.

He pulled the trapped herring up nearer to the boat, when another herring appeared caught up further down the net. His smile grew. He took the first herring over the gunwale, when he saw a third herring on the meshes following the second one. 'This must be my lucky day!' he laughed. 'What are these youngsters on about? Let the old man handle this.'

The first herring rest captured now between his hands, when it suddenly sunk its sharp teeth into his thumb. Viljo squealed in pain, dropped the herring back into the lake and it swam away to freedom.

'That wasn't quite my plan,' Viljo said and rolled his aching thumb. 'Well, at least there's fish in this lake, that's for sure.'

He continued pulling the net up towards him and reached for the next herring on the line. Meanwhile, the first herring that had just escaped Viljo, surfaced behind him. Viljo felt the herring's stare. 'What are you there waiting for?' he turned around. 'You wanna come with me after all? You'd go well on some rye bread and butter.'

But the herring only floated there in safe distance from Viljo, and waited.

Confused, Viljo immersed himself into netting again. Once the second herring was at his reach, on the very last moment, like a contortionist it twisted itself away from the bounds of the meshes. And the third herring escaped by biting itself to freedom. And there was even a fourth herring down below dancing its way out of captivity.

Startled and helpless, Viljo observed this abnormal scene. Being distracted by the insanity of it all, his pipe dropped from his flaccid lips onto his lap burning a hole in his trousers. He swept the ashes on the floor, picked up the pipe, and looked longingly at the escaping fish. In unison, all four herrings tails wiggling like having little engines installed at the rear headed towards the misty end of the bay. 'You wanna play hide and seek? You don't know who you're messing with!' Viljo waved his fist up in the air. He took the oars, slammed the blades in the water and began the chase of the herrings.

Chapter 16

# FISH BITES

'Another! And again, another! I'm back!' Sven announced proudly as he kept filling his and Ida's rental dinghy with tens of trout, haddock and cod.

'I'm happy for you,' Ida yawned, holding onto the oars. 'Shall we go back to London now?'

'A few more and then I'm done,' Sven smiled and cast the bait back in the waters of The Lucky Fish Farm at the Lake District. 'We are gonna have a nice, big dinner tonight of all this fish that I've caught.'

'...and breakfast and lunch tomorrow,' Ida added.

'Absolutely. And the rest we can take back home with us. Guys in Pihtamo will be so jealous.'

'I wasn't really serious,' she snorted.

But Sven wasn't listening as he caught again. 'This is unbelievable! I'm gonna empty the whole lake. Feels like one of the best summers in Pihtamo a few years back when I caught non-stop. Even the scenery here has some familiarity to it. It's like we never left.'

'Exactly,' Ida sighed sarcastically, and looked at the surrounding green hills and leafy forests. However, she couldn't quite agree with Sven about the similarity of the place compared to home. The lake and the shoreline seemed much busier of locals and tourists. There were many unfamiliar languages echoing across the lake. It was usual for the people at and around Lake

Pihtamo to do all the fishing, boating and camping quietly in peace and silence. And there was only one and the same language spoken back home and no dialects. She definitely felt they were somewhere else far away and exotic. She carefully observed every little detail of the ancient woodlands and the mountain ranges in the horizon. The colours were different, more subtle. The light was pleasant, almost dull. The sensation of really being away began to sink in. It was not a dream holiday she had expected, but after all, she had married a fisherman.

She leaned on the side of the boat and observed how the other fishermen and women caught fish reasonably well, too. Sven wasn't the only lucky one. Or skilled. She saw a large family on the opposite shore occupying their own private camping space with tents, barbecues and a motorhome size of a big coach. She sighed again, but this time more positively. She turned to look at Sven who kept swinging his rod back and forth. *What he does the best.* He gave him a flirtatious smile. It made her feel warm, even though she was supposed to be upset. She decided to give him his moment, as she so often did. She looked away and thought whether they would ever have a big family or any children; whether Sven could ever relax from his obsessive fishing habits and they could live at least some brief moments like a normal family. Whatever that "normal" meant for her, she wasn't even sure herself. She assumed something she had just witnessed on the shore where the entire family is truly present in each other's life, experiencing the good and the bad, sharing the life memories, and supporting one another, unconditionally.

Meanwhile, Sven pulled a large, half a metre long salmon on the boat and released it on top of his mountain of fish, already filling the floor. 'We need a bigger boat.'

Ida nodded, and more calmly, turned away again to peer in the horizon. She thought, there was no point arguing. Instead, she scanned the beaches, where a group of kids were swimming and playing in the sand. Even the children seemed somewhat louder and more lively here than in Pihtamo. *Maybe it's the warm climate*, she thought. Then she saw the officer who rented them the boat standing firmly on a jetty. The man wore a grey and dark green uniform. He looked like a forest ranger of some sort. He had a round face, pot belly and a pale skin. He had crossed his arms while observing their relentless fishing success. His face seemed friendly, but when he opened his mouth, his loud voice had an authoritarian quality to it. Then, he beckoned them to return to him.

'Erm... Sven,' Ida muttered and pointed to the shore. 'There's a man on the jetty who wants to tell us something.'

'What does he want? My autograph?' Sven said ignorantly.

'It's the same officer who hired us the boat. But I can't hear well enough. We have to get closer to him.'

'Well, if you wouldn't mind rowing, meanwhile, I keep filling the boat with more fish. I just can't stop now. This is truly amazing!'

Ida snorted and grabbed the oars. 'We probably have to return the boat.'

'Already? It's been only half an hour.'

'Isn't that enough? And we can't fit any more fish on this boat anyway.'

'But we booked an hour. Let's ask him if he has any bigger boats. Or, you ask,' Sven said, totally oblivious to Ida's growing frustration.

A dozen of aggressive strokes later, the officer thought they would be within a hearing distance. He repeated his demands.

'What is he saying?' Sven asked and looked at Ida.

'I think he... wants us to release all that fish back into the lake.'

'What? Why? Is he insane!? Why would anyone do that?'

'Don't ask me. I ain't no fishing expert. He said something about it being their policy. Apparently, that's what everyone has to do here.'

'Over my dead body! I ain't gonna release this catch. Look at it. It's more than I have fished... like ever!'

'The man seems quite serious, though.'

'I would just ignore him. He's not the police,' Sven said, cast the bait, and immediately, caught another one. 'See! This is unreal.'

The man explained the situation again firmly and in more detail. Ida listened attentively trying to understand most of it.

Then, she translated to Sven. 'The man or the water bailiff as he called himself just said that they cannot allow one person to empty the entire lake and keep any of the fish. There has to be fish left for other people as well. They have limited resources in this lake. He is really hoping we'd be willing to co-operate and release all that fish. If we don't comply, there will be consequences. Not sure what exactly, but I wouldn't risk it.'

'That's the most ridiculous thing I've ever heard. Releasing all fish back into the lake once you've caught them makes this whole thing seem as pointless as...'

'Like what?' asked Ida, agitated.

'I don't know... hunting moose... with a paintball rifle?'

'Whatever,' Ida smiled vaguely. 'Why don't you just obey and release the fish? There will be plenty waiting back home.'

'You think so?' Sven said gravely.

'Why so negative, champion?'

'Nothing.'

'Are you really that afraid you can't catch any fish back home? Of course you can. Lake Pihtamo never dries out. Believe me.'

Sven said nothing.

Ida shook her head. Then, she looked at the water bailiff who impatiently tapped his foot on the planks of the jetty. She nodded and chucked the first fishes overboard.

'Are you crazy!?' Sven frowned.

'What's your problem? It's like you haven't seen fish before,' Ida said, teary and threw another few fishes in the water. 'I didn't come here to serve time. The man looks quite serious.'

Sven took a deep breath and had one last look at the riches of the goldmine he had discovered. Mostly, he got saddened by the reality that his brief, successful run healing his wounds after all the recent poor fishing experiences back home was interrupted by a bureaucrat. The amount of fish and the minimal time he had spent to catch them approximated his records at Lake Pihtamo.

Reluctantly, he joined Ida in the mission to empty the boat. The released fishes swam happily away to freedom soon to be caught by another fisherman and another and so on.

The water bailiff nodded approvingly, turned around and

walked back into his office.

'What a waste of time and expertise,' heartbroken Sven dropped his gaze. 'What a crazy system...' He grabbed the largest of the salmons from its tail and chucked it over his shoulder high up in the air. The salmon made a huge splash as it landed on the water. He held back his tears while letting go of the catch of a lifetime. *Limited resources, right? They have no idea what it really means to have "limited resources".*

Chapter 17

# THE FIRST CONTACT

Only a trace remained on the surface after the four herrings dived in the depths of the lake. Determined to track them down, Viljo took the direction towards the dense mist where the fish had disappeared. In a few minutes, he reached the edge of the low lying clouds. Once his boat slowly entered the midst of the fog, the temperature dropped drastically and the visibility dropped to zero. But the splashes of the herrings' wiggling tails and flapping fins got only louder and closer. He followed the sound. Suddenly, though, the air and the lake around him got silent.

He paused rowing. Not even the wind made a hiss. He listened, but heard absolutely nothing apart from his own heavy breathing. The first time since the battles of the world war, he felt the shivers down the spine. The anger and frustration was accompanied by a third, long-lost emotion to him called *the fear*. He leaned over and looked closely at the water. It was as if he noticed a trace of the herrings swimming deep under the surface.

He took another five oar strokes along those lines, until his boat stopped like hitting a brick wall. The collision knocked him off the thwart. Lying on his back on the floor he was kicking helpless like a turtle being turned upside-down. The back of his head leaned against the edge of the front seat. He rolled on his side, held the gunwale and dragged himself on a seated position on the floor. He looked ahead and saw what he had crashed into.

A narrow and slender clinker built Viking style boat

bursting of fish glided past him. So many herrings on the boat that some of them struggled to stay on board. Some clung on the edges by their teeth, the others hung on the sides by their fins. None of the fish wanted freedom though, but the opposite. Some mysterious force kept these herrings on the boat or attached to it in any imaginable way, rather than escaping. The once that accidentally fell out, immediately returned and leaped back to join the ride.

And a grey-cloaked, pointy-hatted, white-bearded and haired fisherman with a silvery fishing rod in his hand, stood firmly on the boat in the middle of all the herrings, spreading his arms like a magician or a ruler of some sort.

'Who are you!?' Viljo screamed fearfully, his head popping above the side of his boat.

The fisherman stood still and looked past Viljo. His eyes were covered by the hat, and the long beard and the hair hid most of his face.

'What have you done to our lake?' Viljo asked, now more firmly. The old knees cracking, he stood up and sway his fist. He looked around, grabbed an oar from the crutch and took a swing with it. But the target was too far away. Once he had fully completed the hundred and eighty degree rotation and missed, his boat rocked from side to side. He took a side step in an effort to regain his balance, but a loose fishing line on the floor got dangled around his ankle. Feet trapped and the boat rocking now to the opposite side, he lost his balance throwing him overboard together with the oar. Head first he dived in the water and the line followed around his foot. As he kicked his knotted legs underwater and swung his arms above, the fisherman raised the silver fishing rod up in the air. The rod started glowing in the mist. Viljo reached out for the only floating device he had taken with him, his wooden oar. He placed the oar under his armpits, rested a little while observing terrified the intentions of the mysterious fisherman who stretched his arms even further out making him look like a wizard. The wizard's rustic boat raised itself above the water about a few centimetres, and with all the herrings, hovered away through the fog and out of Viljo's sight.

'Come back!' Viljo shouted, his mouth gargling the water.

He started swimming towards his boat amongst a few loose stems of reed. Once next to his boat, he reached out and got a hold of the gunwale. He faced one of the most difficult tasks to perform for anyone: younger, fitter or especially someone like him who was eighty-something years old. He had to climb back into his boat.

With both hands he hung on the side and attempted to kick his leg high. But the flexibility wasn't there anymore as it used to be. Only his knees hurt, and his lips and hands had turned blue. The lake had become completely ice free only a few weeks before. The water wasn't freezing anymore, but cold enough for anyone to reach hypothermia within less than an hour. He tried to pull himself up again, unsuccessfully. 'Help!' he screamed from the top of his weakened lungs. His frail cry echoed across the lake. The wizard or anyone else didn't return to save him. In the good old times, there would have always been someone fishing day and night, but not anymore. Lake Pihtamo was a shadow of a paradise it used to be, and now about to claim its first victim sixteen years later since it took the lives of two other greats. Viljo was about to join Carl and Roar as the only drownings ever recorded in the area.

Viljo lowered himself to rest on the floating oar again. Only his head, shoulders and arms were above the surface. The rest of his body had numbed in the cold. He began to feel the symptoms of hypothermia. He knew it was only a matter of time he would begin to sink, similarly to Jack when he lost his grip in front of Rose, except that this was the real deal, not the silver screen. And Viljo wouldn't be getting that last kiss of goodbye. He was alone. But the awareness of joining Aune brought him comfort and warmth in the midst of his body and mind freezing numb. His heart had gone on for so long without her, yet soon they would be back together again. If he was to be accepted at the gates of heaven.

The strength in his arms and upper body was all gone. Slowly, he began sliding away from the support of the oar. He drifted in and out of consciousness, until his body sunk underwater and his mind into another dimension. He couldn't breathe anymore as he floated deeper and deeper. First, everything blacked out, until he saw the light. He heard Aune's soft voice whispering to his ear.

'Viljo. My love. Listen to me. This once. Please. It's not your time to go, yet. You have an important mission to complete. A purpose. The time will tell you more, what and when. Please save yourself for the sake of Pihtamo. And for yourself. And for Carl's memory. He is sending his regards. He is waiting for you, too... But not yet! Save yourself for me. I want you to live. You have so much to give. You're so important that you don't even realise. You have given so much. There is only one thing I ask you to do for me, and I ask you no more. You can. Climb up on that boat of yours, you old hag, 'cause Aune loves you forever!'

Suddenly, he returned to consciousness mouth filled with water. He was drowning, yet he fought against it. He looked up and saw the bottom of the boat above him. He started kicking and flapping his arms like a baby duck learning to swim. Once he surfaced, he coughed his lungs out of water and yellow mucus. He came up as another person, energised and stronger. He flicked his body around slamming his back against the side of the boat. He raised his arms up against the side, turned his wrists and got a hold of the top edge. Then, he raised his both legs up as if doing abdominal curls, but all the way up taking his knees over his head so that in the end his feet touched the bottom of the boat. A full summersault took him around on the boat like performed by a young gymnast. It was an old trick he had learned in the military service more than half a century ago that came in handy for the first time only when he needed it the most – while facing death.

He picked up the oar from the water and placed both of them on the crutches. He started rowing fast to warm himself up. And he seriously considered about retirement, and never returning to the lake again, ever.

Chapter 18

# RUMOURS

Touched by the temperate English sun, Sven's slightly tanned face seemed somewhat exotic in comparison to usual clientele of the Arctic Bar. Jaaku's much paler complexion shone like a lighthouse next to him. Over the years, the seasons in Pihtamo had become more unpredictable and vague. The famous midnight sun and twenty-four hour daylight were often obstructed by grey clouds and heavier rains. The daily highs rarely soared above five to ten degrees Celsius in the summer, whereas winter months had become milder. The chances to get tanned were non-existent.

Sven's and Jaaku's encounter had nothing unpredictable, though. The usual, Arctic Wodka bottle and two shot glasses decorated the bar top under their noses.

'You cannot believe what happened,' Sven said, portraying unusual level of enthusiasm. The holiday break had seemingly energised him. 'We went fishing in Great Britain and...'

'Hold on,' Jaaku interrupted straight away. 'Fishing? On your honeymoon?'

'Yes. And?'

'You know you have a serious problem. Ida must have been absolutely thrilled about that,' he said ironically.

'Actually, she came along.'

'What? Unbelievable! You two are so made for each other,' Jaaku smirked. 'She must love you very much.'

'I hope she does,' Sven said and downed the shot. 'Anyway, I was catching all sorts of fishes. Honestly. My boat was completely full and then this...'

'You caught something? So... you still got it?' Jaaku said and finished his shot, too.

'What do you mean "got it?" I always got it. I still "have it!"' Sven snorted, upset.

'Really? You remember the last time we went fishing together?'

'Ah, that was just an odd day. I guess I wasn't focused. It can happen even to the best of us.'

'You... we caught absolutely nothing.'

'No need to remind me,' Sven said and poured them some more drink.

'The same happened to Viljo as well.'

'Really? Well, I can see that happening. Maybe he's the one "losing it."'

'No. This is something else,' Jaaku said seriously. 'During the week you were gone, no other fisherman in Pihtamo caught any fish. Not a single tiddler.'

'Well, I have to admit that in the meantime, I caught enough for all of us.'

'Perhaps, you did. I am not familiar with the waters in Great Britain. Maybe it's better there. Maybe we should all move there.'

'That particular lake we were on seemed ridiculously abundant of fish. I've never seen anything like it.'

'May I ask if you did anything else apart from fishing?'

'Not really. The problem was that we sort of got caught up in the storm.'

'What happened?'

'Once we finished the fishing tour, we had to stay up north by the lake extra couple of days. All the trains back to London were cancelled, until the day of our flight back home. Apparently, there were leaves on the track.'

'Hold on. Let me get this straight. You travelled all the way to Great Britain... just to stay by the lake? And to fish? You saw none of the famous monuments like Big Ben? Westminster Abbey?'

Sven nodded. 'We saw them briefly... through the taxi

window.'

'Ida must be head over heels,' Jaaku snorted and had his shot.

'Well, I think it's still better than nothing, isn't it?' Sven said. 'And the catch was unbelievable. I'm sure Ida was impressed about that at least.'

*Sure, she was*, Jaaku thought sarcastically and just stared straight ahead, concerned about Sven's indifference in his fresh marriage.

Sven elbowed Jaaku to get his attention again. 'At least someone caught something, ey?' he said encouragingly. 'Gives us hope.'

'I guess,' Jaaku turned to Sven. 'And did they let you bring any of that fish here through the customs?'

'Ah. That is the interesting part. Or sad. They didn't let us keep the fish.'

'Not at all? Who is them?'

'There was some sort of hostile water-police who told us to release the fish back into the lake. All of it. Quite cruel, isn't it?'

'What did you do?'

'I obeyed. And since Ida was there, I didn't want to cause any problems. I think the policeman was armed, too.'

'That's ridiculous! What a waste of good catch.'

'That's exactly what I thought. I told Ida that releasing fish you have just caught is like going hunting moose with a paintball rifle.'

Jaaku's face grew serious. 'What do you mean by that?' he asked while looking away.

'It's a joke,' Sven said and gave a concerned look to Jaaku who seemed distant. 'Is everything alright? I thought it was funny.'

Jaaku's heart beat faster. 'Has someone told you something?'

'You're acting strangely. Too much Wodka?' Sven smirked.

'Probably...' Jaaku let out an uncomfortable chuckle, filled his glass and downed the shot immediately.

'Told me what?' Sven asked.

'Erm... told you about...' Jaaku stammered, but soon remembered, '...Viljo?'

'What about him?'

Jaaku sighed in relief. 'There are rumours flying he saw something on the lake. Something disconcerting.'

'What did the old man see? A fish with three eyes?' Sven smiled.

'I know how you two don't get along very well.'

'Seriously, his binge has lasted long enough to see even Jesus walking on Lake Pihtamo,' Sven laughed.

'Please, could you show some respect towards the eldest. He did after all fight for our country and freedom. We should be grateful for what he has done. And he is a great fisherman.'

'I didn't mean it like that... but it doesn't change the fact that he likes his schnapps every now and then.'

'He likes to drink, yes, but he's not crazy. Just old. Besides, look who's drinking?' Jaaku pointed at their half empty Wodka bottle. 'Would you like some more?'

Sven nodded. 'So, tell me then, what did Viljo see on the lake?'

'This is the interesting part,' Jaaku took a deep breath already anticipating some negativity from Sven. 'Viljo claimed that he saw a some sort of... a ghost.'

'That's exactly what I mean,' Sven's smile widened. 'He's lost it!'

'Or not a ghost, but something like a... grim reaper or... a wizard,' Jaaku said, trying to remember Viljo's story that he had accidentally eavesdropped the day before in the Arctic Bar whilst Viljo shared the details with other town's elderly fishermen. Coincidentally, Jaaku happened to sit on the table opposite to them and hear most of the conversation.

'Was it fishing with a scythe? Slicing the herrings in half?' Sven giggled.

'I know it sounds complete nonsense, but...'

'Please don't tell me you believe him?'

'Of course not,' Jaaku hesitated, 'but whatever it is emptying our lake, we have to find the answer.'

'What else did the old Viljo say? Does the ghost... row a boat?' Sven smirked.

'Apparently, it doesn't row or use any kind of engines.'

'How does it move around then? Use its night gown as a sail?' Sven burst into laughter. He shook his head and had his shot.

'I don't know exactly,' Jaaku remained serious. 'It kind of like... floated above the surface... like a hoverboard.'

Sven stared ahead looking slightly irritated to Jaaku's story. He had a revelation. 'I know what's going on here. It's Viljo's Wodka talking again.'

'Perhaps that as well,' Jaaku nodded. 'We should speak to Viljo directly. He was there. He can explain much better and more than I can. I am only the messenger.'

'The messenger with bad judgement skills.'

Jaaku opened his mouth to say something, but instead, chose to remain quiet. He was losing his strength to discuss about the matter. He knew he couldn't change Sven's unflinching, negative opinion about Viljo. He ordered them another bottle.

They both stared ahead and said nothing. The usual comfortable silence between them suddenly had signs of awkwardness. Sven wiggled restlessly on his seat. Jaaku tapped his fingers on the bar top. The arriving bottle broke the tension.

'So...' Sven said and opened the top. 'That's it?'

'That's it,' Jaaku replied.

'There must be something else. What happened next?'

'He fell off the boat and nearly drowned.'

'The ghost fell?'

'Viljo. He freaked out.'

'Totally unheard-of that something would scare him. I always thought he's the toughest of the tough. Or so he seems.'

'Me too.'

'Then what happened? Viljo was in the water. And the ghost?'

'It floated away with all Viljo's herrings and many other fishes.'

'There were fish? You didn't say anything about any herrings?'

'Apparently, there were loads. Even Viljo caught a few, until they all freed themselves from his net.'

'Freed themselves?' Sven stared at Jaaku with blank eyes. 'Isn't that obvious what's going on here? Viljo must have seen the spirit... of a liquor bottle like a spirit of the lamp,' he smiled.

Jaaku's jaw dropped. He was expecting something more from Sven than just another insult towards the elderly. He stood up, looked down at Sven and said, 'Let me tell you something, Sven. We all know Viljo fought for our freedom as did many men of his generation. They had to pay a high price for that. Many didn't survive. The ones, including Viljo who returned had psychological wounds so deep that never healed. But alcohol was and is the only, if not the best, remedy. At least their generation has an excuse to drink. What is our excuse? What is yours?'

Sven said nothing. Only being shocked at Jaaku's sudden outburst and rant, he looked at his empty glass and the bottle they had just opened. He wasn't used to such an openness, especially from another man. Often such a colourful portrayal of emotions was frowned upon in Pihtamo anyway. The other patrons turned to look at Jaaku.

'What!?' Jaaku yelled openly to the bar. A silence filled the room and the patrons turned their heads away concentrating on their drinks. No one said a thing, neither did Sven. Also, Jaaku turned down the volume and sat back down. 'Nevertheless, whether intoxicated or not, Viljo's opinions have always been highly regarded and respected in our community. He has been fishing these waters for more than half a century by now. He is the head of the fishing board. A champion for fifteen years. I do listen to him carefully and I would too if I was you,' he said firmly, but then his voice got a warmer tone. 'I am only telling these things to you, because I want you to be careful out there. You're my best friend. You're the reigning fishing champion. You work really hard to become even better. I know you're always the first up in the morning trying to find the best possible fishing time and place. And we automatically think we have found all the best solutions. We think we know everything about the lake. Or you do. Or Viljo does. But what if we are wrong? What if there's someone... or something who knows better?'

'There cannot be!' Sven protested, and hit his fist on the table. 'No stranger can know these waters better than any of us. That wouldn't make any sense.'

'Whatever you say... But the only thing I'm saying is that be careful out there on the lake.' Jaaku stood up again and pulled up his hood.

'I will prove everyone wrong. I will go fishing the next thing in the morning.'

'Good luck, my friend.'

'Aren't you coming?'

'Not before I've spoken to Viljo,' Jaaku said, took a twenty-mark note with some change of coins out of his pocket and threw them all on the bar top. He turned away and walked out.

Sven stayed seated, but looked over his shoulder as his friend left the building. When he turned to face the bar, a one mark coin of Jaaku's change kept swirling in front of his eyes. Eventually, the coin landed on its tail side. The glimmer brought back a bittersweet memory of the bedtime story his father used to tell him. 'Bear's Den Mark...' Sven said under his breath. *I miss you, dad*.

Chapter 19

# MEETING VILJO

Jaaku leaned his bicycle against the trunk of one of the apple trees in Viljo's front garden. He always knew where the old man lives, but never came this near. Once he climbed the few concrete steps up towards the house, a musty odour protruded from behind decaying wooden front door. The stench reminded him of his now late grandparents potato cellar.

The anxiety grew to fear as he knocked the door once and waited. No answer. The curtains were open, but the house inside was dark throughout. By the time he knocked the second time, he had already gotten used to the smell. Again, silence.

He pushed the unlocked door open that reminded him about safer times some decades ago when neighbourhood watch wasn't needed, but genuine trust to the community existed by default – much more than in the contemporary Pihtamo. The village wasn't a dangerous place even today, yet the younger generation rather lived somewhat more isolated life than the people at Viljo's age group. The older folk's doors were always open for family, friends and surprise visitors, whereas the younger generation locked their doors and windows in a fear of a burglar, a stranger, a family member or a friend who would pop by unexpectedly. No one visited each other anymore without a warning text message or at least, a phone call. However, not even the war time crimes Viljo witnessed made him more fearful of strangers, but the opposite - more welcoming.

The worst offences ever witnessed on Viljo's property were mainly caused by the town kids stealing fruit from his many apple trees in the garden. Yet, most apples stolen were the ones already fallen to the ground as kids usually couldn't reach the best and the freshest fruit still attached to the tree branches. Unless they had time to shake the trees, which most often they had, when Viljo went out fishing. If he was at home, just seeing his angry face on the window scared the most innocent kids away. Some bullies he had to repel by showing his spear gun. In a way, the little thieves did him also a favour, especially, in his later years, when picking fruit off the ground had become laborious due to severe back pains and bad knees. The kids did the job on his behalf taking care of the apples gone bad.

The hinges squeaked as the front door opened wide. A dark, narrow corridor greeted Jaaku. The temperature inside was about the same as outside. Viljo was known to pinch his every penny in anything: housing, fishing gear, clothing, heating and his boat. Some of the rods and tackles he had used for half a century or more. Having lived through the wartime and worst recessions, Viljo had learned to save, maintain and restore old. Nothing was wasted or thrown away. Not much new was purchased either, only the necessities.

Jaaku's attempt to tiptoe towards the other end of the corridor leading to another doorway failed poorly. The wooden floor planks squeaked under his heavy boots. He felt the indoor temperature rising as he advanced. He pushed the head through the doorway and a glimmer of light in the corner of a dimly lit living room space revealed Viljo sitting on his bed in his pyjamas. A cast iron stove insulated with some asbestos plates generated heat in the room. The flaming wood flickered behind the glass door of the stove.

'Who's there!?' Viljo shouted. He sounded less friendly than expected considering his hospitable open door policy. He held a fishing pneumatic spear gun on his lap.

'It's me... Jaaku.'

'Who?' Viljo grunted. He stood up and squinted his eyes. He took a step forward.

'From the fishing competition. The pie shop owner's son.'

144

'The Eskimo?'

'Well, sir. I guess you can call me that.' Cheeks blushing out of nervousness, Jaaku moved closer to the light from the flames of the stove.

Viljo nodded doubtfully once he recognised Jaaku. He looked at him from head to toes. 'If you came here to apologise, apology denied,' he said bluntly.

'Erm. I came here to talk about the situation at the lake.'

'There's nothing to talk about. Now, get out!'

'But... it's serious. No one is catching any fish. What you saw is...'

'How do you know what I saw? Who told you?' Viljo asked, while steam came out with his breath.

'I... overheard a conversation in the bar,' Jaaku said and looked down to his feet.

'You've been spying on me? Who the hell do you think you are!? Walking here like that,' Viljo pointed the spear gun at Jaaku.

Jaaku looked up again, raised his hands and took a step back. As Viljo caressed the trigger, three soft knocks on the front door caught their attention. Another three louder knocks followed.

'Who the hell?' Viljo took a step closer and glanced over Jaaku's shoulder. 'Did you bring someone else?'

'No. I swear,' Jaaku trembled nervously.

'Quiet,' Viljo hushed and sneaked past Jaaku.

The bittersweet smell of liquor on Viljo's breath reminded Jaaku about Sven's words and warnings of Viljo's heavy drinking habits. He saw an empty Arctic Wodka bottle on the bedside.

Viljo walked along the corridor leading to the front room. He kept the spear gun pointing directly towards the front door. Only a couple of steps away, the door slid open. He stopped and aimed.

'Hello. I know there's someone in there,' a voice echoed before the door opened wide. Sven stood between the frame. He glanced inside, but recognised nothing but darkness. Once he leaped over the doorstep, Viljo came out of the shadow, grabbed him by his collar and pushed him against the side wall of the front room. He pointed the spear gun on his face. 'How dare you sneak into my house?'

'We need to... talk,' Sven mumbled while being crushed against the wall.

'Viljo, don't! He's my friend!' Jaaku appeared in the corridor.

'I know damn well who he is and he shouldn't be anywhere near me! Now, get out of my house, both of you!'

'What are you doing here, Sven?' Jaaku said and joined them in the front room. 'I didn't know you're coming.'

'Why suddenly this congregation at my house?' Viljo grunted.

'I knew this was a bad idea,' Sven said under his breath.

'You're damn right, Mister,' Viljo said and placed his finger back on the trigger.

Waving his arms, Jaaku moved next to them. 'Please, Viljo! Could you put that thing away?'

Viljo ignored Jaaku's cry and focused on Sven. 'Don't tell me you're here, because you haven't caught any fish either... champion?' He pressed the cold tip of the steel spear under Sven's chin.

Sven nodded while sweat developed on his forehead.

'See! I'm not the only one concerned about the situation,' Jaaku said. He sounded slightly delighted having Sven backing up his opinion. 'We have to do something. We cannot go on like this.'

'We? Who's we?' Viljo turned to Jaaku, yet keeping Sven at gunpoint.

'Us three. We are the best there is. We must go and find this... thing that is destroying our livelihoods.'

'I ain't going back there. And besides, I am not stepping on any boat with...' Viljo turned to look directly into Sven's fearful eyes, '...him.'

'Only this once?' Jaaku pleaded.

'Over my dead body,' Viljo said and let go of Sven. He took a step backwards, not lowering his weapon, though. 'I would fear to face the same destiny as my brother when he went fishing with his father.'

'That's uncalled-for,' said Jaaku.

Sven sighed and straightened the collar of his jacket.

'We all know what happened. His father drowned my

brother,' Viljo grunted. 'Everyone knows that.'

'How can you say that?' Sven disagreed.

'Isn't that obvious... you bastard!?'

'My father... disappeared,' Sven hesitated.

'Yes, he did. After he drowned my brother.'

'That's not true!'

'Explain me this then...' Viljo took a deep breath and lowered the spear gun. 'My brother was leading the fishing scoreboard only some weeks left of the current season before the annual fishing final your old man had won fifteen times consecutively...'

'Sixteen,' Sven corrected.

'Shut up! But this time your father wasn't the favourite.'

'What's your point?'

'Your father had always won. That's all he knew in sports and life, being the best. Until Carl stepped in and higher the stakes. You wanna hear what I believe?'

'Not sure if I do,' Sven said bluntly.

'I believe your father couldn't deal with the idea of losing and he tried to get rid of his biggest rival, my little brother.'

'You're insane.'

'Maybe I am. But we all know, the whole Pihtamo knows your father would have lost the title. Carl was on a top shape, but your old man wasn't anymore. He would have lost the year before already, if the judges were not all his best friends.'

'What are you talking about?' Sven asked.

'If you had done your homework, you would know that back then, they also measured the weight of the total catch. Three things counted: the biggest individual fish, the quantity and the total weight. Nowadays, because of the increased number of participants, as we all know, the judges have only time and interest to count the number of fish and the biggest individual fish. The total weight element was ditched years ago.'

Sven looked at Jaaku who only spread his arms. 'I didn't know that,' Jaaku said.

'I thought you kids wouldn't know. Anyway, it was rumoured that your father bribed the judges to give his catch extra weight: the individual and total. Even the real quantities he achieved has been questionable. The judges were all his best mates. He shouldn't have won even the year before.'

'Why should I listen to you?'

'Because I know more than you do, both of you,' Viljo said, oozing confidence. 'How do you explain the footsteps on the snow, the DNA samples, the collision marks on Carl's boat?' he asked, and despicably turned to look at Jaaku. 'And you of all the people, had to buy that boat in an auction. I was prepared to buy it, the boat that belonged to my brother, to my family, but you instead had to bid higher, bid against me. What kind of sick person are you?'

'Yolla was Carl's boat?' Sven looked at Jaaku.

'Well... it was a nice boat, a collective item,' Jaaku said. 'I'm sorry, but it was an open auction. I didn't realise how much it meant to you.'

'Of course it did,' Viljo and Sven said together at the same time, but with different tones. They looked at each other, confused.

'Why you didn't tell me?' Sven asked Jaaku.

'I thought it wouldn't matter. It's all in the past anyway,' Jaaku said.

Sven shook his head in disbelief. 'So, the marks at the bottom?'

'No one knows for sure,' Jaaku replied.

Viljo sighed and shook his head, too. 'You just don't get it. Both of you. You two are here asking me a favour. What were you thinking?'

'Asking a favour not just for us, but for the whole community, including yourself. We can help each other,' Jaaku said.

'We cannot help each other. I cannot take the risk', Viljo said and turned the accusing finger at Sven. 'I know that his father collided with my brother's boat, attacked him and they both drowned. I know!'

'Who cares what you believe!' Sven snorted. 'There is no hard evidence against my father.'

'There is no reason why Carl would have instigated anything. There is no reason why Carl would have had anything to do with your father. It was Roar who started it all. The pressure was on his side. I believe he drowned my brother first and then got rid of his boat, before he drowned himself together with his own sinking boat.'

'You are an old fool! What if your brother attacked and drowned my father? Because that was the only way your brother could ever become a champion. Or what if... you...' Sven looked away.

'Watch your mouth!' Viljo pointed the spear gun again at Sven.

Sven didn't even pay attention to the spear gun anymore. 'Everything you say are only assumptions.'

'Well, that's what we have to live with,' Viljo said.

Sven looked at him in the eyes again. 'I believe us three would have all the knowledge, skills and tools to go and sort the lake out and bring things back to normal... if you stop living in the past.'

'How can I stop living in the past until we know for sure what happened sixteen years ago?'

'We may never find out.'

'That's what you say, because you are afraid of the truth.'

'I'm not! Of course I want to know what happened to my father. Every day for sixteen years I have thought about my father's destiny, as I'm sure you have thought about your brother's. I have dreamed about the day he would just show up from nowhere and tell that everything is fine.'

'How lovely,' Viljo said sarcastically.

'But us arguing here is not gonna bring any of them back. It is all in the past,' Sven said and looked at Jaaku pleadingly.

Jaaku nodded.

But Viljo didn't. 'Yes, for you perhaps it's easier, since you were just a child. But not to me. My brother was my best friend for sixty years.'

'It's not any easier for me. I lost my father, for God's sake!'

'Don't say God's name in vain, son.'

'I'm sorry. I mean... we are all different and I'm not my father. You cannot keep punishing me for whatever he has done or hasn't. We are two different people, me and Roar.'

'I don't need this anymore. I'm too old... as you said.'

'If this is something to do with me winning the

championship...'

'You really believe that you won?'

'Well...'

'You do understand that I would have won if your chubby friend here didn't help you a little.'

'I didn't mean to break the ice,' Jaaku intervened apologetically. 'It was not another one of our evil plans to get rid of you, if that's what you're thinking.'

'Really not? It seemed like a perfect one.'

Jaaku gave Viljo a serious look. 'Of course not. Why do you think everyone is against you? I wanted to win, too, like everybody else. The problem was that there were just too many fishermen around you, following you and trusting you. And I made the mistake that I became one of them. I should have listened to myself and stay away. Or follow Sven who was also doing remarkably well. But my move closer to you on the ice cost us dearly. And it cost you, maybe your championship, maybe not. There were still some time on the clock. Anything could have happened. But I didn't break the ice on purpose. That's just part of the sports, I guess.'

As Viljo listened, his rock solid face softened a little.

'We are begging you,' Sven said. 'We are the best there is, us three. If we cannot solve the issue, no one can and we can all might as well leave Pihtamo and start somewhere fresh. What's the point staying here if there's no fish?'

'He's got a point there,' Jaaku added.

'I really am an old fool,' Viljo said and lowered the spear gun away from Sven's face. 'Where do you need an old hag like me? No one needs me. No one has visited me for last three years apart from Jehova's Witnesses. Now, suddenly, you two barge in here at the same minute wanting something from me.'

Sven sighed in relief. 'Because... you know the lake better than any of us,' he said while swallowing his pride.

Viljo raised his gaze. 'Do you know how old I am?'

'I don't know... sixty-something.'

'Hah! Eighty-four years old.'

'Respect,' Jaaku said.

'Stop it,' Viljo snorted, but soon softened. 'Now, I'm getting your respect, because you need something from me. Where have you been all these years? Where was help when I needed to sort out my dying apple trees? Where was everyone... when I lost my wife?'

'My condolences. When did she die?' Sven asked.

'See! Of course you don't know. It was twenty-four years ago.'

'I was five years old then.'

'Fine! What about your wedding, Sven? The whole town was invited, except me. Everyone's always leaving the old man alone...'

'You were invited.'

'Ah,' Viljo said and looked at the stack of unopened mail in the corner of the room that he hadn't touched for years. Aune always took care of their mail.

'Don't worry, Viljo. That was the worst wedding ever,' Jaaku added. 'You didn't wanna be there.'

'Thanks,' Sven said and rolled his eyes.

'I have been waiting half of my life for some respect and now I'm getting it... almost on my dead bed,' Viljo's voice saddened.

'Please don't say that.'

'The last time was during the war I really felt belonging to something that made a difference. We were respected. We had a purpose, a code of honour, a goal to beat the enemy, or at least, to defend the mother nation to the last breath. Since then, it's been just a struggle, trying to heal the wounds, surviving, paying the bills, slowly losing health and the loved ones around you one by one, until we're all alone with nothing left, but vague and bittersweet memories of the supposedly great times we've lived through. I was expecting more. Fanfares, medals, celebrations, invitation from the president. But after all the glory days, I'm just fighting against the bully kids in the neighbourhood who are trying to steal the rest of my apples. By the way, did you see how my apple trees are suffering?'

Sven yawned. He felt the conversation wasn't really going anywhere.

'We are really sorry what we did to your apple trees,' Jaaku said.

'It was you? Both of you?'

Sven and Jaaku nodded. 'A long time ago.'

'Well, I guess I have to forgive you. There's a new generation now, though. I think it never stops. The apple theft.'

'But... you were the fishing champion. One of the best ever,' Sven said.

'One of the best, but not the best,' Viljo said. His eyes glared in the distance. 'You know very well who was the best. Your father. That's the way he will be remembered, always. Despite, the negative rumours, the uncertainty, the blame. He is ranked the number one in the ice fishing hall of fame and that's the way it will be forever and ever. ' Viljo pointed at Jaaku. 'And by the way, thanks to your friend here I'm not even the champion anymore.'

'That's also part of life... and sports,' Sven said while Jaaku wanted to hide himself.

'True. If anyone, I should know that,' Viljo said. He dropped the spear gun on the side table and spread his arms. 'So, tell me then, youngsters, what do you exactly want from me?'

'To join us this one last time. The only time,' Sven said.

'What's that supposed to mean?' Viljo smirked.

'To join us to solve the mystery ravaging Lake Pihtamo.'

'I mean, the other thing. Are you saying I'm so old that this will be my last time... ever?'

'The last time with us and then you never need to see us again.'

'Until perhaps next year's ice fishing competition again,' Jaaku added.

'Shut up,' Sven said under his breath.

'One last time, you're saying?' Viljo asked.

'Please. We need you.'

'What are we waiting for then?' Viljo said and trotted along the corridor.

'Now?' Sven stepped away from the wall and looked behind Viljo, but he had already disappeared into the living room.

'Of course, you daft!' Viljo's voice echoed through the walls.

'It's almost ten o'clock in the evening. My girlfriend... I mean... my wife is waiting and...'

Viljo stuck his head through the doorway. He was already dressing up warm clothes. 'You two decided to barge in here right now, so I decide that we go right now. We have to be prepared to stay up all night, week or month to catch the monster. Clear?'

'Monster?'

'Whatever it is taking our livelihoods. Are you boys ready?'

'But the best fishing hours won't be until the early morning hours?' Sven looked at his bare wrist.

'I know damn well when the best fishing hours are, but this is about something else. Do you want me in or not?'

'Yes, sir.'

'Then we go now or never. We have no idea what we're dealing with here. No one has ever seen this "thing" apart from myself, and when that happened, I was there early, really early in the morning.'

'What was it exactly that you saw then?' asked Jaaku.

'Something I didn't like. And I have a feeling it doesn't care about the best fishing hours.'

'Let's go then,' said Sven.

'Yes. But if you try any tricks on me, Mr. Sven...' Viljo's face turned grave, '...I'll kill you.'

'Yes, sir.'

'Meet you at my boat in an hour's time.'

Chapter 20

# SALMON FISHING

Punctuality, one of the most highly regarded qualities of people in Pihtamo was never compromised. So-called being 'fashionably late' didn't exist. A chance of running late from a set appointment, even the significant time of five minutes caused immerse stress amongst the one's being late and anger on the other's waiting.

Therefore, none of the three men took risks of upsetting each other by delaying the departure. At eleven o'clock on the dot the same evening Sven and Jaaku met Viljo at his rowing boat. The men were geared up to their best knowledge more for traditional fishing rather than ghost hunting, apart from Viljo's spear gun that poked out of his bag.

'Where do you think you need that for?' Sven said and pointed at the tip of the spear.

Viljo gave Sven a tense look from his head to toes. 'Self-defence, perhaps.'

Sven swallowed and went to mind his own business. He swung past Viljo and gave the old dinghy a disdainful look. 'We are not taking this boat, are we?'

Viljo snorted and pulled the spear gun out of his bag. 'Maybe we should just finish this off right here, right now.'

'What do you mean?' Sven said, alarmed. He took a step back onto the wet marshland.

'Us two have something to settle before we step into that

154

boat together.'

'Not again,' Sven yawned. 'Is this why you asked us to come here? There was no wizard or ghost?'

'This is the least I can do to you,' Viljo said, took Sven at gunpoint and put the finger on the trigger.

'You wouldn't shoot an unarmed man,' Sven said and gave a nervous chuckle. He wasn't sure anymore whether Viljo meant it or not. He seemed to be softening in the house earlier, but now he looked deadly serious.

'What are you two playing again?' Jaaku jumped between the two broilers and waved towards the lake. 'I think the enemy is out there, not here.'

'I will shoot through you if you don't move,' Viljo warned Jaaku.

'Do it then!' Jaaku blustered. 'If you kill us both, you'll be alone trying to fight the enemy... and you know you cannot do it. You need us. We have to stick together as a team.'

'You don't have to do this, Jaaku,' Sven said and tried to push him aside, but he stood rigid in front of him.

'The enemy is...' Viljo paused for a little and then looked down, 'everywhere.' He lowered the spear gun and breathed heavily. He seemed delirious.

Jaaku rolled his eyes and then spoke to Viljo. 'We are here to help you, help everyone, the entire community. Please accept that. We all know what you have gone through in life and we respect that, but seriously, not everyone is an enemy, and especially, not Sven here. He wouldn't hurt a *moosequito*.'

'*Moosequito*?' Sven repeated, confused.

'I mean... mosquito,' Jaaku corrected, blushing.

Sven shook his head and gave Jaaku a suspicious look. 'How many shots you've had today?'

Jaaku laughed nervously as he went for his pocket. 'By the way, I brought this...'

'Don't even think about it!' Viljo raised his gaze again and caressed the trigger.

'It's not what you think,' Jaaku said.

'Take your hand out of your pocket, now!' Viljo ordered and aimed at Jaaku.

'Please do as the old man tells you,' Sven panicked.

Jaaku ignored them both and slowly pulled out a bunch of garlic between his fingers. 'Might come in handy.'

Sven gasped in relief.

'Hunting vampires, are we?' Viljo smirked and lowered the weapon.

Sven gathered himself. He felt less tense now. 'You've seen too many horror films, since you installed that cable TV into your igloo.'

'You never know. It's good to be prepared,' Jaaku said.

'I'm here with a bunch of loonies... and garlic,' Viljo snorted and chucked the spear gun on the back seat. He started unleashing the boat's chain off the birch tree.

'Who's the looney here?' Sven whispered under his breath, still hiding behind Jaaku.

'Did I hear something?' Viljo stopped.

'Nothing. Absolutely nothing,' Jaaku convinced while spreading his arms. 'Must have been the wind.' He turned around and whispered to Sven. 'Now, you shut up if you don't wanna get us both killed.'

'He's as crazy as his brother was.'

'Please don't mention your dad or his brother anymore. Let's just catch the monster and we can all go home,' Jaaku said and rushed to keep the boat steady while Viljo leaped at the backseat. Next, Jaaku took the middle seat.

Sven put his one foot on the bottom of the boat and with his other foot kicked the boat off the grassy shore. Once they were on the move, Sven jumped in and took the front seat. The dinghy glided further out, but no one touched the oars. Everyone avoided eye-contact. Jaaku and Sven shrugged their shoulders. Viljo whistled and went through his fishing gear, until the boat stopped moving. Since the handles of the oars lie nearest to Sven, he decided to grab them. By pushing an oar to the bottom of the lake, he released the boat off the reed patch and away from the shallow waters onto the outer lake.

'Can you ask Viljo where he saw this... thing?' Sven asked Jaaku who became the messenger sitting between the two.

'I can hear you, you coward! Talk directly at me, if you have

156

something to say,' Viljo grunted.

'So... where then?' Sven repeated, looked away and kept rowing.

'I saw it right at the end of the Herring Bay.'

'Really? That's not far from where I live,' Jaaku said.

'Right by the glaciers?' Sven asked.

'More towards the Moose Island,' Viljo said. 'But I tell you more once we get closer. For now, just keep on rowing.'

The sparkling stars filled the pitch black sky. The moon bridge showed them the way. The mild summer wind softly rocked the boat as Sven rowed with his youthful energy. The calmness and silence made the atmosphere somewhat ghastly. There were no signs of life on the lake. No fish jumping, no boats cruising, no fishermen on the shores. Even the birds and insects seemed to have disappeared. Only possible signs of life shone above from the outer space and the sky. One of the liveliest and the most bountiful lakes in the region had turned into a silent graveyard in only a matter of months. The annual fishing contest was only held late the previous year, when the first signs of declining numbers of fish were detected. Since then, the change had been rapidly devastating.

Viljo cast his bait in the water and began trolling. He showed no signs of giving up hope to catch fish. He ran the bait about ten metres below the surface while Sven kept the rowing speed at about three and a half kilometres per hour.

While the current and the former champion worked together, Jaaku in the middle sensed the tension easing. He thought it was a good time to further interview Viljo. 'So, what exactly happened that night?'

'Well... it was like any other night. Dead quiet. Until I caught fish on my net.'

'Are you really saying the lake's not empty?'

'It's not. I had at least four decent sized herrings tangled in my net, but they all escaped. One by one the fish released themselves. I have never seen anything like that before in my seventy years of fishing these waters. I started following their path, but I got caught in the middle of dense fog. The visibility was so poor that I collided into this old, wooden long boat. It just appeared out of nowhere. I have never seen that kind of boat before. I thought I knew every single fisherman and their boats around here. But I guess not. And there was a cloaked man standing on it.'

'A stand up angler?'

'It's not so rare, really. I have met a few. On a small boat, though, it can be dangerous. You need to have an exceptionally good balance. But I don't know what exactly this man, or whatever, was doing. The fish around him, including the ones I had caught first, were like spellbound. They, literally, jumped on his boat without him using any fishing gear, apart from some sort of shiny rod, but the rod had no line or tackle. It was just a long stick he was waving in the air.'

While eavesdropping, Sven couldn't help but intervene, 'Does that make us three like the ghost... I mean... herring busters?'

'Could you please shut it for once and just keep rowing?' Jaaku snorted. 'You were doing so well.'

Shocked, Sven fell speechless. Jaaku, most often the sidekick confronted him oozing unusual confidence. Sven followed his orders and continued rowing in silence, yet not sacrificing the brisk pace.

'Sorry about that,' Jaaku turned to face Viljo again. 'What happened then?'

'The boat and the man disappeared somehow... floating on the surface,' Viljo said as the storm clouds started to gather above them.

'Floating, ey?' Jaaku looked up at the darkening sky and then over his shoulder to rowing Sven. Sven rolled his eyes.

'Not touching the water. Up in the air. Hovering,' Viljo added.

Jaaku gave Viljo an odd look while being doubtful whether the old man had really had a few drinks too many that night.

'I can still somehow feel his presence,' Viljo continued. 'Don't ask me how, but he is still out here. The lake is not empty of fish yet, and I fear this man wants to get everything, every single herring and tiddler.'

'I can also feel something,' Sven snorted. 'Blisters on my

hands. You guys are heavy. What have you been eating? Or more like, drinking?'

Viljo glanced at Sven past Jaaku's shoulder. 'Didn't your friend just tell you to shut up and keep rowing? Two things your forte.'

'What's that supposed to mean... silver medallist?' Sven replied.

Jaaku hid his embarrassed face behind his mitts.

'I'm running out of patience with him,' Viljo grunted to Jaaku. 'I somehow thought his father would have taught him some manners.'

'My patience is put to test here rowing you two,' Sven replied from behind Jaaku. 'I should be the last one of us three wasting my talent by doing this.'

Jaaku gave demeaning glance at Sven. 'Rowing's good for you.'

'I agree. Builds your lousy character,' Viljo said.

Sven scowled. 'Are we there yet?'

'I tell you when we are,' Viljo smirked. 'A few more strokes.'

Meanwhile, the sky had filled with dark clouds. The breeze turned northerly, got stronger and cooler. The first lightning struck in the distance illuminating the horizon. A few seconds later a rumbling thunder followed. The heightening waves rocked the boat. The rain started pouring down.

'I believe this is roughly where I saw... him!' Viljo said hesitatingly.

Jaaku peered around him while holding the boards. Sven stopped rowing, but let the boat glide freely a few more metres. Jaaku picked up a large rock off the floor that was attached to a rope tied around the middle seat. He pushed the rock overboard and let it sunk into the depths anchoring the boat. Eventually, the boat stopped moving further, apart from the rocking and swaying in the developing storm.

'No fish on your line yet, I assume?' Jaaku asked Viljo.

'Not a nibble,' Viljo said and began to retrieve the line.

Freed from the rowing task, Sven took out his fishing rod and cast his reel. 'Let me show you.'

Viljo rolled his eyes in disbelief while Jaaku prepared his

gear.

'What happened a couple of weeks ago cannot be just a coincidence,' Sven said.

'What exactly happened?' Viljo asked.

'I caught loads. More than ever before.'

'Not here. In Great Britain,' Jaaku added.

'Doesn't matter where,' Sven said.

'Ah...' Viljo contemplated when a loud cracking sound interrupted them. They all turned to look how a thick spruce tree got sliced in half by a lightning strike in the distance on the peak of Moose Island. Both sides of the tree trunk fell on either side like a splitting banana. The stormy lake menaced and the skies blackened. 'I have never witnessed a weather like this,' Viljo said.

Sven reeled back his tackle and cast again. This time, though, the strong gust of wind blew the tackle back towards the boat.

'Watch out!' Jaaku ducked down as he saw the hooks of the tackle approaching.

But Viljo didn't see it coming since his eyes were still drawn by the destruct forest on the island. The tackle landed on Viljo's flat cap, grabbed it off his head and threw it on the water. Fuming, Viljo turned around and saw Sven spreading his arms apologetically. 'That's it, boy! I've had enough. That was my favourite hat.'

'Don't worry. It's still attached to the hook,' Sven said and fished the hat back into the boat. He picked up the hat in his hand.

While doing so, though, Viljo had already stood up and fuming he leaned over Jaaku who ducked down in the middle. Viljo raised his arms and clenched his fists. But Sven saw it coming. He stood up, too. He dropped the cap on the floor, his rod on top of Jaaku and then raised his fists for protection. Viljo swung his first, slow and weak punch giving Sven enough time to duck. But as Sven did pull his head down, he accidentally bang his forehead on the top of Jaaku's head, and when Viljo's arm got to the end of the full swing, he lost his balance and landed with full weight over Jaaku's curved back. By that time, Sven had already bounced back upright. A perfect slap stick moment like from any old silent film ended with Jaaku, the impartial third party member taking all the hits and suffering the most - as the innocent often and unfortunately do between the battles of two larger than life egos. Jaaku pushed Viljo off his back. Viljo landed on his seat, whereas Sven in agony stood holding his bleeding nose being cracked open against Jaaku's hard skull. Soon, he collapsed back on the front seat.

'I'm too old for any of this,' Viljo panted, picked up the wet cap and squashed it on his head. He grabbed his reel. The line and his bait were still in the water. Grunting, he retrieved the bait.

The conflict seemed to reach a standstill for the time being. Yet, a sudden gushing rain broke out distracting the men again. The boat floor started collecting water. Sven picked up a plastic scoop from the bottom. The blood dripping from his nose got mixed together with the rain water. Nevertheless, he began scooping the floor, but he wasn't fast enough as the rainfall got heavier. Soon the rain drops turned into slush and snow. Sven wiped his wet face. He could barely see ahead. Next, there were little ice cubes pouring down with a thundery hailstorm. Sven and Jaaku raised their arms over to protect themselves as the hailstones got larger. But Viljo just kept trolling. 'Have we just upset somebody? I haven't seen a hailstorm like this like... never!' Viljo yelled when something was biting. He felt the resistance pulling harder. 'I have caught something...' he hesitated as the line extended fast. He pushed the brake and tried to reel, but the catch fought against him. 'The reel is gonna break! I can't hold it any longer!' Hands beginning to bleed he held onto his trolling device when Jaaku jumped in slamming his hands around Viljo's. 'I told you there's fish in here!' Viljo screamed in both pain and excitement. Sven dropped the plastic scoop back on the floor and tried to join and help the two men, but once he stood up and raised his leg over the middle seat, all the weight of three adults distributed to the back. The boat sipped water. When Sven jumped back on his seat in the front to keep the balance, the fishing line snapped throwing Viljo and Jaaku in the arms of Sven. The boat sipped water again from the front this time. Sven pushed the two men off him on their original positions. The boat stopped rocking and the hailstorm eased turning into a light rain. 'That one was a big fish,' Viljo said, excited.

Sven looked at him doubtfully. 'Well, we never find out.'

'Why not? You still have your rod. Give it a go,' Viljo said.

'Maybe I will,' Sven hesitated while looking at the inconsistently moving surface. The thundery clouds remained. Jaaku picked up the scoop and continued emptying the boat of water. The lake calmed down, apart from a spiral pattern on the surface circulating them. A rotating column of water formed by a sudden whirlwind below them pushed the boat up in the air. The men held the boards knuckles white as the spiralling tower took them higher skywards.

'This must be it!' Viljo screamed, his voice mixed with fear and excitement. 'I told you there's something strange going on here!'

'Not quite what I expected,' Sven muttered as the sprays of water hit his face. The rope holding the anchor snapped and flew past them. The rock remained in the bottom for good.

'Me neither!' Jaaku agreed in a brace position. He let go of the scoop. 'The end of the world...'

The boat kept spinning around, but stopped escalating at about five metres above the surface, whereas the waterspout extended as a funnel rising all the way to the clouds. They were caught up in the middle.

The same process began next to them. Another waterspout developed out of nowhere growing higher.

'Can you see that?' Sven said and pointed up at the peak of the water column.

Viljo nodded. He reached out for the spear gun with one hand while the other was glued to the gunwale. He nearly had it, when the boat shook, throwing the gun on the other end to Sven's feet. Viljo, doubtfully, looked at Sven, who was the last person he wanted to have nearest to the gun. Sven looked back at Viljo, released his hands and threw himself on the wet floor on top of the spear gun.

The turbulent twister next to them created a shadow over their boat. On the peak of the column, a large pink fishlike creature emerged, shimmering brightly and blinding the men. Jaaku took off his woollen mitts and pulled out sunglasses from his breast pocket. 'It's a salmon, a big salmon!'

The gigantic two-metre long pink salmon balanced on top of a spiralling tornado. The monster fish held a brown book between its pectoral and pelvic fins. A golden cross hung around its neck covering the gills. Although fish don't really have necks as such, only a vertebrae, but a pendant resting right below the head made it seem as if this particular salmon had a neck, but a short one. The top of its head was covered with a piece of hair neatly parted in the middle.

Jaaku held the boards firmly and stared mesmerised at the salmon. As the boat spun, Viljo fell on his back and dropped the spear gun on the floor next to Jaaku. The salmon opened the book, raised its gaze and stared back at the men eye to eye. Sven picked up the spear gun and aimed. 'How do you shoot this thing?'

'Give it to me!' Viljo yanked the spear gun off Sven's hands.

Once Viljo had the gun under control again, he aimed randomly. He pulled the trigger, but the arrow didn't even leave the shaft. He pulled again, but nothing happened. He looked at Sven, accusingly. 'What did you do to my gun? It's jammed!'

The shining light dimmed so now they could all see the salmon making a cross sign with its pectoral fin.

The rotation of the boat stopped. Heads spinning, the men stared at the salmon.

The salmon looked down and examined the open spread of its book. 'The Lord is my shepherd...' the salmon read.

All three men's jaws dropped and their eyes widened. They turned to look at each other and back to salmon. Viljo lowered his spear gun, Jaaku took out his sunglasses and Sven sat down.

'Did you hear what I just heard?' Sven asked.

'I'm never gonna drink again,' Viljo looked down.

'What are we waiting for? Let's kill the monster!' Jaaku screamed panting, breaking under pressure. He tried to take the spear gun off Viljo, but Viljo pulled it away from his reach.

'Wait,' Viljo said calmly.

'For what?' Jaaku asked.

'The salmon is reading... the Bible,' Viljo said.

'Is that a good thing?' Sven asked.

'It's supposed to be,' Viljo replied.

'But it's still a fish, a bloody talking giant fish! And we're fishermen,' Jaaku said. 'We know what to do. There's only one thing...' He stood up, pushed Viljo down and yanked the spear gun off his hands.

'No!' Sven shouted, but too late.

As Jaaku got a hold of the weapon and forcefully pulled the trigger multiple times, eventually, the arrow did come out of the shaft shooting towards the salmon, but miraculously stopped right in front of its nose and floated there for a couple of seconds before falling in the water. 'Blimey!' Jaaku said in amaze and lowered the weapon. He dropped it on the floor next to the Wodka bottle. *What do they put in those drinks?*

For the first time, the salmon really acknowledged the men. The salmon opened its mouth again and pronounced more understandable words to a man. 'I walk through the valley of the shadow of death...'

'I think you pissed the salmon off,' Sven said.

'What are you!?' Viljo yelled and stood up.

The salmon slammed the Bible shut and carefully, observed them all one by one settling to Viljo, who asked the question. The lake below calmed and the waterspouts stood still. 'You may call me Psalmon,' the salmon said.

All men looked at each other.

'Psalm...on?' Jaaku pondered.

'Did my old ears hear P. Salmon?' Viljo asked.

'Psalmon,' the salmon repeated and spread its fins wide open. 'Also known as the Priest of Salmons or the Psalm Reading Salmon.'

'What on earth...' Sven breathed heavily.

'Erm... Are you... eating Lake Pihtamo empty?' Viljo asked hesitantly.

Psalmon placed its pectoral fin on the Bible. 'I swear that my deeds are noble and good. You must be referring to the other, evil fish?'

A lightning struck somewhere on the mainland.

'Evil fish?' the men asked.

'I have come to deliver thee a message. I have been send here to warn the brave fishermen of Lake Pihtamo about the danger lying underneath the surface of these once so bountiful waters.'

'You must mean, the danger on the surface?' Viljo corrected.

'Underneath. I am referring to...' another lightning struck right above Psalmon, '...Wolferring.'

'Wolf... herring?' Sven repeated.

'The Evil of the Pisces. The Underwater Nightmare. The Diving Destroyer. A half wolf and a half fish that fears no fisherman. Wolferring.'

'A half wolf?' Viljo said, looking suspiciously at Psalmon. 'We would find that easier to believe if it didn't come from a mouth of a large talking fish.'

Sven leaned over Jaaku and whispered to Viljo. 'Are you sure it was not just a big scary fish that stole your little herrings?'

'I think I can recognise the difference between a bipedal and a fish. It was definitely a man of some sort I saw.'

'I have no good feeling about this,' Jaaku lowered his voice too and raised an eyebrow. 'No matter how many drinks we've all had today or this week, but we shouldn't be having this conversation with... a big salmon. If it's real... I mean... if this is really happening, we should just fish and fry it. That's why we came here and that's what we do best.'

'But... how many times we get to speak to a fish?' Sven asked.

'Or we chat a little while and then kill it,' Jaaku whispered.

'I have to admit sometimes I speak to fish I catch, but they never respond. Until now,' Viljo said. 'This is quite remarkable.'

'I would use this opportunity to interview this salmon as much as we can,' Sven said quietly. 'Jaaku, if you know how to fish it afterwards, feel free. But I assume we had tried that option already and failed.'

Jaaku shrugged his shoulders and shook his head.

'I thought I'd never say this, but... I agree with Sven,' Viljo nodded. 'And I thought I'd never say this either, but let's see what this fish knows.'

Sven nodded and turned to face the salmon again.'Dear Mr. Psalmon...'

'Please, call me Psalmon.'

'Okay. How many of you are there?'

'There is one fish per each psalm.'

'Quite a few then. Which Psalmon are you then?'

'I represent the psalm 6:30-44 Mark.'

'Would it be easier then, if we just call you Mark?' Sven suggested.

'My name is Psalmon.'

'Just thought... we might mix you up with other Psalmons.'

'As we have within all these years mixed up Psalmons,' Viljo said sarcastically. He still couldn't believe his eyes and ears. 'In seventy years of fishing these waters, I have never heard of a preaching fish.'

'The elderly is absolutely right,' Psalmon said. 'It's rare to cross paths with us. We only appear in times of trouble.'

'Why you then of all the fish? Why not some other religious... cod, for instance?' Sven asked.

'Glad you asked, young man. Your curiosity has been duly noted,' Psalmon said. 'Please note there are no other Psalmons. The other preaching fishes have different names and locations. Cod of Thunder is looking after Lake Kihlava. Troutful Christian has just moved to Suolankala. Preaching Pike-y-Perch travels a lot from one lake to another.'

'Okay, okay,' Sven said and raised his palms.

'Since you seem to know your psalms, Psalmon, can you tell us one thing?' Viljo asked.

'Please, share thy worries, grey-haired man,' Psalmon said spreading its fins again.

'What type of fish Jesus gave with bread to five thousand men and their families?'

'Are you Christian?' Psalmon asked.

'Not sure anymore. Used to be more,' Viljo replied, feeling a tad shameful to admit in front of a priest, even though just a fish one.

'One cannot just stop. One either believes or not.'

'But... minds and opinions change once we grow old.'

'What made you stop believing, if I may present you this personal question?'

'I guess...' Viljo paused to think for a few seconds, '...the lack of evidence that God really exists.'

'Until it's proven that God doesn't exist, God can exist.'

'I think the fish is trying to manipulate you,' Jaaku said to Viljo. 'That's what religious always do. Try to convert us.'

'I know what I'm dealing with here,' Viljo said confidently. 'I have had my fair share of Jehovah's Witnesses knocking on my door.'

'My intention is not to manipulate anybody,' Psalmon said. 'My words come genuinely from what I feel inside and what myself and millions of others have discovered through faith. It's something we can only experience ourselves as long as our soul is open and pure. Many who claim themselves as atheists for example express negativity towards religious institutions without themselves really offering any alternatives for giving and educating our future generations good, unified and harmonised values of life. The world don't necessarily have to bury or reinvent religions but only to refresh and update the already existing ones. Many decent values and unwritten rules of life that many atheists try to follow have already been laid out in ten commandments and other religious literature.'

'See! Psalmon's doing it again,' Jaaku grunted.

'I don't know anymore,' Sven said, exhausted. He spread his arms. 'God may or may not exist. But the fact is that we're talking to a salmon vicar here. Who knows what else is waiting for us? Satan in person fishing our lake empty?'

'This is really not the best time or place to debate whether God exists or not,' Viljo said. 'We have a more important mission to complete.'

'God may well exist in all of you,' Psalmon interrupted the men peacefully. 'But answer to your earlier question, what Jesus gave to five thousand men and their families is... herring.'

'What?' Sven's jaw dropped in awe.

'Now you're pulling our... fishing rods,' Jaaku laughed.

'That's not in the Bible, isn't it?' Viljo asked.

'That is the simple truth,' Psalmon said convincingly and pressed its fin on one of the pages. 'It's written here.'

Sven gave Psalmon a suspicious look. 'Are you trying to say that the cloaked man Viljo ran into a few weeks ago was... the Messiah... and he had come to claim all his herring back?'

'To give it to poor?' Jaaku smirked.

'Like Robin the Hood?' Sven smiled, his eyes widening.

'Blasphemy!' yelled Psalmon, furrowing its brows and raising its fins. A large wave developed out of nowhere wiping over the men's boat that soaked them all even more wet. 'Thou shall not mention the name of the son of God in vain.'

All three men shivered in coldness and exhaustion. 'What do you want from us!?' Viljo screamed in agony.

Psalmon calmed down and looked at the men. 'You are the chosen ones. The three wise fishermen.'

'Chosen? For what?' Sven asked.

'Questions, questions... The real question is, what thee want?' Psalmon replied.

'We want all this craziness to come to an end,' Sven said desperately. 'Something is causing havoc on our lake, the ghost, the wizard, Wolferring, you name it. We need help. Guidance.'

'I understand. But, first for you to be able to open up, and accept God's helping hand that will show the direction, and lead the way to salvation, you must have faith.'

'Faith? In what sense?' Viljo asked.

'Take this book and read it,' Psalmon closed the Bible and chucked it across. The book smacked onto the wet floor of Viljo's dinghy right next to Sven's feet. 'The answers you seek are at the end of that book.'

Sven quickly picked up the book from the puddle and felt its weight. *At the end of the book? That's a one big book to finish.* He tried to shake the book dry of water, and looked at Psalmon. 'Is there anything you can tell us? A little spoiler to get started with?'

'In the beginning God created the heavens and the earth...'

'I think we all know that,' Viljo interrupted.

'Good. Then we're making progress.'

'Anything else?' Sven asked.

'Go to the Herring Bay near the six big rocks right at midnight during the full moon and your chances are better.'

'Will you be there?' Sven asked.

'I cannot. I have duties. I need to be at Perkana Lake running a mess for a school of herring.'

'A mess? At midnight?'

'Night mess.'

169

'I understand. Many little ones joining?'

'About twenty tiddlers,' Psalmon replied.

'You must mean, toddlers?'

'Not kids. Fish.'

Sven gave Jaaku and Viljo a confused look. They all shrugged their shoulders and rolled their eyes while the waterspiral underneath Psalmon began its descent.

'But... it's already way past midnight?'

'Read the Bible first,' Psalmon said as the down spiral swirl kept pulling it back down to the surface.

Viljo cleared his throat and thought there was still time for one more question before Psalmon disappeared underwater. 'In the beginning, when we met, you read, the Lord is My Shepherd...'

'Possibly. I cannot remember.'

'I do remember. That's not Mark 6:30-44, isn't it not?'

'You're absolutely right. I might have been reading the wrong page.'

'I think you did.'

'But... a psalm is always a good psalm and that is what the mighty Psalmon does, read psalms. God bless you all,' Psalmon gargled its last words as the ruins of the columnar vortex swallowed its holy pinkness under the surface and back into the mysterious underwater world.

'Wait! Psalmon! Who send you?' Sven yelled, but too late. Psalmon was gone leaving only a foamy spiral on the surface of the lake.

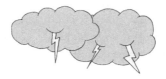

Chapter 21

# SEPARATION

The men's boat also dropped on the lake surface as the waterspout underneath them rapidly retrieved. As they hit the water, the boat bounced up and down on the splashing waves. The men held onto the seats and sides while banging heads to one another. Soon, the lake calmed and the situation returned back to normal. The lake was again like when they had left the shore, as if the biblical sight never happened.

The men returned to their original seats. The confusion was palpable. Viljo panted heavily.

'Are you alright, old man?' Jaaku asked, wiping his wet face.

'Give a me second,' Viljo took deep breaths and held his chest. The intense experience had exhausted him.

Sven instead had his eye on the Bible. The book was drenched. He lay it on the seat to dry.

Without saying a word, Jaaku in the middle grabbed the oars and began rowing back to the shore. No one dared to fish or interact with each other. Everyone sunk into their own thoughts. Incomprehensibility of what they had just witnessed, the fear of the present and what the future may bring, flattened the atmosphere. All their equipment, fishing gear and a spear gun laid useless on the bottom as the men glared in the distance, all in different directions.

As they travelled back down south, the shining stars had faded away, giving space to the rising early morning sun on the east side turning the sky in the horizon a light grey. The moon stayed visible, but lower and not as bright anymore. The best fishing hours had begun, yet all the other boats remained on the shore. The fishermen of the region seemed to have given up hope. Some of them had moved to the other lakes after better fishing grounds, some had completely changed their careers, the others only waited or prayed at home for better times to come.

Sven picked up the Bible and opened it on his lap. 'So... I guess we've got some homework to do?' he said, breaking the silence.

Jaaku looked at Sven. 'Whatever just happened there, I don't wanna talk about it.'

'Viljo?' Sven said, over Jaaku's shoulder.

Viljo took a deep breath. He kept looking away. 'I can tell you, son, that book has no answers, if that's what you're suggesting.'

'But I somehow thought you were more pro religion?' Sven asked.

Still panting from exhaustion and trauma, Sven's question further tired Viljo. Slowly, he turned his grave face to Sven. 'I used to believe more. But unfortunately, God or the strong faith I thought I had didn't save the people I loved.'

'Well, God didn't save my father either, but it's not like I hate or blame religion for that.'

'You sound like a preacher yourself,' Jaaku said in the middle. 'Are you trying to convert us?'

'Or sound like those Jehovah's Witnesses,' Viljo said and looked at both youngsters. 'What do you kids know about religion anyway?'

Sven paused to think, but soon realised his answer would be short. 'Not as much as you do... but I'm curious. I know it has helped me, too.'

'Never heard that before,' Jaaku smirked.

'I look after myself more,' Sven said, deadpan.

Jaaku sneered. 'You go to the gym? Where? In the church?'

'No. But when I was fifteen, during my communion I saw this inspiring image of Jesus Christ on a cross. He had a six pack. I wanted to look like him.'

'That is the silliest story I have ever heard!' Jaaku groaned and pointed at Sven's hanging gut hidden under thick layers of clothing. 'And where's that six-pack of yours now if I may ask?'

'I will get there... next summer.'

'That is ridiculous!' Viljo grunted. 'Would be the easiest then if someone just nailed you on a cross and left you there to rot, until you'd end up with a six-pack.'

Sven snorted, but didn't reply. He fell back into his thoughts as did the others, too. Impatiently, they all stared at the shoreline that grew in their eyes by every aggressive stroke Jaaku took. They all wanted to get out of the boat and go home as soon as possible. There had been enough of excitement and mystery for one night. The Bible, the only physical proof at Sven's hands indicated they had actually met someone or something. Apart from that, they questioned their own sanity or whether they had hallucinated everything or crossed the boundaries of sensible drinking of Arctic Wodka.

A few more strokes and the boat hit the land where they had started from. Viljo sitting at the front was the first one to scramble on the grass. Once Jaaku and Sven climbed up, Viljo took the rope and secured the boat with a knot on a spruce tree. They all picked up their gear, and without summarising the trip in any way or saying goodbyes, Viljo and Jaaku only dispersed to different directions.

'I guess we are done for tonight?' Sven asked, but the two others ignored and kept walking away. Sven followed them. 'But what should we do with this... vampire fish?'

'Vampires, ey?' Jaaku stopped.

'Yeah. Your garlic could work better on this... Wolferring,' Sven smirked encouragingly.

'Very trendy. Girls in town will love to hear more about that,' Jaaku said sarcastically.

'Although now it's all about superheroes, not so much vampires. That was ten years ago.'

'The name Wolferring does sound like a half superhero, a half vampire,' Jaaku suggested.

'And half a fish,' Sven said and raised his voice so that Viljo walking away further in the distance could hear him. 'What do you think, Viljo? What if it was this Wolferring that nicked your herrings?'

Viljo stopped, too. He turned around and gestured dismissively. 'I wish you two all the best. I don't want to be involved in any of this anymore. You can count me out.'

'What do you mean "no more?"' Sven asked.

'All fish has disappeared. What we just witnessed last night should have never happened. And it never did. I am too old and tired of all this madness. I retire. I go home.'

'What about this book?' Sven waved at the Bible in his hand. He did his utmost to keep Viljo on their side despite all the quarrel between them two. 'We must stick together. We can prepare ourselves better. We know so much more. The Herring Bay at midnight. Full moon. Maybe the book has some clues none of us has noticed before.'

'You really trust what you saw and heard last night?' Viljo asked.

'I don't know anymore. But it's all we've got. It's better than nothing.'

'I only heard a pink salmon reading a wrong psalm.'

'We all make mistakes.'

'You know, Sven. I was like you once long time ago, such a long time that I cannot quite remember anymore. I trusted the word of the others, strangers, or I forgave many little mistakes others did or said in vain, and I was always the one who ended up paying the highest price. I should have only listened to myself, but I didn't. Now I do. It has taken a lifetime for me to learn my lesson and it would be too painful for me to stay beside you and watch you doing all those same mistakes. You're stubborn like your father was and I cannot help you or anybody. It seems like you will take the long route and learn the hard way. Feel free to go and learn from your own mistakes, but please don't drag me with you. I am asking you to leave me alone. Please. Leave me alone,' Viljo turned around and walked away to the forest.

'Viljo!'

'Good bye!' Viljo shouted, not stopping anymore. He disappeared into the woods.

'Let him be,' Jaaku said. 'You were right. He's an old fool.'

'I guess it's just you and me then,' Sven said and spread his arms.

'What do you mean?'

'To solve this case.'

'Well, actually, I have some... business I have to take care of,' Jaaku stuttered and took an awkward step back.

'Business?'

'Yes... It's kind of busy times. Work on the igloo... and I have to fix my kicksled and...' Jaaku mumbled.

Sven gave Jaaku a suspicious look. 'If you need time, we can go later in a few days.'

'Go where?'

'Is everything alright?'

'The thing is that... I kinda agree with Viljo,' Jaaku said and looked to the direction Viljo had disappeared. 'Maybe it's time for all of us to think about something else, something new. Explore other avenues. Perhaps, try and really find ourselves.'

'You're confusing me. You sound like a motivational speaker.'

'But it's true. The times are changing.'

'Times may be changing, but we are fishermen. You cannot change that.'

'Change is not so bad,' Jaaku said and turned to Sven.

'Is it not?'

'There must be something else you have always wanted to do in life. Something you never had the courage or chance to try. Viljo is old and I understand he wants to retire, but us two, we are still young, the whole life ahead of us. There are so many other things we could do. Now would be a great opportunity and timing to reinvent yourself.'

'No. I don't understand what you are talking about.'

'Forget about it then.'

'You can tell me.'

'You wouldn't understand. You would never understand,' Jaaku sighed. 'I genuinely hope you find some answers. Take care, Sven.' He tapped Sven's shoulder, turned towards the forest and walked away.

'But... we are the chosen ones, the three wise fishermen...'

Sven pleaded, but Jaaku didn't stop either. He kept walking and disappeared into the forest. 'Jaaku! Come back!' Sven yelled while feeling the pointlessness of it all. But he let him go and turned his back to the forest. He faced the lake. He couldn't hide his disappointment. He didn't know Viljo personally and what to expect of him, but he thought he knew Jaaku better than anyone, who suddenly though, had become unrecognisable to him. Jaaku's aggression and short temper were new characteristics he hadn't come across before. His lecture about change was previously unheard-of. He always thought Jaaku was the man of safety and security. But obviously not.

The night had been long, tiring and full of unexpected surprises. Lake Pihtamo had become an unknown place to him. He felt like a stranger on the waters. Now, he only wanted to go home to Ida, where for the time being, he felt the safest and the most understood.

Chapter 22

# IDA'S SURPRISE

Normally, Sven left fishing not until the early morning hours giving him and Ida the chance to go to bed together the night before. This one particular night, though, Ida had to go to bed worrying and trying to sleep alone. Eventually, she had fallen in a light sleep, until a loud bang on the front door alarmed her awake. Eyes still closed she stretched her arm to the side only to discover an empty place on the bed beside her. The door was being knocked again. A light rainfall caressed the roof. She got up in a fear something had happened to Sven and a messenger or a close friend involved was sent to deliver the bad news. She had those thoughts often, knowing Roar's unfortunate destiny.

She picked up her bath robe from the chair beside the desk, put it over her pyjamas and extracted the furry sheepskin slippers from underneath the bed. She pulled the slippers on, stood up and staggered onto the hallway. Another pounding on the door made her gasp. She slowed her approach. She tiptoed via the living room where she grabbed a steel poker from near the fireplace. She raised the poker up and got back to the hallway and towards the door.

'It's me. Open up,' Sven's weak voice carried through the door.

Ida sighed in relief. She lowered the poker and opened the door to discover wet and shivering Sven standing in the rain.

'What happened? You look like you've been in the war?'

Sven responded with a tired nod. He dragged his sluggish body inside. 'I lost the key,' he said and walked past her.

'Nice to see you, too,' Ida said sarcastically and slammed the door shut behind him. She turned to him as he kept walking away along the corridor. 'I was worried about you. Where have you been all yesterday and last night?'

Sven's wet fishing gear fell off his powerless grip on the hallway floor. He continued into the bedroom without saying a word.

'You could have at least text me. Your phone was switched off,' Ida said and followed him.

Sven crashed on the bed fully clothed.

'Be careful! You wet the bed,' Ida said from the doorway.

'Wouldn't be the first time.'

'Don't be too hard on yourself. You were very ill those couple of days. You are not doing it anymore.'

'I hope not.'

'But you are doing it now with your wet clothes!' Ida jumped on the bed on a sitting position on top of Sven. She took off his wet hat, gloves, and undid his coat. 'Where were you last night?'

'You wouldn't believe me if I tell you.'

'Try me. Is there something I should know?'

'Well, first, my phone battery died when I was in the bar with Jaaku yesterday...'

'Typical!' Ida snorted and stopped undressing Sven.

'It really did happen. These new Mokia mobile phones have the worst battery life,' Sven pulled his drenched phone out of his breast pocket.

'Somehow your phone always dies when you're in the bar,' Ida crossed her arms.

'I think my phone battery is not the main concern here,' Sven said and took off his jacket.

'What is it then?'

'I really don't know where to start. None of this makes any sense. You probably wouldn't believe me anyway.'

'Is it that bad?'

'Not sure if it's bad, but...'

'Why don't you start by telling how much you missed me?'

Ida smiled, releasing the tension.

'Of course I did,' Sven said in relief.

'Well, I have some good news for you to cheer you up, if you're interested?' Ida said eagerly.

'Don't you wanna hear first about my night? Why I was away for this long?'

'Sure I do. And you will tell me. But it's just one little thing I can't wait to share with you.'

'Okay,' Sven nodded doubtfully. He felt as if he was getting away too easy considering he had been gone since yesterday afternoon without telling her anything. After leaving the bar and before going to Viljo's house and later on before meeting the men at Viljo's boat, Sven never went home. Intentionally, he had slowed down and taken his time to travel from one place to another. He felt he needed *me time*. He stayed on his own by the lakeside, reminiscing about the prosperous, bountiful times. He thought about his father. And he wondered what the future may bring, while momentarily forgetting that his future largely will be with Ida, and that's where his focus should be.

'I'm sure this puts you in a good mood,' Ida smiled nervously. She took a deep breath and said, 'I am pregnant.'

Sven's eyes widened, his breathing stopped, nearly his heart, too, yet his face remained serious. 'Really?' he replied blandly.

'Yes. The test shows it.' She leaned over and reached out for the top drawer of the night table. She pulled out a pregnancy test stick and waved a positive result in front of Sven's glooming eyes. 'Are you... not happy?'

'Erm. Of course I am,' Sven's answer fell flat.

'You don't want to have a baby with me?' she crashed landed flat on the mattress next to Sven. 'Why not? We just got married.'

'I do want... but...'

'But what?'

'It's... difficult times.'

'Difficult times? It's always a difficult time for you. When is the right time then? Is it about money? You want to travel more? Experience life more? Meet other women? Go then, but not with me.'

'Please. It's not what I meant. All I'm saying is that we're living a very difficult times in Pihtamo right now. There's no fish in the lake and fishing is what I do. It's my livelihood. How are we supposed to support a family without any income?'

'I can go to work.'

'But even that's not enough. Life here is expensive. The taxes are high, the house prices are rising, the heating and travel costs lot of money. We have to buy a new, bigger kicksled and all sorts.'

'Can't you do something else? There must be some other work you could do.'

'Why does everyone keep saying that to me? I don't want things to change. I don't wanna change!'

'What's the matter with you? I didn't ask you to change.'

'You did! But I am a fisherman and I always will be. It's in my blood.'

'I never said that you couldn't be a fisherman. We get by.'

'I don't want just to get by. I don't want us to be one of those couples that struggle their life through. I want my child and family to have a good life.'

'Me too.'

'But there's no fish! There's no fish anywhere. The lake is empty.'

'If there's no fish, we can go somewhere else to find it. We always have our love to give to the child. That's all the child needs.'

'The child cannot eat love if he or she gets hungry. The child needs food and that costs money. And besides, I don't want to leave Pihtamo. This is my home and has always been.'

'I want to keep this child. I want to have a child with you.'

'Of course we will have the child,' Sven said and forced a smile.

They lay side by side on the bed staring at the ceiling. Even though their shoulders physically touched, emotionally the distance between them two was equal to the distance between two planets.

'Somehow I am not too convinced,' Ida said, disappointment growing in her voice. She turned her back to Sven.

He didn't follow nor touch her, but kept his eyes glued to the ceiling. 'There's only one fish, a talking fish,' he started hesitantly.

'Now you don't make any sense. Are we still talking about the pregnancy?'

'This big fish emerged out of the lake reading this Bible and...' Sven pulled out the damp book off his coat inside pocket and offered it to Ida.

'I don't think I can listen to this nonsense now!' Ida pushed the Bible away and stood up. She left the room slamming the door shut.

'Ida...' Sven sat up on the bed, but didn't go after her. He sighed and let her go. He was too exhausted to make any effort. He collapsed back on the mattress. He looked at the Bible next to him, the famous book, that even out of curiosity, apart from a few forced sentences during the communion at his teens, he never dared to sink into. Whether it was ignorance, laziness, righteousness or the fear of God that had prevented him from reading one of the most well-known publications in the history of the humankind.

Some of the most uncomfortable pitches are done by self-published authors trying to make their friends and family read their masterpiece, or what Christians did in the past while forcing with violence people to believe and read the Bible. But now at least Sven had control. He could choose and form his own opinion. And his best friend didn't write this book. He looked at the Bible and picked it up. He felt the time had come now to open his heart and mind. He had nothing to lose. He was ready. He wasn't afraid anymore to take the step. Leap of faith. He could read the Bible without any fear of being brainwashed or converted. *Only out of curiosity*, he thought.

Thus, he opened the first spread and read the first paragraph which began exactly as the talking salmon had quoted it. Shortly, though, after the first two pages his tired eyes got heavier. The book fell open on his chest, he closed his eyes and drifted to another place - his dreamworld.

Chapter 23

# SUSHI TRAIN

In his dream, Sven found himself in the middle of a dark pine forest. He felt the pressure as if he was being chased by someone or something. He was short of breath and not being able to move properly. As if only he was being slow motioned, whereas everything around him: the tree branches, the birds, the snowflakes, moved at a normal pace. Almost like he was drowning in the air. He came across large foot prints on the snow together with an abandoned luggage.

'Yaaaawnnn!' a loud roar echoed in the forest.

He tried to run away from the voice, but didn't know which direction since the roaring rumbled all around him. He staggered slowly to a direction towards a shimmering light ahead in the distance. His body felt like being partly paralysed as he laboriously threw his one leg in front of another. He heard a loud whistle from where the light shone. He didn't know he was in a dream.

'Yaaaawnnn!' the roaring repeated behind him.

Sven looked over his shoulder, not seeing anything but a dark forest. He continued towards the light which grew larger and larger. Sven could recognise the light came from a steam engine racing on the snow without any visible tracks. The train came straight at him. He got ready to jump aside, but a last second manoeuvre by the engine driver saved him from being run over.

Once the train and its six carriages swung past him, to his

own surprise, he was able to take a giant leap off the ground straight onto the doorway of the third carriage. He didn't know how he did it, but in dreams everything is possible. Yet, he wasn't quite sure at this point whether he was in a dream or not. He started to have his doubts, though.

He landed on a small step outside the sliding door. He pulled a handle and the door opened. He stepped inside the carriage. *A rush hour train*, he thought whilst looking at the commuters of all sorts, shapes and colours, and smelling that typical mixed odour of a crowded train. Once he took another glance, he realised the passengers were not just any regular commuters, but they all had taken a shape and a form of seafood of some sort. A king prawn occupied the priority seat for the elderly. Next to it sat a pink smoked salmon with a pinch of rice on its lap. Two peeled avocados sat opposite them. A group of fresh ginger stood in the middle on their way to school, he believed, looking at their little rucksacks with chopsticks poking out. A big pile of tuna sat on the floor, as if it was not feeling well.

As much as Sven loved the taste of all types of fishes, soon the smell filling his tolerant nostrils became unbearable. He moved down inside the carriage to seek hideaway in the toilet at the end of the corridor. He jumped inside and locked the door behind him. He took a deep breath. Finally alone. Once he opened the lid of the bog, someone's wasabi left unflushed down the toilet made him gack.

'Wake up, darling,' an echoing female voice called out from the carriage loudspeakers. As if the train driver wanted to tell them something. The fast moving train started shaking vigorously. And then it derailed.

He sensed a rosy breath in front of his face. Someone stared at him from a very close distance. Sweat falling off the forehead and onto his eye lids further blurred his sight as he tried to open his eyes. Once he got used to the darkness in the room, he recognised Ida's facial features. 'Where am I?' he asked wiping his wet face.

'You were having a nightmare. It's me. Everything is alright.' Ida put her hand on his restlessly moving chest.

'Sushi train...' Sven said, panting.

'Were you in a restaurant?'

'I think I was... on it,' Sven sat up against the back board of the bed. 'There was a roaring monster chasing me, but I managed to escape to a speeding sushi train.'

'Interesting,' Ida said and switched on the light. She gave Sven a look of concern. 'I think we need another holiday, a proper holiday this time.'

'What was wrong with the holiday we just had? Our honeymoon.'

'I mean, somewhere not by the sea, the lakeside or the riverside, but inland as far away as possible from water and any type of fish. I think we need that. You need it.'

Sven looked drowsy. 'You mean somewhere like... South Sudan?'

Ida shook her head. She sat next to Sven, took his head and pressed it down against her stomach. 'Why don't you go back to sleep? You look so tired.'

'I am not tired,' Sven said, while letting Ida nurture him. 'I hate when people say that, when I actually feel great.'

'Don't argue. You don't feel great. You are tired. Just be quiet and go back to sleep.'

Sven resisted, but Ida forcefully kept his head down. Soon, he gave in. He became quiet and restful.

Chapter 24

# JAAKU'S DOUBTS

Jaaku lay restless on a reindeer skin in the living room of his igloo. The tumultuous past events kept him awake. Moose hunting, the empty lake, Viljo's wizard fisherman and the latest, the most puzzling episode with the talking fish. He felt Pihtamo was in the process of becoming something new and he kept changing with it. A devoted fisherman as he was and had been, didn't feel sure of himself anymore and what he wanted from life. He was losing his identity.

As much as he had been in the shadows of greater fishermen, yet he considered himself lucky. He found his calling at very early age, when many others struggle and remain undecided throughout the lifetime. Little Jaaku's passion for fishing as a child developed to become a lifestyle and later on his work providing him livelihood. From very early age Jaaku knew exactly what he wanted to do. Since his father gave him the first ice fishing rod, he never let go. For nearly twenty-two years he had maintained the same devotion, until these last intense weeks. The brief moments of excitement the moose hunting brought into his life together with a few major setbacks at the fishing front confused him. It was as if he had found a new best friend from hunting while still being connected in some level with the current best friend, fishing. Lately, he had fished only by default from the muscle memory, yet he couldn't stop thinking about the sweet tasting adrenaline rush shooting a large animal offered him. It was a sensation he had never experienced before. To being able to see the target eye to eye, chasing it down and harnessing it at gunpoint provided him the thrills fishing never did. Or perhaps it did years or decades ago which he couldn't remember anymore. He was growing up, moving on. His eyes had suddenly opened. As if he had missed out some stages of life. The idea of monotone, tranquil and repetitive fishing didn't have the same appeal anymore. He had discovered greener grass on the other side of the wilderness.

Even though, Jaaku was the main initiator encouraging Viljo, Sven and him to work together and find those answers to the problems haunting Lake Pihtamo, his motivation to go on with the mission had dropped to zero. He had lost interest in the waters. Neither he felt guilt nor remorse of his growing indifference. His focus was shifting towards something new the moose hunters revealed him. Something he never knew existed. He yearned for the excitement the change could bring him without thinking clearly ahead into the future and the possible consequences. Selfishly, he yearned to experience more of the new world that had opened up for the man known of security, safety and comfort. All of his life he had known exactly what tomorrow brings; where the sun rises and sets; when the ice starts to melt and freeze; when the one and the only Arctic Bar opens and closes. The lack of risk-taking may had been one of the qualities preventing him from ever becoming the champion. He always feared to push himself over the limits, as the other master fishermen like Viljo, Carl, Sven and Roar, had done. If the top fishermen trained for six to eight, sometimes ten to twelve hours a day, Jaaku often settled for three to four hours a day. He also took more days off per year than the others. There was an element of comfort he appreciated more than the others. The last distracting device was the cable television connection in his igloo occasionally taking his time and concentration away from what was important. The time he spent watching television instead of training was another, yet more insignificant reason that may have cost him his lack of ultimate success in the world of fishing.

While being soaked in his fears, doubts and questions,

footsteps on the snow crunching outside the igloo alarmed Jaaku back to consciousness. The times of uncertainty pushed him on the verge of paranoia. He couldn't trust anything or anyone anymore. He stood up and picked up an axe from behind the couch. He listened. The footsteps got nearer. He swung the axe on his shoulder, walked behind the entrance and got ready to greet the uninvited guests.

Chapter 25

# IN LOVING ARMS

Ida's warm embrace was like a vague distant reminder of a motherly love Sven had received as a child. Her heartbeat syncing with his made him feel like a fetus again resting inside the womb or being like a newborn baby being breastfed. However, Ida didn't need to take her breast out, but only caressing the top of his head and fine silky hair sent him back to sleep.

Sven's tired mind started drifting and ploughing through a vast selection of blurry images and randomness, until he ended up dreaming about a circus. Yet, not watching or observing from the audience, but being in the centre of all the attention. He was on stage. Something in the real world while awake he had always feared and avoided, apart from sports competitions where a couple of well-constructed and awkward sentences he occasionally had to deliver as answers to local journalists questions about the aftermath. As much as performing in front of people whilst awake was one of his worst nightmares, surprisingly though, in a dream sequence, he seemed somewhat more confident, comfortable and spontaneous. Like another person.

From as early as the school years, the things he feared the most were speaking in front of the class or acting small parts in school plays, or later on, attending a group job interviews as an adult. The anxiety and the anticipation were unbearable and the uncomfortable moments seemed to last forever. The preparation normally included hours of sitting a nervous wreck in the toilet often causing a strain to his internal organs. The childhood trauma followed to his adult life and he systematically avoided public speaking of any sort. Using spoken words economically was part of his culture and heritage anyway, and making too much noise about yourself and your personal achievements were frowned upon. Shyness was a virtue and keeping silent seen as good manners. *He who has happiness, should hide it.*

Therefore, being in the centre of the attention on stage watched by hundreds of live audience members was one of his worst nightmares about to become true. Something he was already part of. The show wasn't ticketless and free either, but the paying audience with an expectation kept flocking in. Higher the ticket price, higher the demand for quality. Luckily, it was all just a dream. But again, Sven just wasn't aware of it.

To his surprise, he felt light, easy and somewhat confident on stage. The stomach didn't hurt and there was no urge to vomit, at least, not yet.

Before anything, he touched his waist and thighs to make sure he was wearing trousers. Because, almost on a weekly basis in his dreams he found himself constantly in the most awkward public places and humiliating situations waist down naked, like sitting behind the desk in a school class; or behind an office desk; or on a date in a restaurant with a beautiful woman, most of the times the woman being Ida. It was never clear to him, though, how he ended up in these situations without trousers in the first place. He was just there, period. The real challenge was to get away from it unnoticed. Normally, he woke up when he had to make the move, hence never discovering the reactions from the public once getting caught.

The other frequently occurring challenge in his dreams was a stagnated, difficult and slow movability. As in his previous dream, until the big leap onto the sushi train.

This time, though, neither of the oddities applied. He felt fabric instead of skin. He was relieved. He wore something loose. He looked down. Light grey baggy trousers, he observed, with black boots pulled on top of the hems. He checked once more. The trousers were still there. And he was able to move his body quite normally as well. *The worst humiliation cannot happen*, he thought. *Things can only get better.*

Fully dressed in his trousers, boots, a red coat, white gloves, a black top hat and a walking stick, he stared at the cheering audience. A typical looking circus crowd, mainly children clapping hands softly out of sync and the parents beside yawning like walruses looking bored to death while worrying about some petty work issues or relationship problems. Though, a few fresh and young parents hung in there showing enthusiasm, yet unaware of what life has in store for them.

The audience members who had managed to regain their genuine childlike happiness and positivity after the complexities of midlife crisis as the years ahead were running short and teeth count shorter, were the elderly ones. Despite the lack of dentures, Sven could still recognise jolly smiles on the faces of the grandparents from the shape of their mouths, the lips, the gums, the risen cheekbones, and the shining, forever youthful eyes. Observing and engaging with the very oldest and the youngest of the crowd further boosted Sven's level of confidence and enthusiasm, as long as he avoided the eye contact and interaction with the frustrated middle aged, by all means.

Gradually, the empty stage around him began to fill up with colourful boxes of different sorts brought in by his assistants, luggage monkeys. The three monkeys carried one box each which they dropped around Sven, unopened. One by one, the monkeys high-fived him and walked away.

One hand resting on his cane and the other in his pocket, Sven looked at the audience going wild and yearning for more. *But more of what?*

Chapter 26

# VISITORS

The crunching of the footsteps stopped outside the igloo front door. Inside, Jaaku tiptoed towards the door. His heart beat so fast and loud he feared it would be heard through the walls. He squeezed the axe tighter in his palms. Someone stood outside, but no one knocked or rang the doorbell. Slowly, he reached for the lid above the spyhole and raised it. As he did, the lid made a squeaking noise. Panicky, he dropped the lid back down creating another squeak.

'We know you're in there,' a male voice called out from outside.

Jaaku stopped breathing and stood immobile.

'Jaaku. I can see you,' Börje said and knocked on the side window where the curtains were left open. He had a clear, direct vision to Jaaku standing rigid behind the door.

Jaaku sighed in embarrassment. 'The... moose hunters?'

'Yes. Open the door,' the voice came from behind the door that he recognised now was Kalle's.

Jaaku unlocked and pushed the door open. Kalle gave Jaaku a smirk. His breath stank of a rotten cabbage as he revealed his stained teeth while walking inside past Jaaku. Börje followed entering in a more civilised manner. He offered Jaaku his hand.

'How did you know where I live?' Jaaku said and responded to the handshake.

'Shall I say... we have our resources,' Börje said mysteriously.

Jaaku gave them a confused nod. 'Is there... anything I can do for you?' he asked hesitatingly, yet hiding his slight enthusiasm and appreciation of having been surprised by two men he felt were his new friends.

'As a matter of fact you can do a lot. Much more than you realise,' Börje said firmly. He gestured to Kalle. 'Show him.'

Kalle swung a longish leather bag around from his back. He unzipped it revealing two rifles. He grabbed a hold of one of them from the middle section and raised it horizontally in front of Jaaku's nose.

Jaaku gave the rifle an admiring look.

'Take it. It's yours,' Börje said.

Jaaku took a step back and raised his palms. 'I cannot accept that.'

'Trust me. You will be needing it once you hear what we have in mind for you.'

Kalle took a step closer to Jaaku and sneered. He pushed the rifle on his chest.

Reluctantly, Jaaku wrapped his arms around the cold weapon. Although he admired the polished oak stock and the shining high-strength stainless steel barrel. The magazine was on. He caressed the housing and the trigger. His eyes lightened. 'How much do I owe you?'

'Nothing. Consider it as a gift.'

Jaaku tilted his head and looked at Börje. 'Why?'

'We only need you to do us one simple favour.'

Jaaku's eyes wandered back to admire the perfection of the rifle. He stroked the barrel and touched gently on the tip of the front sight. 'I'm all ears.'

'We knew we can trust you,' Börje said. He pulled out a wooden chair covered in reindeer skin from underneath the dining set and sat on it. He took another chair and offered it to Jaaku. 'Take a seat with me and listen. Listen carefully.'

Chapter 27

# THE HERRINGMASTER

A few seconds hesitation on stage felt like hours as the audience waited impatiently for Sven to begin. Drops of sweat developed on his forehead as he tried to come up with ideas. He studied the stage and the props around him. He went to the nearest of the boxes the monkeys had dropped earlier. There was movement inside. He raised the lid slowly. He intended to take a quick glance inside the box before revealing the secret to the audience. However, once the lid was open, each side of the box collapsed in all four directions. As the sides lie flat, one herring revealed itself resting on a little trampoline. Once the herring got under the spotlight, it realised it was the time to perform. It began bouncing and somersaulting elastically in the air.

The crowd applauded faster and louder. Sven gave the audience a subtle smile and a bow.

Heartened by the positive response, Sven moved on beside the next box. He cracked it open to discover inside a beach ball together with another herring. Immediately, the herring jumped on top of the ball upside down and began balancing on its nose around the stage.

The crowd got wilder.

'*Voilà!*' Sven shouted, confidently. *The third one's better be really good*, he thought while letting the crowd's acceptance to sink in.

As expected, also the third box had a herring of a similar

kind and size inside, but with a trapeze, a swing and a safety net neatly packed next to it. And the herring wore a colourful carnival costume. It stood up and pointed at the props with its pectoral fin and simultaneously stared at Sven. Sven glanced around the tent walls and various ropes hanging off the ceiling, where he could possibly hang the trapeze and the swing. The crowd waited on the edges of their seats. He spotted a ladder leaning on one of the poles in the middle of the stage. Halfway up the pole was a little platform as if specifically built for trapeze artist's take-offs and landings. He grabbed the trapeze kit on his one hand and the herring on the other, and climbed up the ladder. Once up on the platform, he put the acrobat herring down while he attached the kit to the bars and the support structures. A few solid knots and the swing sway freely in a soft breeze blowing inside the tent. A couple of firm pushes and yanks tested the trapeze was secure. The herring waited restless as Sven rushed down the ladder to place the safety net below the platform and under the trapeze, in case the herring was to slip its fins off the bar. The deed was more a precautionary measure as he had never seen a herring trapeze artist before and he didn't know exactly how qualified in general they are.

The acrobat herring stood up on its tail fin, got a grip of the bar with her frontal fins and took the first leap. The herring swung on the bar and picked up speed. Sven held his breath, as did the entire audience. Once the speed hit optimal and the bar was in a right angle, the herring let go completing a full twisting double up in the air, landing back on the bar and getting a perfect grip.

The audience gasped followed by a raging applause as the herring returned to the platform.

Sven gave the crowd a big smile, spread his arms and took a bow. Behind him, one herring balanced on a beach ball, another one bounced backflips on a trampoline and the third one flew on the trapeze. If something went wrong, he was the one with a voice, the one to explain the audience, calm them down, take all the heckles and complaints. If things clicked, though, he was the one to take a large piece of the credit. He was the face of the performance, of this peculiar but at the same time magical herring circus. He was the composer of the show. A compere. He understood now. Everything was clear to him. He had the control and the power. He was, after all, the Herringmaster.

Chapter 28

# JAAKU'S MISSION

Hesitantly, Jaaku placed the rifle flat on the dining table and sat next to Börje. He folded his arms and listened.

'First of all, we are aware of the problems at Lake Pihtamo,' Börje started.

Jaaku puckered his eyebrows. 'Your resources again?'

'Well, it's not rocket science to figure out something is badly wrong. Everyone's talking. No one's catching fish anymore, not even the top fishermen like your friend...'

'Sven?'

'Yes, him. And the old man, the former champion.'

'Viljo?'

'He saw something strange out there. And now people have fears. There are lots of theories and gossips what is happening?'

'Like what?'

'From being the devils work to Satan's. Some elderly believe this is the end, the doom date, the end of not just Pihtamo, but the world around us.'

'That sounds a bit harsh.'

'Or a work of... a wizard?'

'Yeah, right,' Jaaku snorted. 'That's what the crazy old man says.'

'Fine. And that's where you come along?'

'How?'

'Next time, when you go fishing...'

'I don't think there will be next time,' Jaaku interrupted.

'Why not?'

'I'm done with fishing. No more. I wanna become a hunter like you, guys. Isn't that why you gave me this rifle?'

Börje turned to Kalle and smiled. Then they both turned together and smiled back at Jaaku. 'That's very sweet of you. In fact, it's excellent!' Börje exclaimed. 'We guarantee you won't be disappointed. That will be the best decision you will ever take in your life.'

'I hope so,' Jaaku said and rested his hands on the rifle.

'But for our friendship's and hunting community's sake, we would need you to make one last, final fishing trip.'

'Why?'

'You must help this mysterious fisherman or whatever to succeed,' Börje said.

'To succeed... in what?'

'Seemingly it wants to empty the lake. It obviously wants all the fish.'

'I'm not sure,' Jaaku said. He felt like an idiot to ask the following, but he did anyway. 'Have you heard of... Wolferring?'

Börje and Kalle paused to stare at Jaaku, until Börje asked, 'What is... wolf herring?'

'A some sort of monster fish that may be also emptying the lake. Or then the wizard. I don't know anymore. It's all getting very confusing. Too strange.'

'How did you hear about all this?'

'From...' Jaaku paused for a moment feeling deep anxiety and embarrassment to say the awkward name out loud, '...Psalmon.'

Börje and Kalle rolled their eyes.

'Been drinking again, ey?' Kalle smirked from behind.

But Börje raised his finger to Kalle and hushed him. He turned back to Jaaku and said more calmly, 'Fine. If you still want to catch salmon, feel free as long as one day soon Lake Pihtamo would become completely empty of fish. Whatever it takes. Go fishing with the wizard if you can or help the wolf herring to succeed. But keep your fisherman friends out of this.'

'Why would I do that?' Jaaku asked and composed himself. 'I don't understand. I know you don't like fishermen or you think fishing is not a real men's game, but by letting the lake become empty would kill the fishing industry. So many hobbies, passions and livelihoods destroyed. It's already happening.'

'It doesn't have to be that way. There are estimated over twenty thousand moose and counting in the area.'

'What are you trying to say?'

'If in the most unfortunate event of Lake Pihtamo emptying of all the fish, there is always work to be done in the vast forests in the region. The moose and the other deer animals are mostly pest and not enough men are hunting them. After the fish is gone, most naturally, people would turn into moose hunting. We can see the change happening already, a growing interest. We are being approached by hopeless fishermen on a daily basis. They want us to recruit them. Teach them about hunting.'

Jaaku's resistance shifted towards intriguing and more positive feel. 'Interesting,' he said and admired the shine of the rifle again. Thoughtfully, he glanced around the igloo walls and the ceiling. The conversation had taken a sudden, unexpected twist.

'Pihtamo is changing. If the push comes to shove, the area doesn't necessarily need fish or fishermen, but brave men who can act, react and adapt to the change,' Börje said with a hint of warmth in his voice. 'You are a moose hunter, Jaaku. Don't deny it. You are one of us. You have always been. We're talking to you, because you're the best of all the new recruits. You have the passion and a real need to change something. You're yearning for respect and recognition fishing never gave you. We can offer all that to you. The moose hunting can.'

'Do it, brother,' Kalle nodded behind Börje.

*Brother from another mother? The best?* The words Jaaku had never heard from Sven. In a moment like this, he felt an enormous distance to his family and his best friend. Having grown up in the same place with Sven, going to the same schools and just simply being the same age had made them friends by default. And the fact that both of their fathers loved fishing as did most men in Pihtamo. But was any of that friendship real and strong enough to last through the changes and the challenges of growing up? Would they have become friends in the first place in another environment where the circumstances were different? He doubted. Their characters were so different. And they had been growing apart while shifting from adolescence to adulthood. Especially, now, Jaaku was changing even more. And he accepted that change. He was nothing like the day they met in the primary school. Or perhaps, he was now what he always wanted to be or become. From the shadows of the others around him, he discovered himself as a hunter with new brothers Börje and Kalle beside him. Not brothers by blood, but by sharing a common cause, a mission and a purpose to change the world around them.

Jaaku stood up and reached out for the top shelf above the dining table. He grabbed a bottle of a special edition Arctic Wodka Sven had given him for being the best man in the failed wedding ceremony. Jaaku slammed the bottle on the table and spread a three shot glasses around. He pulled out one more chair for Kalle and asked him to sit down next to them. He twisted the cap open and filled all three glasses to the top. 'For the new beginning of Pihtamo,' Jaaku raised his glass.

'New beginning,' Börje joined by taking one of the drinks.

Kalle followed and grabbed the last, remaining shot. In a perfect harmony, the three hunters downed the shots.

Börje gave Jaaku a satisfied look. 'Once all this is over, you will discover that your actions will revolutionise the local economy. The weapons, the ammo and the hunting gear trade will start blooming. The quality of the local meat in the restaurants will improve. We also need to gain access to better four-wheel drives to reach remote areas, forests and swamps. There's so much more we can do,' Börje talked encouragingly. 'But there is one thing you oughta know...'

'You can tell me anything.' Jaaku refilled their glasses.

'There's one man that has to be taken down.'

'Don't worry. Sven is totally harmless. I can take care of him. And Viljo is an old fool. I think he retired anyway.'

'Neither of them. I am talking about a special man who plays a pivotal role within the moose hunting community. He is the great leader of all the moose hunters, a character who has become a legend of its own, a mythical, worshipped ruler, almost like a godlike figure to many. There are books about him, his words and actions. He has written rules and commandments moose hunters follow. If you break them, it is believed you will end up living a troubled life.'

'Sounds like quite a character. What should I do with him?'

'Stop him. He is a traitor. He has turned against the traditional hunters who have always thought it is better to keep hunting and fishing communities separate, whereas he wants to unite us all. He has a vision where us all could live in a perfect harmony. Obviously, that is not possible in any circumstances. There have been riots already and the situation is getting worse. He's already on a mission to chase and stop this wizard, and help the fishermen to prosper. But since you are an expert at the waters and the lake, you can help the wizard to succeed.'

'Why fishermen and hunters couldn't live or work together? Or do both at the same time?'

'Dream talk. It's not possible. No man has the time or the resources for both activities. It has been tried before. It has to be one or the other. Otherwise, the quality of the work will suffer. And, realistically, there aren't enough men in Pihtamo to hunt and fish at the same time, even separately. Most importantly, dead moose provides much more food on the table than fish. We can get up to two hundred kilograms of meat out of one bull moose. How much you have to fish to get the same amount?'

'I see. Interesting,' Jaaku said and looked outside the window. 'So... how can I help you?'

'Destroy our ruler. Eliminate Mooses. Also, to prove you're a worthy hunter.'

'Moses? Like in the Bible?' Jaaku said while an image of Psalmon came to his mind.

'Mooses as if in moose.'

Jaaku nodded, confused.

'But be aware of Mooses' powers. He is not just a normal man. In fact, no one really knows who he is or where he comes from. Most of the stories of him are based on mythologies and random, unconfirmed sightings.'

'Have you ever met this Mooses?'

'Once, long time ago, when we became moose hunters. He

gave us our hunting permits.'

'I assume you would join me on this mission?'

'To be able to chase Mooses as well as to protect the wizard, you need to be on the waters. It's rumoured that Mooses is keeping base on Moose Island.'

'Moose Island? In the middle of the lake?'

'Yes. And we won't step on any boat, never. We cannot stand water and we have no clue how to swim. That's why we need you, someone who knows the lake. If you need help from someone, lure your friends along, but make sure the right target gets eliminated, and that is Mooses. Keep the wizard safe and let it finish its duties. Or wolf herring. But the bottom line is: get rid of Mooses and make sure the lake becomes empty. Once those goals are reached, only the sky is the limit for you and us, for the hunters.'

While listening to Börje, Jaaku sank in a deeper confusion. *First, Psalmon and now Mooses. As if a doom day was set to arrive with all the biblical figures popping up. Or maybe the salvation date?* Nevertheless, his gut feeling told to trust the moose hunters. He thought their story made more sense than any other alternative he had heard before either from Sven, Viljo or the talking salmon.

He felt the temptation. Despite the long lasting friendship with Sven, converting into moose hunting could offer him the new beginning he had longed for as well as the exit from the shadow of the top fishermen. If he was to choose the side of the hunters, he hoped him and Sven could somehow maintain their friendship. Whether Jaaku would be viewed as a traitor on one side or a hero on the other side, didn't play a big importance to him anymore. Selfishly, he needed that change for himself, and simultaneously, he convinced himself that the community has to change and evolve anyway into a new and a better direction. He trusted the ones who really knew him, would understand him and accept the change. Gradually, everyone involved would follow him to become hunters themselves. Once the mission to exterminate Mooses was completed, the lake mysteriously emptied and most of the godless fishermen had been turned into hunting, he would be remembered as the one who changed the history of Pihtamo. He would be hailed as a hero with a statue erected in the middle of the town centre square. *The man who saved Pihtamo*, the plague would say. The generations to come would read about Jaaku the Great Hunter who revitalised the area and brought new winds as did his likes of Gorbachev and Hasselhoff while breaking the iron curtain. Wind of change started to blow in Pihtamo and Jaaku was in the frontline of the revolution.

Chapter 29

# SEEKING ANSWERS

The turmoil had settled between Ida and Sven as the weeks passed. He gave her the promise to apply for real jobs, which he hadn't done since finishing secondary school. After twelve years of being a fisherman and nothing else, updating the old, dusty curriculum vitae turned out to be an easy, yet slightly depressing task. He was nearly thirty years old without any notable work experience.

Once he finished typing his resume in the late evening, he joined Ida in the bedroom. She rested in her pyjamas back against the backboard of the bed. She read her favourite paper, Hejpodej, a monthly glossy gossip magazine of the latest celebrity news from Pihtamo - which was also one of the thinnest publications in the world. Sven lay beside her and picked up a Ice Fishing Monthly magazine from the top of the night table. He randomly opened a spread with an article stating that Lake Pihtamo was now officially empty of fish according to the marine biologists, scientists and researchers. The reasons were unexplainable though. No pollution or erosion were discovered and the high quality of the waters seemed unchanged in comparison to the measurements taken within the last decades. The possibility of still using the lake for recreational purposes existed and it was believed the lake could have a future of some sort as a platform for businesses offering water sports, water skiing, wind surfing and so on. None of which Sven was merely interested.

The article came as an unnecessary reminder of the lake he had not thought about for weeks. Ida's early pregnancy as well as the idea and the process of applying for jobs had taken his time and thoughts away from fishing.

He turned another page with adverts about rowing boats, boat engines and augers while Ida's snuffling beside him indicated she had drifted to her dreamworld. Frustrated of reading the news, he stuffed the magazine inside the drawer of his night table, when under the unopened junk mail and a few bills gloomed a corner of the Bible. He moved the magazine onto the side and stared at the book. He looked over his shoulder and checked if Ida was really asleep. She tucked herself deeper under the duvet. Her eyes were shut tight. Sven turned his back to Ida and pulled the Bible out for the first time since his first failed attempt to read it, when he fell asleep in a matter of seconds. The answers the book may contain started to puzzle him again as much as he wanted to forget and leave it all behind him for Ida's and their future's sake. He placed the book in front of him on the mattress. As he opened the first chapter, the hardened, dried out pages let out a mouldy smell in the air. He took a deep breath and prepared himself mentally for a long, complex and enduring reading process.

He opened the first spread. The famous opening sentences and a couple of first paragraphs seemed to be in the scope of his understanding. He nodded and moved on, delicately turning the scruffy pages that had suffered in the midst of the dramatic trip on the lake with Viljo and Jaaku. The ink had spread at places, but the text hadn't lost its readability. As he reached the page four, Ida turned her side and threw her arm over him. Her hand slammed on the book.

'What are you reading?' she mumbled with a sleepy voice, yet keeping her eyes closed.

'Erm...nothing,' Sven said and moved her arm away. Slowly, he closed the Bible and began to move it towards the drawer.

Ida raised her head up and opened her eyes a little. She saw Sven sliding the Bible back into the drawer. 'You were reading that book again?'

'I wasn't,' Sven denied defensively.

'It's absolutely fine. I just didn't know that you're into that sort of stuff,' Ida said and dropped her back onto the pillow.

Sven put the book back into the drawer and drew it shut. He slid himself under the duvet keeping his back to Ida. He switched off the light. He lay sideways wide awake. He wiggled his legs back and forth.

'You can read if you want,' Ida said, sensing Sven's restlessness.

'That's fine. I can read later. Good night,' Sven said briefly, trying to avoid further investigation.

'Is there something you want to tell me?'

Sven's breathing got heavier. *Why cannot she just let me be?*

'I remember, you brought that book with you the night you came back from your last fishing trip. Where did you get it from again?' Ida said, and switched on her night light. She sat up on the bed and poked Sven at the back. 'Who gave the Bible to you?'

Sven peered over his shoulder, but turned away from her again. He took a deep breath. 'This preacher called... Psalmon.'

'I cannot recall Pihtamo has any priests called Psalmon?'

'That's the name of the priest.... that is also... a fish. A salmon. A religious salmon,' he said quietly.

'Look at me,' Ida's voice grew serious. 'Can you tell me one thing?'

Sven turned around to face Ida, yet avoiding eye contact.

'How much did you drink that night? Please, be honest.'

'I didn't!' Sven cried. 'Or, I don't know about the others. Viljo might have had a few too many, but he's always like that. Me and Jaaku had a couple of shots earlier that day in the bar, but that's all.'

'A couple? How much?'

'A bottle.'

'Each?'

'Yes.'

'So, you were all quite drunk when you saw this fish?'

'I wasn't drunk! We all three saw and heard this thing rising from the water with our bare eyes!' Sven screamed spreading his arms to demonstrate the length of the salmon.

'Okay. Calm down,' Ida said, looking suspicious.

'This towering tornado lifted our boat ten metres up in the

air and there it was, Psalmon, right in front of us like sitting on top of a water fountain, preaching on us and telling about a monster fish that is emptying our lake,' Sven's heart pumped faster as he explained about the nightly events.

'And this Psalmon told you to read the Bible?' Ida smirked.

'Psalmon said that "the answers to our questions are in the back of that book." The Bible. Yes.'

'What are your questions then?'

'About the lake. The problems. The lack of fish. The mysterious fisherman. Everything, I guess.'

'In the back, ey? Why don't you read the back first then?'

'Very funny,' Sven said sarcastically. 'That's not the way to read a book. I don't think I would understand the end if I didn't read the beginning first.'

'Shoot yourself. That's a long and tiring book. I tried to read it once and I only made it to the Epistle to the Romans.'

'Well, I should have all the time in the world to read, since the lake is officially dead now,' Sven said.

Ida sighed, inhaled heavily and rubbed her stomach. She turned her back to Sven again, switched off the light and closed her eyes. 'Good night,' she said and pretended to fall asleep.

'Good night,' Sven replied. He sat up for a while and waited and waited, until he heard Ida's nose whistling, confirming she had fallen asleep again. He pondered for a while whether to sleep or not. However, the curiosity won. He reached out for the top drawer and pulled out the book together with a small torch. He was even wider awake now, ready to sink himself into the depths of the Bible to seek those answers.

Chapter 30

# VILJO'S RETIREMENT

One of many problems aging Viljo had was lack of sleep. On an average night, he went to bed around half past ten and got up the next morning between two and three o'clock. And he wasn't able to fall asleep again, giving him three to four hours of solid sleep per night that wouldn't be sufficient for most of the growing people. But he seemed to be doing fine as long as he got his black cup of coffee and a bowl of barley porridge with some freshly picked raspberries or blueberries mixed together with crystal white sugar first thing in the morning.

After Aune's passing, though, not only his peaceful sleeping patterns suffered, but the berries were not freshly picked anymore, but bought from the local supermarket by himself or sometimes brought to his doorstep by the home delivery service. His deteriorating back prevented him from going into the forest and pick berries or mushrooms himself anymore. Therefore, he had to rely on imported groceries that he wasn't too fond of in the beginning, yet gradually, he adjusted to the process of aging and accepted some realities of life and mortality. Like the fact that he couldn't enjoy everything fresh anymore.

As a young man, Viljo used to spend effortless eight to ten hours, sometimes half a day on the boat fishing, smoking, eating packed lunches prepared by Aune, drinking a little and catching large amounts and different types of fish every single time without exceptions. The recent years, though, he was able to get up only four to five times a week to fish about three to four hours each time. There were better days sometimes when he could stay a good six to eight hours if he felt less pain at his back and knees, and his head was clear and he felt no dizziness. He never discovered, what caused those good or bad days. He had never spend a day in a hospital or needed medical attention. He didn't know if there was something more seriously wrong with him, if his body was rotten inside. Neither did he bother. He had lived a life long enough not to care. He had been very lucky.

Nevertheless, every morning, day and night used to be different for Viljo in the good old times when Aune was still alive and accepting his misbehaviour and mistakes. She loyally waited for him at home with a cooked meal ready and a clean house after long days he had been away fishing, or sometimes, hanging out with other fishermen in Pihtamo Bar, until the early hours of the morning. From his point of view, the times were very different and more glorious in the past, when Lake Pihtamo was crammed with fish and men had all the power in and outside of home.

Now, almost ten months after the loss of his championship and the last time he had caught any fish, and a couple of months after the last fishing trip with Sven and Jaaku, as well as his decisions to give up fishing, Viljo's life had become quiet and dull, and each day, similar to each other. To fill the enormous gap quitting his lifelong passion had left in his life, a retired widow without other hobbies and interests, had rummaged through the old closets, the attic and the basement, where he discovered his old, dusty sixteen hole chromatic harmonica - an instrument he hadn't played for nearly fifty years. He blew the harmonica a couple of times from the distance to clear the dust particles away. Once being cleared, he sealed his lips with a deep relaxed embouchure around the mouthpiece. A few rusty notes in the beginning, until he got the hang of it. As much as the sound brought old hidden emotions back to surface, somehow though, the first mellow tunes didn't feel the same as he remembered from his adolescence. The dream of becoming a global harmonica superstar and phenomenon wasn't a realistic option anymore. And his inspiration and only fan, young Aune wasn't there listening to him as she did in their younger years before fishing started to take all his time.

He took the harmonica with him downstairs to his living room. He sat on the arm chair and kept playing. More he did, more melancholic sadness did his songs capture with the only audience member being his half full Wodka bottle beside helping him to forget his excruciating feeling of loneliness.

While he played, the downbeat sounds travelled him back to his childhood, his late teens and the first dates with Aune where he lured her to open her heart to him, to young, charming Viljo by playing more upbeat songs once upon a time. *The happiest times of his life*, he recalls, an era, where the emotions and hormones run the wildest leaving memories and scars that will last a lifetime and follow us in our hearts no matter how old we are or become. The skills he learned and the passions he enjoyed at those heated years of adolescence had never left him. Even some vague signs of an early dementia hadn't faded those early, happy memories. He was still that same, passionate Viljo, only the objects of his affection and desire had disappeared around him, those being fishing and Aune. Not quite sure which came first, though.

As firm as his decision to quit fishing was, the dramatic events on the lake and the words *the chosen ones, the three wise fishermen*, still haunted him.

He quit playing the out of tune harmonica and glanced around his bookshelf. On the bottom corner rested an old, white miniature version of the Bible that him and Aune received when they married more than fifty years ago. The book was never opened since. He got off his chair and walked to it. He put the harmonica aside and reached out for the Bible. The cover was under a thick layer of dust. His hands were shaking, either from the old age or nervousness.

'The answers you seek are in the back of this book,' he quoted, whispering. He wiped the dust away with his palm. He turned the cover, browsed the untouched, white thin pages all the way until the last pages. He opened the last spread and took his reading glasses from the book case. He scrolled and browsed through the last spread. 'Nothing here... or here.' He glanced at the blank back cover. He sighed, closed the book and put it back on the clear spot surrounded by more dust where it had been untouched for more than half a century. 'I knew it,' he snorted, picked up his harmonica and slouched back on his rocking chair. Another low key tune drifted him back to his happy youth with Aune and bountiful of fish. He felt teary, but his supply of teardrops were long gone and dried up.

Chapter 31

# THE LETTER

The pages of the Bible kept turning faster as Sven's yearning for answers grew. Whenever Ida was gone, or at nights once she had fallen asleep, he reached out for the night table, quietly opened the drawer, picked up the book and read. Days had turned into weeks since the interpretation of the Bible turned out to be a laborious task. Although the search for the truth had somewhat filled that missing gap withdrawal from fishing had left in his life, yet it didn't pay his bills.

Towards the end of the book, he began to understand the old language better. Yet, to his disappointment, whether there were any direct answers or solutions to the problems they were facing, was debatable. He undoubtedly had become more aware of the story of the Old and the New Testament, yet he wasn't capable of connecting the dots with any of the recent events at the lake to the story of God, Jesus Christ or his disciplines. He began to suspect whether they actually had hallucinated in their drunkenness the event of hearing the salmon talk, or if someone only wanted to spread and force-feed the message of God and Christianity as mostly Jaaku had suspected. He almost felt as if he had been tricked into reading the entire book and his valuable time had been wasted.

Only a few pages remaining, he lay on the sofa reading. Ida was away in the supermarket doing the groceries that gave him the space and time to hopefully finish the book before she returns.

He got to the second to last spread. His frustration had reached its limits. Having compromised time sending out resumes and seeking for jobs only to read the Bible made him feel like a fool. The times of uncertainty gloomed ahead. He started seriously stressing and fear about an employment he may have to find from other industries. But the questions was, what industries? He wasn't skilled in anything else than fishing. Or further education was the other option, Ida had suggested him. But that would cost time and money, when especially the latter he did not have. Yet, she had both, or at least for another few months she had time, until the baby was due. Money she had been given enough by her family, but he could never accept her to support him. And if her family was to find out her even considering spending her money on him, they would do their utmost to stop her.

He felt lost, as he held the last two pages between his fingers. Anxiously, he turned the last spread open in front of his tired eyes. A dried up, wrinkled envelope rested on the right side of the spread blocking the page he tried to read. He moved the envelope on the coffee table thinking it consisted an old bill or something from the drawer, which had accidentally ended up between the book.

He finished reading the last page all the way till the last sentence. To his disappointment, he didn't feel he had found an answer to anything in particular or felt any sort of enlightenment.

He slammed the book shut and chucked it on the living room floor. He sat up and dropped his head between his arms. He pulled his hair, whimpered and moaned. He didn't get up, but kept his head down, when a small breeze blew the envelope on the floor between his feet right under his vision. He examined the envelope. It was old, dried and hardened. There used to be writing on the cover, but it was mostly washed away and unreadable. Only a few ink stains were left on the worn texture. The envelope was sealed, though. He observed more carefully. It was not a utility bill, he recognised. He picked it up, slid his finger between the seal and ripped it open. The inside revealed a piece of paper partly torn apart. Carefully, he pulled the fragile paper out. It read:

*For those brave men fishing these waters, save yourselves from the monster...*

The hand writing had a peculiar familiarity to it. As if he had seen a similar text before. His heart beat faster as he rushed to the bookcase. He reached out for the folder with all his most important documents, bank statements and old bills. Most importantly, though, he located his birth certificate. He pulled the certificate out and placed it next to the old letter from the envelope. He looked at the letter again.

*... I pray for my family, my son. For those about to judge, I wash my hands to declare my innocence...*

The letter contained three simple sentences, until the ripping had cut the rest of the writing away. The text may had continued, he couldn't tell. Apart from that, there was only a date and a year scribbled on the top corner. The letter was dated two days after his father's death.

Chapter 32

# MAN'S GOTTA DO...

The front door slamming made Sven jump on the sofa.

'Honey, I'm home!' Ida's voice carried from the corridor.

Sven sat quietly. He fought to swallow his tears. He rested his elbows on the coffee table on both sides of the letter and the birth certificate. He breathed heavily.

'There really is a monster fish,' he whispered to himself.

Ida walked to the doorway. 'Ah, I didn't know you were here.'

'Where else would I be?' Sven said, staring at the table.

'I thought you had a job interview?' Ida said and walked around so she could see his face. 'How did it go?'

'I didn't go.'

'Why not?'

'Who wants to hire a fisherman?'

'Is everything alright?'

Sven pushed both papers towards her at the corner of the table. Slowly, he looked up at her.

'What are they? Why there are tears in your eyes? More bills?' she said and rushed to embrace him. 'We will get by, don't worry. The baby isn't due for another three months. I have some savings we can use. My family has been very generous.'

'Read the letter, please,' Sven said quietly.

'What is it? Don't say we have been evicted?' Ida said and grabbed the letter off the table. 'We have always paid the rent on time, have we?'

'Be careful! It's an old piece of paper.' Sven jumped up.

'What's the matter with you?' Ida pulled away and read the letter. 'What is this?'

'I found it folded inside an envelope at the back of the Bible,' Sven said and sat on the sofa again.

'Is this the answer? There is a... monster fish?'

'Possibly. But most importantly, the letter is written by... my father.'

'Oh, dear Lord,' Ida said, feeling shivers down her spine. She sat beside Sven. 'How is that possible? How do you know?'

'It's his handwriting,' Sven said, picked up the birth certificate and put it side by side with the letter.

Ida nodded suspiciously and shifted her focus back on the letter. 'He is claiming he's innocent?'

Sven stood up again looking somewhat more determined. He composed himself and wiped his teary face dry. He walked to the window and pushed the curtain to the side. He looked outside and nodded to himself. The winter months had arrived while he had been studying the Bible, yet not as cold or snowy as usual. 'What I find the most interesting is that the letter is dated two days after my dad's and Carl's disappearance. So, it means that him or they both were still alive for at least two days after their departure and believed time of drowning.' Sven pulled the curtain back and walked to the storage closet. He opened the door and began examining his fishing gear that had been packed away for months, longer than ever before.

'Unbelievable! I don't know what to say.' Ida shook her head. 'I guess I owe you an apology.'

'It doesn't matter. I would have done same if I was you. Who would believe a crazy drunk fisherman telling he has met a preaching salmon?'

'What are you doing?' Ida stood up, looking concerned while Sven plough through the closet.

'I must go to Herring Bay.'

'I don't think it's a good idea.'

'I know, but someone's gotta do it.'

'What about Jaaku? Or Viljo?'

'They've pulled out. Both of them.'

'It's dangerous. You should think about me and us. About our future. Our child.'

'That's why I am doing it.'

'Please...'

'I will return.' Sven turned away and started putting together his neglected fishing gear. Ida walked behind him and tried to touch his shoulders, but he pulled away, ignored her and kept packing his bags. Once his fishing gear was ready, he pulled over his winter coat, boots and a hat.

'Are you going... now!?' Ida said, still standing behind him in the hallway. 'It's eight o'clock in the evening!'

'I know. I have to be fast. Apparently, the best time is at midnight.' Sven pulled the rucksack on his back and took a couple of fishing rods with him. 'If I won't be back by tomorrow midday, post my wish list to Santa will you, please. I know tomorrow the letters are due.' Sven gently touched Ida's cheek and turned away to the door. He pushed the front door open. A cold breeze slapped his face blowing further inside to give Ida the shivers.

'Please, don't go,' Ida walked behind him and grabbed his sleeve. 'You cannot do it alone.'

Sven turned to look at Ida over his shoulder. 'You used to always support me. Always. What happened?' he said disappointed.

'But... I'm really afraid to lose you. I have always been. But now our child needs a father. If anyone, you should know what it's like to grow up without one.'

Sven turned to face Ida. 'That's unfair to bring that up. I am not going to disappear. But I have to go. I know what I'm doing. And it's the full moon.' Sven leaned over and kissed Ida on the cheek. 'Trust me. I am... The Herringmaster,' he said confidently, turned around and walked out of the house.

'Where did that come from?' Ida pushed her head out of the door, but saw Sven already in the distance speeding away on his kicksled.

'Don't forget to post the letters to Santa!' he shouted and waved, eventually, disappearing behind a curtain of fog and snow fall.

Chapter 33

# THE BEGINNING OF THE END

Apart from the sound of Sven's heavy breathing and the wind gusts embracing his crisp red cheeks, the silence on the lake was haunting as he departed the shore. Only a couple of weeks to Christmas, yet the waters were ice free. The shockingly warm temperatures had left the land and the forests around the lake green and barren of snow, apart from a few scattered wet white piles on the ground and on top of the bottoms of the abandoned fishing boats flipped upside down. He even had to dump his kicksled half a kilometre away and walk the rest of the way to reach his boat. Even the most remote Arctic haven had not been safe from the effects of global warming, whereas the mystery terrorising the fishing industry kept the fishermen away for good.

At the safety of home and in the presence of Ida, Sven thought he was fully prepared and confident to face the creatures of the night alone, yet, whilst the eerie wind whistled, and foamy waves and rapidly shifting currents rocked the boat, he began to develop doubts. More than five months had passed since the last time he had been on the lake, the longest period ever in his life. He felt somewhat rusty and out of touch. The rowing felt laborious as he moved slowly against the strong currents.

*I hope Ida will forgive me*, he thought, as the last image of her standing in the doorway, looking disappointed and not responding to his wave never left his mind.

He started by following the southern coastline towards west, but eventually his plan was to turn up north west past Moose Island to Herring Bay. He got near the south end of the lake, when he saw movement on the coast. He couldn't see clearly. 'Another fisherman?' he rejoiced. *Not everyone has lost their hope.* He wanted to speak to the man, share any knowledge, warn him. Once he turned the boat towards the shore, the northerly gusts eased his effort. The tail winds carried him closer. Before the last few strokes, he looked over his shoulder and recognised the man. The man stared back at him. It was Viljo by his boat, a pipe in his mouth, a cap on his head and a spear gun in his hand. He looked serious. Sven wasn't sure if he was delighted or not as he pulled the boat next to him. 'What are you doing here?'

'I could ask the same question from you,' Viljo said and took a step closer to Sven's boat.

Sven stood up and jumped beside Viljo. 'I never said I'd given up.'

'I didn't give up either. I retired!' Viljo grunted. 'I am still allowed to come here, am I?' He took another step towards Sven making him feel uneasy. Sven backed off ankles into the water. He heard a slur in Viljo's voice and an odd distant stare in his eyes as if he was outraged, heavily intoxicated or both. Viljo looked around, pointed the spear gun at Sven's face and said, 'I guess it's just you and me then.'

'What are you saying?' Sven asked nervously.

'Like sixteen years ago,' Viljo said, eyes glooming, 'but now the roles have changed. This will be a revenge on behalf of my family. And nobody has to know what happened, because no one will ever come to the lake anymore. Your body would never be discovered. And the justice would have happened.'

*Not again,* Sven thought. He shook his head and raised his arms. 'Please, Viljo.'

'I really do hope you read the Bible, because now it's time for you to say your prayers for the last time,' Viljo said and wrapped his shaky, wrinkled finger around the trigger. 'Like father like son, ey? I despise your dirty little plot with your idiot Eskimo friend to drown me and strip me from the championship. As if I haven't suffered enough. How much you paid your friend to break the ice? How much!?'

'I know now what happened. I know!' Sven said urgently and afraid these would be his last words.

'You don't know a damn thing, boy. You should only be ashamed.'

'I read the entire book and...' Sven said, dropped his one arm and slowly reached out for the side pocket of his coat.

'Get your hand away from those pockets,' Viljo barked and poked him with the tip of the spear.

'It's just the book, the Bible.'

'Good. You'll need it in the afterlife if there is one.'

'I found something.'

'From the Bible?'

'Yes.'

'I knew it! You were brainwashed to read the book and now you're trying to make the others do the same. That's the way of the religious. Trying to convert us, too.'

'No. I found this letter inside the book,' Sven said, clenching his teeth. 'I want you to read it.'

'No poem is gonna save you.'

'It's not a poem, but something much better. A message. A clue,' Sven said and turned his side to Viljo. 'You can take it yourself, if you want.'

'What have you got there? A mouse trap?'

'Could you please stop being so suspicious? Just take the piece of paper and read it yourself. It's folded between the pages.'

Eyes glued to Sven's, Viljo reached out for the pocket. He lowered the spear gun to point at Sven's stomach. He pulled out the book, opened it from the spread in the middle of the book where the piece of paper rested on.

'The letter was inside an envelope between the last spread.'

Viljo stared at the paper, yet didn't want to release his hand from the weapon. He focused, but his long-sightedness made the text unreadable. He didn't bring his glasses with him either. He pushed the letter in front of Sven. 'Read it for me.'

Sven took the letter, unfolded it and read the three sentences. Once he had finished, he looked up at Viljo, pleading.

'Is that all?' Viljo snorted.

'Yes. But you know the date? It's two days after my dad and your brother went missing.'

'So?'

'The person who wrote this letter is... my father.'

'Your father?' Viljo laughed. 'Not in a million years.'

'I believe so. I compared the handwriting. Look.' Sven pulled his birth certificate from another pocket and held it beside the letter.

Viljo gave him a suspicious look. He yanked the paper off Sven's hands and zoomed onto both documents. First, he got closer and then pulled away, until his blurry eyes focused. He couldn't compare the two texts in perfect detail, but he sure did notice overall similarities between them. He looked up at Sven. 'What are you trying to tell me?' he asked, more calmly.

'My father didn't drown your brother. The letter suggests that it was something else. A monster fish?'

Viljo lowered his gaze together with his spear gun. He sat on the tree stump next to him and sighed. He breathed heavily. 'Is this real? You didn't make this up yourself?'

Sven took a deep breath of relief. Once again, he believed he had escaped a near death experience. 'Why are you really here? You are not here to kill me, are you?'

Viljo looked up at Sven next to him. There was sadness in his eyes. 'It got too quiet. I just cannot stop. I tried not to think about what happened, leave it all behind, fishing, everything we have seen and experienced. But I couldn't. I need to be in the middle of the action, where the fish is. But where is the fish?'

'Tell me about it.'

'I don't care what the scientists or researchers say. They have no idea. This lake is not empty. I was prepared to go out there on my own, find those answers, face the horror and be ready to die, if it comes to that. Who cares if I die anyway? At least I would do it for the sake of people in Pihtamo, so that our future generations can enjoy a bountiful, fish-filled lake for years, decades, maybe even centuries to come. Besides, I have my other foot in the grave already. There wouldn't be anyone really missing me anyway. I could might as well go, go to hell, but before that I would offer the evil or evils terrorising our lake the fiercest resistance they ever can imagine existed. I would show them hell, hell on earth, and they would all have to be ready to die for what they believe in... because I am ready to die for what I believe in.'

Sven stood in silence and listened to his ranting. He thought now it was his moment to speak, take a brave step closer to someone who had always kept him as an enemy. 'You're not alone. We can do it together,' he said and put his hand on Viljo's shoulder.

'No!' Viljo protested. 'You have a life ahead, a future, a beautiful wife. You are not coming with me.'

'There's no way you can stop me. I need the lake as much as you do,' Sven said.

'You remind me of someone,' Viljo said, thoughtfully. 'Your father.'

Sven's eyes lightened. 'You knew him well?

'Well enough to know that he was as stubborn as you are.'

'I have also discovered within these last few months that fishing is all I know. I guess once you lose something, you understand how much you needed it. If I can't fish here, I might as well choose hell with you.'

'I always thought that I am the only crazy person here, but you...'

'Perhaps we are not so different after all.' Sven offered Viljo his hand that he accepted. Sven yanked him on his feet. 'So, should we use mine or your boat? Or should we use both of the dinghies?'

Thoughtfully, Viljo examined the boats. He shook his head. 'Neither of them.'

'You don't wanna go now?' Sven asked, confused.

'I wanna show you something. Follow me,' Viljo said and stepped away. He started rambling through the trees and bushes along the coastline. Sven tied a quick knot on the nearest tree and left his boat there half of the hull in the water. He rushed behind the old man who seemed to be moving surprisingly smoothly for his age.

'Wait!' Sven shouted and returned to grab his fishing gear.

Viljo looked over his shoulder. 'If you get lost, just follow my footsteps.' He pushed through and disappeared into the vegetation.

Sven rambled behind soon catching up with Viljo. 'You know we haven't got much time. It's midnight soon and we still have to get to Herring Bay.'

'I know very well. Trust me,' Viljo said and picked up pace. 'Speaking about lack of trust, have you seen your friend Jaaku lately?'

'Not since we all met at the lake three months ago. Why?'

'I don't trust him.'

'Is there anyone you do trust?'

'Don't push it, son. I'm here with you, alone, even though you're the last person I should trust,' Viljo snorted. 'Not only that your friend sunk me in the competition, but the last time us three met, your friend showed up without proper fishing gear and he talked about moosequitos.'

'I remember,' Sven said. 'I think he was only joking.'

'Or was he on drugs? Isn't that what you youngsters do?'

'I don't think so. At least I have never taken anything,' Sven said, feeling slightly hypocritical thinking about the amount of Arctic Wodka him and Jaaku had downed within their adult lives. That, however, was not classified as a drug, even though it probably should have been. 'He can be a little bit quirky sometimes. To be fair though, I'm not sure if I can trust anyone here anymore either. The past events have been just beyond comprehension.'

'Fair enough,' Viljo's voice softened. 'I never thought I'd say this, but I have to admit that I do respect you in some level. You beat me in the competition. It's something no one still alive today has achieved, except you now. Whether your friend helped or not. Whatever the conditions were, you got the gold medal and that's what the public remembers and will read about in days to come. That's all that matters.'

'Well, thank you,' Sven said, flabbergasted. In return, he tried to think of something nice to say about him. 'You probably know without saying that... together with my father, you are one of the inspirations for my fishing career. After his passing, I secretly followed and idolised your techniques. I have learned a lot from you, believe or not.'

Sven's complementing words were the heart-warming credit Viljo had been longing for. Having lived in the shadow of the success of Carl's and Roar's outstanding careers and later on the myths of their dramatic disappearances, he felt he never received the full appreciation and recognition for his long lasting career. Sven's kindness momentarily lifted him up. 'By the way,' Viljo said, 'we may never find out what really happened between your father and my brother... and I think we should leave it as it is. Leave it all behind us. Let them rest in peace.'

Sven never thought to hear these words from Viljo. Like a large rock had been just moved away from his chest. He had butterflies in his stomach. 'I agree,' he stuttered. Viljo's sudden softness gave him the peace of mind. He felt as if this could be the beginning of a new chapter in their lives.

A long period of silence followed after the brief moments of openness and forgiveness. The forest got denser while the moon shining above gave them guidance. The coastline remained in the vicinity. Shadowy areas behind the thick tree trunks kept parts of the forest cooler. Their winter boots sunk deeper in the snow.

'So, where are we going exactly?' Sven asked, breaking the silence.

'Patience. Won't be long,' Viljo said, while pushing branches to the side.

Suddenly, a loud gunshot following a whistling bullet flew through the trees and trimmed down needles on its path right in front of the two trekking men. Both men dropped down on their knees, and from there, threw themselves flat on the ground. They crawled on the snow to hide behind a dense clump of shrub.

'What was that?' Sven let out a panicky whisper.

Rustling footsteps approached them from the distance through the bushes. Without making a sound or taking a breath, Viljo sat up against the tree trunk and pulled out his spear gun as Sven clinched his fists. Once the shooter walked past the bush they were hidden, Sven stood up, attacked the gunman from behind, pushed him to the ground and jumped on top of his back while twisting his arms. Viljo followed pressing the spear gun to the man's neck.

'Please. No!' the man screamed and gargled snow while lying face down.

'Jaaku?' Sven said, and eased the hold of Jaaku's arms. 'What are you doing here?'

Jaaku turned his head followed by his body as Sven loosened the grip, yet Viljo kept pointing the spear gun at him. Jaaku's face was wet and red. 'I... I thought I saw... Psalmon,' he muttered.

'Where? In the forest?'

'Erm. I mean... Wolferring,' Jaaku said nervously. 'These things... rifles... have a long range.'

Sven stood up and pointed at the weapon next to Jaaku. 'Why are you carrying a gun? I thought you hate all sorts of firearms.'

'I've been thinking lately... it's about time... to arm ourselves with... weapons. Yes, more weapons, ' Jaaku explained. He wiped some snow off his clothes and stood up. 'We can do so much more. There's enemy lurking... everywhere. We don't know what to expect anymore and we must be prepared. Ghosts, monsters, vampires terrorising our livelihood. It's a tough against tougher. If the traditional methods don't work, we must try something new.'

'Where did that come from?' Sven said condemningly.

'Fishermen don't need firearms,' Viljo added.

'Speaks a man holding a spear gun,' Jaaku said and gestured towards Viljo.

'Spear gun is a fishing tool,' Viljo grunted.

'So are firearms suitable for a certain type of fishing,' Jaaku answered.

'Not in Pihtamo. You don't need a firearm to catch fish here,' Sven said.

'Times could change. Obviously, times have already changed. How were you thinking about catching all these... monsters? With a worm or a crawler?' Jaaku smirked.

'You're always talking about change.' Sven raised his eyebrow.

'Who knows. Tonight, we may need to fire a few bullets and you might end up thanking me for that. A few shots won't hurt anyone.'

'It does exactly that. Hurt.'

'Cross fingers we hit the right target.'

'I have my fingers crossed already. You almost got us killed,' Viljo said. Then, he whispered to Sven, 'I told you I don't trust him,' and picked up his gear and continued the journey through the forest leaving the two friends behind. Sven gave Jaaku an odd look and followed Viljo. Jaaku saw the two men disappearing into the forest. He shook the rest of the snow off and followed them.

Soon, the forest got nearly impenetrable and the rustle of the dead branches louder. After an hour or so of floundering around the spruces, pine trees and through the bushes, Lake Pihtamo opened up in front of their eyes again. A narrow strip of coast revealed itself behind the dense Arctic vegetation. And an old fishing motor boat parked next to a short wooden jetty. The three men lined up side by side facing the lake.

'Is that... yours?' Sven said, suspiciously looking at the old fishing boat.

'Yes,' Viljo announced proudly. 'That's my Aune.'

'You named it after your ex-wife?' Jaaku asked.

'She's still my wife!' Viljo grunted and grabbed Jaaku by his collar.

'Sorry,' Jaaku spread his arms and tried to pull away, but Viljo held him tight, until he let go and pushed Jaaku a couple of steps backwards.

Viljo ignored Jaaku and walked down towards the boat while he explained, 'This boat has the size and all mods and cons to help us complete our mission.' He took a step on the creaking planks of the jetty. Sven and Jaaku followed behind him, looking at each other, not knowing how to react. The boat seemed to them like it had its best years way behind. Although all three cramping into a small rowing boat to hunt for a monstrous fish didn't sound ideal either. Viljo hopped at the rear of the boat while Sven and Jaaku stayed on the jetty observing. Spreading his arms proudly, Viljo began the presentation, 'As you can see, her spacious aft and fore decks give any hard-core angler that extra room to reel in larger-than-life catch. A full walkaround cabin with big plate windows gives the helmsman three-sixty degree visibility. The cockpit has the latest multiscreen radar-plotter-sounder-sonar equipment.'

'The latest?' Jaaku smirked under his breath.

'What was that?' Viljo stopped.

'Nothing. Go on,' Sven intervened.

Viljo gathered himself. 'Where was I? Ah, yes. The hull is hundred percent oak extending to six and a half metres in length with a two metres beam,' he said and walked around the cabin. 'The stainless steel hand rails circling the boat are recently fitted.'

'Recently?' Sven said and leaned forward together with Jaaku to get a better view, but all they saw were rust covered railings that probably were stainless long time ago.

Viljo kept moving reaching the bow. 'I have single-handedly rebuilt the engine with a new crankshaft. I also rebuilt the gearbox and rewired everything. The inboard six cylinder diesel engine gives eighty horsepower that should be enough in these waters.'

'It's definitely better than oars,' Sven said supportively.

'Indeed,' Viljo nodded approvingly and turned to face the lake. He leaned on the railing. 'Top speed was as far as I recall... about thirty knots.'

'And the mast?' Jaaku asked, peering above.

'Yes, the mast,' Viljo looked up, 'I added to observe.'

'Observe... what exactly?' Sven asked.

'Since the drownings of my brother and your father, I wanted to do something about it. Find them. Discover their bodies or at least some evidence. I thought a viewing deck would bring me to new heights to observe better what lies beneath the surface.'

'I guess for that you'd need a submarine or to be a diver.'

'Thought about getting a submarine, too. But I was never comfortable underwater. I rather stay above the surface. So, I installed the viewing mast towering up to three metres in height.'

'Did it work?'

'Obviously, not. Otherwise, I wouldn't be here with you tonight, if I had discovered something. Since you showed me that letter from your father, I am not here anymore just to hunt some big scary fish, but also to find more answers.'

'Me too,' Sven nodded.

'So, shall we go? We haven't got much time,' Viljo said.

Sven took a step forward and jumped at the rear deck, whereas Jaaku stayed on the jetty.

'I actually haven't sailed this boat for nearly a decade,' Viljo said and joined Sven at rear.

'Nice to know,' Jaaku yawned, 'but can we go back now?'

'Back where?' Viljo asked.

'I believe we have a mission to complete,' Jaaku said.

'Yes, we have. That's why I brought you here.'

'We are not going to take that old tin can, are we?' Jaaku said arrogantly and looked at Sven, but he only shrugged shoulders behind Viljo.

'Fine. You can stay on the shore and practice shooting squirrels,' Viljo smirked at Jaaku and then turned to Sven, 'but we're gonna take this real boat, right?'

Sven nodded hesitantly.

'We have no idea what is waiting for us out there,' Viljo continued. 'Last time our tiny rowing boat was taken twenty metres up in the air by a tornado. That was enough of excitement for me. I believe for all of us. This time we need something stronger and sturdier that gives us the edge.'

'I have to admit I agree with Viljo,' said Sven.

Viljo began unleashing the rope that was frozen stiff and cracked. 'Is your friend coming or not?'

Sven gave a concerned look at Jaaku who nervously examined his rifle. Jaaku knew he couldn't back off anymore. He had to join them to complete his own mission initiated by his new moose hunter friends. Sven and Viljo could lead him to the source without realising it themselves. This may be his last chance to make use of their knowledge and help to locate Mooses. He observed the rust on the bottom as he took steps closer to the boat. 'When was the last time you sailed this thing again?' Jaaku mumbled and decided to hop on board to join the two fishermen.

Viljo pulled the rope inside the deck and moved into the cabin behind the steering wheel. *I really wish Jaaku would have stayed on the shore*, he thought and light the pipe.

Chapter 34

# A HESITANT STOAT

After multiple failed attempts, the boat engine clunked into life. The hull cracked, and the railings and the mast rattled as they pulled away from the jetty. Having a larger and faster boat than any of the rowing dinghies was supposed to ease their task, but so far Sven and Jaaku were not convinced.

'I'm afraid this may be our last journey,' Sven whispered his fearful regrets to Jaaku as they held onto the sides and stared longingly at the waning coastline behind them.

A tiny short-tailed weasel appeared from the dark forest onto the jetty they had just left. Its white and shiny coat reflected brightly off the moonlight and contrasted against the brown planks as if an angel had appeared to send the men farewells. The stoat stretched its long back, short arms and yawned mouth wide open. 'Erm...erm...' It made a peculiar sound, which however, disappeared under the loud noise of the diesel engine.

Sven responded with a friendly wave. Jaaku didn't pay attention, but sat down on the deck back against the cabin wall. Viljo only looked ahead and pressed the throttle further down. The boat picked up speed.

'Erm...erm...' the stoat repeated, raising its voice. It kept waving its one paw, but the other pointed along the coastline.

Bemused, Sven stopped waving, but kept staring curiously at the stoat. From the distance, it seemed like a fur coated miniature air traffic controller pointing its paws to different directions.

Sven wasn't familiar with the forest wildlife and how they were supposed to behave. *Was this normal?* The stoat began jumping up and down on the spot while swinging both arms around. The stoat looked concerned. Along the railings, Sven balanced himself carefully to the doorway of the cabin. 'You'd better stop the engine and come and have a look at this?'

'What is it?' Viljo asked, dumbfounded. 'I cannot stop the engine now. I'm afraid it may not start again if I do.'

'Can't you keep it running on neutral or something? There's an animal of some sort on the shore, that is to my understanding, acting strangely?'

Viljo shook his head, but listened. He slowed the speed and eventually the boat stopped, yet he kept the engine running.

Meanwhile, Jaaku had picked up his rifle and taken the stoat at gunpoint.

'What are you doing!?' Sven yelled, spotting Jaaku's mean deeds.

'Target practicing,' Jaaku said and aimed.

'Are you crazy!?' Sven jumped from behind and knocked the barrel up making Jaaku fire towards the skies. The echoing shot got the stoat leaping backwards and blocking its ears with its paws.

'Why did you do that for!?' Jaaku shouted.

Viljo came out of the cabin. 'What's going on here?'

'Jaaku tried to kill an innocent animal,' Sven said.

'You kill fish. I can kill a stoat,' Jaaku said. 'It's the same thing.'

Viljo and Sven looked at each other and back at Jaaku. 'Where did you learn that?' Sven asked.

'Erm...erm...' the stoat interrupted the men with more waving and bouncing up and down.

'That is a very strange noise the stoat is making,' Viljo said, being able to hear now while the engine hummed quieter at the background.

'As if it's... trying to say something?' Sven said.

'There's something not right about this,' Jaaku said concerned while caressing the rifle.

The stoat stopped moving and focused. It waved its paw

more gently now. It opened its mouth wide and let out a sound, 'G-g-greetings to... you... a-a-all.'

Once the stoat formed understandable words to a human, Viljo's pipe fell off his mouth onto the deck floor. He rushed to the cabin to turn off the engine. Jaaku lowered his rifle together with his jaw. Eyes wide, Sven took a step forward and leaned on the railing to get a better view.

'Y-y-you... are g-g-going the...the...the... wrong... way,' the stoat hesitated.

Sven looked over his shoulder at Jaaku standing behind him and Viljo who returned outside. 'Can you hear what I hear?'

Viljo and Jaaku nodded in awe. They both joined Sven on the railing.

'Another chatty animal?' Sven asked dumbfounded. He glanced at the men either side of him. 'And we haven't been drinking?'

Bewildered, Viljo and Jaaku nodded again.

'Just a tiny bit,' Jaaku said.

'A bit more,' Viljo said, shaking his head.

'Well, I haven't and I can still hear,' Sven said and turned to look at the stoat. 'Who... What are you?'

'I am... Erm...ine.'

'Ine?'

'Erm...ine.'

'It's ermine,' Jaaku said. 'That's usually how you call a stoat in its pure white winter coat. I saw one when I went hunt... I mean... Hungary.'

'You went where?' Sven asked, confused.

'It's... erm... long time ago,' Jaaku panicked.

'N-n-no. Erm...ine,' the stoat repeated.

'Yes, 'Jaaku nodded, relieved about the interruption. 'We understand. You're an ermine,'

'W-w-ith the... pause in the... m-m-middle. Erm...ine,' Erm...ine explained.

'Erm...ine?' Sven asked.

Erm...ine nodded.

'But are you also an ermine?' Jaaku asked.

Erm...ine nodded again.

'I'm not following,' Viljo shook his head.

'Doesn't matter if you don't,' Sven said with more sarcastic, yet fearful tone. 'This is just unbelievable. We haven't even really left the shore and this happens. I am dying to see what's waiting for us tonight. Or not.'

'The forests are vast and more mysterious than we realise,' Jaaku said.

Sven turned his suspicious eyes back to Jaaku. 'Is there something we should know?'

But Jaaku ignored Sven's question and only kept his eyes glued to the stoat. 'Not that I was paying that much attention at school, but I cannot remember any biology or even elocution teacher telling about stoats that stutter.'

'Well, considering that we've already met a talking salmon that threw us with a book, so far this one is child's play,' Viljo said, looked around and spotted his spear gun leaning on the cabin wall. He picked it up and hid it behind his back. 'So, tell us something, Erm...ine. Are you the little bugger eating all our fish?'

'N-n-no. I wo-wo-would never... do anything... like t-t-that!'

'Fine. What do you want from us then?' Viljo asked anxiously. 'Did you just come and wish us a good journey? We have no nuts or anything else to give you, whatever you Erm...ines eat.'

'I-I-I have some...thing to t-t-tell you,' Erm...ine stuttered gravely.

'Pardon?' the three men asked in unison.

Exhausted, Erm...ine repeated the same sentence twice, until the men understood. It wasn't always easy to be a stoat with a speech impediment. 'We... h-h-have a co-co-common... interest. T-t-the evil... man... is not only... interested about... f-f-ish. H-h-he tried to... k-k-kill me!'

'The evil man?' Jaaku asked.

'The... m-m-man with... big... a-a-antlers.'

'Can't recall seeing any antlers on the wizard,' Viljo remembered.

'I-I-I reckon he... wanted my f-f-fur,' Erm...ine said, fearfully rubbing its hairy chest.

'What about... big fishes? Have you heard or seen any?' Sven asked. 'Does Wolferring ring the bell?'

'Or Psalmon?' Viljo added.

'S-s-salmon? Wolf... herring? T-t-there's... definitely no fish... left a-a-around here. I-I-I wish there... was. I'm s-s-starving.'

'Where did you see this... antler man?' Sven asked.

'On... the w-w-west coast... n-n-near the Three A-A-Apostles.'

Viljo rushed to the cabin and brought out a map. He spread the map on the floor in front of them.

'We were supposed to go to Herring Bay tonight. That's straight up north,' Sven said while studying the map.

'Exactly. And that's also where my herrings were stolen,' Viljo added.

'Viljo, your sighting was half a year ago,' Jaaku said. 'And besides, what if the antler man and the man who stole your herrings are two different people?'

Both Sven and Viljo turned to Jaaku.

'What makes you think so?' Sven asked.

'Do... w-w-whatever you t-t-think is... best,' Erm...ine intervened, dropped its head down and walked away while the men debated. 'I'm... just a h-h-hungry... messenger.'

'B-b-but...' Sven stood up stuttering, but too late. Erm...ine had disappeared into the dark forest.

'What d-d-did we d-d-do?' Viljo stammered.

'Why... a-a-are we all... s-s-stuttering?' Jaaku said.

'It's... r-r-really catchy,' Sven replied.

'Stop it!' Viljo grunted. 'This is becoming like some weird kids animation.'

'So... we were going to the wrong direction then?' Sven questioned.

'Why would you trust a little stuttering stoat?' Viljo snorted.

'Stuttering doesn't make Erm...ine less credible than any other...' Sven started.

'Any other speaking animal?' Viljo continued and laughed. 'Right. We have been advised now, twice, by talking fauna who has given us two completely different instructions.'

'Erm...ine talked about a man with antlers,' Sven said.

'The man I saw was definitely wearing a pointy hat,' Viljo remembered.

'Maybe there were antlers hidden under the hat?' Sven suggested.

'There's only one way to find out,' Jaaku said.

'That means you boys wanna listen to Erm...ine?' Viljo asked.

'I would rather cut in the middle straight to Herring Bay,' Jaaku suggested and peered at the map thinking that route would take them nearer to Moose Island where his target is more likely to hold base. Although that contradicted with what Erm...ine had just said about "Antler-Man's" possible location on the west coast, yet Jaaku trusted more in his fellow hunters' knowledge.

'Can we go around both destinations?' Sven said.

'I doubt we have enough time, if we're supposed to get to Herring Bay before midnight,' Viljo explained, 'and as nice and quality this boat is, I wouldn't necessarily take it on a long journey straight away after such a long break. We can do one or the other,' but then, he softened to suggest, 'however, to help make up our minds which direction to choose, we can always try and spin the herring.'

'Spin... what?' Sven asked, dumbfounded.

'The herring,' Viljo said proudly. 'It's an old, traditional way to navigate, when the modern methods don't work, let you down or you end up undecided with multiple choices, as we have now.'

'That's the most ridiculous thing I've ever heard,' Jaaku laughed.

'Yes. I still understand fishing and eating fish, but not playing with it,' Sven added.

'This is not a game, kids,' Viljo said and raised his index finger. 'Spinning the herring has saved me from trouble dozens of times. You spin the herring on a flat surface and where the nose points once the herring stops is the direction you will take. I'm sure this is a method even your old man never knew.'

'Probably not,' Sven smirked.

'I remember once in nineteen fifty-three, when...'

'Fine. We'll spin the herring,' Sven interrupted, knowing the lengths and the amount of details Viljo's old stories could contain, which they didn't have time to listen at this point. 'Whatever it takes for us to start moving onto one direction or the other.'

'But there's only one problem,' Jaaku said. 'Where do you think we get a herring, since the lake is empty?'

'Is it really so?' Viljo asked. 'We are the top three... I mean... top two fishermen in the area...'

Viljo's words made Jaaku grimace.

However, Viljo didn't stop, but went on while he moved inside the cabin. 'If we cannot catch one single herring from one of the most abundant lakes in the known world, then we are all doomed and we can all might as well go home and start knitting or something.'

Dumbfounded, Jaaku and Sven looked at each other.

Viljo came out with his fishing rod. He cast the lure a fair distance away. 'So, you two are just gonna stand there and look stupid or you'll join me? We haven't got much time to lose.'

Sven nodded eagerly, took out his fishing rod and cast on the opposite side from Viljo.

However, Jaaku who had only brought his rifle with him, stood awkwardly in the middle.

'You can borrow my spare rod.' Sven pointed at his remaining gear on the floor.

Jaaku nodded, placed the rifle on the floor and picked up Sven's rod. He cast off from the bow, so that men's rods pointed at all three different directions.

'If we catch nothing in the next fifteen minutes, then we just toss the coin,' Viljo said.

Sven and Jaaku didn't reply. They all stood quiet lures in the water waiting for the miracle to happen. Silence took over all around them. They were set like for a final battle from an old Spaghetti Western cowboy film, except that these participants were looking away from each other, not towards. Who will draw the herring out of water fastest would be the winner. It got so quiet that they could almost hear each other's thoughts.

Sven's mind was filled with guilt of how he had ignored Ida recently leaving her alone at the time she needed him the most. He hoped the mission was soon over and he would be back home by sunrise.

Jaaku had only one, obsessive goal in mind: to hunt down the leader of the moose hunters. He felt no quilt or remorse. Fishing of the herring was only part of the game he had to play, not to cause any further suspicion amongst his fellows. However, it seemed like a waste of time, when they should be concentrating on more important things. He had an idea where to go look for Mooses, but he hadn't figured out yet how to phrase that to Sven and Viljo.

As Viljo reeled, he reminisced the golden era of fishing and the best years of his life. The good old times, so to speak. How the fish would catch non-stop. How Aune would wait for him day after day, no matter what. She stood by her man as many women of her generation did despite their men's imperfections. The motor boat was the last reminder of their happiest times together. In his mind, he still saw images of her sunbathing on the foredeck in her black one-piece bathing suit. Whatever was the outcome of this final attempt to catch something, nevertheless, he felt less lonely by the lake and he always would, until it's time for him to go. As if the wind sometimes whispered his name, even though it didn't. As if he was in the presence of someone else, whether there was company or not, or fish or not. He felt calm and relaxed by the water and the mellow waves. As he did with her.

'What if the herring's nose, once we spin it, points at... let's say... east?' Sven broke the silence with his pondering. 'As we know, based on the advice we've been given, we only have two options: west and north.'

'We pick the closest direction,' Viljo replied.

'Naturally.'

The men fell into silent mode again. The seconds turned into minutes. The surface of the lake that used to have fishes jumping continuously as far as the eye could see, had flattened to resemble a mirror. The early morning hours had a ghastly feel. The fog developed around them. The wind picked up a little and the waves began to rock the boat. The clouds gathered above them like on the night they met the previous time. The men gave a concerned glance up on the darkening skies.

'That's enough,' Jaaku said and retrieved the line. 'Who's got the coin, we toss it now.'

'It's not quite fifteen minutes yet,' Viljo said.

'There's nothing in here,' Jaaku snorted. 'Can't you see? Look around us. Or listen. It's all dead. That lake hasn't got a single living thing in it. Accept it.' He dropped Sven's spare rod on the floor next to his rucksack and picked up his rifle.

Viljo's head sunk in disappointment. Sven looked at them both, but wasn't sure which side to take. He wanted to agree with Jaaku, but he felt as heartbroken as Viljo about the situation. He wanted to go on for another ten minutes and another few more. It was difficult to accept that this would be the end of an era. *There is no fish.*

'Only a couple of more minutes, please,' Viljo pleaded, grinding his teeth. 'We're the best there is...'

Jaaku sat on the floor in the corner of the deck, arms crossed. 'No more for me, thank you.'

Viljo turned to Sven with his old, sad eyes.

Sven nodded discreetly at him and then looked back onto the lake. He had given it all. He felt as empty as the lake. 'I'm sorry, old man. I cannot do this anymore,' Sven said. Once he finished reeling, he threw his fishing gear on the floor and walked inside the cabin. He sat on a chair and hid his face behind his palms.

Somehow, Viljo had trusted Sven would go on longer than him and be the last one to give up. But to see the young champion he dearly admired and respected, stop fishing, broke his back bone. He sighed heavily and gave one more glance at the waters. *Lake Pihtamo is dead*, he accepted. As he began reeling his tackle out of the water, he felt resistance. The line became heavier, as if something was holding it on the other end. When he tried to pull, the rod arched.

'Stuck in the bottom, ey?' Jaaku smirked.

The pulling motion became rhythmically repetitive. Viljo struggled to hold the yanking rod in his palms. 'This is not the bottom!' he screamed while fighting against something extremely lively. The u-shaped rod sway from side to side. Knuckles white, he squeezed the handle. The odd movement of the catch pulled him towards the railing. He smacked stomach first against the steel bar, yet holding onto the rod and not letting go.

Sven heard Viljo's grunt and rushed outside to assist him. They both held onto Viljo's rod and fought the resistance.

Meanwhile, Jaaku aimed his rifle roughly at the point where the fishing line met the surface.

'Wait!' Viljo ordered Jaaku not to fire yet. Being squashed between the railing and Sven behind him trying to help, Viljo was losing his breath. He squeezed the rod so hard his hands began to bleed.

'Let go!' Sven pleaded. He felt and understood the remarkable strength of the *thing* at the other end of the line. 'Fire, Jaaku, fire!'

Jaaku nodded and aimed at the water. Simultaneously, though, the agreement with the moose hunters affected his action. His true goal was not to help Pihtamo anymore, but the opposite. He had given his vow. *The new beginning.* He worried about the consequences of this one shot. *What if it's Wolferring?* He was supposed to save the monster fish.

'What are you waiting for!?' Sven screamed.

Viljo dangled on the edge, his upper body bent around the railing and hanging largely outside the boat. He had stopped breathing. He was falling unconscious. The handle of the rod and his sleeves were covered in blood.

'Let go, old man,' Sven whispered calmly to Viljo's ear. 'You can't win. It's gonna take you. Take both of us. Please.'

Viljo never let go, but a fire blasting off Jaaku's rifle snapped the fishing line. The sudden release of tension threw Viljo and Sven against the cabin wall and from there they fell on the floor. Viljo landed on top of Sven.

'Nice shot, Jaaku,' Sven panted from underneath Viljo.

Jaaku saw a stream on the surface of the lake rapidly disappearing onto the horizon. He glanced at the blazing gun. His hands shook nervously. He was uncertain whether his shot helped the mission or helped to ruin it.

Sven pushed Viljo up on his feet and got up himself, too. 'Everything alright, old man?'

'Of course,' Viljo shook his head and wiped his bleeding

hands on his trousers. And then he pointed at the water. 'What was that?'

They all stared at the vanishing stream on the surface.

'Wolferring?' Jaaku said.

'Or Psalmon?' Sven said.

Meanwhile, a little herring pushed its head on the surface, right in front of the boat and the men. '*Buenos dias!*'

Confused, the men peered ahead and behind them at the boat.

'Did one of you just speak Spanish?' Viljo wondered.

'*Sí! Español!*' the herring conversed from below.

Eventually, the eyes of all three men found the source of the voice. Astonished, they spotted the herring. Immediately, Jaaku aimed his rifle at the herring, but Sven pushed the barrel away again before he could pull the trigger. 'Not so fast! That's not what we're looking for,' Sven ordered.

'How do you know what we are looking for?'

'That doesn't look like a monster.'

'Who knows what a monster looks like anymore? Anybody can be a monster,' Jaaku said.

'Yes. Anybody,' Viljo gave Jaaku a serious, long look.

Jaaku sighed and lowered the weapon.

'That can't be Wolferring, though,' Sven said.

'*Jajaja!*' the herring laughed like Spanish do. 'Me? No. But you had the monster on the hook, until you fired a shot.'

'I shot... Wolferring?' Jaaku asked nervously.

'*Sí.* Or wounded. *Pero Wolferring se puso arrecho!* Wolferring, very angry! But you gentlemen saved my life. I am forever grateful. *Muchos gracias!*'

'Saved your life? We did?' Viljo asked, confused. 'Unheard-of that us three would save fish. We are fishermen.'

'With the shot, you scared the monster fish away that was chasing me,' the little herring said enthusiastically with its alluring Spanish accent.

'So the monster is still out there,' Viljo said.

'Wounded,' Jaaku added slightly relieved that his shot wasn't lethal.

Sven gave the herring a suspicious look. 'And what brings

you here? I've never come across any... Spanish fishes at these Arctic latitudes?'

'*Mi amigos*. Let me explain. This may sound crazy, but lately I've been hearing these voices,' the herring said, lowering its own speaking tone.

'Voices?'

'I come all the way from Venezuela. *Hola!* First, I had an epiphany. An urge to follow the sound, a luring, almost magical voice that was calling me. And now, four months later, I am here. I believe I am very near, since the voices are getting stronger. Perhaps, I have reached my destination. Now, I'm just waiting for a sign.'

'You swam half the world to come here in the middle of nowhere just by following some voices inside your head?' Sven said in awe.

'It's something I couldn't resist. I had no control over it. I left my neighbourhood, other fish...'

'What other fish?' Sven interrupted.

'Salmon, a whale couple, trout, *uno* mahi-mahi.'

'What about other herrings?'

'I was the only herring in my neighbourhood.'

'So, all the other fish stayed?'

'Yes, I believe so.'

'Someone out here likes herrings in particular.'

'What do you mean?' Viljo asked.

'The fish that escaped your net, Viljo, were all herrings, right?' Sven gathered.

'Yes.'

'Venezuelan herring swam here across the globe, but all the other fish stayed. Psalmon has been left alone, since it's a salmon. The very few last fish I caught months ago were cods. I think you, our Latino friend, are swimming into the dragons den by coming here.'

'You must mean, Wolferring's den?' Jaaku suggested.

'Do you think it was Wolferring sending those luring messages, calling you to swim all the way here?' Sven asked the Venezuelan.

'*No sé!* I can't say. The only thing I know is that I couldn't

239

resist the sound. Thank God, you saved me. I'm forever grateful. From now on, I will be your most humble servant.'

'Can you describe those sounds? Not that us humans are necessarily even able to hear them, but out of pure curiosity.'

'It's like... meditative music. It puts you in a trance. It's been like attending a yoga class for four months twenty-four seven.'

'You must be quite relaxed then,' Jaaku said.

'I think I am. Us Venezuelans tend to be quite chilled out anyway.'

'If you still hear those voices, can you follow them and lead us the way?' Sven asked.

'*Sí! Sí!* That would be an honour,' the herring nodded confidently.

Viljo glanced at the herring and said under his breath, 'Can't say I have a good feeling about this either.'

'You generally have a good feeling about... nothing,' Sven replied and moved closer to him, 'The herring has swam ten thousand kilometres to find Pihtamo. That's a bloody good reference to me, better than your idea about spinning the herring. The Venezuelan can possibly lead us straight to our target. It may have done it already once, but Wolferring managed to escape. However, Wolferring may be wounded now somewhere and easier for us to tame and catch.'

'Fine. Let's follow the Latino,' Viljo snorted. 'Another conversing animal. This is becoming totally normal to us now, right?'

'Thank you,' Sven said and turned to the herring. 'Now, listen carefully for those voices and we shall follow.'

'Most certainly,' the herring answered. 'I will do my best... if you tell me what's in it for me?'

'For you? You just said about being our servant?' Sven asked, baffled.

'But a little compensation from my hard work would be...'

'We let you live,' Viljo interrupted. 'If I was a little herring myself, I wouldn't mess around with three fishermen. You show us the way and you won't get a hook in your mouth and end up in a marinade, you got it?'

The herring gulped nervously.

Sven gave Viljo a disapproving look, yet condemning the herring's arrogant approach. 'Go on then and we follow,' he added to encourage the herring. 'Don't worry about the old man.'

The herring nodded while Viljo went inside the cabin and attempted to re-start the engine.

'After you, Mr...' Sven gestured.

'Arengue.'

'Of course.'

The herring swam around the boat to the front, dived underwater and occasionally kept popping its head on the surface so that the men could see its winding path. Sven and Jaaku followed to the bow to observe the route. The engine coughed and rattled, until it stayed running and didn't stop. Viljo took the course following the herring.

Sven panted excitedly while observing the herring's winding path. He turned to Jaaku who sat down on the floor. 'A fish at Pihtamo... Unbelievable!'

'Amazing,' Jaaku replied unenthusiastically.

'What's the matter with you? Are you not interested?'

'Of course I am,' Jaaku said, staring ahead glassy-eyed. 'But it's not really a type of fish that belongs here. We still don't know if there's any native fish left. Venezuelan is here only visiting. Or basically, because it got lost really bad.'

Sven glanced at him concerned and turned his eye back to the jolly herring.

'*All Night Long...*' sang the herring and wigged its oiled tail smoothly like salsa dancers move their elastic hips and torsos.

'The herring's travelling north,' Viljo observed from the cockpit.

'Good. That goes with what Psalmon said,' Sven said. 'Herring Bay.'

Next, though, the herring took a sudden turn. '*Uno, dos, tres, cuatro!*'

'Now it's going west,' Viljo said and turned the wheel.

'Well, that'll do as well. Isn't that what Erm...ine advised?' Sven said.

'This is going to be a long journey,' Viljo grunted.

'Let's give the fish a chance,' Sven said. 'Not that we have too many options anyway.'

'Three opinions,' Viljo sighed. 'All from animals that talk.'

Suddenly, the herring appeared at the back of the boat heading towards the starting point. Viljo made a u-turn while Sven held onto the railing. They followed, and soon, saw the departure jetty in the vicinity. The herring came to surface, began spinning around and doing flips, like a synchronised swimmer. Viljo slowed down and brought the boat to a halt. Sven leaned on the railing and sighed. 'Perhaps, this wasn't such a good idea.'

'I'd say we spin the herring and we spin it now,' Viljo's voice echoed from the cabin, until he stormed out with his spear gun. 'Where is the little bugger?'

Chapter 35

# SPINNING THE HERRING

It was the time of the year when the sun didn't rise, but looking at the dark grey skies, the men could tell the night was turning into early morning. They had already lost hours finding Viljo's boat, chatting to the stoat and now following the jiving herring. 'We are gonna be late,' Sven said. 'We haven't got time to spin anything. We must go. Now.'

'Don't worry. The full moon is supposed to be visible until early afternoon.' Viljo peered at the water and spotted the herring partying alone.

'*Bailando, bailando...*' the herring sang and danced totally unaware of the men's plans.

Viljo supported his spear gun on the railing and aimed.

'There must be some other way,' Sven said. 'Can't you spin a living herring?'

'What are you talking about, champion?' Viljo snorted. 'You're the number one killer of fish in the region and now suddenly you grew a conscience?'

'No...but...'

'Is it because the fish talks?'

'Well, look at it. How happy it is. It's having the time of its life. The fish here are not like that. They are all dull, lifeless, emotionless, introverted. Somewhat boring.'

'You must mean, normal?' Viljo said. 'As fish should be.'

'Yes, but at least once we have a colourful and interesting

fish here. Why kill it straight away? There must be some other solution. Knock it unconscious? Isn't that enough? It must be very difficult to shoot such a small target with your spear gun anyway, right?' Sven's need to protect the unique species sidetracked him from his usual instinct to catch everything. Something had changed in him. The recent encounters with conversing stoat and fish proofed that animals can have a personality, thoughts and feelings that a human being can understand and relate to. Such a simple gesture as being able to express themselves and communicate had helped these poor animals convince the superior, in this case the humans, not to hunt or kill. Conversational skills and being an extrovert had saved lives. As it does similarly help many of humans to succeed in life. Or some, survive.

Jaaku stood up and slammed the rifle next to Viljo's spear gun. 'I know I can hit the target.'

'*Que!?*' the herring screamed.

'No!' Sven protested. 'Can't we just ask it to stay still while we spin it?'

'I doubt there's anything we can say to stop the movement and rhythm running in its veins,' Jaaku said. 'We must paralyse it somehow. I would suggest shooting is the way forward.'

'Hold on. There's another thing we can try.' Viljo put his hand inside his coat and pulled out a flat pocket flask. 'Wodka. Perhaps, that will immobilise the Venezuelan.'

The herring gave concerned glances at the men debating about the next steps.

'Great idea!' Sven said, pleased. He was not alone with his protective thinking. 'But what if alcohol will make the herring even more lively and in the end it just wants to keep on dancing?'

'I wasn't thinking about just one or two shots, but the whole bottle. Or at least half. The Arctic way.'

'Ah, yes. You mean, first bottoms up, and then the bottom's down on the floor and the four-wheel drive is on.'

'Exactly!' Viljo exclaimed, uncorked the flask and sprinkled a few drops overboard on the tip of the herrings curious nose. The herring seemingly enjoyed the first taste of the sea-buckthorn flavoured, strong liquor. It swam closer to the boat and opened

244

its mouth for some more. Viljo clocked the herring requesting for another sip. He poured a mouthful. Venezuelan ingested everything following a series of coughs. Tears ran down its face. The burning sensation in the digestive system made its body shake from head to tail. It began swaying and bouncing on the water in a way that resembled an exotic rain dance of some sort.

'*Despacito!*'

'Not enough. We have to give the fish some more,' Viljo said and looked at Sven. 'Meanwhile, can you try and catch it?'

'I can still shoot it,' Jaaku snorted.

'No!' Viljo ordered. 'The herring must be alive while we spin it. It's absolutely fundamental for the technique to work. I just remembered now.'

'But you said earlier...'

'I was wrong. I forgot. The rule is that the herring has to be alive,' Viljo said with a softer tone.

'This game has the silliest rules ever,' Jaaku sighed. 'Someone must have been really drunk who invented them.'

'Actually, that was me,' Viljo said.

'How about just a flesh wound?' Jaaku said eagerly.

'Wodka will take care of this. Trust me.' Viljo gave the herring a few drops more and the private party got even wilder.

*Maybe Viljo has got a heart after all*, Sven thought, satisfied. He went to pick up his fishing rod. 'What does your rule book say about spinning the herring that has passed out?'

'Erm... That should be fine,' Viljo hesitated. 'Or we'll find out. I haven't finished the book yet.'

'You're writing a manual?' Jaaku smiled while lowering his weapon.

'Yes. How to Spin the Herring,' Viljo said quietly. 'This shall be part of my research.' He emptied the rest of Wodka on the herring while Sven from the other side cast the tackle right next to the drunken herring.

'*Olé, olé! Puerto Rico!*' the Venezuelan gargled the alcohol before swallowing. Its head spun around a few times, until spotting the luring, colourful lure floating beside. The herring thought to be in heaven. It had long forgotten the calling sounds that had attracted it to Pihtamo in the first place. There were no external disturbances what-so-ever. It even stopped paying attention to the three men and their steaming boat. It was a party time. The herring was the centre of attention. There was unlimited amount of free alcohol and the buffet table had been laid beside. What else could one ask for? The herring opened its mouth wide and sunk its teeth into Sven's tackle. '*Mamma mia!*' The herring squealed in pain as the hook penetrated its jaw tissue.

'I'm so sorry. It will hurt only once,' Sven said regretfully. 'It cannot be worse than being at the dentist.' He yanked the dancing herring up in the air and pulled it towards the bow. The herring flew over the railing and smacked on the cold deck floor. The party had ended in tears of pain.

'It's still too lively. We have to give it more.' Viljo pulled out another bottle and opened it. He had the first sip.

'Wow. You were really prepared,' Sven said as he released the hook and held the herring still.

Viljo wiped his mouth. 'I thought we'd be here for a while.' He poured some more on herring's mouth. 'But my plan wasn't to give it all to one herring, which I seem to be doing now.'

The herring's body functions began to slow down. The fluent Spanish turned to jibberish like babies or sleeping talk. The tail fin stopped flicking and the body went limp.

'We haven't got much time. I'm not sure how quickly fish sober and wake up,' Viljo said.

'Fine, old man. It's your show. Show us how to spin the herring,' Sven said.

Viljo nodded and took an old rag. He wiped the limp fish dry off grass, mud, water and alcohol, and then picked it up. 'This is where you start Spin the Herring. Its body must be placed in the middle of the front deck for navigational purposes. Once the spinning stops, the end position the nose is pointing at indicates the direction we should be heading towards,' he explained. 'To begin with, the nose has to point the direction we've started our journey, which is south. The herring has to rotate at least three full circles anti-clockwise. Anything less and the end result doesn't count. You should not influence on the spin in any way or make the herring stop in the direction you wish. In any instance, a minimum of three full three-sixty degree circles are required.

And last but not least, always, the oldest in the presence does the spinning. In this case, that'll be me.'

'Naturally,' Sven smiled.

'Will you just spin the herring, please,' Jaaku snorted.

'Patience, young men. This has to be done right. Otherwise, it's waste of our time.'

Sven and Jaaku nodded together in a perfect harmony.

Viljo placed his large palm on the body of the floppy herring lying flat on the wet floor. He squeezed the fish a little and released. He raised his arms and spun his shoulders around a few times. He rotated his wrist around to warm-up a bit more, until he brought his hands back down. 'Let the spinning begin,' he announced and flicked the fish.

'One, two, three...' Sven counted the spins.

'*Ay, Ay, Ay!*' Squealing, the herring recovered after five spins and counting. On the eight spin it began to slow down and on the ninth, it stopped to point directly ahead. '*Por qué?*' it cried and puked some half-solid grey liquid on the floor.

'The herring's pointing up north east,' Jaaku observed.

'Which means it is closest to north,' Viljo said. 'And that is one of our options. Herring Bay. I can live with that. I will start the engine. I told you it works.'

'That'll do,' Jaaku said, also seemingly pleased with the result. He made his way up to the viewing tower.

'I must say this is such a nonsense,' Sven snorted. 'Look at the herring. It's suffering.'

'Well, it's either the word of a religious salmon, stuttering stoat or the result of Spin the Herring?' Viljo shouted from the cockpit and started the engine. 'Who would you trust the most?'

Sven gave the nauseous herring an empathic look. Then, he raised his gaze up on the horizon. *None of them really. We're on a very thin ice here... or surrounded by it, literally. And it's late. Early morning. I hope Ida isn't angry.*

Chapter 36

# WISH LISTS

Birgget's wooden red hut in the middle of the forest had all the simple comforts she needed for herself. The interior was warm, rustic and timber. The kitchen had a small masonry oven and a hole-in-the-floor underground cellar. An outdoor privy stood hidden behind the cabin on the edge of the woods.

The cabin was ideal for single living. However, the amount of details, and fascinating handcrafted items and decorations the house held inside made it undoubtedly an exciting place in the future for the grandchildren to explore. Not that she was aware yet of the upcoming grandmotherhood, which Sven and Ida had kept a secret from everyone for all these months. *He who has the happiness, should hide it.*

She drew open the flower embroidered curtains and saw Ida waiting outside in the darkness. Ida stood behind her kicksled steering bar rummaging through her handbag filled with Christmas cards and letters signed and ready to be delivered to friends and family, as well as hers and Sven's wish lists to Santa. A crisp early morning air made her cheeks blush. Every time she exhaled, her breath came visible into the cold air.

Covered with a long wool coat and a fur hat, Birgget came out of the hut and greeted Ida with a warm hug. 'Looking so lovely today,' Birgget said and smiled.

'You as well, always,' Ida replied and leaned over to embrace. Her thick winter clothes covered her pregnancy of six months.

They let go and she gestured at the chair. 'You can sit in the front.'

'Very funny. Thank you, though.' Birgget said while hearing seriousness in Ida's voice. 'Is everything alright?'

'Yes. Fine.'

'How is Sven?'

'Fine. Let's go,' Ida said briefly. 'The post office closes earlier today.'

Birgget looked at her suspiciously, but decided to let her be. She sat on the tiny wooden front seat, the one and the only chair traditional kicksleds tend to have. Once she was comfortably seated, Ida offered her handbag to her lap. Birgget squeezed both of their purses tight and nodded Ida she was ready. Ida waited a few seconds and then she pushed the sled onto motion. Once they picked up speed, she stood on both runners. She raised her other foot and used it to kick more speed.

'I was actually expecting you to come with your snow mobile,' Birgget said.

'I returned it to my parents. I decided I don't need anything from them anymore. It's time for me to make it on my own.'

'Brave decision.'

'Or stubborn,' Ida said and gave the icy ground another kick.

After the long driveway, they entered a forest path beginning with a downhill. They could both relax and enjoy the slide.

'Was it difficult to decide what you want for Christmas?' Birgget asked, keeping her eyes on the path. Her cabin was further away from the coastline and deeper in the forest, hence more snow in the area.

'Always,' Ida replied. 'There are so many things I want in this life.'

'Who wouldn't. I used to be more like you,' Birgget stared in the distance. A little sadness filled her eyes. 'I've become such a realistic though.'

'Maybe that's better. Does save you from many disappointments. But you know what I'm like. I am a dreamer. I have always been,' Ida glanced at the dark grey skies.

Birgget looked at Ida over her shoulder and gave her a smile. Ida responded with a half-smile.

The slope became a flat terrain filled with spruces and pine trees as far as the eye could see. They were heading into the darkening forest. Winding foot and paw prints of wildlife of all sorts broke the thin layer of snow on the ground. There were signs of small mammals, foxes, moose, weasels, some large animals, perhaps even bears, leading to different directions.

'I may need your help soon to tell which turn to take. The forest seems so different this year,' Ida observed the view ahead.

'It's because there is less snow. Global warming, they say.' Birgget looked around at the scenery. 'But snow or no snow, I would know the route to the post office by heart - even when I'm asleep. By this age, I have done the trip so many times. And maybe soon do it for grandchildren's sake too,' she turned to look at Ida again and winked her eye.

Instantly, Ida stopped the sled flying Birgget off her seat into the snow face down.

'I'm so sorry.' Ida rushed by her side, helped her sit on the ground and wiped the wet snow off her face with her woollen mitt.

'Why did you do that for?' Birgget pondered while spitting the watery snow off her mouth.

'Has Sven told you something?'

'Something? About what?' Birgget stood up and wiped her clothes.

'About... wanting to have children?'

'No. But I assume he would want one day,' Birgget kept answering, confused. 'Are you alright? Do you want me to ride if you sit?'

'It's fine. I can do it.'

Birgget gave Ida a concerned nod, yet sat on the chair. Ida kicked the sled on full speed again, while Birgget guided them on the right path. They entered the deep forest. The kicksled zigzagged between the trees and the dense bushes.

'You want to have children, right?' Birgget broke the moment of silence.

'Yes. More than anything,' Ida said melancholically.

'What's the matter, love? You know you can tell me anything.'

'I'm just concerned about the men. We have really no idea what we are up against. I am afraid of the unknown and fear for the worst.'

'Tell me about it.'

Ida took a deep breath. 'Sven didn't come home last night. I hope nothing happened to him.'

'Don't worry. Roar was sometimes away for days,' Birgget said thoughtfully. 'Always fishing, apparently. Or so he said.'

'I'm sorry. Of course, you must know exactly what I'm going through. You must have felt the same every time he went away.'

'Always. I never really wanted him to go, but I understood he had to. Obviously, that was his livelihood, lifestyle and passion. Unfortunately, he was not a nine-to-five accountant working in an office or a chef in a restaurant. I had decided to marry a fisherman. Our life revolved around his career. Sometimes, though, after big arguments, that we had a few, I wanted him to go, but I always felt regretful soon after. Once he shut the door and vanished, I began missing him immediately, and when he returned, I felt a huge sense of relief.'

'You still miss him?'

'Of course I do. The pain never goes away, but you just learn to live with it.'

'You think he is still alive?'

'You mean if he disappeared?'

'No. I didn't mean to say that he wanted to leave. I meant that... there's always hope.'

'To be honest with you, we were not at our happiest at the time, if that's what you are asking for. Some years after the incident, I thought about that option too, of him disappearing, leaving his family, since the body was never discovered. Although if he did run away, it was wrong for Sven, no matter how unhappy he was with me. He shouldn't have ran away from his only child, and especially at a time the child needed the father the most. Although Roar I thought I knew would have never done that. He may have wanted to leave me, but not Sven. Never. I believe he was taken by Lake Pihtamo, where his heart and soul belonged.'

'It must have been difficult for Sven. He never really talks about it.'

'The men here don't seem to talk too much anyway. It always makes me wonder what those men talk to each other on their fishing trips.'

'Maybe they don't. Only grunt,' Ida smiled.

'Or they talk about their kicksleds, teepees, boats...'

'...ice hockey, Wodka, fishing,' Ida added.

'Let's hope this time they're too busy for conversation and they would rather find those answers and solve the problems,' Birgget said with conviction. 'All three of them are highly skilled men.'

'This time, though, Sven went alone,' Ida said gravely.

Birgget sighed in surprise. 'Sorry. I didn't know,' she said more worriedly.

Ida said nothing, but kicked the sled to top speed. She felt uncertain whether Sven really understood the challenges he may be facing on the lake alone. She prayed for him.

Once the forest ended, the town limits appeared in front of them. First came the church reminding about Ida's and Sven's embarrassing wedding, yet an event Ida had begun to remember with more warmth and hilarity. At times, she was even able to laugh about it. After all, she had married a fisherman and offering his bride a fish on the altar was something one can expect. *I should have seen it coming*, she almost blamed herself.

After passing the church, they reached the high street. The town centre, sleepy for about eleven months a year, had turned into a bustling shopping district for these very few weeks preceding Christmas. Tens of people wandered the streets and visited the few shops in a struggle to find presents for their loved ones, friends and family members. Although the hardest part of the shopping was not being noticed and get caught by the ones the presents were meant for - such a small place Pihtamo was. Today, though, since it was Saturday, the early closing hours of the shops forced people back into their homes sooner to heat up their saunas and enjoy the rest of their weekends. The high street was getting emptier. The last remaining open facilities were the post office and the Arctic Bar.

The post office was on the first floor of a two-storey building situated opposite the pie shop on the corner of the 1st and the 2nd streets. In front of the building there was a line up of kicksleds of different colours: red, green, orange and one black with flames painted on the wooden side bars. Ida parked hers extending the row with one more. Birgget hopped off the seat and together they went inside without locking the kicksled. The town was considered as a safe haven and commonly people didn't lock anything. The trust to the community was strong; the theft of kicksleds non-existent. Rarely, though, kicksleds were stolen by punters of the Arctic Bar who after a long night out were too intoxicated to walk home and they had to "borrow" someone else's kicksled to get home. Usually, after a day or two, though, in remorse, the stolen kicksleds were returned to their original owners either voluntarily or after a polite recommendation from the town sheriff.

The narrow entrance to the post office was decorated with handmade paper snowflakes and carton Christmas elves. In the lobby a real living and modestly decorated Christmas tree stood proudly in the corner, and next to it, a fully blazing fireplace maximised the heat and cosiness of the shop. The only waiting seat angled diagonally near the fireplace was occupied by one of the town elderly and her shopping bags, while she waited for her siblings to conduct their businesses by the counter.

Despite the high season, the office counter had only one staff member left to serve. She was Marjukka. The other worker had been sent home early. The queue behind the counter nearly extended outside. Ida and Birgget were just about able to shut the entrance door to fit inside and join the back of the line. The central heating turned to the maximum took an immediate effect on them. They took off their thick mitts, hats and opened their coats. Momentarily, Marjukka stopped serving the customers. She stood up and walked by the entrance. She was a tall and handsome lady at her mid-thirties. She had a dark, shortish hair, a rarity and somewhat exotic in Pihtamo where the majority of the people were blonde. She wore modern glasses, a purple Christmas jumper and black trousers. The clothes seemed to fit her surprisingly well and the materials were better than the average quality, Ida observed. Considering how the entry level staff of many corporations are often being dressed up in ill-fitting and uncomfortable uniforms making them look less glamorous to save costs, Marjukka was in a better position. She was the manager, and perhaps that gave her the edge and the privilege to wear something more suitable.

'Good timing. You're the last of our customers today,' Marjukka said politely to Ida and Birgget and snapped the door lock shut behind them. From now on, the only way was out. The access from outside was denied and the ones arriving later had to wait until next year to post their Christmas letters, or post them the next day with a high risk of the letters not arriving on time - a risk Ida and Birgget were not willing to take.

Chapter 37

# THOU SHAN'T CONTEST

Viljo kept the speed on half throttle to save the old boat and its fragile engine. He steered to the direction pointed by the stiffened body of the unconscious herring. Sven clung to the railing while observing the view ahead, yet struggling to keep awake. All the nights of studying the Bible had taken its toll. Jaaku, on the other hand, stood the most alarmed and awake on the viewing tower looking through his telescope lens at the Moose Island looming ahead. His rifle rested against his thigh, loaded and ready to take down Mooses. No signs of the hunters' leader, though. Jaaku nervously thought about the options of how to make Viljo stop by the island. This may be his only opportunity for long time. They were so close. He couldn't be too forceful, though, since that would cause suspicion. Not that Sven and Viljo hadn't already raised concerns about Jaaku's erratic behaviour.

'I thought I saw something,' Jaaku created fake news hesitantly while observing the still trees and the silent bushes. 'On the island. Some movement.'

'Moose Island?' Sven asked and looked up at Jaaku.

'Yes,' Jaaku said, determined. 'As if I saw a glimpse of antlers.'

'The Antler-Man?' Sven whispered to himself and turned to Viljo who had left the cockpit side window open. 'We must stop on the island. Jaaku saw something there.'

'But what about Herring Bay? It's only half an hour away,' Viljo said.

'I saw it again,' Jaaku said, not even looking through the telescope, but peering down at Sven and Viljo.

Sven raised his gaze and peered towards the island, but couldn't see a thing, besides the coastal cliffs with pine trees and spruces on top, and a grassy shoreline stretching around the backside.

'I think I see something, too,' Viljo said.

'You do?' Sven looked harder.

'...ahead of us,' Viljo continued, stretched his arm and pointed his finger towards the horizon.

Sven turned to look ahead and saw a boat approaching in the distance. 'Jaaku? There is something coming towards us from the direction of Herring Bay. Is that what you were talking about?'

Jaaku sighed disappointed and turned to face the front. He looked through the lens. 'I can see that. As if there's someone... standing on the boat.'

'Standing, ey?' Viljo said, tried to focus ahead, but couldn't see that far away. Frustrated, he pushed the throttle to the bottom.

The boat hit the maximum speed, knocking Jaaku over on his bottom on the viewing tower while Sven hung to the side railing. They raced further away from Moose Island and towards the solitaire boat on the mouth of Herring Bay. Longingly, Jaaku glanced behind them at the island. He sighed, and composed himself back on his feet. He pulled out his telescope to get another glimpse ahead. 'I can see better now. This man doesn't really seem to be fishing at all. He's just waving at... some sort of stick.'

'A fishing rod?' Sven asked.

'More like a... wand.'

'Sounds familiar,' Viljo whispered with a hint of concern.

'I can see it now. Viljo, can you see?' Sven asked.

'We have to get closer.' Viljo only recognised a blurry figure. 'You remember what I told you about my sighting a few months ago?' he said louder so that both Sven and Jaaku could hear over the howling wind. The water sprays swept past them as they sped through the rocking waves. The bottom of the boat bounced and smacked against the rough surface.

As they got closer to the standing fisherman, him and his

boat's appearance became fully visible to the bare eye.

'What a cool boat!' Jaaku said.

'Look at all that fish!' Sven said in awe.

'That's him! The same man I saw,' Viljo screamed and stopped the engine. 'He's stealing all our fish! He tried to kill me!'

The cloaked and pointy-hatted fisherman ignored them, though. He had spread his arms open wide, holding a lineless rod in his hand. He had more fish on his Viking boat than any top fisherman could ever dream of; more than the three men on Viljo's boat had ever seen in their lives.

'Is that the... wizard?' Sven asked. 'It sure looks like one.'

Viljo ran outside on the deck with his spear gun. 'Doesn't matter what it is! It's bad news. We have to get rid of it! I believe we're in a good shooting range.' He glanced up at the viewing tower. 'Are you ready, Jaaku? Finally, you can be useful here.'

'Sure, boss,' Jaaku gulped and checked if the rifle was still loaded, yet simultaneously he thought about the promise he had given to the moose hunters to help the wizard to succeed by protecting, not shooting him. He didn't know how to get away from this all, but he had to play along. He picked up the rifle and aimed at the wizard.

Sven gave both men with weapons a concerned look. 'There must be some other way to solve this. Perhaps, we can try and talk to this man first. We really know nothing about him.'

'Fine. You do the talking. We do the shooting,' Viljo said and winked at Jaaku. Jaaku responded by nodding uncomfortably. 'We know enough that he's stealing our herrings. Can't you see?'

The wizard still didn't pay attention to the men or show any interested towards their intentions. He was purely focused on his unusual and unexplainable fishing techniques. Luring without a lure. It was a miracle to follow, yet causing envy amongst the three men, who all thought to be the best there is. Obviously, they were not. The man on the boat was proving otherwise. They may had met their match. As if all herrings had a desperate need to be close to the wizard, which was a special skill the best fishermen could only dream of. The most confident fishermen like Sven, or Viljo at his peak, believed their skills were beyond human comprehension, until they witnessed this particular illusionist at work. Sven had to rub his eyes a few times, but the nightmaric scene never disappeared. They only had to admire the wizard in envy - a feeling that soon turned into frustration.

'It's time to end this game,' Viljo said and put his finger on the trigger.

'Let me say something before you shoot. Please.' Sven spread his arms. 'At least, he's got fish.'

Viljo nodded and aimed. Reluctantly, Jaaku followed taking the wizard at gunpoint.

'Erm... Sir. Excuse me, sir,' Sven started. 'May I ask what exactly are you planning to do with all those herrings?'

The wizard ignored his cry, remained sideways to the men and kept filling the boat with fish.

Sven's attempt to negotiate was failing before it even really begun. 'I don't think we've seen you here before. Are you local?'

The wizard remained silent.

'You know... in these waters you need a fishing licence. I believe the amount of fish you have on your boat... exceeds the daily quota per fisherman,' Sven stammered.

'Where did that come from? We're not the coast guard,' Viljo snorted.

'Well, I don't know. I've never done this before,' Sven said. 'I thought since you're the head of the fishing association, you might have the power to control licensing.'

'Well, I do, but...' Viljo replied, 'I doubt this creature is interested about rules and regulations. He seems to have acquired his own licence... to fish.'

'Fine. You do the talking, then,' Sven snorted.

'I'd say we let the spear gun do the talking,' Viljo said and fired.

Sven and Jaaku gasped.

However, the arrow landed on one of the side planks of the wizard's boat. The boat rocked slightly, yet the wizard kept his balance. Although the shot caught his attention. He bent down, pulled the arrow off the side and chucked it in the water. Then, slowly, he turned to the men, yet his face was still covered under the hat, the long hair, and behind the thick beard.

Viljo gave his spear gun a confused look and then up to Jaaku who stood static and frozen. 'Are you gonna do something about this?'

Jaaku nodded nervously, still aiming at the wizard.

The wizard spotted the rifle. First, he raised his gaze up to Jaaku, and then lowered to Sven. The wizard said nothing, hardly moved a muscle, yet stared at Sven with his silvery blue eyes glooming behind his grey eyebrows. He raised his arms a notch higher and squeezed his wand harder. His knuckles turned white.

'Please, surrender your fish!' Viljo shouted. 'If you don't obey, there will be even more serious consequences.'

'Maybe he doesn't speak our language,' Jaaku said, trying to buy him more time to keep him from firing. 'What if the wizard's foreign?'

'I think he understands... more than we realise,' Sven said thoughtfully while holding the eye contact with the wizard. 'I just can't figure out what it is he really wants.'

'Jaaku, just shoot, will you?' Viljo said. 'Shoot the devil!'

'Really? Now?' Jaaku stared at the wizard through the front sight. His panting made the rifle shake.

'Yes. Now!' Viljo shouted, aimed and fired again, but this time the arrow missed dearly. Eyes wide, he stared at his weapon. 'Jesus! I never miss.'

The wizard's narrow boat began gliding towards the men. Jaaku wiped sweat off his forehead as he cocked the weapon. He caught an eye contact down with Sven, who seemed concerned and hesitant.

Sven turned to look back at the wizard that had arrived dangerously close. 'How on earth does that boat move?' he asked, dumbfounded.

'That's exactly what I witnessed the first time,' Viljo panted. 'The boat just disappeared without any oars, engines.'

'But now it's floating... towards us!' Sven said in panic.

'Jaaku, shoot, will you or do I have to climb up there to shoot the damn thing myself!?' Viljo screamed, waving his fists below the viewing tower.

Hands trembling and forehead dripping of cold sweat, Jaaku fired. He had no other choice. But being devoted to the moose hunters, he missed purposely. There was a loud splash behind the wizard as the bullet landed on the water. The whistle of the gun shot, though, made the wizard stop his approach. As a self-defence, he brought his rod in front of his body. He stretched his arm forward and responded to the men's hostility with a glazing beam firing off his magic rod. The bright beam hit straight on the top of the spar pole supporting the viewing platform. The platform fell, sending Jaaku flying down the deck. He landed on top of Sven, knocking them both on the floor.

'My boat,' Viljo cried, looking at the falling mast, yet showing no concern over the two men.

Thick winter clothes saved Sven from the worst bruises and Jaaku was saved by Sven's body that softened the landing. Jaaku pulled himself upright before assisting Sven. Then, Jaaku picked up the rifle off the floor again and aimed at the wizard. He started getting second thoughts whether he should trust the moose hunters anymore or just shoot the wizard. Since sparing the life of the wizard in devotion to the moose hunters' wish had nearly cost him his own life, he thought he was making a mistake. He was against a difficult choice: to fulfill the mission or save himself?

'Stop it! Don't shoot,' Sven pushed the rifle barrel down. 'He's gonna destroy the whole ship. Kill us all!'

'Who are you!?' Viljo screamed at the wizard. 'What are you doing here!? What do you want from us!?'

Slowly, the wizard brought his arms and magic rod down next to his hips. The men waited impatiently and frightened. There was a complete, sudden silence, until the wizard spoke out.

'I am... the Lord of Herrings.'

A fierce lightning out of the dark but cloudless sky struck in the middle of Lake Pihtamo.

'A Lord of... what?' asked Sven, still holding his pelvis after getting squashed by Jaaku earlier.

'The Lord of Herrings,' the wizard repeated.

'Is he... drunk?' Jaaku chuckled nervously.

'Not sure, but he looks serious. Very serious,' Sven said while looking deeply through the windows of the wizard's soul; his eyes.

Chapter 38

# POSTAL SERVICES

From the back room of the post office, an abundance of red envelopes, Christmas cards and personal gift parcels flooded under the feet of Marjukka while she simultaneously clung behind the counter serving the last customers on the queue. The mailing department had been stretched to the limits by the Christmas fanatics that Pihtamo was so greatly filled with. However, Marjukka handled the stress well with years of experience in the postal industry: first as a trainee, then as a regular staff and now managing the shop independently. Apart from the seasonally decorated branch she had created for herself and the customers to enjoy, she further boosted the festive atmosphere by popping on a red hat with a fluffy ball at the tip for the last few minutes before the closing time.

The attention to detail of the shop décor was immaculate, yet keeping the interior cosy and warm. The room was dimly lit, walls dark timber and all furniture sturdy and solid wood. The red handmade decoration gave the walls and windows a colourful edge. There were white knitted snowflakes and angels in the windows, red round shaped metallic ornaments hanging off the ceiling. The Christmas tree in the corner was the brightest object in the room. The tree had real living candles. Silver and golden ribbons hung shining on the thick branches as did red, silver and golden baubles. The dark green needles seemed well and healthy. The tree stand was already covered with a few presents, yet Marjukka had planned that more was yet to come.

Birgget and Ida examined their hand bags and collected all the letters and packages they were supposed to send while the last customers ahead of them, a family of four, were being served. The mother stacked an enormous pile of cards and letters on the counter, as if the family were supposed to remind the entire world of their existence. *They simply cannot know that many people*, Ida thought and sighed. She looked at the few items in her hand and thought if she had forgotten someone. But she couldn't think of any. She, and especially Sven, lived a less sociable, modest and quiet live. She had cards for her parents, her sisters, her uncles, her aunties, her best friend Ronja, and both hers and Sven's letters for Santa.

While waiting, a tray laying on top of the counter caught Birgget's attention. She reached out for the tray filled with Christmas cookies of different shapes and sorts: stars, angels, elves, hearts, pigs. She picked a star for herself and offered an angel to Ida. Ida accepted with a smile. A steaming pot of hot glowing wine whistled next to the tray. Ida did as the "Help yourself" sign next to the pot suggested and poured them two full cups. Two small plates beside had a handful of flaked almonds and raisins on display. Ida added hint of both of the spices on their drinks. '*Kippis*,' they cheered.

As the family ahead of them had finished and were exiting the post office, the swinging of the outdoor pushed a cold breeze inside. A large gulp of hot Christmas drink and a taste of sweet ginger biscuits helped them to fight the shivers. They stepped on the counter and handed over their mail to Marjukka. They were the only remaining customers before the closing. Or so they thought.

Chapter 39

# THE MIGHTY LORD

'My intentions are good and noble,' the Lord of Herrings announced with a voice echoing authority and determination.

'As if I've heard that before,' Viljo mumbled to himself and then continued on more confrontational note, 'I'm afraid, sir... Lord... but we have our doubts.'

'I have come to save Pihtamo,' the Lord of Herrings continued.

Viljo turned to Sven and Jaaku. 'I don't feel good about this.'

Sven hesitated and spread his arms. He didn't know what to think or say.

'He's got all our fish. Look at his boat. It's bursting,' Viljo lowered his voice to whispering. 'Jaaku, try and shoot again. Isn't that why you brought the rifle here in the first place? Show us what you're made of. Do Pihtamo a favour and blow up that crazy old hag.'

Jaaku nodded under pressure, took position at the bow, but accidentally stepped on the tail fin of the Venezuelan.

'*Ayayay!*' the herring squealed and returned back to consciousness.

'Sorry. I forgot you were still here,' Jaaku said, took a side step and leaned further away against the railing.

The Venezuelan calmed down, looked up and saw the Lord of Herrings. Suddenly, it started rolling on the deck, threw itself over the edge into the water and swam towards the Lord of

Herrings' boat. Soon, the Venezuelan joined the other herrings wanting to be part of the wizard's success story.

'Did you see that?' Sven looked, amazed, but soon, was disturbed by a blasting rifle.

Jaaku's shot missed metres from the target. This time so badly that the Lord of Herrings didn't even bother reacting. Instead, Viljo and Sven did. They both rushed to the bow with different intentions.

'Now, give me that rifle! You're useless,' Viljo said and grabbed the gun together with Sven. But Jaaku fought back and didn't let go either.

As all three of them battled for the rifle, an accidental shot fired through one of the cabin windows. The glass shattered in hundreds of tiny pieces.

'I would strongly advise you mortals put down your insignificant weapon,' the Lord of Herring administered and brought his rod forward again.

The men stopped wrestling, Sven ending up with the rifle.

Panting, Viljo pushed Jaaku to the side and faced the Lord of Herrings. 'Why are you emptying our lake!? You're tearing Pihtamo apart!'

'I, the Lord of Herrings have helped the tiny community of Pihtamo for generations to come.'

'And how exactly have you helped us?' Sven asked with a great suspicion, while keeping the rifle away from the other two.

'I have single-handedly taken the responsibility for transporting all of the fish away to safety.'

'We simply cannot allow that,' Sven said. 'The damage you have already caused is irreparable. People are suffering.'

'You would all be doomed without the existence of the Lord of Herrings.'

'We are doomed already!' Viljo screamed having had enough of the wizard's smooth and eloquent talk. In frustration, he yanked the rifle off Sven's hands. 'Since Jaaku don't know how to shoot, here's how to do it. Watch and learn!'

'Don't!' Sven jumped on Viljo, but too late as the Lord of Herrings responded with another, yet more powerful beam shooting straight to the hull of *Aune*. The boat capsized flying all three men and their gear overboard.

'How dare you contest the mighty Lord!'

Panicking, the three men gargled the icy cold water and waved their arms as the Lord of Herrings calmly observed the situation. The men paid the highest price for obstructing him and failing to obey his command. Sven and Jaaku stayed afloat, but Viljo began to sink. First, he gasped air when his heavy clothes began to pull him underwater, but soon after he felt no regrets, yet a bliss. He had had his lifetime of battles and enemies, but now it seemed he had met his match. In the shores of Lake Pihtamo he was born, he had fished every fish, and in Lake Pihtamo he was to drown. The circle of life was becoming complete. He accepted his destiny. He let his limp body sink deeper and soon he'd be together with Aune again.

Instead, Sven's and Jaaku's fighting for their own lives with their youthful energy continued and distracted them from even noticing Viljo's disappearance. They swam to the capsized boat. Sven got a hold of the edge when Jaaku clung to the propeller. Meanwhile, the Lord Of Herrings' narrow boat changed the direction and floated away.

'Viljo!' Sven screamed, realising the old man had not surfaced. He let go from the edge of the boat and began swimming around. He kept popping his head underwater to get a glimpse of Viljo's body. He reached the point the men flew overboard. He dived deeper underwater, but saw nothing. The visibility was poor. In the recent decades, the water had turned murkier and more brown. The surrounding agricultural pollution was to blame. There were also lots of currents. He bounced back on the surface breathing heavily. The freezing water began to slow his body functions. 'Help us then if your deeds are good!' Sven screamed while waving his arms and fists at the Lord of Herrings.

But the Lord of Herrings showed no interested to turn around.

With his last strength, Sven returned to their vessel and hung on the edge together with Jaaku. 'We lost Viljo.'

Jaaku nodded briefly to Sven's shocking statement, yet he was too preoccupied holding the propeller and trying to save himself. There wasn't much time before hypothermia would start to set in. They lacked strength to climb on the side of the boat. The surface felt too slippery as Sven reached out his hand. Soon, their lips turned blue and limbs numb. As if everything had been just a bad dream. Or so Sven hoped. Like the Herringmaster had been a dream, even though it felt so realistic to him at the time. *Was I not the Herringmaster after all?* The dream that didn't come true, like most of them don't. He felt stupid, nothing like a master. He was more a traitor. A bad influence. He felt responsible of Viljo's drowning and soon his own together with his best friend's. If he had just left the case as it was. If he had listened to someone else, listened to Ida. Or change as he had been advised to do. Do something else for living. Start a new life. Get a real job. If he had never taken and read the Bible. His stubbornness to solve the mystery had led to a disaster. His child would have to live without a father, like he had to most of his life.

'I cannot hold on anymore,' Jaaku's voice trembled.

'No! You must stay! Look at me.'

'I can't. My eye lashes are frozen together,' Jaaku said, blinded.

As Jaaku began to lose his grip, a powerful lightning strike illuminated another figure. A bearded man with raised arms stood on the hilltop on Moose Island and looked out towards the stormy lake. He wore a helmet on his head that was decorated with a ginormous moose antlers.

'Not so fast, the Lord of Herrings!' the antler man shouted and took a few steps closer to the island shore.

Chapter 40

# ARCTIC CHARM

'Did you leave any for me?' a gentle male voice called out from behind Ida and Birgget at the counter.

Ida felt a tap on her right shoulder. They both turned around. 'Christian?' Ida blushed. 'What are you doing here?'

'Am I not allowed?' Christian smirked, towering behind the two women.

Ida rolled her confused eyes and wiggled uncomfortably.

'I came to deliver my family's Christmas letters. Just made it on time,' he smiled, looking into Ida's eyes. 'And you?'

Ida waved the letters in her hand. 'The same...'

'What a coincidence,' he winked his eye.

'You two know each other?' Birgget snorted for being ignored and left out of the conversation.

'Ah, yes. He's a... friend,' Ida stuttered. 'This is my... I mean... Birgget.'

'Pleasure,' Christian took Birgget's hand and kissed it softly. 'Are you two... sisters?'

'Please,' Birgget chuckled, and gently touched the tips of her hair.

'You could say that,' Ida smiled.

Christian stepped closer behind Ida forming a little queue again. His tantalising cologne tickled Ida's sensitive olfactory system. Nevertheless, Ida kept facing the counter.

However, Birgget's curiosity grew. She wanted to find out

more. 'I thought we were the last customers,' she said.

'I managed to sneak in when the last family opened the door and left the shop,' Christian replied.

Birgget nodded. She measured him from head to toes. Then, she saw the mail in his hand. 'And you only have... two letters?'

'True. One for Santa and one for...' Christian looked at Ida, 'someone special.'

Ida kept staring ahead, her eyes smiling.

Birgget elbowed Ida on the rib cage. 'What a charm he is,' she whispered, making Ida squeal and blush. 'Just friends, right?'

Once Marjukka had handed Ida and Birgget their change and receipts, Ida turned around, but Christian's firm stance blocked her. They stood dangerously close. She felt his heartbeat. 'Well, it was nice... to see you again,' she said, shivering. She looked up at Christian who was nearly one head height taller than her. 'I wish you a... Merry Christmas,' she smiled.

'Yes. Merry Christmas, Christian,' Birgget said, grabbed Ida and pulled her away.

'Merry Christmas, ma'am,' Christian nodded and turned around. 'And Merry Christmas, Ida,' he said with glistening eyes, 'and a Happy New Year.'

'You too,' Ida said while Birgget dragged her away.

'I wish you receive all the happiness and joy,' Christian continued. 'You deserve it.'

'Could I have those letters, please?' Marjukka said, tapping her fingers impatiently on the counter.

Christian ignored Marjukka's anxious request. Instead, he looked to the exit where Birgget reached out for the handle and Ida hung around her arm.

'Excuse me, sir. Did you want us to post those letters on time?' Marjukka asked again. 'We are closing.'

Christian didn't reply, but only kept his eyes glued to Ida. 'Wait, Ida! Please. I have something I wanna tell you,' he said and took a step away from the counter towards her.

'Oh, boy,' Birgget snorted and saw Christian coming.

'Please, let me go home,' Marjukka said under her breath.

Ida fought herself off Birgget's armlock and approached Christian.

Chapter 41

# GENESIS

Jaaku squealed in pain as he forced his frozen eyes open. He could see again. 'Mooses? It's true?' He gazed at the antler horned man wandering on the island shore.

'What are you saying? You know the antler man?' Sven panted with his last strength.

'Mooses is bad news,' Jaaku said.

'Mooses?' Sven said baffled. 'But he seems to wanna fight the Lord of Herrings. That's a good thing, right?'

Mooses had reached the shore. He waved and circled his walking stick up in the air. The wind blew stronger and the waves began to develop. The gusts reached the Lord of Herrings, blowing his hat off and releasing his long white locks. He stopped advancing.

'This is not helping us!' Sven screamed as the heightening waves pounded their frozen bodies against the hull.

As Mooses spread his both arms wide to the sides, Lake Pihtamo began to divide in a biblical way, starting from the point where Mooses stood and cutting between the men's and the Lord of Herrings' boat. Two separate waves pushed the men together with the motor boat on one side and the Lord of Herrings to the other, revealing the bottom of the lake with a few boat wrecks, hidden waste barrels, rubble and rocks. In the middle of all the junk, Psalmon rested on a bed of weed reading the Book of Psalmons. And next to Psalmon lay sunken Viljo

coughing his lungs out. The Lord of Herrings lost his balance and flying disappeared behind the wall of water. The other wave threw Sven and Jaaku to the opposite direction towards the island where Mooses controlled the spectacle. Jaaku landed softly on the meadow near the shore, but Sven got caught on the branches of a small pine tree. He felt one of his rib bones cracking. With a little help from the wave, Viljo's boat turned back upright, soaked, and having completely lost her viewing mast. The boat floated about fifty metres offshore.

Mooses took a step on the path on the bottom of the lake he had created in between the towering walls of water. He walked towards Psalmon in the middle who wiggled on its bed.

After being beaten by more powerful forces, the only thing Sven could do was to cling onto the branches, observe the spectacle and shake his head in confusion. *The Lord of Herrings and the Antler Man or Mooses are two different characters?* Suddenly, though, he became uncertain about the men's real intentions. *Who is the good guy? Is there one? Are we all losing our minds?* Again, it was impossible to trust anyone or anything. A life in Pihtamo, that was considered normal, had turned into a something from a fantasy movie or animation. 'If there is something you wanna tell us, Jaaku, tell us now,' Sven peered down to the ground.

However, Jaaku ignored Sven's question and only observed Mooses trotting down towards the deep bottom of the lake.

Viljo seemed to be the most calmest of all three fishermen, despite the most horrific pain. Although he truly believed this was the end of the world. The walls of water on each side created a shadow over him. He felt he already was on the "other side". Neither did his knees nor bad back hurt anymore. He only coughed out some last drops of water he had inhaled, but apart from that, he felt peaceful. 'Am I dead?' he asked to himself while pinching his arm. The muddy and bare bottom of the lake felt like a soft mattress of a coffin. The religious figures had come to claim him to eternity, heaven or hell. He somehow believed he would be ending up to the latter.

Sven spotted Viljo's body moving at the bottom of the lake on the path Mooses had created. 'Nice to have you back!'

Viljo's eyes lightened as he saw Sven hanging on the tree. 'I already thought I had joined my brother!' he shouted and showed Sven thumbs up.

'Not yet,' Sven replied, feeling Viljo's painful state. He attempted to climb down the tree and help the old man, but as he did, he felt agonising pain himself. As if parts of his body were poorly damaged.

Viljo wasn't as broken as it may have seemed. He got up on his feet and started limping away from the bottom towards the island while Moose came down towards him.

Jaaku, on the other hand, had finally found the right target. The wrong man, the Lord of Herrings, had been taken down, whereas Mooses was still standing. Jaaku scanned the beach and saw the rifle being swept on the shore some stone's throw away.

Sven rolled his eyes in confusion as he saw Jaaku limping towards the weapon. 'Who is he gonna shoot now?'

Jaaku picked up the wet weapon covered in weed and aimed at Mooses who was just about to walk past Viljo.

However, Mooses showed no interested towards Viljo, neither did Viljo care anymore or feel threatened about anything. If someone or something wanted to take his life, it was theirs to have. Only their eyes met as they passed each other. As Viljo looked straight ahead again, he saw Jaaku pointing the rifle to the direction he was coming from. 'What is he doing now!?'

Jaaku aimed at Mooses and pulled the trigger, but as he did, the rifle malfunctioned. Cold water, weed and leaves burst out of the ruined mechanism.

'Are you out of your mind!?' Sven screamed down at Jaaku. 'Mooses saved us all!'

'I knew he was trouble from the start,' Viljo whispered under his breath as he dragged himself forward.

Dumbstruck, Sven observed the scene from the tree as Jaaku tried to recover the weapon by shaking and wiping it dry. Despite the pain, Sven felt he had to do something to stop the craziness. He dropped himself down from the tree ignoring his hurting back and chest.

As Sven hit and fell on the soft moss, the Lord of Herrings appeared slowly floating above the gigantic wall off water, making eight circles with his magic rod. 'Antler Man! You have upset the mighty Lord of Herrings!'

Meanwhile, Mooses had reached beside Psalmon. He spotted the Lord of Herrings returning. 'I need a psalm. Give us a psalm. Now!' Mooses ordered Psalmon.

Psalmon composed itself, stood on its tailfin and nodded. Psalmon began examining the Book of Psalmons.

Sven got himself up and quietly limped behind Jaaku.

However, the true power struggle was at the bottom of the divided lake between the two waves that Mooses kept apart with his powerful faith. Mooses at the bottom and the Lord Of Herrings on the top of the wave were set for the final battle.

Jaaku on the shore aimed at Mooses again, when Sven reached out for his shoulder. He flipped Jaaku around and punched him on the face. Jaaku's nose made a loud cracking sound. The rifle flew off his hand on the meadow. Blood dripping, Jaaku bent down when Sven landed an uppercut on his forehead that dropped him to the ground.

'Yes! I wanted to do that long time ago,' Viljo celebrated while watching the two brawlers from the distance. Seeing Jaaku receive the punches brought a long gone smile on his otherwise grave face.

'I don't know what you've been up to, but it must stop now,' Sven pointed his blaming finger at Jaaku who groaned in pain, blood bursting out of his nostrils.

As Viljo reached the dry land, he turned to face the divided lake. 'Oh, dear lord. What is happening here?'

The Lord of Herrings descending the wave towards Mooses who was adjoined by Psalmon studying the book vigorously, was a spectacle no match for. Sven stopped tormenting Jaaku, and instead watched the apocalyptic sight developing.

'I found a psalm that could work,' Psalmon said.

'Excellent! Read it out,' Mooses ordered.

'Thus a noble men should be honoured, not a creation of devil...' Psalmon preached with determination and dedication. 'The fishes of the bountiful lake belong to the men of faith, who shall follow the righteous path to salvation...'

'Is that in your book?' Mooses asked, dumbfounded. 'The

Book of Psalms?'

'Psalmons. Yes, it is. Here. Look.' Psalmon flashed a spread.

Mooses rolled his eyes. 'Fine. Go on.'

Gradually, the force of the psalm and the devout delivery of Psalmon raised the Lord of Herrings together with his boat ten metres up in the air. His boat began spinning faster and faster as, line by line, Psalmon progressed with the psalm like exorcist at work. Every sentence, word and syllable was like a knife stab wounding the mighty Lord of Herrings. From being superior godlike figure, he gradually shrunk closer to something mortal. So did his boat transform from a glorious Viking vessel to a small fishing dinghy. The reading of Psalmon brought the Lord of Herrings down to his knees. The good had beaten the evil. In a matter of minutes such a powerful, fearful figure had turned into an average, old and vulnerable man. Once Psalmon finished preaching, the Lord of Herrings' limp body fell down and landed back first on the middle seat of his boat. A loud crack of a spine echoed across the lake. The remaining herrings pulled aside to save themselves. Most of the herrings had already escaped once his boat shrunk to one third of its original size. He had no power over the fish anymore either. The Lord of Herrings groaned in pain.

'Give us another psalm. The Lord of Herrings is not finished yet,' Mooses said.

Psalmon did as ordered and browsed through the book further with its handlike fins.

'How about this one, sir?' Psalmon pointed a text from the book.

'That shall seal his fate,' Mooses chanted devilishly.

Psalmon began, 'The Lord of Herrings is NOT my shepherd... '

With his diminishing strength, the Lord of Herrings raised his weak arm over the side of his boat. He waved a white handkerchief in his hand. 'Wolferring... fears... no... fisherman,' he panted. 'You all be doomed. Wolferring will come... and destroy you... all!'

'Did I just hear him say Wolferring?' Sven said to himself while the Lord of Herrings fought for his life. *What were his good intentions? No one ever dared to ask him. The Lord of Herrings knows about Wolferring? And what was wrong with Jaaku? Why does Jaaku want to save the Lord of Herrings and kill Mooses?* A long list of questions puzzled Sven, as Psalmon went on with the psalm that slowly sucked the remaining life out of the Lord of Herrings. 'Stop!' Sven screamed. 'Psalmon, stop reading that psalm! Please!'

Psalmon raised its nose off the book and turned its gaze to the shore. 'Why, sir Sven?'

'I think his intentions may be... genuinely good. Noble,' Sven said hesitantly.

'What makes you believe so?'

'He may be the wrong man or... wizard we're after. Just listen to him. He said something about Wolferring. You said yourself, too. He knows something.'

Psalmon raised its eyebrow, closed the book and turned towards Mooses who seemed dissatisfied.

'What are you doing out there!?' Viljo screamed, disagreeing with Sven. 'Kill him! Kill the Lord!'

'Yes, Psalmon,' Mooses agreed. 'Open the book and keep reading. Finish the Lord of Herrings!'

However, Psalmon didn't need to go on as the Lord of Herrings' boat together with all the remaining herrings rolled uncontrollably down from the edge of the wave hitting the muddy bottom. The Lord of Herrings' body got thrown off the boat, slamming flat on the ground next to Psalmon and Mooses.

Immediately, Sven started limping along the bottom path towards Psalmon, Mooses and the Lord of Herrings, who now lay face down on the mud. His cloak was torn to pieces and magic rod split in half.

Psalmon looked at Mooses inquiringly, but Mooses only extended his arm and raised his palm as a sign to halt all action. He became curious and calmer. He felt the Lord of Herrings was no longer a threat. Psalmon's psalms had effectively worked, even though not finished him off, yet.

As Sven reached beside the Lord of Herrings, Sven tensed his fists ready to protect himself, even though he believed he already had two more powerful figures present to defend him.

'Don't be frightened, Sven. We have stripped him from his evil powers,' Psalmon said. 'If he is still breathing, from now on he will be living his life just as an ordinary fisherman, like all of you. I wish you'd leave him alone, don't haunt him, don't make him pay for what he has done. He's an old, sick man and won't live that long anymore. There's nothing he can do to hurt you or anyone.'

'I guess I should be... grateful to you two,' Sven said to Psalmon and Mooses before kneeling next to the Lord of Herrings' limp body.

'No,' said Mooses. 'You, three brave fishermen lead us to the Lord of Herrings. I have been chasing him for more than a decade. Without your help and persistence, he would still be causing havoc and trouble amongst the fishing population in Pihtamo. Not anymore, though.'

A shrivelled man, once known as the mighty Lord of Herrings coughed his lungs empty, turned around on the ground and opened his eyes. Fearfully, he looked up with a blurred vision at the figures daunting him with their intense stare. 'I'm sorry. I'm sorry... about everything,' he said, trying to catch an eye contact with Sven.

'Pardon?' Sven replied.

The old man sat up. 'You have no clue how sorry I am. I have no words.'

Sven acknowledged his stare and recognised something familiar in the eyes as he got closer.

The old man wiped his muddy appearance, pushed his long hair to the side and revealed the rest of his face.

'Father!?'

'Yes, my son. It's me, Roar.'

Chapter 42

# UNDER THE MISTLETOE

Ida and Christian stood face-to-face by the counter.

'I am thinking about you all the time,' Christian blurted out.

'Please, Christian. Don't do this,' Ida replied.

'I think it's better if I leave you two alone,' Birgget snorted from the exit, but Christian and Ida ignored her anyway. She walked out of the door and went to sit on the kicksled, yet her eyes peered through the window.

'How are things between you and... him?' Christian asked.

'We are... just fine.'

'Didn't sound that convincing. Is everything alright?'

'I'm sorry to bother you, but we are closed now,' Marjukka stood up behind the counter. 'You have to come back on Monday.'

'Just give us a minute, okay? It's Christmas time,' Christian pleaded.

Marjukka snorted and got back to her routine of cashing out while giving them an occasional frustrated look. *What Christmas has to do with any of this?*

Christian took Ida's hand and escorted her to the open lobby by the Christmas tree to gain more privacy. 'You're not happy with him, am I right? I can feel something is not right.'

'I am... We are... doing alright.'

'Just alright? Don't you want more. I know you do. I know you better than he does. You want... everything. You always have.'

277

'My... mother-in-law is waiting outside.'

'That was Sven's mother? I didn't recognise her,' Christian said and looked outside, where Birgget gave a smudge face. 'It doesn't seem to bother her that I'm talking to you. Or, perhaps, she doesn't care about her daughter-in-law that much.'

'Please, don't say that.'

'My mother adores you.'

'I get along with Birgget very well. By the way, I told her we're just friends... as we are.'

'Are we? You don't believe that even yourself.'

'What do you want from me?'

'I want...' Christian took a step closer to Ida. He moved his hands on her waist.

'What are you doing?' Ida looked down on his firm hands and then back up to him.

Christian took another small step towards Ida. He glanced above and saw a mistletoe hanging above them. He moved his body against hers, leaned forward and pressed his lips to hers.

Chapter 43

# THE REVELATION

Sven stood face-to-face with a man claiming to be his long-lost father. He examined every detail in him. His sharp cheek bones protruded under a thin beard. There was familiarity in his eyes, even though the years had passed and worn him out. The family, your own blood is something you should never forget, yet Sven remembered his father differently: as a strong character who he had idolised, whereas the man in front of him seemed like a shadow of what Roar represented at his prime. Once-proud posture had curved, well-build frame thinned and his bright eyes lost their shine.

The old man in rags, or Roar, formerly known as the Lord of Herrings, examined Sven in return. Roar's dry and chapped lips curved into a subtle smile. But the joyful expression on his face soon turned fearful and angry. He stretched out his arm and pointed a finger towards Mooses who had taken steps aback towards the shore. 'Don't trust that man!'

Mooses' face tensed as he sped away from the bottom, swinging around his walking stick.

'He wants to destroy Pihtamo,' Roar revealed.

Sven and Psalmon gave a confused look at each other and then to escaping Mooses. Mooses didn't look back, but kept climbing up the path.

'What are you saying?' Sven queried Roar.

'His mission is to wipe out all fishermen and give full power to the hunters of Pihtamo. That's the reason he was after the Lord of Herrings as well.'

'But what were you then... or I mean... the Lord of Herrings trying to achieve?'

'That has nothing to do with Mooses or any of you. I did my utmost to save all the fish of Lake Pihtamo from the monstrous claws, teeth and sideburns of Wolferring.'

By the time Roar finished his sentence, Mooses had already reached the shore, where Jaaku stood holding his broken nose and Viljo with his wobbly knees. 'Thank you, you silly little helper,' Mooses nodded to Jaaku.

Baffled, Jaaku followed with his gaze as Mooses swung past him.

Dumbfounded, Viljo looked at Jaaku and spread his arms. 'What is Mooses thanking you for? I don't understand.'

Jaaku ignored Viljo and followed Mooses' intentions.

Mooses climbed up the hill, turned himself towards the split lake and raised his walking stick up in the air. The waters began to rumble on either side of Roar, Sven and Psalmon down at the bottom.

'See what I mean!' Roar said alarmingly.

Sven spun around and saw the walls of water starting to collapse on both sides of them. Mooses was about to bring the divided lake back together as one. 'Run!' Sven screamed.

'I don't need to run. I'm a fish,' Psalmon smirked, puffing its gills and making no effort to move. 'I am fine here. You save yourselves, humans!'

Sven rushed up the path, but Roar didn't follow. He attempted to get up, but couldn't move a muscle. Sven looked behind him and saw Roar lying on the ground holding his back. He stopped and returned to Roar. Sven grabbed his limp and wet body, and pulled him up on his shoulders. The old man felt light. Last time they met, Roar had carried Sven to bed after he had fallen asleep in the living room watching television. Now the roles had changed and the circumstances become more serious.

Sven raced for life carrying his father on his shoulders as the colossal walls of divided lake on each side got closer. The first sprays of water sprinkled on them. The muddy bottom and the weight of Roar's soggy cloak took the challenge on another level.

'It's too late. We cannot make it,' Sven slowed down and looked behind at Psalmon who had sunken to study its book. 'Is there any psalm to stop this?' Sven asked, panting.

'I'm just looking. Give me a second,' Psalmon flicked through the pages.

Simultaneously, the two waves collided sinking Sven, Roar and Psalmon in the deep embrace of the lake waters.

'Hahaha!' Mooses let out an evil laughter. 'You fools!'

'How dare you!?' Jaaku screamed at Mooses. 'You were supposed to bring peace between fishermen and hunters!'

'Is that what Börje and Kalle told you, you stupid ice fisher? Have you ever heard the saying: "Don't trust the hunter?"'

'You betrayed us all.'

'No, Jaaku. You did. You brought them all to me. You could have shot me if you wanted, but instead, you protected me,' Mooses said and walked away into the little forest in the middle of the island where he had appeared in the first place. One could only hear him chanting as he disappeared into the woods, 'Long live the moose hunters, long gone the fishermen!'

Jaaku dropped down on his knees and cried. A mixture of tears from his eyes and blood dripping from his nose fell on the grass. 'What have I done?'

The collision of the waves launched a storm that ravaged the lake. The violent scene got Viljo moving. He began wading towards his boat that floated freely and upright near the shore. Jaaku gathered himself up and trotted behind Viljo. One by one they climbed on the boat. Once they rolled on the deck, the waves pushed them towards the island, whereas the next current pulled the boat further away again. Viljo crawled to the cockpit and got a hold of the wheel. The steering felt pointless as the boat only drifted aimlessly. Miraculously, though, the boat stayed upright. He tried to start the engine, but it made no sound.

Jaaku peered the menacing surface in a hope of getting a glimpse of Sven and Roar. He saw his telescope rolling back and forth on the deck. He threw himself next to it and captured the telescope under his palm. He fought his way up against the cabin wall and looked through lens. 'It's Sven!' he yelled after spotting a blue soggy winter hat popping in the middle of the foamy waves.

About hundred metres away bound by the waters, Sven waved his hand up high. His other hand tried to keep Roar afloat.

In the seventh attempt, Viljo managed to start the engine. He revved and tried to steer towards them, but the storm angled the boat off course. After a banana-shaped curve and a few steep turns, the boat reached near Sven and Roar. Jaaku located the lifesaver attached to a rope that he threw overboard. Sven got a hold of it and Jaaku reeled the two men on the boat.

Sven and Roar crashed soaking wet on the deck floor. Sven coughed heavily, until he let go off Roar who collapsed beside him unconscious. He leaned against Roar and tried his pulse. He felt nothing. 'Does anyone know CPR!?' Sven clamoured.

Viljo rushed out of the cockpit to join the men. 'I do,' he sighed and knelt in front of Roar's lifeless body. He took a deep breath as he prepared to do something he never thought he would have to even in his wildest dreams: to try and save the life of a man he had hated for all of his life. But what else could he do? Viljo was a human after all and this proved it. He began pumping Roar's chest accordingly and rhythmically. No result. He pumped more, but still nothing. 'Okay, here we go then.' He rolled his eyes and pressed his mouth on Roar's. He gave him breaths, until the chest rose. Suddenly, Roar sat up, coughed water out of his lungs, and then some more solid liquid followed. He collapsed back on the floor panting and breathing heavily.

'Are you okay?' Sven asked Roar and patted his chest.

Roar nodded and drooled the last drops on the floor.

Viljo stood up, wiped his mouth and walked away. He believed the dirty job had paid off. Although he wasn't quite sure whether he was pleased to see Roar alive or not, but this time he had saved Roar for Sven's sake and for his only.

'I'm sorry about everything, son,' Roar whimpered. 'I hope Birgget is well. How is she? Is she well? I should have never gone away that night. I shouldn't have. Forgive me, please.'

'Hush. Keep quiet,' Sven said calmly. Suddenly, he forgot the tiredness, the injuries, the feeling of sickness and coldness. He wasn't thinking about the violent lake. The familiarity of his father's pleasant voice he remembered. *It's really him.* Sven's eyes filled with tears further wetting his already soaked face. He examined his father's aged features that were much more obvious and clear now as his hair and beard were slicked back and wet.

'I have missed you, son, so badly,' Roar said and slowly sat up beside Sven.

'I have missed you, too.'

Roar responded to Sven's embrace. Momentarily, the warmth of the reunion made them ignore everything else around them.

Meanwhile, Viljo dragged Jaaku away to the stern. He grabbed Jaaku by the collars and lifted him against the stump left of the mast pole. 'You have some answers to give! Did you know the Lord of Herrings is actually Roar?'

'Erm... no,' Jaaku replied.

'Then, how come you understood not to shoot him?'

'I missed on purpose.'

'On purpose! You're not good enough shooter that you could choose whether to hit or not.'

Viljo's ranting interrupted Sven's and Roar's special moment. 'Will you excuse me for a moment... dad,' Sven said with a sense of awkwardness calling someone his dad for the first time over sixteen years. He let go of the embrace, and holding the railing wobbled around the cabin.

'Aren't you glad that I missed the shot?' Jaaku asked Viljo.

'Obviously, I am glad,' Sven intervened standing beside Jaaku and Viljo. 'But how? Any of this makes no sense.'

'Let me explain,' Jaaku said apologetically, and raised his hands while being interrogated now by both Sven and Viljo.

'You'd better, boy,' Viljo said and let go of Jaaku.

'The moose hunters gave me the rifle,' Jaaku said. 'Börje and Kalle.'

'Why would you take anything from those two idiots?' Viljo snorted. 'Why would you even talk to them?'

'I was an unhappy fisherman. I wanted change. Something new. Something different.'

'I remember you told me,' Sven said.

'Meeting Börje and Kalle made me feel like reborn,' Jaaku opened up. 'I had never won any of the competitions. It's been always Viljo or now you, Sven… and then in the last competition, I ruined everything. I almost drowned half of the best fishermen in town. You have no idea how I felt.'

'I can imagine,' Sven empathised.

'You can't. You don't know what it's like to be… a loser. You've always won. Got what you wanted.'

'I haven't. I lost my father. And Ida.'

'But you got them back, both. You're the luckiest man alive.'

Sven looked away on the moving horizon. He began to feel sea sick, which he never thought he could. But the heights of the waves had reached the level he had never being exposed to before. The lake had had storms, but nothing like they were witnessing today. He squeezed the railing harder. 'Why then… I don't feel like I'm the luckiest man alive?'

'Because you don't appreciate what you have. You have everything. But me instead have always been in the shadow,' Jaaku said. 'So, I met these two hunters and they made me feel special. Hunting made me feel special. I thought I wanted to become a hunter instead and maybe that would be something nobody can take away from me. Not you. Not Viljo. But instead, I ended up ruining everything. Again,' Jaaku whimpered, and sat down leaning against the wall.

'Not true,' Roar interrupted, after having dragged himself behind Sven. 'Sorry, I don't even know your name?'

'Jaaku.'

'I remember you,' Roar nodded. 'As a kid, you always hung around in your parents pie shop stuffing yourself full of pies.'

'A memory that I'm less proud of,' Jaaku looked away.

Roar smiled, his teeth chattering from cold. 'I wanted to say that past is past. Now, we have survived and we can only make the most of it. But first, I'm getting pretty darned cold out here. Are you?'

They all nodded.

'There's a heater in the cabin,' Viljo said and went to switch it on. 'But we have to take turns, because there's not much space. And by the way, one of the windows is broken. It's still better than nothing.' Viljo came outside and gestured Roar and Sven to go in first.

284

Once Roar and Sven settled inside, Roar returned to the conversation through the doorway. 'Nevertheless, Jaaku, what you've done today is something you can be proud of whether you did it intentionally or not. As long as you understand the consequences. You saved my life. Without the manipulation from the hunters that made you act the way you did, I would be long gone. Possibly, all three of you would have wanted to wipe the Lord of Herrings off the nautical charts of Lake Pihtamo.'

'Luckily, Jaaku is such a terrible shooter,' Sven smirked.

'No. As I said, I missed purposely,' Jaaku corrected. 'I wanted the Lord of Herrings to succeed, to empty the lake. That was part of the mission initiated by the hunters.'

'How about killing Mooses then?' Sven asked. 'You were supposed to shoot him for real?'

'I was, but the rifle malfunctioned. So, I guess you're right. I should stay away from firearms.'

'Perhaps this proofs that you're a fisherman no matter what,' Sven said encouragingly.

'I think we all four are,' Roar said. 'There are certain things you cannot change.'

Meanwhile, Viljo pointed at the lake. 'You'd better have a look over there.'

The men turned to look at the horizon. It seemed as if the water level had risen dramatically. Sudden loud and eerie noises started rumbling in the direction of the north shore. Another set of thundery sounds followed, even though the sky was clear.

Sven and Roar came outside as well to get a better look when the horizon began creating a dark blue, rising canvas that approached them alarmingly fast.

'The lake's coming right at us,' Viljo shouted. 'The wave!' he jumped into the cabin, took the wheel and manoeuvred the boat to the opposite direction.

Soon, they raced away being chased by a rolling Arctic tsunami. However, the twenty-metre-high wall of water moved four times faster than the boat's top speed, catching them up life-threateningly. The engine roared and let out extra dark smoke.

'Can't we go any faster!?' Roar yelled and held onto the railings.

Jaaku jumped up and wrapped himself around the remains of the mast pole. Sven hold onto the ropes used to tie the boat on the jetty. Viljo squeezed the wheel knuckles white as the wave grabbed the boat and lifted it up towards the peak like an ascending roller coaster. They smoothly rode on the wave like surfers and dolphins do. As they reached the peak, the water masses rolled over Moose Island they had just been castaway, and where Mooses had hidden himself. The boat went flying over the island as the wave underneath them pulled off trees and bushes. Sven and Roar looked down and thought they saw a glimpse of Mooses's cloak, antlers, and the man himself waving his walking stick, before he was gone in the depths of the tsunami.

'Karma,' Roar said while looking down on the drowning Moose Island and its only known resident.

The watercoaster ride came to its final stretch when the boat begun its descent. Butterflies developed on the men's stomachs as the boat landed on the flat surface of the lake, whereas the wave kept rolling non-stop towards the mainland.

'That was close,' Viljo exhaled in relief.

But the feeling of excitement and thrill suddenly turned into concern as they realised, the enormous wave showed no signs of reducing in size, when it head towards Pihtamo town centre. They had just witnessed an entire island being wiped away in only a matter of few seconds, but how prepared the town's people and the infrastructure were for a tsunami of that magnitude. No one knew since the area hadn't witnessed anything like this before as far as the history records showed.

'Ida. Mum,' Sven whispered with a voice filled with worry.

Chapter 44

# THE WAVE

Christian wished the kiss would never end. Even though, she didn't even respond with her lips. Neither did she resist. She just stood rigid in front of him eyes wide open, partly feeling confused and shocked, and part of her guilty for enjoying the forbidden intimacy between her and an old crush. She knew what they did was wrong. She loved Sven and that was all that mattered. Or should have.

As Ida pulled her lips away and pushed him farther, the whole post office building began to shake vigorously. Some pencils, notebooks and envelopes flew off the shelves on the floor. The windows clattered. The tremor lasted a few seconds and then stopped.

'Did you feel that?' Ida asked, still holding onto Christian.

'Ah, boy, did I? Amazing!' Christian smiled.

'No. I mean... the earthquake?'

'Don't be silly. There are no earthquakes here.'

Marjukka bent down to collect the notes and receipts that had flown off the desk. 'What was that?'

As Christian reached out to hold Ida's hands, even stronger earth movement followed bringing the Christmas tree down on their feet. The living candles decorating the tree set it on fire like a dry forest can lit on a hot summer day. The boiler pot and a tray of cups filled with hot wine fell off the counter, colouring the floor dark purple. Christian and Ida kept their balance by holding onto each other tight, whereas Marjukka fell and slammed the back of her head on the desktop screen.

Outside, Birgget started tapping the outdoor glass with her mitts. The door was still locked. She was trying to tell them something, but it seemed to the people inside as if she only mimed. The triple glass windows insulated not only the coldness but the sounds away, too. She was waving her arms and pointing the opposite direction away from the post office. She pulled the handle, but in vain. She had clearly reached the panic state. She had to get inside. She banged the window now with her fists. Ida clocked her concern and rushed to help, but she couldn't open the door from inside without keys. 'Marjukka!' she yelled and looked behind towards the counter, but couldn't see her anywhere.

'Let me in!' Birgget knocked the door louder and stronger, but her cries remained isolated outside the shop.

Marjukka's hand appeared on the counter from underneath. With her other hand she held her bruised head.

'We need to let Birgget in. She needs to get back inside!' Ida screamed while staring at Birgget through the thick glass. There was terror on her face. Both of their faces. Ida only didn't know what for, whereas Birgget seemed to know something.

Marjukka forced herself up and rushed to the door. She pushed Ida to the side and went through her pockets as the top of her head started to bleed. She pulled out a large set of keys, many different sizes. Panicky, she went through them all. A procedure she had repeated smoothly hundreds of times, every time at the closing time of the shop, but now she struggled to find the right key. Her hands shook. She tried one, and another, but none of them worked. Birgget banged the door harder while yanking the handle up and down.

'What's the matter? It shouldn't be that cold outside.' Marjukka pushed another key into the hole, but the door remained locked. Birgget stared at them behind the glass door as if she was experiencing the end of the world.

'We'll get you in soon, don't worry,' Ida said. 'What is it? A polar bear?' she tried to mimic a large animal by making some mean facial expressions, raising her arms up and curving her hands like they were claws.

But the rumbling noises coming from behind Birgget distracted her to glance over her shoulder. Ida, Marjukka and Christian felt the heightening tremor as well.

'What an earth is that?' Christian said, standing behind the women.

They all looked outside. A high pitched screeching noises as if metal or cars were being crunched became more audible. The loud rumbling sound was accompanied by a towering wall of water. The compound of lake water, ice and rubble quickly filled the high street. The fast moving wave grabbed a hold of kicksleds parked on the pavements, street signs, benches, Christmas decorations and trees in front of the shops and along the streets. The water mass took anything and everything with it and stopped for nothing or no one.

'Water!' Ida screamed, staring through the glass. The wave was heading directly towards the post office.

'I know!' Birgget replied after being able to read Ida's lips.

'Oh, dear Lord...' Marjukka glanced up while attempting to find the right key. Pleading, Birgget turned to look through the glass door at Marjukka who still struggled with the set of keys. Their desperate eyes met. The pressure of the situation made Marjukka drop the keys on the floor.

Ida grabbed the handle and jolted the door back and forth. Christian joined her, but the door was too strong built. It didn't move or open.

'Damn Arctic building standards!' Christian snorted as he manhandled the solid door in vain.

In shock, all three inside the post office saw how the wall of water created a gigantic, dark blue backdrop behind Birgget.

'Run! Run upstairs! Save yourselves!' Birgget screamed, but again her cries were blocked by the thick insulation. Panicky, she glanced around and spotted a row of kicksleds parked on the pavement. The adrenaline rush she was experiencing made her react rationally and fast, rather than shutting down her body functions or mind. She knew this may be the last, the only thing she could ever try before the masses of water and rubble would slam her body against or through the post office walls and windows. She grabbed the nearest, unlocked kicksled and with all her strength lifted it up in the air.

'What is she doing?' Ida gasped, pointing at Birgget who stood upright holding the kicksled above her head like a wrestler holds his or hers opponent on straight arms.

'I think we'd better move out of the way,' Christian said and took Ida to the side.

Marjukka got off the floor after picking up the keys and saw Birgget turning the kicksled front facing the window. 'No! Don't! I think I have the right key now.'

'Step away! She's got a better plan,' Christian repeated firmly, and yanked Marjukka away from the door.

Birgget took a few steps back, and then sped up towards the facade and launched the kicksled against the glass door. The first hit cracked the window from one corner to another, but didn't break it. As she picked up the sled again, her feet started getting wet. She looked over her shoulder. The wave had broken moments before and flattened, but the foamy water masses didn't stop moving. She waded towards the door in the knee high, freezing water. The door started to leak from the bottom. Not even the firmest possible insulation stopped this amount of pressure. Now, as she released the kicksled, it shot through the window and inside the post office shattering the glass into dozens of pieces.

Birgget climbed inside through the window frame while Christian rushed to assist her. She cut her hands in the piece of broken glass left hanging on the frame. She was in Christian's arms now. They all looked outside as the water level kept rising. One smaller wave on top of another advanced.

'Upstairs! Now!' Marjukka ordered. She began wading through and leading the group towards the back of the office. The water entering the building suffocated the fire on the burning Christmas tree and on the presents around it. The envelopes, empty carton packages and other stationery products floated on the soaked floor. Marjukka peered into the stairwell leading upstairs. 'Follow me, if you don't wanna drown,' she said and waded towards the staircase, the others following behind her. A few steps further up they reached safety from the rising water. As they climbed up the steps onto the hallway of the first floor, another tremble knocked them all down. As if the whole structure got off the ground.

The masses of water underneath and around begun to carry the entire post office, turning it into a water raft on its way to the destination unknown. As the building floated away, Marjukka jumped behind one of the doors on the hallway and pulled the set of keys near to the key hole. This time, she found the right key on her first try. She pushed the door open. 'Don't worry about taking your shoes off,' she said and went inside.

Holding the walls on either sides, the others balanced their way through the doorway and followed Marjukka into a small flat. The apartment had already suffered from the sudden impact of the wave. One bookshelf had crashed on the floor together with a flower vase. The water and the soil had spread all over the carpet.

'Who lives here?' Ida asked.

'I do,' Marjukka said with a sadness in her eyes while looking at her messy flat.

'I'm so sorry. This is just horrible,' Birgget said.

'What should we do now?' asked Ida.

'I guess, we just wait,' Marjukka said.

'...and pray,' Birgget added as she stumbled towards the window.

A glass framed painting came crashing down on the floor. 'Let's keep away from the furniture and paintings on the walls,' Marjukka reasoned.

'...and the ceiling lamps,' Christian observed above at swaying chandelier.

Birgget looked outside the window. Another wave slammed against the facade accelerating the building's journey. The water splashed against the apartment window. Another painting fell on the floor. As did the chandelier, too. Christian pulled himself away in the last second. The walls were empty and white now. Miraculously, though, the Christmas tree stayed erect. All the power went off, yet the grey sky shed some light. It was early afternoon, but no signs of the sun yet for another couple of months.

As the building drifted, the group tried to hold onto

whatever they could. Ida and Christian jumped on the sofa embracing each other. Marjukka joined Birgget, and together they held onto the window sill. Physically, the ride had turned into something like a funhouse of an amusement park without any fun and amusement associated with it but only horror.

'There's something wet on the floor,' Christian said and spotted water rushing at his ankles.

They turned to face the door where the water came bursting through the narrow gap underneath. 'The flood water has reached this floor!' Marjukka panicked. 'We must go higher!'

Chapter 45

# AFTERSHOCK

The wave was long gone. Only screeching thunder-like noises rumbled in the distance. Screams of people echoed across the lake. The four men on the boat feared about the scale of damage the impact may have caused and there was nothing they could do about it. Viljo stood in the cockpit and the other three on the deck, all in silence watching the horizon and feeling the helplessness of the situation. The joys of discovering Roar and wiping out Mooses were short-lived as the celebrations turned into the worst horror imaginable.

Gradually, the noises died down as the lake calmed. It became morbidly silent. All the visible landmarks around them including Moose Island where Mooses himself had disappeared, had vanished from the face of Lake Pihtamo, apart from a few pointing tree tops and pieces of ice drifting around them. The water level had risen dramatically. In a few ravaging moments, the lake had become unrecognisable to the most experienced fishermen on the boat. Such a familiar environment for all four men who used to know every island, rock and meadow, had turned into a something that resembled of a vast and flat ocean. The weather calmed. A softly caressing wind cleared the clouds away, yet the sky remained dark. The air was crisp. In more delightful circumstances, the moment could have been even romantic, but the men on board found the catastrophic situation far from magical.

'What was that?' Viljo asked.

'Tsunami?' Roar said.

'There are no tsunami's in Lake Pihtamo,' Sven said.

The men knew the town of Pihtamo had no tsunami or flash flooding alarm systems in place. And everything happened so suddenly, unexpected, hence there were no chance to warn anyone.

Jaaku cleared his throat. 'No, but the possibility exists. The glaciers and the ice bergs on the north shore are fragile. The heavy storm that Mooses created may have broken some of the icy walls. When the large cubes break and hit the water, the impact may cause high tidal waves. We may have just experienced one.' As he spoke out, he started worrying about his parents' pie shop. Luckily, though, the shop as most of the high street stores closed early on Saturdays. But the possible damage caused to the property can be insurmountable. His own and his parents' residence as well were high up on the glaciers which should have been a safe ground. He was mainly concerned about his brother, Aariak, the town sheriff. He may had been on duty when the wave hit. The police station was situated right in the centre of the town.

'The Eskimo may be right,' Viljo said, feeling concerned about his home that he had cherished, built and rebuilt for past fifty years. Only a building it was, yet containing so many memories. The house kept inside an entire human lifespan of experiences: as a safe haven where he married, witnessed wars, raised children, drank, partied, cried, fought, struggled and grew old as a widow to end up on a fishing boat with his worst competitors and a man who he still believed had something to do with the drowning of his brother. Most of the things from the past he wouldn't want to relive, yet the experiences had a sentimental value of invaluable amount. The thought of having lost the best reminder of the past, the house, devastated him. That was all he felt he had. No close family members or that good friends to worry about, but only a house that may have been wiped out by a single wave.

After being gone for sixteen years, Roar feared mostly for the lives of innocent people, including a young woman as he remembered Birgget: his first crush, a girlfriend and then, wife. Unfortunately, though, he believed she had moved on in her life long time ago, perhaps several times. But he hadn't. His time away never changed his feelings for her. But he was certain she would never forgive him for what he did to her, his son and the family. He was certain she had found someone new, but didn't dare to ask Sven about it. He didn't want to know. The life had moved on. He had to accept that. It was such a long time. Everyone had moved on, except him. 'Ida?' Roar asked like cutting the silence with a knife. He turned to look at Sven who stood next to him on the railing staring in the calm horizon. 'Your... girlfriend?'

A sudden question awakened Sven out of his deep thoughts and concerns. 'My wife,' he answered briefly. At the same time, he realised that for Roar he still may be that twelve year old boy. It struck him how his father doesn't know a thing about him as an adolescent or young adult.

Roar looked down at the water. His eyes filled with a mixed expression of joy and sorrow. Joy of his only son finding the true love, and sorrow of missing all those important moments in his son's life of becoming a grown-up man.

'She is amazing. Everything I have. I would do anything for her,' Sven said teary.

Roar raised his arm and gave him a little, awkward pad on the shoulder. He also forced a shy but a proud smile. It was difficult to know how to be with him, with a son that had suddenly grown mature and independent. Sven seemed like an improved version of him as the younger generation are supposed to be anyway. Much more confident, and stronger physically and emotionally what Roar remembered himself to be at Sven's age. Perhaps, it wasn't fully true. Some parents may feel less of themselves while comparing to the faster developing children. He genuinely wished though that the younger generation would learn from history and not repeat the mistakes of the older generation. Roar could only hope and pray Sven not to repeat his mistakes. So far it seemed he hadn't.

'There is one thing I need to know,' Sven said seriously.

'I believe there are many things you want to know... as I do, too. What is it... son?' Roar asked anxiously.

As much as Sven had missed his father all these years, it took some time to get used to hearing someone calling him *son* again. He twinged. 'Well... Roar... How did you become this... the Lord of Herrings... or what was it again you called yourself?'

Roar sighed in relief once he heard the question. For all these years, he had been dying to share the whole story with his loved ones. Finally, he was free to tell the world, and settle the account of what really happened that night and all these years. 'You remember the night I disappeared?'

'How could I forget?'

'That night I ran into Carl, who was my fiercest competitor at the time...'

Viljo heard the key name, his brother's, being pronounced outside. He stopped the boat and left the wheel alone. He began steaming towards Roar and Sven. 'The moment we've all been waiting for!' Viljo rolled up his sleeves.

Roar and Sven looked confused as Viljo stepped between them two. He pushed Sven aside, grabbed Roar by the collar and pushed him against the railing. 'What did you do to my brother? What happened? You killed him!? Didn't you!? Admit!'

Sven bounced back and wrapped his arms around Viljo's neck. But Viljo didn't let go of Roar. He was furious and out of control. Sven jumped on Viljo's back his arms strangling him, while Viljo tried to strangle Roar with his bare hands.

'No! Sven... Viljo...' Roar gasped. 'Let go... I can explain... everything.'

Even though Sven hung around Viljo's neck with his full body weight, Viljo was strong for his age. Like a raging bull, he fought back. For a moment, they wrestled around the deck, until Viljo gave in and collapsed on his knees to the floor. Sven released his hold and stepped next to them like a referee before or after the boxing bout.

Viljo coughed and rolled on the floor, but soon he composed himself, stood up and pointed his blaming finger at Roar. Sven stepped in the middle keeping Viljo and Roar apart.

'Speak up, the Lord of Herrings!' Viljo screamed. 'Now, you tell us every single detail!'

'Fine. May I sit down?' Roar said, panting. 'It's gonna be a one long story.'

'I believe we all have time now,' Viljo glanced at him intensely and then gestured at the vast waters.

'Well, not so much,' Sven said worriedly. 'We must go, find land and look for survivors.'

'Yes, we will. But, first the story. I believe we all want to hear this. You too,' Viljo demanded and looked at Sven.

'Of course I do,' Sven nodded, after being shaken again from Viljo's unpredictability.

Everyone gathered around Roar as he sat down, took a deep breath and began explaining. 'That night me and Carl disappeared, I ran into him by accident. We happened to be leaving around the same time to go fishing. We were the first ones up, way before the so-called best fishing hours.'

'As always,' Sven said and gave a little smile.

'Yes. You're right. That's why I think we were the best at the time. It was mostly about timing.'

'Cut the crap,' Viljo grunted. 'What happened?'

'Well... your brother... Sorry. You don't mind if I go next to the heater again. I'm freezing,' Roar said apologetically.

Viljo shook his head as Roar stepped inside, but kept the door open.

'So, Carl left the shore about ten minutes before me. I let him go. I wanted to keep the distance to him and I am sure he felt the same way towards me. The same happened on the lake once we began fishing. There was a reasonable distance of some hundreds of metres between us. But then I saw Carl catching something really big. Of course I had mixed feelings about that. I was always interested about what others were catching as well. Even though he was my fiercest competitor, I wished him success, too.'

'That is not true. You were afraid of him,' Viljo argued.

'Please. Give him a chance to explain,' Sven said.

'May I tell the story?' Roar demanded.

Viljo nodded.

'So... by that time, I had achieved everything, any accolade you can as a fisherman in Pihtamo. There was no reason for me to have any quarrel with your brother or anyone. Believe it or not, I was tired of winning.'

Viljo sighed in disbelief.

'It could make sense, if it was the other way around.'

'What are you trying to say?' Viljo asked, raising his eyebrow.

'Nothing. I am only saying that I was happy about your brother's success. And I was that night, too, when he was about to catch that enormous fish. But soon what seemed to be the catch of a lifetime turned into a biggest mistake of our lives, mine and Carl's, that eventually took his life, and took me away from my family for all these years. We always pushed ourselves closer to the edge and this time we crossed that limit.'

'What happened?' Sven listened attentively.

'The fish Carl had caught was strong and powerful. He didn't have any control over it, yet his fishing rod was strong enough to last. He was strong, too. So strong, in fact, that he kept drifting around with his boat for good half an hour behind the fish. Physically, Carl was always stronger than me. I admired his physique. The pulling of the fish began to move Carl and his boat across from side to side, even though it was supposed to be anchored. Even the heavy weight of the rock didn't hold the fish. The strangest thing happened when I felt a similar pull on my fishing line that seemed to come from the same source where Carl's line was set. I began to fight back, too. We thought we had hit the jackpot, a school of gigantic herrings of some sort. We were excitedly sharing the moment. For the first time we felt as if we were not competitors, but literally pulling the same cord, or in this case, a line. It became like a team work. Soon, our boats collided and they stayed side by side, yet us doing none of the manoeuvering. All the controlling came from underneath the surface. We thought we were about to capture the biggest catch, but in fact we were the ones being caught. We just didn't know it yet. The pulling of the fishing lines and the rods took us around the lake in circles. We followed, not the fish. The mistake your brother did that he never let go. We were there side by side like in any competition the years before and would have been only weeks after the incident. But this time despite the sensation of working as a team, he really wanted to beat me without realising what we were up against. I let go of the rod my hands cut and bleeding. I simply couldn't hold on anymore. But Carl kept holding his rod hands bleeding and suffering enormous pain. All I could see was blood dripping on his sleeves and the boat seats. I pleaded him to let go, but he didn't. He looked at me, straight into my eyes, first with anger and arrogance that slowly turned into fear and desperation. The fact he never let go cost him his life. He wanted to beat me so bad. The fish yanked him overboard, and in just a matter of few seconds, he had disappeared underwater and never surfaced. Only parts of his life vest did.'

Speechless, Sven, Viljo and Jaaku stood in the doorway as Roar got to the bottom of the tale. After living with all doubts, gossips and speculations, they had finally heard a version from the mouth of someone who was there in person. The story sounded credible and Roar's delivery believable enough for even Viljo not to contest immediately.

'Wolferring really exists?' Sven asked.

'Yes, my son. And Wolferring took Carl's life.'

Viljo's jaw dropped. The answer had come to him, suddenly, after sixteen years of agonising unawareness. His frustration and anger turned into a mixture of sadness and relief.

Even though Sven got his father back, he had to refrain from celebrating too much for Viljo's sake. However, Viljo comforted himself with a thought that when a person goes missing, there's always that glimmer of light and hope shining in the end of the tunnel that the person may be discovered or just turn up on your doorstep one day. As Roar had just now, then why not Carl as well? Nevertheless, a stone fell off Viljo's chest, too. He knew now at least a one version of the story. For so many years he had prepared himself to receive these negative news. The day had arrived. He believed Wolferring might as well as exist, since they had already witnessed the existence of so many mythical creatures no one had ever heard of. He genuinely wanted to believe Roar's explanation, since there was no other story available, apart from the investigators' vague conclusions. Viljo wasn't easy to fool, though, but he trusted Roar had a good, honest heart and soul. He accepted that his brother had been taken to the eternity by doing something he loved so much he was willing to die for. He would have had probably done the same in the same situation. A feeling of grief turned into some form of serenity.

Sven sensed he could open his mouth again. 'What happened to you then?'

Roar sighed and looked away.

'Why you never came back? Why did you... leave me and mum?'

'Okay. Here we go. I saw this coming,' Viljo interrupted. 'That's something I leave you two to sort out, because I think we have a rescue mission ahead, right men?'

'True,' Roar said.

'We have this boat that still seems to work reasonably well, despite all minor damage it may have suffered in the storm,' Viljo pushed past Roar into the cockpit. 'I suggest we go and go now to see what destruction the wave has caused and save whatever there is to be saved.'

Roar stepped outside and joined Sven. They moved to the bow and looked in the direction they believed was the town of Pihtamo.

'I will speak to you later, dad, right?' Sven asked and looked at Roar.

Roar nodded subtly. He kept his eyes firmly on the horizon.

Chapter 46

# UPWARDS

Suddenly, a loud bang echoed and the post office came into halt. Birgget fell on her bottom on the wet floor. Ida rushed to help her back on her feet. As she pulled her upright, they saw water outside the window as far as an eye could see. The water masses had transported the entire building to another location, but finally something ahead blocked its advancement. Everything from sign posts to tree trunks, branches, skis, kicksleds, snow mobiles and ice floated around. Rubble mixed together in a complete disorder. Silhouettes of a few roof tops surfaced in the distance that may have been the town centre where they had departed.

'The end of the world,' Birgget gasped desperately.

The women looked down and saw the current hitting the wall underneath Marjukka's flat. The water wasn't far from entering the flat through the window.

Christian gave a concerned look at the doorway where the water kept rushing inside the flat. Marjukka waded past him in the ankle deep water towards the hallway and the staircase. The flooding had completely filled the ground floor and the stairwell. Her workplace for many years was ruined. Marjukka ran back inside the flat. 'We have to climb further up.'

'Further up? What's there? An attic?' Christian asked.

'The roof... unfortunately,' Marjukka said, and determined, she waded next to the fireplace by the Christmas tree. 'The only problem is that there are no stairs to the roof,' she looked up through the chimney flue, 'so, we have to go through here.'

'But we will freeze outside,' Christian said.

'And we will freeze and drown here,' Marjukka said. 'I have plenty of blankets and warm clothes we can take. But we have to do it fast. We still have some time to save us supplies from my wardrobes and closets before the water reaches them.'

'I guess we have no other choice,' Ida said hesitantly and moved closer to Christian. She grabbed a hold of his arm. A gesture made them seem like a couple to the outsider, which they had been in the past. He turned to look at her where she only responded with a sigh. He felt a warm sensation, whereas she felt awkward and sad. She let go and went to help Marjukka who was going through her wardrobe. They began carrying stuff out on the sofa: woollen mitts, jumpers, blankets, duvets, socks, boots, wellies. Everything more or less thick, warm and woollen. The uncertainty of how long the situation would last made Marjukka pack everything they could possibly carry.

'You can take anything from the kitchen,' Marjukka delegated Birgget.

Birgget rushed to the kitchen with Ida behind her. They located shopping bags from the drawers and began filling them up with food from the fridge and the cupboards. They took plates, cutlery and cups. They even emptied most of the freezer hoping that the food items would survive outside in the coldness.

Christian joined to assist Marjukka with packing the clothing and blankets into her suitcases and bags. The water reached their knees now. 'We must go!' Marjukka ordered as she zipped up the last, bursting suitcase.

'Shall I go first?' Christian said and pointed at the fireplace.

'What a gentleman!' Marjukka snorted.

'I mean, if I can fit my shoulders through, then we all do. And it's probably the best that I'm there reeling you ladies up one by one. If you give me a piece of rope, I can drop it down for you once I'm up there.' Christian bent down and pushed his head to the chimney pipe. 'Looks... dark.'

'Well, that is the only way,' Marjukka reasoned.

'Great,' Christian said sarcastically and grabbed the rope. He leaped onto the fireplace that was still dry while being protected by sidewalls, normally, meant to keep the sparks away from flying to the carpet and beyond. He gave another glance at the group before disappearing inside the chimney flue. With his leather gloves he tried to hold onto the inside walls. He could see the dark sky and a few early bright stars appearing above. He thought this is what action or superheroes must feel like. However, the stunts he had seen performed in the movies seemed much more effortless than his painfully slow ascent.

Halfway up the chimney, his hand slipped, releasing the other end of the rope straight down in the fireplace, nearly hitting Marjukka's face who was peering up the flue. Luckily, he held the other end of the rope with his one hand while his other hand and both feet were firmly glued to the walls like suctions cups.

'Are you there, yet? Can we start climbing? Is the rope secure?' Marjukka asked nervously and softly yanked the rope.

'Don't touch the rope!' Christian's voice echoed.

'I guess not yet,' Marjukka spread her arms and looked apologetically to Ida and Birgget behind her.

Christian wrapped the end of the rope around his wrist and kept on ascending. A few more pushes lead him closer to the roof. He reached out his arm on the edge of the crown. He pulled himself up and leaped on the roof where the chaotic view truly opened up and struck him. He spun around. The waters were around him three hundred and sixty degrees with a few visible roof and tree tops. Rubble was scattered all around. Once the safe haven, a quiet Arctic village, had suddenly turned into a catastrophic area. He rubbed his eyes as he couldn't believe the sight. Nor did slapping his cheeks or pinching help. The view remained the same, a nightmare where he never woke up.

'Are you still there?' Ida's voice echoing through the chimney pipe brought Christian back from the shock to reality. He felt pulling on the rope that was still tied around his wrist. He untied the rope and tied it around the masonry instead.

'Who's next?' Marjukka looked at Ida being the closest. Ida nodded hesitantly.

Ida went up flying with Christian's assistance from the top.

She was a light weight to handle. Motivation played a big part as well for him to get her up as fast as possible. Christian reached for her hand, put his other hand on the arch of her back and raised her from the chimney flue in his arms. She felt like a feather to him. Her nose and cheeks were black from soot that made her even cuter in his eyes.

'Thank you,' Ida said shyly as his firm, but gentle hand caressed her lower back and neck area. 'You can drop me down now, please.'

Christian did as she requested and lowered her on the roof.

'Oh, dear Lord!' Ida gasped, after releasing her eye contact from Christian and realising the level of destruction around them. She broke into tears. The seriousness of the situation finally struck her. And the immediate concern and question over the destiny of the most important person to her, Sven. *Where is he?*

She sought for consolation from Christian being the nearest. They embraced tightly.

'The water is really filling up this place! We need to get up!' Marjukka's desperate voice from downstairs interrupted them.

She let go of him and just stood there staring in the distance. She tried to let it sink in, but it was impossible. Too soon, too much. The dark afternoon made the sight even more disturbing. All the street and shop lights were gone. The only dim light came from the outer space above. The surface of the lake was messy and the waves hit from all directions. Ida's heart jumped, again, when Christian came standing behind her and put his hands on her waist. 'What do you think you're doing!?'

'I'm sorry, but... I need the rope back.'

'Ah. Of course,' Ida looked down and touched her hair gently.

He untied the rope from her waist while caressing her hips and lower back. 'Thank you,' Christian whispered in her ear.

Ida gave her an odd look. As Christian stepped away from her, the sensation of horror completely took over when faced with the vast waters.

Birgget was the next one to come up bringing supplies with her. Marjukka sent the rest of the necessities they thought they

would need for survival before herself ascending. She left a bitter and heart-breaking goodbyes to her flooding home. She glanced around the living room for the very last time. So many important things and sentimentally valuable objects she couldn't rescue: old photo albums, souvenirs from family members and friends, letters from ex-boyfriends and lovers. An entire history of a small, average adult human being wiped away in a few minutes. The moment made her, one person, feel so miniscule and worthless against the nature that will take what it would need without asking.

Once Marjukka had completed the outward journey on the roof, they all stood in silence for a moment just staring at the vastness of the lake. No one knew what to say or where to start. Although the adrenaline rushing their veins made them all momentarily forget the pains and coldness. They were all just dumbstruck by the sight they wished they never had to witness.

'What shall we do next?' Christian made an attempt to break the tension.

'I guess... we just wait,' Marjukka said.

Chapter 47

# NAVIGATIONAL DISPUTE

'I'm afraid I have some bad news,' Viljo stuck his head out of the cabin window after steering the boat in circles for hours.

'What could be any worse than this?' Sven snorted.

'The navigation system is out of order.'

'Do we need one?' Roar said from beside Sven.

'Look around yourself,' Viljo said. 'There really are no landmarks left to follow. I used to know these waters by heart.'

'Me too,' Sven said.

'True,' Roar added. 'It's too dark even to recognise the mountains in the distance.'

'Exactly. And the low lying clouds don't help at all,' Viljo said and pulled his head inside. He took the map out and placed it against the dashboard. The sound of paper crumpling got Roar and Sven curious. They squeezed themselves to the cabin doorway when Viljo pressed his finger on the map. 'This is the island where Mooses first appeared and then got taken by his own wave.'

'Okay,' Sven took a step inside the narrow cabin. 'But we must have drifted kilometres away from there.'

'We may have, but let's assume not quite that far away,' Viljo said. 'Logically, we should have travelled along with the wave towards the town centre.'

'Why don't we navigate following the stars?' Roar suggested.

Viljo and Sven turned to Roar, curiously listening.

'As the Lord of Herrings...' Roar coughed, 'I usually drifted around this lake at night time in a complete darkness to avoid being seen. While doing so, I develop a skill to find my way around by looking at the stars. I had no modern equipment like now you have in this boat.'

'Modern equipment which doesn't work?' Sven smirked.

'Hey kid, because of this boat we're all still here and alive!' Viljo barked. 'Think if we had taken your tiny little dinghy, we would be long gone.'

'Do you two wanna argue or hear me explain?' Roar sighed.

'We have to wait for the clouds to clear out first before we can see any stars,' Sven said.

'You can see some of the stars even now,' Roar said and looked up at the sky. 'If you first locate the Plough or the saucepan or however you wanna call it... which is right there... and then you look at the two stars on the right edge where you would normally pour the sauce. Right below that bottom star is the north... or in fact, the direction towards the North Pole.'

'Good, dad.'

'Fine,' Viljo said. 'So, let's assume the star Roar explained is north and based on that knowledge we keep that star to our left, we should be heading east where the town centre is located.'

Sven turned around and stepped away from the cabin.

'What should we set as our priority then?' Roar asked, clocking Sven's discontent. 'Saving the town or finding individual residences of people we... or one of us may know?'

'Well, don't ask me,' Jaaku interrupted, standing behind Roar on the stern. 'All my family live up on the mountains and the glaciers. I'm hoping they'd all be safe. Also my parents' pie shop was closed when the wave hit. Most of the shops in the town centre were supposed to be closed early anyway, except the pub and the church, I think.'

'What about your brother?' Viljo asked.

'I just remembered he doesn't work on the weekend's anymore, since his daughter, my niece, was born.'

'I have no preference either which direction to start heading,' Viljo said. 'I have just an old house filled with old, useless junk. If that's gone, then it's a big shame. I have no one in particular I have to save. Just anyone, really.'

All eyes turned to Sven as he stood alone at the bow. He felt the stare at his back.

'What's your opinion, Sven?' Roar asked.

'Does it matter?' Sven said.

Viljo came out of the cabin. 'Your house is not far from the town centre, right?'

'What are you trying to say?' Sven said and turned to face the men. 'That we should head to town? I thought we have already done our duties here. And enough damage as well. We found out that the Lord of Herrings is my father. And he's alive. We found out what happened to your brother. Sad news. We're sorry about that. Why don't we all just go home? This was not supposed to be a rescue mission. We are done here. Besides, my house is quite far from the centre, but not sure if far enough.'

'Since we were all partly responsibility of what has happened, the least we can do now is to help the others,' Roar said.

'What do you mean by "all?"' Viljo asked, showing discontent.

'Perhaps, this disaster could have been prevented by dealing with Mooses in a different way, more diplomatic manner,' Roar suggested.

'Hold on, Mr Lord!' Viljo grunted, pointing his finger at Roar. 'You're the one who started this! Your crazy idea to empty the lake of fish!'

'The fish are all safe,' Roar said calmly, 'in a better place.'

'The fish are still alive?' Sven asked.

'My... I mean, when I was under the spell, my intentions were genuinely good. All the fish I caught, I only saved them from the lethal claws of Wolferring.'

'Where are the fishes now then?' Viljo asked eagerly.

'I will show you once all this is over. But now I do think that we should aim to rescue as many survivors as we can. There may not be many other boats around. Not to point fingers on anyone in particular, but our actions have partly caused the tsunami and we are survivors with a decent sized boat. It would be stupid and selfish not to head to the direction we believe have the most population affected. Sven, I understand your concern over Ida and Birgget, but for the sake of the community…'

Viljo looked at Roar suspiciously as he explained. He still felt discomfort in his presence.

'You do as you wish,' Sven said, leaned on the railing and stared far in the horizon towards the direction he believed his house was on the south coast.

'What should we do?' Viljo asked openly from everyone.

'As long as we find land,' Jaaku said.

'I have shared my opinion. We have the stars to guide us,' Roar said, left the doorway and joined his son at bow.

Viljo restarted the engine and randomly took a direction he felt the most comfortable with.

'The problem is not the house, but… who's in it, am I right?' Roar asked and put his hand on Sven's shoulder.

'You're right. I left Ida there last night when I departed on this journey. And I didn't even say goodbyes. I just left doors banging and slightly upset. She didn't want me to leave. And she was right. I shouldn't have.'

'Don't say that. We found each other.'

'We did indeed,' Sven said and gave Roar a little smile.

'And your mother? I mean, Birgget. Where does she live nowadays?'

'She lives north of the town, which doesn't make this any easier. Every one of us comes from different parts of Pihtamo.'

Roar rolled his eyes. 'Now I understand your reaction. Do you think we're making a mistake?'

'It's one or the other. The family or the community. We can't have it all. Don't worry. I have learned that early in life.'

'I'm sorry. What do you think we should do? Really?'

Sven took a deep breath. 'I never thought I'd say this, but… let's just find land. We look up on the sky, follow the stars and aim to town. As you said, we have to think of a greater good and pray for our loved ones.'

'Are you sure?'

'No. But I have spent most of my life on the water and now suddenly I feel like I miss land, soil, green grass, trees, even the wildlife, birds singing. I feel so distant from everyone, everything. Look at the horizon, just water everywhere. It's like

Lake Pihtamo has turned into an ocean. I'm not a seaman.'

'Me neither. I agree with you, son. I have missed land for all these years and I would like to come home, but at the same time, I know the place I used to call home doesn't exist anymore.'

'The place is still there. Has always been. Not perhaps as you remember it, but there is home for you. We have just plenty of catching up to do.'

'Alright, gentlemen,' Viljo raised his voice over the roaring engine. 'Have we made up our minds?'

Sven and Roar looked at each other. Both nodded and then Roar said, 'Viljo, we respect you being the oldest and the most experienced on board. Therefore, feel free to navigate to your best understanding. If you want to follow my method of looking at the stars, be my guest. I would appreciate that. And I am happy to assist you with that. However, if you want to use the map or any other method you may find more efficient, I won't contest you. As long as we find land, eventually. Nonetheless, as a good citizen, I think our responsibility is to rescue anything or anyone along the way. You have our mandate.'

Roar's clear and precise response silenced Viljo. The announcement wasn't quite what he expected. He processed the answer for a moment until nodding hesitantly. He looked at Jaaku who responded showing only thumbs up.

Instead of feeling a sense of relief once being granted a full navigation responsibility, pressure began to crawl up on Viljo. The expectation was laid upon him. Now, he just had to do what he felt was right.

Chapter 48

# SLEEPING ROUGH

It had become the darkest time of the year, the day of the Winter Solstice. Ida sat up on the yoga mattress observing the calm, flooded lake with all the rubble floating around. Christian had fallen asleep beside her. Birgget lay under a thin feather duvet staring at the sky. Marjukka was already up standing on the edge of the roof. She peered towards the town. Or where she believed it was. The moon and the stars gave them some light from between the clouds. The post office had shifted some hundreds of metres from its original position, whereas the rest of the town not so much, if not at all. Luckily, they had been in one of the tallest buildings in Pihtamo at the time the wave hit.

It was as if Marjukka recognised the silhouette of the church spire, the tallest structure in town, rising above the water. She believed the church was exactly where it had been for last couple of hundred years since the day it was built. The quality of the structures constructed in the good old times couldn't be beaten even by tsunami waves. All one-storey high buildings had drowned, though, no matter if young or old.

'I think the water level has stopped rising,' Marjukka said and walked to the chimney pipe. She nodded as she looked down the flue.

'Everything okay?' Ida asked.

'Could someone please lower me down again? Christian?' Marjukka said, walked to him and tapped his arm.

'What? Now?' Christian mumbled and turned his side.

'Yes. I have some more things downstairs that we can use. The water can't be deeper than waist-high in my apartment.'

'It's freezing water,' Christian said.

'I'll be quick.'

Christian turned to Marjukka and opened his tired eyes. 'If anyone goes back down, that's me.'

'I appreciate that, but don't worry. It's my apartment. I know the best what and where to look for. I'll be fine,' Marjukka said and chucked the end of the rope on Christian's lap. She tied the other end around her waist and went to wait by the chimney.

Christian gave Marjukka a concerned look, shook his head and kissed Ida on the cheek.

'Why did you do that for?' Ida looked puzzled.

'Erm... just to wish you good morning,' Christian smiled a little and stood up.

'I wouldn't call this a "good" morning,' Ida snorted and wiped the moist but warm kiss off her cheek.

'I'm sorry. I meant, it could be worse,' Christian said and grabbed the other end of the rope.

'How could this be worse!?'

'Well... at least, we have each other. You know...' Christian mumbled.

'Right,' Ida stood up and walked away to the opposite corner.

Christian stood up, confused, and went to tie the rope around the masonry. He took a firm grip of the rope between Marjukka and the chimney pipe. Marjukka leaped over the edge and began lowering herself down the pipe towards the fireplace while Christian made sure the rope was secure. As she reached the apartment, the fireplace had flooded, too. The spark protectors hadn't kept the water masses away anymore. She sunk her lower body in the water while observing the destruction in the flat. Her heart was broken. She sobbed as she waded through the living room. Only the things above the waistline on the cupboards and wardrobes had survived the water damages. She opened one of the closets, rescued another woollen blanket and a couple of pillows. She tied them on a rope and sent up to Christian. She moved on towards the kitchen and grabbed some of the intact food items.

She packed them in bags and sent up as well.

'How about the Christmas tree?' Christian's voice echoed from above.

'Are you crazy!?' Marjukka snorted.

'In case we end up staying up here longer, maybe we can... spruce up things a little bit,' Christian said and looked at Ida.

'You must mean... spice up?' Marjukka said.

'That as well. It could be nice.'

Despite the water starting to freeze the bottom half of Marjukka's body, the idea made her smile. She liked it. She waded next to the half sunken Christmas tree. She got a hold of the trunk, raised it above her head and carried it by the fireplace. She flipped the tree upside down and tied a knot around the thicker bottom part of the trunk. She figured the tree would be easier to pull up the bottom first, letting the branches bend in the direction of the growth. She hailed Christian and up the tree travelled, a few wet needles sprinkling down the flue. Marjukka went to pick up a few of the Christmas presents floating in the water. She put the presents in the big carry bags and sent up to Christian. Pointless, perhaps, since soaking wet and ruined they were, *but better than no presents at all.*

'Who has ever celebrated Christmas on the roof?' Christian said, trying to lighten up the mood, as the Christmas tree appeared at the end of the rope. He flipped the tree upright.

Birgget stood up and said, sarcastically, 'Not yet... and I hope I never have to.'

'Don't be so negative, Birgget,' Ida said. 'He's only trying to cheer us up.'

'Exactly,' said Christian. 'We can try and celebrate a little, in case we end up staying here longer.'

'Celebrate!? For what?' Birgget snorted. 'My son, her husband is out there and we don't know where or if he's still even alive... and you want to party? And what about us? Besides, Christmas is three days away. I wish we'll be out of this roof by then.'

'I'm sorry, ma'am. I didn't mean to upset anyone,' Christian said.

'Please, Birgget. It was just a nice, genuine thought from him,' Ida said.

'You two have fun decorating your lovely tree then,' Birgget sighed, turned her back and moved to the corner edge of the roof. She looked away thoughtfully.

Christian shook his head. He heard Marjukka calling at the other end. He jumped on the rope and pulled. 'Look! There's presents, too.'

Ida stepped closer to Christian and hushed him pressing her finger on his lips. She gave him a little notch before moving towards Birgget. She went to stand right behind Birgget. 'I know the men are out there somewhere... safe. I can feel it.'

'Can you? Really?' Birgget asked doubtfully. 'When Roar disappeared, I also thought I knew lots of things. I waited, believed in miracles... which just never happened. There are no miracles in this life. It's just hard, cold facts. Life is not easy.'

'Sven is young and strong,' Ida said.

'Now, pull me up!' Marjukka's scream came from the chimney. 'I'm getting really cold and wet here.'

Once Christian felt the weight on the rope, he started assisting her ascent. As she got back on the roof, she hid herself behind the chimney pipe to change her wet clothes and dry herself with a towel. Her lips had turned blue. She was shaking.

Christian picked up a thick, woollen blanket and went to wrap Marjukka inside it whilst taking her into a full embrace. The colour of her lips began to return back to normal and she stopped shaking. She pressed her head against Christian's chest and calmed down. A single tear drop fell from her eye on his overcoat.

Ida glanced over her shoulder and saw Christian and Marjukka having their moment.

'Roar was once young too,' Birgget returned to the conversation with Ida. 'You have no idea. I thought he was a... demigod. Everyone wanted to be like him. People loved him. Every man wanted to beat him, too. He had enemies as well, because he was so good. The best. But then once he disappeared, a few days waiting turned into weeks, weeks turned into months, months into years. I found myself thinking less and less about him as each day passed by, yet, never forgetting. One day, after so many years, I woke up in the morning not having had any nightmares about his disappearance or any thoughts about him the first thing in the morning. I felt so light. A little bit guilty, too. As if I had accepted his drowning, his death. Finally. It was a relief, but a sad one.'

Ida stared to the same direction as Birgget. She felt teary. 'Why are you saying these things?'

'Don't worry. It's just me. I used to be like you. I can see myself in you. So positive, full of hope, everything still ahead, a little bit naïve sometimes. I don't want to take that... innocence away from you.'

'Then, don't,' she sobbed. 'I don't want you to... prepare me for anything. Or patronise.'

'No. I just want you to know that life is difficult. The long life has made me such a realistic.'

'There's always hope.'

Birgget didn't respond. She only stared in the distance with her tired eyes.

Ida waited for a few moments in silence, but since nothing happened or more was said, she turned away. She went to open one of the boxes Christian had just pulled up. The box was filled with Christmas decorations. Meanwhile, Marjukka let go of Christian. She gave him a satisfied smile before stepping away and giving room for Ida and him to start "sprucing up" the tree.

Chapter 49

# ROAR'S STORY

Occasionally, tree tops, or something, hiding underwater scratched and knocked the bottom of the boat. Viljo had taken the direction, he believed, where the town centre was. Roar snoozed on a seated position against the outside cabin wall. He had wrapped himself in a thick rescue blanket. He looked wizened. A long, solitaire struggle on the lake as the Lord of Herrings had taken its toll.

Sven observed his sleeping father who had aged more than he would have ever expected. It was hard to tell, though. At least, when spending time together with the loved ones on a daily or weekly basis, the aging process can go unnoticed while the eye adjusts, whereas a break of sixteen years felt like a time warp. Distant memories and a few old photographs where Roar looked at his prime had glorified the image Sven had of him. For the first time, Sven felt the balance between them two might have shifted to him, a son, being physically more capable. Whenever Sven saw his father's return in his wildest dreams, he was always meeting a young, strong person he was at the time of the disappearance. Now though, in front of him, was almost totally another man. A shadow of the glorified memory. An old, weak and malnourished man. Somebody that resembled more of Roar's own father as Sven remembered him as an elderly, his now late grandfather.

'Dad,' Sven said, poking Roar on the shoulder.

Roar opened his swollen eyes a little.

'You know there's one more thing I wanted to ask you.'

'I know,' Roar muttered and closed his eyes again.

'Why? Why, dad?'

'It's a long story,' Roar said.

'We have time now. All the time in the world.'

'Where should I begin?' Roar opened his eyes.

'Is it really true what happened on the lake sixteen years, two months and five days ago?

'You remember,' Roar said, stunned, 'precisely?'

Meanwhile, Viljo pushed his head closer to the window to hear a glimpse of the serious sounding conversation between Sven and Roar. There were still many facts and details he was uncertain or unaware of. He also yearned for more answers.

'I have been waiting every day for you to return,' Sven said.

Roar's eyes lightened. 'Well, here I am.'

'Nothing is worse than the unknown, not knowing what, where and why? There were no signs, no clues, nothing where to begin the search, apart from Carl's boat. Everything was just blank, emptiness. As if you were abducted by the aliens.'

'Sometimes I did feel like I had an encounter of the third kind,' Roar smirked and looked up. He tried to remember the events in the right order as they unfolded. There were so many years in between. 'For me it was just a normal fishing trip like any I had done hundreds or thousands of times before. That night, I had already caught dozens of normal fishes. Salmon, pike, lots of herrings... until that one herring,' Roar said, his voice turning serious and face grave.

'Wolferring?'

'Correct. After it took Carl underwater, I jumped behind him and tried to rescue him. I saw Wolferring eye to eye. It's furry coat. Long and sharp claws. Thick sideburns. Fortunate for me, not for Carl, its mouth was already full. While I was trying to climb back up on the boat...' Roar said and leaned over his right foot and pulled the trouser hem up to reveal a wooden leg.

'It bit your... leg off!' Sven gasped and looked away.

'Unfortunately.'

'I had no idea,' Sven sighed and turned back to Roar. 'There was no one around to help you? No one heard your scream?'

'No. You remember I always went fishing earlier than anyone else.'

'Not really.'

'Of course you don't. You were always sleeping that early.'

'Sure. Too early for a young fisherman.'

'More like a fisherboy,' Roar corrected. Sven tried to smile, but couldn't stop staring at his father's artificial leg. Roar noticed Sven's shocked expression. He pulled the trouser hem back down. 'So, while Wolferring took out Carl, I panicked and climbed to the closest boat possible, and that happened to be his Yolla. Once Wolferring was finished with Carl, it got absolutely mad and tried to eat me. It began chewing Carl's boat where I was hiding. That's where the scratch marks on the sides come from... and possibly my DNA. I spent a fair amount of time on his boat with the stump left of my leg bursting blood all over the floor and the seats, giving the impression there had been a struggle between me and him. And since it was his boat where this all happened, it must have seemed I had attacked him. But it was just me alone struggling for life. Gladly, though, Carl's hard plastic dinghy was too tough to chew, even for Wolferring, who eventually gave up. I assume it hurt its teeth or something. Anyhow, once it got silent and I thought Wolferring was gone, I leaped back onto my boat. Neither of the boats had oars left, but I decided to stay in mine as I had all my gear there. After a while I began to feel very weak since I was losing blood constantly. At some point, I must have fainted, until I woke up on the banks of River Pihtamii.'

'That's hundreds of kilometres away!'

'Four hundred and something. I woke up inside a Teepee of this local, indigenous tribe and their village. A local medical healer guru was giving me some herbs, berries and reindeer meat. They also made me drink this yellow liquid that afterwards I thought might have been reindeer's urine.'

'Hope not!'

'I was so thirsty, hungry and weak that I didn't care. I was ready to eat and drink anything they gave me. And they took good care of me. They even made me my first wooden leg.'

Sven nodded. His eyes widened in disbelief. 'What... an amazing story.'

'You don't believe me?'

'Well, I do...' Sven said, eyes wondering. 'But I still don't understand why you never came back? Back to us? Your family?'

'Fair enough. I thought people wouldn't believe me as I feel is still happening right now.'

'I do... believe you.'

Roar looked at Sven with a suspicion. 'There was a moment of hesitation there.'

'Sixteen years ago I would have believed you straight away. Mum, too. If you'd come back immediately, tell the story the way it was, that would have been different. But sixteen years is a long time.'

'Really? You would have believed my story that a monster fish suddenly appeared in the most peaceful lakes, probably, in the whole wide world, to drown my fiercest competitor who would have very likely taken my title only weeks after the incident.'

'There are also other monsters like... Loch Ness?'

'I doubt Loch Ness really exists,' Roar snorted. 'Besides, at the time I was not in my best shape for fishing. I had been neglecting training. I had become too confident and comfortable with all those championships. Carl would have beaten me, no question about that. The whole town knew that he was on a top form and I wasn't. Even the betting odds were against me. The people of Pihtamo, the fishing community, the fans, everyone was yearning for a new champion. But there was no trace of him left, apart from his boat that was filled with scratch marks and my blood stains. I even took his gear with me once he was gone in case I needed supplies. At the time, if I'd turn myself in, people would have slaughtered me. A jealous champion ready to do whatever it takes to keep himself in number one position. Even willing to kill his contender.'

'Even willing to lose his leg?'

'Carl always carried an axe on his boat. He often axed the fish once he caught them.'

'Sounds like a very unusual method.'

'It was not unusual at all twenty, thirty years ago. Viljo was well aware of this. They would have brought this up against me that Carl had acted in self-defence against me trying to drown him. During the struggle, he sliced off my leg and I sunk him underwater. After, I had nicked his gear and ran away.'

'And they never discovered his body.'

'Exactly. I knew straight away when I saw Wolferring's fierceness that they may never discover Carl's body. I would have been accused of getting rid of it.'

'But there was no real evidence against you. You were innocent.'

'It doesn't matter. There was enough evidence to have a believable theory, a conclusion. The public, and especially, the media would have loved the story. Nothing exciting ever happened in Pihtamo and still doesn't, I presume. It would have been sensational, if they caught me. I would have had no future in Pihtamo. I would have had to flee and the family, too. There must have been quite a few gossips in town against me, am I right?'

Sven falling silent confirmed Roar that he was not completely wrong.

Roar nodded subtly.

'I could have ran away with you,' Sven said.

'No. Neither you nor your mother. You don't like change anyway. You never did when you were a child. And look at you now. You're still here in Pihtamo. You have never left.'

Sven didn't say anything, instead, he looked away knowing Roar was right again.

'Besides, when I became under the spell, which again is another story, I felt I had a mission and a responsibility that without completing, I had no business to return home. And I didn't. I was in another world.'

Sven gave a confused nod, while Viljo on the other side of the wall felt the serenity creeping in again. The story made sense as unbelievable it may have sounded like. Wolferring's existence was confirmed now by many resources, not only by Roar. Viljo himself may have had Wolferring caught up on the bait, while they found the Venezuelan Herring.

Viljo stepped back behind the wheel.

'Land! I can see land!' Jaaku screamed from the top of his lungs while peering through the telescope.

Chapter 50

# SPRUCING UP

'Is everything alright between you and Birgget?' Christian whispered to Ida as he leaned over to grab more decoration out of the box.

'Don't worry. She has her past as we all know,' Ida said while raising a bauble on one of the top branches. As she stretched her arm, her bare left hand revealed the wedding ring.

Christian spotted the glow. 'You would have at least deserved a proper ring,' he smirked, agitated.

'Please, Christian,' Ida sighed and pulled the hand away inside her pocket. 'I am really sorry that things didn't work out between you and me.'

'We could still make it work,' Christian said quietly and moved closer to her. He took some silver ribbon and wrapped it around Ida's waist.

'Just friends, right?' Birgget snorted from the opposite corner. 'This is a large rooftop, but not that large. Behave yourselves, kids.'

Ida rolled her eyes and manoeuvred Christian behind the tree to gain some privacy. 'What do you think you're doing?' she whispered, holding his arm in one hand and another bauble in the other.

'What?'

'We've been just hit by a tsunami and you... I'm with Sven now. We are married.'

'But... what kind of man gives his bride herring on the wedding day?'

'We all make mistakes.'

'I doubt that's the only mistake he has made.'

'Nobody is perfect. Besides, you know nothing about him,' she said defensively.

'There's so much you don't know about me, either. It's been such a long time since us two really dated. I have changed. Grown. So much good has happened. Look. I am even here protecting you and your family.'

'Us trapped here together is a pure coincidence,' she said with a growing suspicion and anger. 'Or is it!? Did you follow me here to the post office yesterday?'

'No...' Christian said and looked down to the roof.

'And please, I really don't need any reminders from you or anyone else that my husband is not here. That he might be somewhere... drowned! Is that what you want!?'

'I'm sorry,' he said, trying to touch her shoulder, but she pulled away. 'I didn't mean it like that. I just thought we had a good thing going on. I like you very much and I thought you liked me, too.'

'I think you're great, but...' she sobbed, 'me and Sven are meant to be together.'

'Whatever you say,' Christian said, came around the tree, leaned over to another box and picked up a candle set.

'And I am...' Ida started, keeping herself tucked away hidden behind the tree. Christian could hear her weak voice through the branches. She rubbed her stomach.

'What are you?' he asked and waited her to speak.

'Nothing,' she hesitated. 'Let's just finish decorating this tree and... have a jolly time,' she said sarcastically and wiped the few tears off her cheeks.

Christian obeyed, and soon the tree began to look more festive. Once they picked up the last ribbons out of the box and began wrapping them around the tree, a male voice echoed in the distance. 'Is there anyone out there who can hear us!?'

The group on the roof top froze. They looked around to all different directions, but saw only darkness. Accidentally, Ida's hand slapped a bauble off the branch, smashing it broken on the roof. Marjukka jumped up next to Birgget. Slowly, all four survivors huddled closer together while glaring ahead in the direction they believed the voice came from. But they could only recognise shades of the church spire and one roof top - which they believed was the Arctic Bar, one of the few two-storey high buildings in the centre. Apart from that, a few tree tops together with a couple of broken street lamp posts had remained standing and visible above the surface.

'Hello!' the same male voice repeated. 'Anybody?'

'Hello!' Marjukka replied.

'We are here... on the roof of the Arctic Bar,' the male voice said.

Christian turned to the ladies and smiled. 'Seems like we're not alone.'

More positive vibes spread amongst the survivors. Hearing other voices gave them hope. As if they were one step closer to the end of this horrific episode in their lives.

'Who is there?' Marjukka yelled out.

'It's Aariak, the town sheriff.'

'And Tomas from the bar,' another male voice joined in. 'Who is there?'

The four shouted out their names in turns.

'Have you got any supplies?' Marjukka asked.

'We have... twenty bottles of Wodka,' Tomas replied.

'Anything else?' Marjukka rolled her eyes. 'Anything warm?'

'I managed to take a couple of reindeer skins from the bar seats before we rushed upstairs and onto the roof,' Tomas added.

'We cannot see you,' Birgget said.

'We cannot see you, either,' Aariak said. 'It seems like the post office drifted quite far away. All new buildings seem to have shifted. The Arctic Bar is an older structure and therefore remained in its original position. As did the church, naturally.'

'Can you see any other survivors?' Marjukka asked.

'There weren't that many people, if anyone else, in town when the wave hit,' Aariak said. 'The only places open were the post office and the bar. And even the bar was just closing. I was the last customer. Or, well... I only came to check everything was fine here at the bar,' he added, embarrassed to admit he had actually stopped for a few at the bar while on duty.

Tomas smiled and nodded next to him.

'Thank goodness for that,' Ida said.

'How are you coping there?' Tomas asked.

'We are...' Christian looked at the ribbon he still held in his hand, 'decorating a Christmas tree.'

Tomas and Aariak looked at each other and rolled their eyes.

'And how about you?' Marjukka asked.

'I guess we'll just have to wait and hope someone will find us,' Aariak said. 'That's all we can do here.'

'And if it gets too cold, start drinking those bottles,' Tomas added. 'It's all on the house now.'

'Wodka sure does keep you warm,' Christian said and threw the last ribbon around the tree.

There was no answer.

Chapter 51

# MORE WEASELS

To men's disappointment, the sighting Jaaku had earlier called 'land', only turned out be a tight group of spruce and pine tree tops growing densely together above the surface. There probably was land of some sort, but somewhere deep underwater. Viljo slowed down once the bottom of the boat started hitting unfamiliar objects again. The familiar waters had become an unknown hazard zone even to the most skilled navigators. He turned off the engine and let the boat drift closer to the trees that now seemed more like a mangrove growing in the middle of the vast lake. There were no birds or owls singing, though. It was dead silent apart from the branches rustling and an occasional pine cone splashing on the water. The men observed the trees if there were any signs of life, any survivors, people hanging onto them, until they spotted three stoats sitting on the branches.

'Isn't that one in the middle, Erm...ine?' Jaaku said.

'Erm...ine?' Sven repeated.

Roar gave both Sven and Jaaku confused looks.

Viljo slowed down and swerved the boat colliding to the tree. The three stoats held on tighter as their trunk shook. Viljo looked outside. 'It sure is Erm...ine.'

'You must mean, ermine?' Roar asked.

'No. Or, we're not quite sure. Anyway, she calls herself Erm...ine,' Sven explained, 'with the pause in the middle.'

'That is the craziest thing I've ever heard,' Roar said baffled.

'Says a man dressed up in a wizard's outfit,' Viljo snorted, 'shooting laser beams off his magic rod.'

Viljo's witty remark silenced Roar.

'Most of tonight's events don't really make any sense anyway, except in some loony cartoon world,' Sven said.

'H-h-hello, my... dear f-f-friends!' Erm...ine interrupted the men while being a little shaken from the collision.

Roar stared at the stoat mouth wide open and then he looked at the other men.

'What's wrong, dad?' Sven asked.

'It's just that...' Roar muttered.

'What?' Viljo snorted. 'How can you be so shocked, the Lord of Herrings? You must have seen this and that.'

Roar sighed and looked at the trees, where Erm...ine stood on a separate branch from the other two stoats. She jumped on a lower branch, then on another, and in the end, on the boat deck.

'Erm... How good... to s-s-see you a-a-all!' Erm...ine said and spread her paws.

Roar took a step back behind Sven.

'Pure luck that we found you,' Viljo said.

'M-m-meet... my two... f-f-friends, Less Weasel and More Weasel,' Erm...ine pointed at the two stoats on the trees, who responded with a friendly wave.

Sven responded to the wave and addressed the smaller weasel, 'You must be least weasel, am I right?'

'Less Weasel,' the little weasel replied. 'Unfortunately, we haven't seen least weasel for ages. He moved further south years ago, where the air is warmer and the drinks are colder. Good for him, though. Saved his tiny, furry bottom from this troubling flood. Least weasel has always been the least interested about the cold weather. Least interested about anything, in fact.'

'I...I...I miss... least we...we...weasel. He... he was so much... f...f...fun to-to-to be a...round,' said Erm...ine.

'More fun than us?' queried More Weasel.

'Less fun... of co-co-course. He w-w-was the least f-f-fun of you... three,' Erm...ine smirked.

Roar shook his head while listening to the most awkward conversation. Having experienced many odd things in his lifetime, his eyes and ears just couldn't comprehend the scene. 'I guess I've been too focused only on fishing all these years,' he said, flabbergasted.

'Tell me about it,' Sven said.

Sven, Jaaku and Viljo seemed to have adjusted to this new reality of having conversing wildlife around that they found it somewhat normal. Nothing really seemed to shock them anymore and Roar was afraid to be joining the same bunch of *loonies*.

'But, hold on,' Sven said. 'We met Erm...ine where we left the shore and where this boat was parked. Are we back in the same place?'

'It can't be. This is nowhere near the coast,' Viljo said.

'The-the coastline... h-h-has shifted,' Erm...ine explained.

'That means it has shifted...' Viljo looked up at the horizon, 'for many kilometres!'

The stoats nodded.

'That's right,' Jaaku said and peered through his telescope. 'These are the lowlands. The wave has travelled far especially in this area.'

'And it also means that we are nowhere near the town!' Sven raised his voice and turned to Viljo. 'We have come back towards the south west coast. We were supposed to head east!'

'I know very well where we have to go,' Viljo said calmly. 'Do you want to take over the wheel? Or you wanna row? I know you're pretty good at that.'

Sven shook his head and stepped on the edge as the stoats waited to be rescued. He stretched his arm and one-by-one helped the two stoats on the boat.

'The stars were not visible all the time. I had to improvise,' Viljo snorted and went to start the engine.

Roar stared at the three stoats, amazed, as they chattered cheerfully amongst themselves after finding rescue. 'Sven, did you know about this? Talking fauna in Pihtamo?'

'It's all new to me, to all of us,' Sven said, grabbed Roar's arms and pulled him aside, 'as was a laser beam shooting wizard.'

'You're hurting my arm,' Roar said, concerned.

'I'm sorry,' Sven loosened the grip. 'I mean, your magic

powers. Where did you gain all that? The way you used the magic rod or steered the boat without an engine or oars?'

'You're confusing me now. I have no clear recollection of how I did those things.'

'You understand that while you were being the Lord of Herrings, you were performing some extraordinary acts, something unknown to any normal human being.'

'I can remember feeling very powerful. I was in another world. It's all very blurry to me. Almost like a dream sequence or a... nightmare. Repeatedly, I kept seeing this... I think it was a dream. I was working in a circus as a ringmaster.'

Sven's heart started pumping faster. *The dream*, he remembered. 'You mean... Herringmaster?'

'That's it! Good, son. How did you know?'

'Erm... Wild guess,' Sven said, disturbed, and rather tried to think of something else to talk about. 'What else do you remember?'

'I was following a mission to save Pihtamo. Some mysterious force inside me told to fish and keep fishing until the lake is completely empty. That process took more than a decade - most of my time away. But not to gut, kill or fry any of the fish, but take them all to safety away from Wolferring.'

'Who told you that?'

'I first thought something had happened to me, something had changed after Wolferring bit my leg off, that I had developed a defence mechanism to protect myself and the entire community. But now I've become more convinced that the time I spent in that indigenous village changed me. I don't know how or why, but somehow I felt... the enlightenment when the chief sent me on my journey. They didn't necessarily just heal me, but they...'

'Drinking that reindeers urine gave you superpowers?'

'I don't know. I can't remember. And I don't feel so powerful now, but the opposite. I may have lost them.'

'But you said you do remember where you have taken all the fish?'

'I'm not quite sure if I do.'

'Try. It can save the future of Lake Pihtamo.'

Concerned, Roar looked at the lake. 'Not sure if Pihtamo really has a future.'

'Any help is welcomed.'

'I will try my best,' Roar said, looking puzzled like a sufferer of dementia. He paused for a second and gathered himself. 'May I ask you a question, too?'

'Just one,' Sven smirked.

'How is mother... I mean... Birgget? Your mother.'

Sven stared away in the distance. 'She's fine... I hope.'

'And your wife?' Roar asked, forcing some excitement into his voice while the sadness of missed years overwhelmed him. 'You said you got married?'

'Yes. Last summer. We even went to England on our honeymoon.'

'Well, congratulations! I wish I was...' Roar said, hopelessly spreading his arms.

'I know,' Sven said flatly.

'My son, such a globetrotter,' Roar said proudly.

'It was a great trip. The fishing scene there was absolutely fantastic.'

'Wait a minute! You took your newlywed bride for a fishing trip?' Roar asked, stunned.

'Why does everyone have a problem with that? Did you take mum somewhere special on your honeymoon?'

'I think... we had none,' Roar said sadly.

'And why is that then?'

'Because...' Roar had a little pause before admitting, 'I had a fishing competition the next day... and the day after.'

'Here we go,' Sven looked at him judgementally.

'Like father like son,' Roar sighed. 'I'm sorry. At least you two went somewhere else together. How was the catch in England then?'

'Surprisingly, better than anywhere else ever before. My boat filled up with fish over its edges, until this security officer ruined everything and ordered me to release all the fish that I had caught back into the lake.'

'That's a disgrace! Sounds to me like... hunting rabbits with a paintball rifle.'

'That's kind of what I thought. That was the only incident that laid a little shadow over the trip and the fact that we got caught up in the storm and flooding afterwards. Otherwise, I thought it was a great honeymoon.'

'Like us now getting caught up here.'

'Indeed. We just haven't caught any fish though.'

'You must miss her.'

'I miss her like crazy.'

'We have to find her.'

'Both. Mum and Ida.'

Chapter 52

# WAITING GAME

Another dark dawn broke on the roof. Or so the survivors believed. They began to lose track of time. The amount of light between the night and day had not much difference, if none at all.

Birgget and Marjukka had taken one side of the chimney pipe as their resting area, whereas Christian and Ida stayed on the other.

Ida had already woken up, but she kept her eyes shut. She only tucked herself closer to Christian's warm body. They lie sideways, him holding her from behind, only their blankets and thick winter clothes separating them.

Both Ida and Christian opened their eyes and looked at each other. Christian smiled at her, but her eyes only widened. She couldn't remember how all of this had happened. How they ended up sleeping so close together?

'What a beautiful morning,' Birgget cleared her throat sarcastically, as she peered at Christian and Ida from behind the chimney.

Dumbfounded, Ida composed herself and pushed away from his arms. She stood up and replied formally, 'Yes. It feels like it could be morning.'

Birgget just glanced at her, turned away and walked to the pile of supplies near the chimney pipe. She started going through the grocery bags that mainly had dry food and a couple of fruits left, and, ironically, bottled water, when they were surrounded by unlimited amounts of fresh water. *Should be one of the only things that doesn't run out*, she thought. How drinkable the lake water was though with all the rubble floating on it, was questionable.

The surroundings were quiet and peaceful though, apart from some loose planks floating on the light waves and gently hitting the outside walls. As if the nature was also tired from the recent disaster and needed time to rest and recover.

Slowly, Ida walked around the edges of the roof scanning the horizon hoping to spot a glimmer of light, any sign of life, anywhere in the distance. But only a vast and dark emptiness filled the scene. She saw a silhouette of Aariak and Tomas. Aariak seemed to be waving at her. She responded with a wave.

Christian got up as well and walked to Ida. He stood behind her and touched her shoulders. 'I'm sorry about last night.'

'No. You're not,' Ida said and lowered her arm.

'Nothing happened.'

'I sure hope not!'

'We just fell asleep after we finished decorating the tree. That's it. You were so tired you nearly collapsed.'

'And, you thought it's better if I sleep next to you?'

'You fell in my arms,' Christian said defensively. 'And to be honest, you seemed quite comfortable.'

'How can you say that? I had literally passed out.'

'That's just... how I felt.'

'Well, I have no recollection of anything. Let's just leave it as it is. From now on we sleep in separate mattresses.'

'As it is?' he wondered. 'How is it?'

Ida didn't answer, but instead she heard Marjukka getting up as well. Ida ignored Christian and walked to her. 'Morning, Marjukka. How long you think we can survive here?' she asked bluntly.

'Good morning to you, too,' she said sarcastically, and rubbed her eyes. 'Well, I would say we have food supplies for another day or two. That one bag next to the chimney pipe has a couple of slices of rye bread left. I also managed to grab a little bit of Christmas food, like smoked salmon and a jar of garlic herring.'

'I wasn't really thinking about food, but thanks for clearing that out. I thought about the weather. It's really cold and neither the nights nor days are getting any warmer.'

'I thought about that last night. There may be a way to light a fire in the fireplace. The chimney pipe would heat up as well as the roof once the flat gets warm underneath.'

'Isn't the fireplace all flooded?' Christian asked and stepped closer to the ladies. He placed his hand on Ida's lower back. She glanced at him, but let him keep the hand where it was.

'We could try and place the spark protector around the fireplace, empty the fireplace of water, use it again to burn some wood and hope the spark protector would keep the flooding away,' Marjukka suggested.

'What can we burn there?' Ida asked.

'Furniture.'

'Furniture's all wet,' Christian said.

'Not the top parts,' Marjukka said. 'I have a big wardrobe and a book case that have only bottom parts underwater. We can still chop the wood off the tops and burn it all. All the rest, I think, is underwater.'

'What a great idea,' Ida said. 'You really are an angel, aren't you?'

'I'm not an angel. I'm just a woman from the post office who wants to live another day. Survive. No matter what.'

'You're something else. You're special. You have saved our lives and we all should be forever thankful for that,' Ida said and smiled.

Christian agreed with a firm nod.

Marjukka blushed, embarrassed. It was very early in the morning for her to receive compliments, as if any other time of the day would make it easier.

'But... how do you think we can chop those furniture into smaller pieces?' Christian asked. 'You need some sort of tools to do it.'

'I have some tools in the bottom drawers in the kitchen. I recall there should be an axe and a saw, at least,' Marjukka hesitated.

'Bottom? That means underwater?' Christian pondered.

'I would say so.'

'So someone should dive in there... in the freezing water?'

'To get the tools, yes. And chop the wood, too. Someone would have to wade in the water.' Once Marjukka replied, everyone stared at her, but she only rolled her eyes. 'I ain't going down there anymore! Besides, I have no spare clothes left.'

All pleading eyes turned to Christian. 'I will... think about it,' he hesitated and walked to the other side of the roof to ponder. *Not that I or anyone else have spare clothes.*

Ida stayed with Marjukka and gave Christian his privacy.

'So, what's the thing between you two?' Marjukka asked quietly, making Ida wiggle uncomfortably. 'I'm sorry about the direct question. I know you have been coming to the post office for many years... and we have never really spoken and...'

'And now you thought is the right time?'

'I just thought... since it's obvious you two are...'

'There's absolutely nothing going on between us two!' Ida raised her voice alarming Birgget. Birgget's head appeared again from behind the chimney pipe. She was peering curiously at the two women. Ida had to lower her voice. 'Me and Christian only dated long, long time ago. I am married now and my husband is somewhere out there.'

'I'm sorry. I just...'

'Have you got someone to look forward to? Your own sweetheart out there you're worried about or perhaps he's worried about you?' Ida gestured randomly at the lake.

'Unfortunately, no,' Marjukka looked down on the roof.

'I didn't mean to...' Ida said apologetically.

'I broke my heart years ago. I was with someone. You remember, Anders from the supermarket?'

'I'm not sure. From the bakery section?'

'Fish and poultry. Doesn't matter. We were supposed to get married and have children, but then he got promoted to the head office of the supermarket almost thousand kilometres south from Pihtamo. He chose his career instead of life here with me. We tried to make it work long distance, but obviously, it didn't.'

'You didn't want to follow him?'

'Absolutely not. Pihtamo is my home and has always been. I have my job here in the post office that I wouldn't give away for anything.'

'You sound like my husband.'

'Sven.'

'You know him?'

'Not personally, but everyone knows who he is. The champion.'

'Indeed, he is. I never thought he would be so famous around here or anywhere.'

'As famous as a person can be here. Like his father, Roar, who in fact, was a legend.'

'You knew his father as well?'

'Again, not personally, but as a customer, yes. I remember him, too. And Birgget, of course,' Marjukka said, lowering her voice almost whispering as she spotted Birgget still eavesdropping. 'They used to come together to the post office. I had just started working there. They seemed happy. Until he disappeared. She kept coming back alone, yet she wasn't the same anymore. There was sadness in her eyes, even when she tried to smile. I can still see that in her. She hasn't recovered.'

'She says she has left it all behind now, but you may be right.' Ida turned to wave at Birgget. Birgget gave Ida an enquiring look, but Ida only responded by shrugging her shoulders.

'Don't be afraid, Ida,' Marjukka said encouragingly. 'There's always hope.'

'Hope?'

'That your husband is still out there.'

'Yes. He went all alone to find answers why the lake was running short of fish. He only had a small rowing boat. We saw the size of the wave. It is a miracle if he had survived. I wish I was stronger. I wish I'd stopped him from going.'

'Don't feel guilty about it. You know very well what the fishermen can be like.'

'Stubborn.'

Marjukka nodded. 'I dated one. Jaaku was his name.'

'Really? He's Sven's best friend. I wonder where he is now.'

'Small world,' Marjukka smiled. 'Actually, we only chatted

online. But he only kept talking about ice fishing the whole time.'

'Sounds like him.'

'Fishermen!' Marjukka snorted.

Christian came beside Ida and Marjukka. He had done his thinking. 'I will do it.'

'Light up the fireplace?' Marjukka said, her eyes glistening.

Christian nodded unenthusiastically. 'Not right now, though, but later. Soon. Once we start to feel unbearably cold. We must wait till the last minute. And this is not it, yet. Am I right?'

'I agree. Thank you,' Marjukka smiled. As Christian walked away, Marjukka looked at him admiringly. She elbowed Ida. 'But I have to admit, he's quite something, isn't he?'

Ida joined with a nod. 'He's alright. Not bad at all.'

They both chuckled.

Chapter 53

# SMOKEY PEANUT

The boat with three new passengers, the weasels, advanced full steam ahead. It had become impossible to take guidance off the land as the floods had pushed the nearest, southern coastline too far away. They had to rely on the stars again.

A floating log or a piece of a spruce tree top they had picked up from the mangrove where the stoats huddled replaced the broken viewing mast. They had tied the trunk upright with ropes as an extension to the stump left of the original pole. As usual, Jaaku had climbed on the summit to view and help navigate the route ahead. He sat above the thick upper branches looking through his telescope. 'A meteorite!' he screamed and saw arching white trails or contrails descending directly towards them. 'Save yourselves!' he pulled his arms above his head.

'What is he talking about now?' Viljo looked outside.

Sven, Roar and the three weasels looked up. Ahead of the white trail, a brown flaming dot got larger and closer. Sven embraced Roar and pulled him to the railing. The weasels pressed themselves against the cabin outside wall right before a foot long peanut smacked from the sky like a meteorite, burning a black circle shaped stain on the floor in the middle of the foredeck. The smoking peanut shell snapped in half. A tiny, brown rodent jumped out energetically. The rodent raised its little right arm and clenched its little paw to demonstrate a superhero posture. It wore a bright red cape and had a little S-shaped red hairpiece circling its muscular chest.

'Squirr-El!' exclaimed Erm...ine.

'Well spotted,' Roar said. 'It sure is squirrel.'

'But not just any squirrel,' More Weasel added. 'She's Squirr-El.'

'What's the difference?' Roar looked at Sven confused.

Sven spread his arms dumbfounded.

'Behold, fishermen and weasels,' the squirrel started.

'Not again,' Roar sighed and shook his head. 'Another chatty animal?'

Viljo's sigh could also be heard from the cockpit.

The squirrel ignored the men's negativity as it said, 'My furry eyes have witnessed many terrible sights whilst flying above this lake. The dark green forests around Pihtamo are vast and hide many extraordinary species of fauna that were forced to reveal themselves on the brink of danger. Your vessel may be the only hope for the wildlife population affected by these horrendous floods. '

Viljo turned down the engine and stepped outside. 'We appreciate your feedback, little flying fellow, but this is not a rescue boat. This is only an old, now badly damaged fishing boat. Secondly, we haven't got the supplies to go on much further and, especially, if we start picking up more passengers. We don't even know if we can save ourselves. The navigation system is already down, we haven't got enough life vests and...'

'When was the last time you old man changed your undergarment?' the squirrel interrupted wittily while scanning Viljo from head to toe.

'What's that supposed to mean?' Viljo frowned.

'Nothing.'

'What a rude, little squirrel!' Viljo shouted. He took a step closer to the squirrel, leaned over and attempted to grab her on his palm, but the squirrel was too fast. The squirrel rushed from between his legs behind him and back to front again, until Viljo's head spun, got dizzy and he fell on his bottom. The floor underneath made a loud crack as if he had farted. The other men and weasels chuckled. 'This is not funny!' Viljo waved his fist while holding his sore bottom with his other hand.

'Very entertaining,' Sven smiled, perfectly used to the fact that another animal with a voice had arrived.

While Viljo got a hold of the railing and slowly pulled himself up, another small rodent dragged itself out of the steaming peanut shell. The rodent had a withered coat. It was carrying a long stick. So long, in fact, that everyone wondered how the stick fit inside such a small shell. As if they were watching a magic show of some sort.

'Ah, there you are,' the squirrel clocked the little rodent.

Roar dropped down to his left knee in front of the two rodents and asked them politely, 'So, where have you two come from then? Who or what are you?'

'You can call me, Squirr-El,' the squirrel replied.

'The-the-the... Squirr-el of S-S-S-teel,' Erm...ine added.

'Squirr-El of Steel?' Roar repeated. 'So, it was not just Erm... ine talking, but that's actually your name?'

'Correct. I have been blessed with unique powers. But now, I need help. Your help. The tallest tree of all in Pihtamo was my home which I had to abandon once the tidal wave hit. My home has been destroyed. While seeing the first wave approaching, I panicked and saved what I could. I grabbed my cape and this one peanut which now lies burned and battered here on your front deck. Once I escaped the tree together with my neighbour, Sergei here,' Squirr-El pointed at the stick carrying rodent who joined beside her, 'we just kept flying and flying, because the lake had turned into an ocean. The waters seemed to never end. And two of us flying inside the peanut shell was too much. The weight must have brought us down and we crash-landed here on your boat.'

'You were lucky to find us then,' Sven said.

'Yes. There was nothing else around,' Squirr-El said gravely. 'But I have failed in my duties.'

'What are your duties?'

'I am Squirr-El, the Squirrel of Steel, and I have a great responsibility to protect the rodent communities in the area. But instead, I escaped and left them all behind when they needed help the most.'

'Hold on. You have exactly... what kind of powers?' Sven

asked.

'Like some sort of... supersquirrel?' Roar asked.

'I don't wanna go too much into details now... but I can, for instance, crack a peanut shell with just one tap of a tail.'

'That's it?' Viljo laughed, still holding his hurt bottom.

'Obviously, I can fly,' Squirr-El added.

'I thought quite a few other squirrels can fly too,' Viljo argued.

'Pteromyini can fly just a little while, but that's about it,' the little rodent with the pole intervened.

Everyone fell silent. They turned to look at the rodent.

'And, who are you again?' Sven asked.

'I am Sergei,' the rodent replied with a strong Eastern European accent. 'But my friends started calling me Pole Vole after my emigration. They think I live in the North Pole.'

'Well, not far,' Roar said.

'Let me guess. A Russian rodent?' Sven asked.

'Ukrainian.'

'And, what about the long stick you seem to be holding on so tight?' Roar asked curiously.

'I use it to pole vault.'

'Naturally,' Sven smiled.

'Mainly to jump over larger animals and other obstacles.'

'And what about you, Squirr-El, do you have x-ray vision, too?' Sven asked, leaning closer.

'Why?'

'You said Viljo has dirty underwear,' Sven whispered. 'How do you know?'

'No,' Squirr-El laughed. 'I can't see a darned thing. He just looked like a kind of a grumpy old man who doesn't perhaps change his underwear that often.'

'What was that?' Viljo snorted.

Sven and Roar looked at each other and smiled.

'Do you need a hand, old man?' Sven offered to assist Viljo.

But Viljo only pushed his hand away. 'I can look after myself!' Viljo grunted and finally managed to get up fully on his feet.

'But despite my unique powers, as I said, I feel I have failed poorly,' Squirr-El continued.

'You saved one of your kind,' Sven said and pointed at Pole Vole. 'That's always better than nothing.'

'But there are so many more out there who need my help,' Squirr-El said longingly.

'Great power comes with...' Roar started.

'Lots of crap. I know. So many lives to be saved,' Squirr-El sighed. 'Right before I fell down from the sky, I saw a large group of you... people having escaped to safety on the mountains.'

'That's good news,' said Roar.

'And earlier, we saw a few of you trapped on the roof top of a tall building,' Pole Vole added.

'So, you have seen land and rooftops,' Roar pondered. 'But why you didn't stay there rather than flying back here in the middle of the lake?'

'I couldn't. I felt like I had to save some more lives. But then, as I said, I just ran out of steam. Trying to fly carrying a peanut shell that size with Pole Vole inside it was too much. I overestimated my strength.'

'You said... a tall building?' Sven intervened. 'Was it pointy like a church spire?'

'We saw the spire, too. But, no. The roof beside it was more flat, I would say,' Squirr-El said.

*The post office*, Sven thought and remembered. *The Christmas letters.* 'Did you see anyone in particular?'

'As I said before I can't see very well. And all human beings look the same to me anyway. If I look at you all four, you could be related.'

Sven and Roar looked at each other approvingly being the father and son, but then they looked at Jaaku and Viljo who responded with a stare. They all understood how small the community of Pihtamo really was and the possibility they all were related in some level potentially did exist. However, they all shook their heads and tried to erase that disturbing thought of their minds.

Chapter 54

# BODY HEAT

Again, Christian and Ida ended up sleeping next to one another. The coldness made her adjust. Her head rested heavy on Christian's arm who was already awake. Gently, Christian pulled his numb arm away and raised himself up a little to see if anyone else was up yet. He saw Birgget sitting on the edge of the roof, staring into the distance. As if she was praying. He thought it's better to leave her alone.

Ida opened her eyes and tapped him on the shoulder.

'Ah. Hey. This might sound a bit weird, but...' Christian started, 'if something even worse is going to happen, I am here for you. I can always look after you and your family.'

'What do you mean by "my family?" Happen what?'

'I mean you and... Birgget.'

'Well, she can look after herself,' Ida snorted.

'And you?'

'I can... look after myself too,' Ida said hesitatingly, placed her hand on her stomach and rubbed it.

Christian gave Ida and her awkwardly wandering hand an odd look. Then, he raised his gaze again. 'I was thinking, because... we've been, who knows for how long trapped on this roof. We may all have to start all over soon. This may be the new beginning for Pihtamo. For all of us,' he said gravely.

Ida turned away from him and burst into tears.

'I'm sorry,' Christian said and embraced her from behind.

'No. Don't be,' Ida wept and let him hold her. She took his hands and pressed them tighter on her waist. She tucked herself closer to him and took his hands around further onto her belly.

'There's something you should know...' Ida hesitated.

'You know you can tell me anything.'

'I'm... I'm...' she stuttered, 'very confused.'

'Me too. Trust me. It's difficult times for all of us.'

She nodded. The unbearable guilt about how comfortable she felt with Christian while at the same time, not knowing where Sven is, ate her from inside. If nothing else, she could have been just a friend with Christian, but she knew Christian wasn't capable of that. He wanted more. She didn't want to tell Christian or anyone about the pregnancy either. Something stopped her. The uncertainty about everything, about Sven's survival, the happiness and the future of their marriage. Was it meant to be? Were they really that happy? Could she live all of her life with a fisherman, who clearly chooses fishing over her, and will keep doing so? Or was this even the right situation or time to think about these issues? *Is there a right time?*

She thought it was too soon from Christian to suggest they all may have to start again. It was too early to give away hope. But, what if Sven never returns, like his own father didn't? What if their child has to live without a father and experience the same doubts and fears as Sven did? Her mind was filled with hard questions. She didn't want the same destiny for the baby. Sven had suffered enough in his lifetime for not having a father. *Could Christian be the one... to take over the responsibility if needed? If so, do the outsiders need to know who is the real father of the baby as long as everyone is happy? Would it make mine and the baby's life easier if Christian was the "father?"* She blushed. *Nobody has to know. Nobody knows.* Her heart beat faster.

'Are you alright?' Christian asked and rubbed her belly gently.

She took Christian's wrist, moved his hand to the side and said, 'Just hold me please. I feel really cold.'

She closed her eyes, and in a matter of seconds, fell asleep in his arms. He gazed in the distance. *Soon, she will be all mine.*

Chapter 55

# THE ICE BERG

Suddenly, the hull started to rise and tilt onto an angle. The bottom of the boat made vile screeching sounds. There was a loud thump as Viljo fell off the wheel onto the cabin floor. Roar and Sven slid across the deck floor on their bottoms. Jaaku had slipped from the tree top mast with his feet tangled between the branches. He ended up hanging upside down trapped from his boots. The stoats and the rodents rolled on the side deck towards the stern.

The boat came into a halt its nose being lifted up in the air in a forty-five degree angle.

Viljo shook his head, yawned and rubbed his sleepy eyes as he composed himself back behind the wheel. He wiped off the drool on his mouth, picked up his pipe and began evaluating the situation around, as if nothing had happened.

The boat rested diagonally shipwrecked on a piece of ice size of a little island centred by a snowy hill, also made of ice, or so it seemed.

'Where did that come from?' Viljo said, astounded. 'I have never seen that before.'

'I bet you haven't,' Sven snorted.

'I mean... I have never, as long as I have sailed these waters, seen such a large ice berg in Pihtamo,' Viljo corrected.

'Did you fall asleep in there?' Roar said and rubbed his tired eyes.

'Did you?' Viljo grunted.

'Well, I think we all did,' Sven said and looked up.

'I didn't. Seriously,' Jaaku answered while hanging upside down. He tried to use his abs to raise himself back on the top, but the gravity kept pulling stronger. The thickest branches saved him as he could have landed straight on the deck head first.

Sven started climbing up the tree. As he was near the top, he looked at Jaaku. 'I will pull your boots off.'

'Are you kidding me? I will hit the deck!' Jaaku screamed, blood rushing to his head.

'Should be fine now. The boat is at an angle. The snow looks soft underneath you,' Sven said and began untying Jaaku's shoelaces.

'Don't you dare...' Jaaku started, but too late. As the second boot loosened, his feet slipped off and he came shooting down, missing the boat by centimetres and landing on the edge of the ice. But the surface wasn't quite as soft as it may have looked like from above. Jaaku's body bounced and rolled off the edge straight into the ice cold water.

Luckily, though, Jaaku was a strong swimmer. He had already proven that during the ice fishing competition. In the worst scenario, Jaaku's waterproof seal skin suit would also function as a floating device. Jaaku took a few strokes back to the edge of the ice, but couldn't climb on a slippery surface.

Sven picked up Jaaku's boots, came down the tree and together with Roar hopped on the island to help pull Jaaku out of the water.

Jaaku stood up and shook his whole body dry like a wet dog. 'There must have been another way!'

'Sorry. I thought that was the best thing to do,' Sven said. 'But how did you manage to get yourself in that position in the first place?'

'I was doing my... morning exercise,' Jaaku said, touching his sore neck after the fall. 'I pushed my feet between a couple of branches and tried to do... crunches hanging upside down.'

'I didn't know you exercise.'

'Why not? Because I look fat in this outfit?'

'No need to get sensitive about it.'

'Before this journey, I was training every day.'

'Well, if you'd concentrated more on navigation than your body, we wouldn't be in this situation in the first place,' Sven said and looked at the empty piece of ice.

'Now, it's my fault?' Jaaku said, frustrated. 'What were you all doing then? Sleeping?'

'So, that... we can take turns,' Sven stammered.

'Turns in what!? You were all asleep! Besides, none of you have ever been up there in the mast,' Jaaku yelled.

Viljo and Roar looked away, ashamed.

'Erm...' Erm...ine cleared his throat. 'M-m-may I... interrupt?'

All heads turned to the little stoat.

'I...h-h-have a bad feeling... about t-t-this place. I can... s-s-smell some... thing is... n-n-not right.'

'It somehow smells familiar to me,' Jaaku sniffed the air.

'We have to get the boat off the ice and get out of here,' Viljo intervened..

'Should we give it a push?' Roar suggested.

Viljo nodded.

The four men lined up beside the hull and pushed, but the boat didn't move a centimetre. They gave it another push while the little animals on board watched impatiently.

'Should we ask them to step out as well?' Jaaku suggested.

'I doubt our little passengers weigh that much,' Viljo panted and stopped pushing.

Roar and Sven gave up once realising the pointlessness of it all. Jaaku also let go.

'What about Squirr-El? What were your superpowers again?' Sven asked.

Squirr-El appeared on the edge of the deck. 'I can wrestle any marmot to the ground,' she announced proudly.

Sven sighed in disappointment. 'What should we do?'

Suddenly, a loud roaring alarmed the men and little animals on board. They all looked to the direction of the island.

A two, ginormous white polar bears stood near the hillside, however, not paying attention to the surprise visitors, but only eating something and stretching their bodies upright.

'Are they eating... pies?' Jaaku observed.

Sven and Roar nodded next to him.

'I don't care,' Viljo grunted, climbed back on the boat to fetch his spear gun.

'My family pies,' Jaaku said. 'That's the smell I recognised.'

'We cannot be that far away then!' Sven said excitedly.

But the polar bears heard Sven's voice. They gave the men a little glances, but soon focused back on their pies.

'They must really like them,' Jaaku said proudly.

Viljo joined the other men on the ice with his spear gun.

'Could you for once put that thing away?' Sven snorted.

'Look who's talking! Our wildlife activist,' Viljo smirked. 'Of course, not. I'm hungry. We need food.'

'But, but...' Sven panicked and looked at the others.

However, Viljo wasn't listened but only aimed.

Pleading, Sven looked at Jaaku and Jaaku nodded as a response. Together, they jumped on Viljo and wrestled him to the ground.

'No more shooting!' Sven shouted as he twisted Viljo's arm while Jaaku retrieved the gun.

'What are you doing!? But... they are dangerous!'

'No. They seem quite friendly,' Sven said.

'Maybe, because they are eating quality pies,' Jaaku smiled.

'Maybe, they could help us push the boat off the ice,' Roar suggested.

'What a great idea,' Sven said and slowly released Viljo. 'What do you think, old man?'

But Viljo only snorted and looked away. 'Do as you wish, you crazy people.'

'And then, if they can help, we will take them with us,' Sven suggested.

Everyone gasped.

'I don't think that is such a good idea,' Jaaku said.

'Fine. But once they run out of the those pies, what will they eat? There's no fish left in these waters. There's nothing. They'll end up starving. We must take them somewhere where there is food.'

'Don't worry. Polar bears can swim long distances. They can

find their own food,' Jaaku said. 'The shoreline cannot be that far away.'

'Can these polar bears swim that far? With the energy they get from those pies?' Sven asked doubtfully.

'Listen,' Viljo interrupted. 'If we take them with us, they'll definitely gain more energy by eating us all alive, especially, the little weasels and rodents.'

'So, are you saying that we are only saving the little animals? Isn't that a bit unfair?'

'Life is unfair, sometimes,' Viljo snorted.

'Dad, you have some experience with polar bears. They can be friendly, right?'

'I only know the sleeping ones can be,' Roar said. 'But I have to admit, these ones seem quite calm. And they don't really seem to be that bothered about us.'

'There's only one way to find out,' Sven said, took a deep breath and started walking toward the polar bears.'

'Wait...' said Roar, but Sven was already on his way. He sighed and felt, he couldn't let his son go alone.

So, together, the father and son approached the two polar bears. First, Sven went to offer them his hand. One of them responded with a smile and took it. 'Look,' Sven smiled back. 'Easy.'

'I have no good feeling about this,' Roar said, eyes wide open.

'Do it. Bring the other one,' Sven said and started walking the polar bear back towards the boat.

Roar shook his head but slowly offered his shaking hand. The other munching bear seemed friendly, too, and accepted his hand. *Viljo will be thrilled for this surprise,* he thought, sarcastically whilst escorting a gentle polar bear three times as big as him.

'They mean no harm. They are friendly,' Sven yelled at the passengers on the boat as he came closer.

'You're not seriously bringing them here?' Viljo shouted back.

'Where else? They need to be rescued, too, like any other animal we have so far.'

'But, this is their natural habitat...'

'These seem to behave well as long they have food.'

'Well, we have no food,' Viljo said. 'We hardly have anything to eat for ourselves. I don't understand how you think we can feed two polar bears?'

'The boat is still stuck, right?' Sven pondered as they got closer.

Viljo nodded.

'I believe these two furry fellows are stronger than all of us together. I'm sure we could use some polar bear strength,' Sven suggested.

'Be my guest. If you can make them do it,' Viljo said.

'And, if they can push the boat off the ice, we take them with us?' Sven pleaded. 'We just have to find them food. Perhaps they can smell the food from the distance.'

'My boat is not an ark if that's what you were thinking?' Viljo said. 'Have you been reading the Bible again?'

'I promise these are the last animals we take on board. Only people next if any.'

Sven and Roar arrived by the boat with the two polar bears. Everyone seemed uneasy, especially, the little animals who huddled behind the cabin trying to hide.

'Well, if we take those bears in, we cannot fit much more in the boat anyway,' Viljo said and softened. 'We take them if they can release the boat. But remember, you're responsible of them.'

'Yes, sir,' Sven nodded, and went to demonstrate the polar bears how to push the boat off the ice. The other men lined up next to him. Obviously, the boat didn't move a millimetre, until one of the polar bears got the idea, put its paws on the corner of the hull and pushed. The other bear joined in and the boat started sliding like its bottom had been oiled and the polar bears didn't even struggle or make a face.

Sven spread his arms proudly as a sign of victory. Roar nodded approvingly, whereas the weasels and rodents couldn't quite share the joy of having two new guests from totally different end of the food chain.

As the boat sailed back in service, Sven and Jaaku escorted the two polar bears on board. Discomfort drove the little animals to the front, while the polar bears conquered the entire back space. The weight of them raised up the bow and sank the stern deeper.

'Could one of the bears go to the front and one stay at the back?' Viljo suggested.

'I'll see what I can do,' Sven said, tried to grab one of the bears' arm, but it only growled back at him. Sven rushed away and took position at the bow. 'I think it's better we leave them alone. They seem quite... inseparable.'

'Fine.' Viljo locked himself inside the cockpit after Sven's failed attempt to demonstrate how harmless the polar bears were supposed to be. He was also given his spear gun back, but he promised not to use it, unless the situation gets "out of control". Jaaku climbed back up on the tree top viewing mast where he thought he would be safe. Roar together with the little animals joined Sven on the front deck to keep the boat in some sort of weight balance. The sky in the distance was turning light grey. If they hadn't completely lost the track of time, they believed it was supposed to be getting near to Christmas eve.

Chapter 56

# FIRE

Whilst Birgget and Ida were still huddling in the warmth of their blankets, Marjukka had already begun lowering Christian down the chimney pipe. He descended at the fireplace and sunk his wellies in the water. He untied the rope and let it hang loose inside the flue. He leaped over the spark protector. The water level was above his crotch and near to his waistline. Breathing heavily, he waded towards the kitchen door. After a few steps, he kicked his knee on some living room furniture underwater. *Perhaps Marjukka should have done this*, he thought while biting his teeth in pain. But it was too late for regrets. He was in too deep, literally. He tried to ignore the pain and focus on what was important: their survival. He looked around at the furniture he could start chopping, once he had located the tools. There was a large wooden wardrobe still one third above the surface. Also a couple of veneer plywood shelves were attached to the walls that he could possibly pull out. And apparently, there was more furniture in Marjukka's bedroom.

He reached the kitchen and located the sink. Below the sink, there was supposed to be a plastic bucket that he could use to scoop the fireplace empty of water. He took a deep breath and squatted. As he went down, he felt how the cold water rose against his stomach, bellybutton, then the rib cage and the heart, nearly, stopping the beating. He couldn't breathe. He reached out for the handle, opened the door and put his hand inside the little closet. There were some plastic bottles that he thought were cleaning products. He waded his arms around and felt different things, like wet sponges and drain pipes. He lowered himself even more. The cold water entered his jacket through his collar. He was neck deep in the water. Below the bottle tops was something that felt like could have been a bucket. He grabbed the edge of it, pulled it out and raised it up. It was a bucket filled with cleaning products. He tilted the plastic bottles away and raised the empty bucket above the fridge. Next, he located the oven fan. Below the fan, he felt the oven that was underwater. Next to the oven, there were a set of drawers. In the largest of the drawers at the bottom, there were supposed to be some tools. Christian took a deep breath and bent down, since he wasn't keen to squat again. But his arms only reached for the third drawer from the top. He had to get to the fifth one. He had to sink down further. And he did. He had no choice. He was so close. He was panting. Eyes wide he fought the freezing pain as he dived deeper. He was one drawer away. He had to sink his head. And he did. He took a deep breath and dived completely underwater. Ears blasting and ringing, he couldn't see a thing. He felt the knob of the bottom drawer. He pulled the drawer open and felt the inside. It was a mixture of metal and rubber. With both hands now, he grabbed whatever he could. He felt excruciating pain. Something sharp cut his hand. Was it the saw or a knife, he didn't know, but he didn't care either. He kept going, blood mixing with the water. He took a pile of tools in between his hands, stood up and stacked them on top of a fridge. The water had turned red. His left hand fingers and palm were bleeding all over. But most importantly, he had picked up an axe, not a saw. That was good enough. He had no intention to reach for that drawer anymore, ever again. Hand bleeding, he put the axe in the bucket, took it with him and waded back towards the living room. This time, he managed to dodge the obstacles underneath the water. He placed the axe on the mantelpiece, climbed over the protector and started scooping the water away from the firebox. Ignoring the coldness and the loss of blood, he worked and worked. There was only one thing in his mind. *Fire.* After tipping tens of buckets of water over the protector, the brick floor underneath became visible. A thin layer of water remained that he wasn't able to scrape off. He had to leave it there at the bottom, hoping he could find enough wood to cover the wet patch. And there should be, as long as he will get a hold of it all.

For a few seconds, he enjoyed the feeling of standing on something dry. Soon though, he felt the wet clothes against his body. It didn't make much difference whether he was out or in the water. Between two bad options, he chose the latter. They needed the fire.

Suddenly, he remembered how Jaaku plummeted through the ice during the ice fishing competition. He felt much more empathy towards him. He wasn't aware, though, that Jaaku's clothes were waterproof, unlike his.

He raised the axe above his head and waded by the large wardrobe. He held the top with his free hand and with the other holding the axe took a great swing. A large chunk chipped off the corner. He pulled the piece of wood off and threw it in the fireplace. As he hit the second time, the whole top came off and the entire structure started collapsing. Immediately, he threw his arms around and gave the wardrobe a big embrace. That seemed to hold it in one piece. He couldn't let go, though. Otherwise, the wardrobe would fall apart and sink underwater. The metal bar inside holding Marjukka's clothes came off its wall mounts and fell down. He thought he could still rescue one side wall and keep it dry, which was better than nothing. As he released his one arm, the other side of the wardrobe collapsed in the water. He pulled the other side panel away and carried it to the fireplace. He chopped the dry top part off and chucked it on top of the other pieces of wood. He looked behind him and saw the back veneer plywood panel of the wardrobe leaning on the wall. He thought he could use parts of that as well. As he also used the shelves attached to the walls which he could only yank off with force. But he saved the world atlas map book resting on the shelves to be burned later. He stuffed the book in his rucksack. Then, he went to the bedroom where he was more successful. He managed to secure the whole top part of the wardrobe and keep it dry. Finally, he even chipped some wooden bits of the bedroom and kitchen doors. He was swinging that axe like a proper lumberjack.

Marjukka's well-decorated, modernised flat seemed like a ruin now. Parts of the destroyed furniture floated in the flooded rooms. Christian examined the flat, but couldn't see any more dry things to be burned. He was glad Marjukka wasn't here to see the destruction.

He leaped over the spark protector back inside the fireplace. Some of the small pieces of wood he packed in his rucksack to be used later on. They could drop them from above onto the burning fire. A few bigger pieces he tied on the rope.

'I'm ready!' he exclaimed in the chimney. 'You can pull up the rope. There's some dry wood coming up.' He waited for an answer. Nothing. A moment of silence. He yanked the rope once. It felt loose. 'Hello!?' he raised his voice, only hearing his own echo. He started to feel the early symptoms of hypothermia, like shivering and fast breathing. His lips were trembling. Suddenly, he felt really hot and cold at the same time. His hands and legs were shaking. He looked at the wood stack he was standing on. He took off his rucksack and pulled out a newspaper. The lighter in his trouser pocket was all wet. 'I need a lighter too. Drop me a lighter, please! The one I took is all wet... Can anyone hear me? Please! I'm freezing down here!'

Another moment of silence, until Marjukka's reply came, 'Excellent! You're a hero!' The pieces of wood in the rope began moving upwards. 'I'll drop you a lighter.'

Christian sighed in relief. He began crumpling the newspaper before tucking it in the gaps between the wood stack. Soon, the rope dropped down again with a little bag attached to it. There was a lighter and more newspapers.

'Christian! There's a ham in the fridge. A Christmas ham,' Marjukka yelled.

'And?'

'Could you bring that as well, please?' Marjukka asked, being totally unaware of Christian's severe condition.

Christian stared at the water on the other side of the spark protector. The thought of returning to the kitchen didn't appeal to him, but he knew well they were short of food supplies on the roof. Soon, they would need any food source there was. Someone would have to come down again. A Christmas ham would provide sustenance for some days.

He put the remaining pieces of newspaper and a lighter away on the mantelpiece. He held his breath and took a giant leap back into the water. To his surprise, he didn't feel the pain. His body had numbed and slowed down. He waded across, bumping into the furniture again and forgetting that it was still there. He didn't really care anymore though.

As he reached the kitchen, the fridge was mostly under water. He pulled the door open and soon located the vacuum packed, uncooked ham on the bottom shelf. It was heavy, about five kilograms of solid meat with a bone sticking out. Although he felt so weak that the real weight of the ham could have been half of his estimate. Struggling, he raised the pork leg over his shoulder and carried it towards the fireplace. He couldn't feel his lower body anymore. He stick his head inside the chimney and shouted, 'What do you want me to do with the ham?'

'Ah, you got it. You're amazing!' Marjukka replied.

*Don't feel particularly amazing,* Christian thought.

'Tie it in a rope and I'll pull it up,' Marjukka said. 'We can lower it down later for roasting once you've made the fire. You must be freezing down there.'

'Freezing is a mild way of putting it,' Christian mumbled to himself as he tie a knot around the bone of the ham and hung it upside down. 'You can pull now!'

Marjukka pulled. Soon, she lowered the rope again. 'Could you do one more little thing since you're down there? I promise this is the last one.'

'What!?' Christian shouted.

'You see the dining set right by the fireplace? It's probably mostly underwater, but at least it's very near. You probably don't even have to go back into the water to pick it up. I could reel that up here.'

'The whole thing?' Christian asked, dumbfounded.

'Yeah. It won't take long. I thought it would be nicer to have some Christmas food on the table, rather than on our laps. We already have some cutlery and plates here.'

'Women...' Christian snorted and sunk his arms in the

water. One by one, he reached out for the pieces of the dining set for four and sent them individually to the roof, first the chairs and then the foldable table.

'Amazing!' Marjukka said and dropped the rope. 'Please make the fire now.'

'I will!' he shouted, grabbed the pieces of newspaper and a lighter. He stacked a few pieces of wood together with Marjukka's team building exercise t-shirt that she had left for him to burn. He lit the paper and the fabric. The wood caught fire. He chucked a few more pieces of wood and paper on the fire. Simultaneously, he grabbed the rope. Instantly, he felt the heat. He was so frozen he wanted to stay seated on the fire. 'I've set the fire. I'm coming up now. Pull me up, please!' He hung on the rope with his weakened arms as the burning sensation caressed his bottom. Fortunately, his trousers were so wet they had become temporarily fire proof. 'Pull faster! I'm roasting here!' Panicky, he kicked the walls of the chimney pipe as the rope slowly took him higher and away from the blaze. His own ability to assist the ascent was non-existent. He had no strength left. He was on the brink of hypothermia.

Ida and Birgget helped Marjukka to pull the rope. Palms blistered and bleeding, all three women slowly brought a limp, nearly unconscious adult man up the chimney. The heat rising from the fireplace gently restored Christian's body functions, yet soon the smoke began to fill the pipe. The oxygen ran out. He couldn't breathe. His cut hand dripped blood on the fire. *How much more can a man take?*

Once he reached the top, his limp, shaking body collapsed over the edge of the masonry onto the roof.

'We have to strip him off those wet clothes!' Ida rushed first to help him.

'Yes!' Marjukka said, determined.

Together, the three women started tearing his clothes off, revealing his shaking, ripped body. Once he was fully undressed, they dried him with towels and wrapped him with still warm blankets from their own body heat. He couldn't feel the difference anymore whether he was being naked or wearing wet clothes. He passed out.

Ida held his head in her arms as Marjukka covered him in more blankets. 'His sacrifice may have saved us all,' Marjukka said, looking at the ham resting next to Christian.

'Or at least, given us more time,' Birgget said.

Ida kept stroking his head. She kissed him on the forehead.

Chapter 57

# A TIRED MONSTER

'I have good and bad news,' Jaaku announced from the tree top. The expression on his face showed more worry than satisfaction, though.

Sven looked up, anticipating. 'Since I believe nothing can really shock us anymore, let us hear the bad news first then.'

'The polar bears have nothing left to eat,' Jaaku said and pointed at them sitting at the back and licking their empty claws. They seemed agitated.

'We must have some food left we can give them?' Sven turned to Viljo in the cockpit. 'Any pies?'

'Pies on-board?' Viljo snorted. 'I have to apologise, but we don't serve pies on this cruise. Would some caviar do?'

'We must find food, quickly,' Sven said. 'We can't take any risks with them getting hungry. The hell may break loose. We have to find your parents' pie shop, Jaaku.'

'Do they have to be pies?' Viljo asked.

'Or any food,' Sven corrected. 'Although we can all tell for sure those polar bears like pies. And there's not much left to eat anyway, even for us, if I'm right?'

'You are right,' Viljo grunted. 'It was your idea to take those monsters on board in the first place.'

'What else can we do?' Sven asked. 'Only rescue small animals?'

'Well, this is a small boat if you haven't noticed yet,' Viljo said and took a step back from the wheel. He opened the grocery cabinet and browsed through the inside. He looked concerned. He pulled out a packet of cereal and waved it upside down outside the window. A few crumbs fell on the deck. 'This is everything.'

'That's all?' Jaaku squealed.

Viljo nodded, stuffed the box back in the cabinet and grabbed the wheel again.

Sven looked up at Jaaku. 'Your parents' pie shop may be our only hope. Or Arctic Bar. They have a kitchen, too.'

Jaaku spread his arms. 'Or supermarket. If they're not all complete drowned by this flood.'

'Sven, you really wanna find the post office?' Viljo said.

Sven shrugged his shoulders. 'Sure. Why not? Anything. Doesn't matter. Enough of this empty lake.' He rested against the railing. He had just said something he never thought he would. As much as he had devoted his life to fishing and being out on the lake, for the first time ever he genuinely missed land. People. Family. Normal things. Mainly, though, he missed Ida, her presence, her voice, her touch and her scent. He looked ahead. The sky in the horizon seemed dimly lit. 'Is that... the good news then?'

'Yes. The daylight is returning,' Jaaku said. 'Or, well, in a couple of months time.'

They all turned to witness a thin wedge of a grey shadow rising over the horizon. A silence fell upon the men, the rodents, the weasels and the polar bears. They knew the sight wouldn't last long, until the light was taken over by darkness again. The days were getting longer again, but painfully slow.

Anywhere else, in the safety of intact homes and dry land, the conditions on a day like this would have been perfect for a traditional Christmas celebration filled with jolly activities and family fun. Sven thought about people and families somewhere farther unaffected by the disaster, happily building snowmen and snow castles, going sleigh riding or having snowball fights. For the ones trapped on the boat, though, all that was just a dream. Survival was the only goal. Then, his mind drifted back to Ida and his mother, and if they were at this very moment watching the same dark coloured skies and thinking about him in a same, warm way.

Jaaku's thoughts were with his family, too. This was the first Christmas ever they seemed to be spending apart. He prayed they were safe on the mountains. The pie business may have been lost or damaged, but that was all fixable.

Viljo was the least bothered where he would spend his Christmas. Since Aune's passing, long holidays hit the hardest. The feeling of loneliness multiplied during those odd few days, when everyone else disappeared to their loved ones. In some peculiar way, though, he felt less lonely having had to spent this Christmas trapped on a boat with a bunch of acquaintances and a few strange animals. At least there were some company around distracting him from almost two decades of solitude.

Sven gave Roar a glance. He saw a subtle smile on his dad's face. Roar may have felt the luckiest of them all. He had nothing to lose, but only to gain. He had gotten his life back, and his only son. However, all that came with a high price, which lay in front of their eyes as a flooded Lake Pihtamo. Suddenly, the feeling of guilt took over turning Roar's face serious.

As the low lying clouds from either side curtained the dimly lit horizon, a loud roar from the back of the boat broke the peaceful moment. The polar bears' calm faces turned hostile. They stood up. They needed to be fed.

Panicky, Sven grabbed Roar with him and they both squeezed themselves inside the cockpit, despite Viljo's resistance. Sven slammed the door shut. The three men were rammed inside like sardines in a can. They could barely breathe.

'There's too many of us here! Get out of here!' Viljo screamed and panted, but in vain. The men behind him didn't move. They were stuck.

Jaaku was left outside on the tree. The polar bears spotted him sitting alone at the top. They attempted to climb the mast, but the surface was too slippery and wet. They tried again and again, but always landing on their bottoms on the deck. In frustration, they kept punching the air.

'I was thinking...' Viljo tried to speak, his face squashed to the front window, 'there are some eggs and flour in the kitchen corner.'

'You have a kitchen here?' Roar asked.

'Well, a portable oven with one hot plate on top. Beside the door. Can you see it?'

'I think... I may be sitting on it,' Sven said, feeling something hard under his bottom.

'What are you suggesting?' Roar asked.

'Does either of you know how to make those damn pies? Or anything?'

'I believe Jaaku does,' Sven said hesitantly.

'Very funny,' Viljo smirked. 'That's not gonna help us at all. He's trapped on top of the tree and soon be eaten by the polar bears if we don't do something about it.'

'I can't cook,' Roar said, 'apart from preparing fish.'

'Me neither,' Viljo said. 'Aune always did all the cooking in our house.'

'Ida always makes these amazing pies at Christmas time,' Sven remembered longingly.

'Do you have any idea how she makes them?' Roar asked.

'I have seen her doing it. She's definitely using eggs and flour or something. I'm not sure.'

'Or, we just shoot the bears?' Viljo snorted.

'No!' Sven said alarmingly. 'I haven't seen a one single shot here that has done any good.'

'That's because we've always missed, but I guarantee this time I won't,' Viljo said and moved his hand around to look for the spear gun.

'No more shooting, please,' Sven said firmly and kicked the spear gun to the opposite corner. 'I will try and make those pies.'

'Fine,' Viljo snorted and stopped searching for the weapon. 'We have nothing to lose. Open the cupboard below where you're standing.'

Sven shifted his bottom away from the hotplate and stepped down, squashing Roar against the opposite wall, who again pushed Viljo to the dashboard and front window. Sven opened the cupboard underneath used for storing cooking utensils. A small egg carton and already opened flour packet lay on the edge of the shelf inside. He picked them up and turned the oven to hundred and fifty degrees Celsius, based upon his vague memories of Ida's baking. Also, he was almost certain there were some whisking involved. He mixed all four eggs with all the flour in a bowl and began whisking. 'Sorry,' he kept apologising repeatedly, as his elbow kept hitting Roar's ribcage.

'Don't worry about us,' Roar said, enduring the pain. 'Just bake like it's the last day of our lives.'

'It may as well be,' Viljo said gravely.

Meanwhile, outside, the polar bears were ready for another attempt to catch Jaaku. Rather than avoiding the claws, though, Jaaku leaned down, putting himself in danger. 'Add salt! Add salt!' he yelled, after seeing Sven with a bowl and a whisk. But the polar bears roaring covered Jaaku's cry.

Sven's mixture was ready. He located a can of tuna from the same cabinet. He mixed the tuna in the dough. As he opened the oven door, a hot baking tray waited inside. He spread the dough straight on the tray.

Jaaku witnessed the baking tray and the dough mixture flying in the oven. 'Bake thirty minutes in two hundred degrees!' he screamed, but again in vain. Although he feared they may not have half an hour. The polar bears would rip the boat apart in any minute or second.

'How long do we have to wait?' Roar asked.

'I don't know... ten to fifteen minutes,' Sven estimated.

'Not sure we have that long.'

Nervously, Sven tapped his fingers on the oven glass. The smell began to spread around the cockpit, bringing back sweet memories from Christmas time. The delicious taste of Ida's pies crawled on Sven's tongue. As they say, *the way to the man's heart is through his stomach*. Ida was a magnificent cook. He licked his lips. His heart ached.

A loud thump from the roof of the cabin alarmed the men crammed inside. As if someone heavy walked on top of them. Sven looked through the back window. One of the polar bears had disappeared from his sight, soon, landing at the front deck in front of Viljo's view.

'Er...er...' Erm...ine panicked, not even being able to stutter properly as she faced the angry polar bear.

Beside Erm...ine, Less Weasel tried to pull a hatch open on

the deck floor, but it remained shut. More Weasel came to help, but the lid was too heavy to handle. As they yanked again, the other polar bear also jumped on the foredeck. The boat's nose dived and the bow sipped water.

One of the polar bears stretched out its arm and grabbed Erm...ine in its palm, examining her like King Kong holding hostage the female characters.

Between the feet of two polar bears, Squirr-El felt the responsibility to use the power invested in her. After all, she was a superhero and she had to live up to the expectation. She couldn't let the others down. She had to react. She shook her head and puffed her chest. She opened her mouth wide and sunk her sharp front teeth on the big toe of the polar bear closest to her. She bit as if she was chewing a hard nutshell.

The polar bear's painful roar made the other polar bear freak out and drop Erm...ine on the floor.

Squirr-El thought now was their time to hide. She jumped on the hatch, and with all her strength and her tiny palms ripped the hatch open just enough for all the small animals to sneak in. One by one, they hid, Squirr-El being the last cramming herself inside the bow deck storage box.

Fuming, the polar bear with a broken toe turned to the cabin where Viljo's face was pushed against the steamy, front window. The polar bear took a step forward and tapped the glass with its sharp claw. Viljo almost felt the claw scratching his nose through the window. The polar bear tapped a couple of times more and pondered, whether it would be possible to penetrate the glass with a single blow.

'Sven... I don't think we have much time,' Viljo said, staring at the polar bear eye to eye. He sounded calm but fearful, like a person who knew something bad was about to happen.

'It's been only... eight minutes,' Sven looked at the ticking clock on the front panel of the oven.

'You should take the pies out...' Viljo requested, but before he even managed to finish the sentence, the polar bear punched its fist through the front glass. The window shattered in little shards right next to Viljo's face. Luckily, though, all sharp pieces of glass dropped downwards and away from his face. But his neck got a tight embrace from the polar bear's claw. Its nails scratched his upper back. He could barely breathe.

Viljo's gagging got Sven panicking. Prematurely, he yanked the oven lid open, grabbed the tray on his thick sleeves and kicked the cabin door open.

'You made them!' Jaaku acknowledged out of sheer joy. Soon, his excitement, though, shifted into a slight disgust. 'They look... interesting.'

'Looks don't matter! It's a matter of life and death now,' Sven shouted and rushed around the cabin to the front to meet the hungry polar bears.

The polar bear released Viljo once Sven came out with the tray. Viljo collapsed in the arms of Roar, whereas Sven placed the tray on the deck floor and slid it across towards the polar bears' feet. They examined the pies carefully, mouth dripping. They began savouring.

The set-up at the bow was like an idea for a new cooking or baking reality show, where Sven as a contestant waited for the judges' verdict. Judges being the two, starving polar bears. Only a decent cooking could win the judges' hearts and save the lives of everyone on board. Or at least, buy them more time. *Was he voted out or chosen to stay?*

The polar bears took mouthfuls and chew. Both of them nodded satisfied.

'I think you did alright,' Jaaku gave Sven thumbs up.

Everyone looked attentively at the polar bears, like watching two babies eating, hoping them not to cry, but be quiet and in the end, fall asleep. But that vision only belonged to the perfect world, since after the third bite the bears' eyes widened and faces turned sour. Their stomachs growled loudly for everyone to hear. In anger, they chucked the half eaten pie *à la Sven* overboard. The polar bears stood in their towering heights, howling in culinary pain.

'You didn't add salt, did you?' Jaaku asked.

'No,' Sven said. 'Should I have?'

Jaaku nodded.

The polar bears started spatting everywhere. They stretched their long necks over the railing and sunk their faces in the icy cold water to gargle the disgusting taste away. They brushed their teeth with their hairy fingers. They coughed and gagged.

'You tried to poison them?' Viljo said.

The polar bears stood up straight, faced Sven and gave him looks that could kill.

'Save yourselves!' Jaaku screamed.

Viljo grabbed his spear gun and rushed outside. 'Pie polar disorder!'

'You can't,' Sven said, slowly losing faith on his own message. 'They're... endangered.'

'But we are in danger,' Viljo said firmly, and aimed.

Pleading, Sven looked at Roar, but Roar only nodded approvingly. 'Sorry, son. He must. Otherwise, we won't make it. None of us will.'

'Shoot them!' Jaaku chanted from above.

As Viljo put his finger on the trigger, a humming sound from the skies above caught their attention. In the distance, a small propeller plane pulled behind a black line of smoke. The engine of the plane kept cutting off.

'A rescue plane?' Roar pointed at the skies and waved his arms. 'Do you think they can see us?'

'The plane's coming towards us... very fast,' Jaaku said.

The cluttering sound of a broken engine got louder as the black smoke embraced the plane's body. The plane kept diving directly towards the boat.

'I have doubts whether that plane is here to save us,' Roar said and pulled Sven down with him. 'I... love you, son.'

'You think this is it?' Sven asked, but wasn't quite ready yet to confess his love.

Ignoring all his pains, Viljo threw himself flat on the floor and covered his skull under his palms as he had learned during the war to protect himself from airstrikes.

Jaaku came down the tree, hid inside the cabin and slammed the door shut.

Only the polar bears remained standing tall at the bow, unaware of the approaching danger. The poor giants had never seen a plane before. They couldn't comprehend what it meant and what the consequences may be.

As the plane swung past only centimetres away from the boat, one of its wings, however, caught one of the polar bears and took it away. Supported by only the wing, the polar bear flew above the lake, until the plane crash landed in the distance on the same icy island they had taken the polar bears on board earlier on.

It was quiet again. The noises the plane made had muted. The remaining polar bear sat alone at the bow whimpering. The inseparable couple had been divided.

'Are we still alive?' Sven whispered on the floor.

Jaaku gathered the courage to open the back door. 'The plane just caught one of the bears,' he said as he walked out, after having witnessed everything through the cabin window, 'and the plane was flown by... a hairy giant.'

'What!? You saw the pilot?' Sven asked and stood up.

'Look yourself,' Jaaku pointed at the ice berg where the plane wreck rested.

Viljo and Roar stood up, too, and they all looked at the direction they had sailed from. They saw a gigantic, hairy pilot jumping off the driver's seat. Its weight cracked the ice a little. There was smoke coming out of the plane.

'What is that!?' Sven said, stunned.

'No wonder the plane crash landed. The pilot's weight alone must have brought it down,' Roar said, equally amazed.

The pilot picked up its two, large suitcases and walked towards the edge of the ice, where the polar bear had fallen. From the back seat of the plane, a large cat-like figure jumped out carrying a small laptop case.

'There's two of them,' Jaaku noticed.

The pilot took off the helmet and goggles revealing its white, hairy face and a big head.

'Looks like some sort of... snowman?' Sven pondered.

'A yeti?' Roar suggested.

'Oh dear. This is the last thing we need,' Viljo sighed.

Look! The pilot's lifting the injured polar bear up on its shoulders,' Sven said. 'Now, it's looking this way. It's waving... to us?'

'Don't try and suggest that we should go back there,' Viljo

said, unimpressed.

'But it does kind of look... friendly,' Sven hesitated.

'So, did the polar bears, first.'

'Yaaaawnnn!' the monster pilot roared and spread its long, hairy arms.

# Chapter 58

# THE HAM'S COOKING

Christian opened his sore eyes. His vision was blurry. 'Am I in heaven?' A shadow appeared in front of him. Someone took his hand. 'Ida?'

'Christian!' Ida rejoiced. 'I thought... we thought we've lost you.' She squeezed his hand tighter, leaned over and kissed his cheek. A kiss, that warmed more than any woollen garment could ever do. Quickly, Ida pulled away. 'I'm sorry,' she said and looked away, but smiling subtly. Her cheeks turned rosy.

'No. Don't be,' Christian said, thinking, whether the kiss was only between two friends with the intention to nurture, or something more. 'What happened?'

'You went down the chimney into the flat last night, you remember?'

'I remember that, but... what about now? You seem so... happy.'

'Nothing,' Ida replied briefly and kept looking away.

Two thick blankets separated them. Christian was tucked in the warmth of both of them. He ran his hands under the blankets to feel his own body. He was bare chested. He moved further down and felt the skin of his thighs. 'Why am I... naked?'

'You nearly suffered hypothermia,' Ida said, blushing more.

Confused, Christian tucked the edges of the blankets under his body. 'But you've taken all my clothes away?'

'It was... erm... Marjukka.'

'What is it?' Marjukka appeared right behind them after hearing her name being pronounced. She wore an apron. 'Nice to have you back, hero. You did us a big favour, big boy,' she said, pointed a wooden cooking spoon at Christian and winked her eye at Ida.

'What's the smell?' Christian sniffed the air.

'We are preparing Christmas dinner,' Marjukka said proudly. 'We have lowered the ham down in the chimney above the fireplace for roasting, the ham you rescued. It should be ready in about four to five hours, perfectly for dinner time.'

'Impressive, how you still keep track of different meal times,' Christian smiled.

'Well, my stomach is telling me it's supposed to be lunch time now, but I'd say it's better we wait and all eat together once the ham is cooked. Birgget there has been very helpful. It won't be only ham we're eating, though. I told you I managed to bring some other food with me on the first journey up.'

Christian licked his hungry lips. 'I didn't know we have so much food.'

'We don't, really. This is all we have. Just about enough for one proper meal, perhaps some leftovers for tomorrow.'

'Last supper,' Christian said more gravely.

'Indeed,' Marjukka nodded.

'Well, then, I guess the only thing we can do is to enjoy and celebrate as if this was our last day,' Christian said and looked at Ida. Finally, she turned to him and nodded. She gave him a subtle, but melancholic smile, when a jolly singing from the distance caught their attention.

*'Ice on Lake Pihtamo, is life left well behind…'* drunken male voices howled from the lake echoing a famous wartime song.

'What is that?' Ida turned to face the lake.

The singing got louder, but slurred. The lyrics became beyond recognition.

'Aariak? Tomas?' Marjukka said. 'I totally forgot. They've been on the roof for all this time.'

'Hello!' Christian called. 'How are you coping, guys? Guys!?'

The singing stopped followed by a loud echoing hiccup. 'Never… better,' Aariak replied, sounding drunken.

'Are you sure?' Marjukka asked, concerned. She looked onto the direction she heard the responses coming from. 'What have you two been doing?'

'We've been mostly... drinking,' Tomas shouted jollily.

'We can hear that,' Marjukka replied. 'You must be starving?'

'Well, what can you do? We still haven't got any food here,' Aariak said.

*And we have more than enough*, Marjukka thought and looked down at Christian. 'There's no way we could get them some food?'

'How? Throw them?' Christian said. 'They are too far away. We cannot even see them. And please don't ask me to swim all the way there.'

Marjukka sighed in desperation.

'But it doesn't matter anymore,' Aariak added calmly but with a hint of hopelessness in his voice. 'The Wodka seems to be taking all the pain away, anyway.'

The survivors on the post office roof heard Aariak's and Tomas's glasses clinking. And the singing begun again. *'We've been bumbling here and tasting liquor, yeah...'*

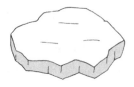

Chapter 59

# THE ARK OF PIHTAMO

'We are not going back there,' Viljo said while staring at the ice berg behind them.

The monster on the shore stared back at them for a while, but since nothing happened, it got distracted. It dropped its suitcases to the snow, opened one of them wide and pulled out a small foil tray. The monster offered the tray to the injured polar bear.

'It's... feeding the polar bear?' Roar observed.

'Airplane food?' Sven said. 'I was given one of those on my flight to England. I had to pay a fortune for that though, and it tasted like cardboard.'

'Poor polar bear,' Jaaku said.

'Do you think that white "gorilla" would have more food? Food for us?' Jaaku suggested.

Meanwhile, the little animals hiding in the storage box assumed the long silence above meant it was safe to surface. Squirr-El being the strongest took the responsibility to open the hatch again. She took the first glimpse. The route seemed clear. She pushed the lid fully open, and one by one, the rodents and weasels sneaked out of their hiding place. Even the remaining polar bear totally ignored the little animals sneaking around her feet while she was being transfixed to follow the destiny of her mate.

'Erm...' Erm...ine tried to catch the men's attention, but was ignored.

Pole Vole climbed on his pole to get a better view. Once he found his balance, he could just about to see over the railing. His face lightened. 'Are my little eyes lying or is that... Yetilag?'

'Yeti... what?' Sven turned to look down at the balancing Pole Vole. 'And where have you been hiding?'

'Ah. We totally forgot your existence,' Viljo snorted.

'You could have ended up as polar bear food,' Sven said. 'Be careful though. There's still one up there.'

'Luckily, we are very small. We can hide in many places,' Squirr-El said proudly.

'Is that also one of your superpowers? Being invisible?' Viljo smirked.

Squirr-El crossed her arms, offended.

'So, are you saying you recognise the monster pilot?' Sven asked Pole Vole.

'It's definitely Yetilag. Or a tired monster. Not even a monster, really, but very friendly and casual.'

'You mean, a yeti... with jetlag?'

'Kind of. They're tired all the time, because they travel long distances. Or long haul, as you call it. You only have to look at its baggy eyes. And it yawns a lot.'

'It's got baggy eyes for sure,' Jaaku confirmed through his telescope.

'How do you know all this?' Sven asked.

'In my home country of Ukraine, people of the nation believe in Yetilag's and talk about them in traditional folk tales. The stories tell that "they live in the vast plains and snowy mountains of Kazakhstan." No one has ever seen one though, neither have I. I have only seen artistic interpretations of them... and what is out there standing in front of our eyes is a very accurate portrayal from the drawings and paintings.'

'You believe in those stories?'

'Now I do. In fact, this is an amazing experience. A historical one. If I get a picture of that, I would make a fortune back home.'

'So, you think... yetilags are harmless?' Roar asked.

'Absolutely. Should be...' Pole Vole hesitated. 'In all those tales, they are always very friendly creatures. The only problem

I recall is that they get agitated when they get too much sleep. They should always be kept a little bit sleep deprived.'

'There we go. I think it's better to sail away,' Viljo said and took a step closer to the cabin.

'Hold on,' Sven said and raised his finger.

'What? You're not believing that random Kazakhstani bed time story?' Viljo grunted.

Sven pointed at the island while looking at Viljo. 'Look what Yetilag is doing to the polar bear. Giving food. And its twice as big as the polar bear. What if it has more food - food for us? Who knows what its big luggage have in store for us.'

'Yeah. Who knows?' Viljo said suspiciously.

'What about the cat?' Roar asked and pointed at the little, spotty feline next to Yetilag. 'What does your folklores tell about cats with... what is that... a computer?'

'Never heard,' Pole Vole said, squinting his eyes. 'But they seem to get along well. Seems like Yetilag's co-pilot.'

'Let's go back then,' Roar said, determined. 'Viljo, get your spear gun ready, just in case.'

'What are you... in charge now?' Viljo said anxiously.

'Well, isn't it obvious that we must go back there. Firstly, we cannot separate the two polar bears. Secondly, this Yetilag may actually have food for us,' Roar explained.

The other men, even the little animals nodded. That's how desperate they had become.

Viljo shook his head, but obeyed. Submissively, he steered the boat back towards the ice berg. This time, though, he was well awake and approached the shore more carefully.

Meanwhile, the polar bear finished the leftovers of Yetilag's airplane snack. After the meal, the polar bear rested calmly against Yetilag's shoulder. Only having just met, the two giants seemed like best buddies already. Yetilag's gentle nature and generosity became even more noticeable as the men got closer.

'Is... Y-y-yetilag... a c-c-carnivore?' asked Erm...ine.

'They should be vegans, which may partly explain their constant tiredness,' Pole Vole explained.

Yetilag picked the injured polar bear on its shoulder and began walking towards the approaching boat. The large cat walked next to them.

'The cat looks like a lynx,' Roar said.

'I can't believe we are really doing this,' Viljo said under his breath as he stopped the boat, just in case, a few meters away from the edge. The massive, intimidating size of Yetilag became more apparent. Jaaku squeezed the tree branches tighter underneath him. Viljo came out of the cabin with his spear gun. Squirr-El puffed her chest. Sven and Roar looked tensely.

'Yaaaawnnn!' Yetilag repeated its animalistic roar.

'I still don't feel good about this,' Viljo said.

'Actually, that was its expression of happiness,' Pole Vole translated.

'Is that what it said? That it's happy to see us?' Sven asked.

'Yes. You got it spot on.'

'Yaaaawnnn!' Yetilag added.

'Doesn't sound happy to me,' Viljo snorted.

'It said that they started flying from Kazakhstan three days ago.'

'Really? I think everything Yetilag roars sounds exactly the same,' Viljo said.

'It's all about the variation in intonation,' Pole Vole clarified. 'A different pitch and tone in Yetilag's voice can change the meaning of the message.'

'Strange. An animal that doesn't talk, technically,' Sven said.

'As it should be,' Roar added, '...in reality.'

'But this animal flies planes,' Viljo said. 'So, there goes your reality out of the window.'

'I think reality has gone out of the window a long time ago,' Sven added.

'I'm pretty sure there was someone who said that monkeys don't fly planes in Kazakhstan?' Jaaku pondered.

'It's not a monkey. It's Yetilag, 'Pole Vole said. 'Abominable but tired monster. Rare species. One of its kind.'

'Abominable? Where did you learn such a word, Pole Vole?' Viljo asked.

'Wikipedia.'

'Yaaaawnnn!'

'Yetilag says they had to have a stopover in Amsterdam.'

'Is that why they crash landed? They've been smoking something,' Jaaku smiled.

'Yaaaawnnn!'

'No. The plane ran out of petrol.'

'Off all the places in the world, they had to crash land here. Why?' Sven asked.

'Yaaaawnnn!'

'They were on a journey to see the real Father Christmas.'

'You are making this up, Pole Vole?' Viljo smiled.

'Honestly. That's what Yetilag said.'

'And the little friend?' Roar asked.

The lynx stepped away from Yetilag's shadow.

'Yaaaawnnn!'

'Her name is Links, computer literate cat, co-pilot, responsible of navigation.'

They all greeted Links with a wave.

'Navigator, you say? Computer literate, too?' Viljo said, suddenly oozing curiosity. *That might come in handy*, he thought. 'I think we should offer these creatures... a lift.'

'Why such a sudden generosity?' asked Sven, surprised.

'The navigation system is down,' Viljo whispered to Sven, 'and none of us has really any idea where we are. I never thought I'd be saying this, but that big cat may be our best chance, if she can really navigate.'

'That we shall find out soon,' Sven said and turned to face the island again. 'Would you two like to join us?'

As the side of the boat gently touched the shore, Roar stepped out to meet and greet the newcomers.

'Be careful, dad,' Sven said and followed him.

'Don't worry. I have a good feeling about this,' Roar said confidently over his shoulder.

Immediately, Viljo welcomed Links straight into the cabin and prepared her a desk next to the malfunctioning navigation system. The others observed dumbfounded Viljo's sudden politeness.

The polar bears felt re-energized once being reunited. They took over the entire stern again lifting the bow up. Fortunately, both of them seemed tamed and submissive in the dominating presence of Yetilag. The polar bears sat quietly at the back, despite their rumbling, hungry stomachs.

Yetilag with its enormous sized luggage was welcomed to the front to distribute the weight evenly. Everyone gasped, when the boat sunk half a metre, the sides nearly edging the water level. The weasels and rodents occupied the roof of the cabin. Jaaku remained in the tree tower. Viljo, together with Links and her equipment filled the cabin space.

'We have a slight problem,' Viljo said, concerned. 'We haven't got much space left. And the boat is nearly sinking.'

Sven and Roar still standing on the ice looked at each other. All the rest already on the boat looked at Sven and Roar and then at each other.

'There must be something we can throw away? Something, we can get rid of?' Sven suggested.

'Yetilag's luggage?' Jaaku said.

'Yaaaawnnn!' Yetilag waved its fist.

The eyes turned to Pole Vole to hear the translation.

'That's all it's got left, its assets.'

'Well, we have nothing left either, or do we?' Jaaku said.

'That we only find out once we discover land and understand the scale of this flooding and destruction,' Sven said.

'I meant, on this boat,' Jaaku added.

'I'd say we get rid of the suitcases,' Viljo suggested.

'Yaaaawnnn!' Yetilag sounded confrontational.

'But those suitcases contain...' Pole Vole explained seriously, 'the remaining artefacts, historical items and documents the small community of Yetilag's has left behind. It's the last of its kind remaining after the evil hunters destroyed the few other remaining Yetilags. They are hunted for food, or just for being misunderstood as savage and hostile creature, which they are not.'

'You must be kidding?' Viljo said.

'It's true. If this luggage is left behind and lost, the entire historical evidence of the existence of Yetilags will be gone forever and never retrieved.'

'We have Yetilag itself. Isn't that evidence enough?'

'Yaaaawnnn!'

'But all those items will outlive us all and carry the legacy long after us mortals are gone.'

'How about any food in those bags?' Viljo asked.

Yetilag shook its head and looked down.

A loud crackling noise from the island caught their attention. The weight of the crash-landed plane cracked the ice and it began to sink. Yetilag's saddened eyes observed, how only in a few seconds the wreckage of the plane disappeared through the ice in the depths of the lake. Its potential travel methods were suddenly limited to just one: the boat. Yetilag slumped miserable on the floor next to the luggage.

'Fine. We understand,' Roar said calmly. He observed the boat bursting of passengers. There was possibly one space for one average size man on top of Yetilag's luggage, if they can bare the weight. 'Son, if Yetilag don't mind, you climb on the suitcases... and I will stay behind.'

Yetilag nodded approvingly.

'What?' Sven said, shocked.

'We must save everyone already on board. But we cannot take any further risks. If one of us can't come, I shall be the one to stay behind.'

'There has to be another way. Rock, paper, scissors? Throw away something else? There must be other unnecessary things in this boat we don't need.'

'We have gotten rid of everything,' Viljo said. 'We have no food left. And since the lake is empty, we can't even fish for our survival. The only thing we can do now, is to sail, and sail as fast as we can, which won't be that fast considering how full this boat is, and hope we find something that would save us within next few hours. Otherwise, we'll all be doomed.'

Roar examined the creaking boat. 'The front is filled with Yetilag and the luggage, the stern with polar bears, the little animals have taken the roof, Jaaku is at the tree tower, Viljo and Links with her computers needs to be in the cabin. Son. It's my time to step aside,' Roar said and held Sven from the shoulder.

'Why not me?' Sven pleaded.

'Because, you're young. You have all your life ahead.'

'But... I have only just found you... to lose you again.'

'As Viljo said, the lake is empty. We are trapped here... and it's all my fault. I will take the responsibility of my actions now by giving space to the ones who deserve it.'

'But...'

'Listen! It would be wrong to leave anyone else behind. Yetilag saved all of us by calming down the polar bears that are all endangered and have to get to safety. Links can help Viljo and Jaaku to navigate, I am confident about that. And you're young. There's someone who cares about you, is waiting for you and you can share a life with. Everyone on this boat is more important than me. My actions has caused nothing but trouble and headache. The least I can do now is to sacrifice for the sake of making this world a better place. We must protect the vulnerable, weak and young. The future. That is all of you, not me.'

'But...but...' Sven lowered his voice while biting his teeth, 'Viljo is even older than you and more miserable.'

'Viljo has done so much good in this life, unlike me. He's a war hero. He was there standing with all the brave men shoulder to shoulder protecting the home land and risking his own life. And most of all, he has been there competing against you, making you a better fisherman without you necessarily even realising it. His fierce attitude to challenge you in all those competitions made you the best. Whereas, I wasn't there for you when you needed me the most. In a strange way, he has been the father figure, an example and an idol for you that I should have been. He even joined you to find out what was wrong with Lake Pihtamo. Because of him, you found me... And most of all, he's the only one who can really steer this boat.'

'Don't say that. You were always there with me. In my heart. It's not your fault that you were not physically there. You were taken away from us.'

'Maybe, I was. Maybe, I wasn't. Maybe, it was something I subconsciously wanted to do.'

'To be... the Lord of Herrings?'

'Not that,' Roar lowered his voice together with his gaze. 'To be very honest, me and your mother were not at our happiest at the time. I felt like I was failing as a father. I think I wanted...

something else from life.'

'You got that for sure. Did it make you happy?'

'It may sound like every fisherman's dream to have all that power I had as the Lord of Herrings. But it wasn't so. I was lonely. I always knew my actions would cause controversy, even though the intention and basic principle was good. And I am sure not just myself, but many others as well do blame me from this catastrophe. I don't want to be remembered this way.'

'But you said the fish are all safe? That is a good, heroic deed.'

'Yes. But I also took all the fish away from your reach, all fishermen, without communicating with the community. I just did it, because I was able. I had the power. It was a very selfish act.'

'Not selfish at all. You were thinking about the best of Lake Pihtamo.'

'But I didn't tell anybody. I had this idea the Lord of Herrings was above all and doesn't need to be accountable to anyone. Very egoistic thing to do. But I paid a price for that. Eventually, my actions caused the battle with Mooses and Psalmon that launched the entire cycle of these natural disasters. Perhaps, any of this wouldn't have happened, if I let Wolferring eat Lake Pihtamo empty. Who knows, maybe someone else would have come up with a better solution. Maybe, someone would have just hunt Wolferring down, stick a sword through its heart and fry it in a pan, or whatever it takes to get rid of that monster.'

'Apart from us now, no one has ever done anything about it. At least, you were trying to do something, dad.'

'Please, don't. I have been away for so long and no one would notice me being gone. No one would remember whether I am here or not. No one cares. Seriously.'

'I remember. I care.'

'I am forever grateful you do and I hope you carry no hard feelings towards me.'

'I forgive you, dad.'

'Thank you. That means a world to me.'

'So... you'll come with us? We'll find you space.'

'I cannot. It's too risky for all of you. The boat simply cannot take it. But your forgiveness heals my soul. Tell your mother how sorry I am for not being there for you two. I would do nothing to hurt my family.'

'Dad...'

'And tell her I forgive her, too.'

'You forgive her?'

'There's something we never told you, and I assume she still hasn't told you either.'

'Told me what?'

'Since you're a grown up man now, I can tell you that your mother had sort of an... entanglement with this one Italian singer, Mr Martello.'

'Lumbardi Martello?'

'Yes. You know him?'

'I remember when I was little, you and mum listened to his C-cassette's.'

'He was a great singer and did well here in Pihtamo. I guess he wasn't that appreciated back home in Italy and that's why he left to come here up north where his exotic dark brown eyes, slick black hair and adoring accentuated singing voice were highly appreciated, especially, amongst the female population of Pihtamo. Women absolutely worshipped him.'

'My mother? I cannot believe it!'

'It was a difficult time for both of us. Not just for us, but all men and couples in Pihtamo. The women went crazy about Martello. They were out of control. His romantic Italian ballads melted a woman after woman, married or not. That one night Birgget went to see Lumbardi's gig with her friends, but she didn't return home until the early hours of the morning. I knew something was wrong. The rumours started to spread. However, it took nearly two years for her to admit what had happened. I assume, she just felt so bad about it that she couldn't hold it inside any longer.'

'I don't know what to say. I thought you both genuinely liked his music, only the music.'

'We did enjoy his ballads. The tunes had something familiar to the music from our region, but with a little exotic spice added to them. He did lots of tango, waltz and good dance music. But most of the men in Pihtamo were naïve and didn't understand the power he had over women. We were all fools, unable to sing, talk, dance or look after ourselves and our other halves. Most of the gigs us men were too drunk to understand how simultaneously our partners had fallen under Lumbardi's spell. Unfortunately, your mother was one of those women affected amongst with, I believe, most of the women in the village.'

'I'm sorry, dad.'

'Don't worry. It happened long time ago. And it was just one night - or so she claimed. In the end, I think she understood once the rumours about him started to spread that he was untameable womanizer and not worth breaking a marriage or a family.'

'You believe her?'

'I don't know what to believe anymore, except that she was a good mother and has raised you well.'

'She is. She has.'

'And that's why I forgive her.'

'If I'm right, nowadays this Mr. Martello works as a pizza chef in an Italian restaurant that opened in the outskirts of Pihtamo a few years ago. He's hosting a monthly karaoke night there.'

'Really? He's still around? Must be him then. I doubt there's too many Italian's at these latitudes. Too harsh environment for their sensitive souls, I believe.'

'I agree. But it seems, he has lost lot of that charm over the decades.'

'You've met him?'

'Well, actually... erm... he sang... in our wedding.'

'Ah.'

'Sorry, dad.'

'No. Don't worry. You couldn't have known. I just wish I was there.'

'You were there... in my thoughts. And besides, we didn't plan Mr. Martello to be there. It was just one of those ready-made wedding packages where they provide everything, even the singer. All you have to do is turn up.'

'Don't tell me you went to Lasi Vekasi?'

'How do you know!? I didn't even know the place exists.'

'You won't believe, but... me and your mum got married there! It had just opened... twenty-nine years ago.'

'I cannot believe it!'

'I can't believe the chapel still exists! I have to say, though, I somehow always hoped my son would have... how should I say... more glamorous wedding.'

'Trust me. Lasi Vekasi worked much better for me. Like father, like son... And what comes to Mr. Martello, I wouldn't be too concerned about him either. He weighs about hundred and forty kilograms nowadays and there's only a few grey strands left of that thick dark hair he used to have. And he can't quite hit those high notes anymore as he did when he was a young man.'

'Well, God bless him. The time does the trick for all of us. But I have to admit that I can't blame him. I probably would have lived like Lumbardi when he was younger, if I had the same talent, looks and confidence.'

'You were very handsome. You still are.'

'Thank you, son.'

'Dad. Please don't go. We'll find another solution.'

'Now, listen to me. You MUST lead everybody else on this boat to safety and do it now. Between you and me, I think you're the only sane creature on that boat anyway. Then, if you or someone can, you'll come and get me later. You understand? Keep on sailing as long as you find land. We are surrounded by mountains and some of those peaks must be above the surface for you to hang on, wait till the water level drops, or if it comes to that, you will start a new life in a changed environment. There is always hope, even when the hope is gone.' Roar took Sven in his arms.

Sven responded squeezing even harder, never wanting to let go. 'What about... catching the last herring? Or Wolferring?'

'You can do it without me. You know you can do anything you want. You have the powers unimaginable, yet undiscovered.'

'What about all fish from Pihtamo? Where should we start looking for them? Are you sure you haven't got any recollection?'

'Ah, yes. Glad you reminded,' Roar said, released his hold of Sven and began ploughing through his trouser pocket. He handed Sven a piece of paper and whispered, 'Here. Take this map. It shows the exact location of the pond where the fishes are hidden. Don't show or give it to anyone else. The amount of fish there is priceless. It's a gold mine. People would kill to get a hold of this information. But do remember that map was drawn before any of this flooding happened, so things can look a bit different today.'

'I thought you couldn't remember.'

'I did, but I didn't want the others to hear. That piece of information is worth a fortune. Keep it to yourself,' Roar said, took a step away from Sven and gestured him to hop on board.

Holding his tears, Sven climbed on the front and squeezed himself as the last passenger right under Yetilag's hairy armpit and onto his luggage.

'We'll come back and get you, dad!' Sven shouted.

'First, do as I told you. Find Ida. Your mother. Everyone. Don't worry about me. I will survive. I always have.'

'I will. Thank you for this short time we spent together. I will always love you, dad.'

Standing on the edge of the ice, Roar waved as they sailed away. Sven couldn't hold back his tears anymore after losing his father for the second time. This time, though, he feared, would be the last. Suddenly, Sven was saddened by the words he remembered from the Bible he had so carefully examined. *We don't get a second chance.*

Chapter 60

# LAYING THE TABLE

As Marjukka pulled the rope, a steaming lump of hot foil rolled over the edge of the masonry. She unwrapped the foil, revealing a juicy glistening ham with a golden crispy skin. The temperature reading at the meat thermometer sticking out of the flesh indicated the pork leg was well done. Grease and fat had dripped on a tray tied underneath the ham. She swiped some of the fatty liquid on a baking brush and spread it all over the skin. While licking her lips, she finished the surface with a thin layer of mustard before wrapping the ham back in the embrace of the foil to rest.

Birgget was setting the dining table when out of the corner of her eye, she noticed Ida and Christian close together again. They sat side by side looking out onto the horizon. He put his arm over her shoulders like dating couples do in the cinemas. Birgget took a pause and cleared her throat noticeably. 'Sharing body heat again?' She gave her a judgemental glance.

Ida looked over her shoulder and their eyes met. Slightly embarrassed, Ida turned back to Christian. 'It's dinner time soon.' She kissed him on the cheek again and walked to Birgget.

Christian observed her from behind as she walked away. Her hair was messy, teeth not brushed for days and clothes all wrinkled. But he wasn't bothered about her scruffiness. Everyone on the roof had had equally rough time and didn't look their finest. Their outer appearance were the least of the worries.

Christian saw her as beautiful as the first time they had met at high school.

'Do you need help?' Ida asked as she parked next to Birgget.

Birgget said nothing. Only one of the plates slipped out of her hands and smashed into pieces against the rooftop.

Christian and Marjukka turned to look. Ida responded to them with a gentle nod, indicating that everything was "under control". Then, she turned to face Birgget again. 'Are you alright?'

Birgget watched quietly how some of the shards of the broken plate fell into the water. A few bigger pieces remained tangling on the edge of the roof. She didn't bother picking them up. She only sobbed. Ida stepped closer to comfort her, but she pulled away. 'I dropped a plate! Why is that such a big deal?'

'You were thinking about Sven, were you?' Ida asked.

'Of course! I think about my son every minute,' Birgget said, fuming. 'How about you? How do you feel? What's on your mind!?'

Ida looked at her, dumbfounded. 'I feel... awful,' she said and looked away.

'You're still married, you remember?' Birgget whispered viciously and saw how Christian turned his back to them. 'Sven may still be alive, out there, looking for you.'

'What's that supposed to mean?' Ida also glanced over at Christian and then back to Birgget.

'My son has been gone for a few days...' Birgget started louder, but then lowered her voice again, 'and you're already in the arms of someone else.'

'Someone else?'

'He likes you. A lot. And he wants more.'

'Christian? Nah,' Ida said and flipped her palm towards her. 'We're just friends.'

'You've said that before, but you two sure don't act like one. The way he's looking at you, the way he's holding you. It all makes me cringe.'

'We're only victims of this... absurd situation,' Ida explained. 'The body heat is so important. He could have lost his life.'

'Please! Don't tell me about body heat,' Birgget raised her

hand and pointed a finger at Ida. 'He's taking the advantage of the situation. Of you.'

'This... armageddon!? He's not a monster. He wants our best. To protect us.'

'Sure he does. As all men do,' Birgget sighed.

'I'm sorry if we've made you feel uncomfortable, but...' Ida lowered her voice to whispering. 'Please be aware that I have no feelings for Christian. I'm thinking about Sven as much as you do, I swear. But I feel lost. And Christian has been a great support, a special friend I need, we all need now in these difficult times. I hope you understand.'

Birgget said nothing. She only picked up some more plates and chucked them at designated places on the table.

'When you lost Roar, you must have needed someone near to support you?' Ida asked hesitantly.

'Yes,' Birgget snorted. 'But it took years that I could have ever considered another man, not days! And don't talk like Sven has disappeared, please.'

Quietly, Ida observed as Birgget aggressively swung some cutlery near the plates. Ida didn't know what else to say or do. Nothing came to her mind. She stared at the horizon, but even the vastness of the lake gave no guidance. Even the singing of Aariak and Tomas from the roof of the Arctic Bar had muted. Only darkness and silence all around them, apart from the clinkering noises Birgget made while finishing setting the table.

Marjukka arrived breaking the tension between the two by placing the ham tray in the middle of the table. 'Let it sit there for another ten minutes and then we can start,' she said, sounding overly excited. 'In the meantime, I will go and make myself ready.'

'Make yourself ready?' Ida repeated, but by the time, Marjukka had already disappeared behind the chimney pipe.

From under the pile of the remaining supplies, Marjukka pulled out a make-up bag. From the bag, she revealed a little mirror, hairbrush, a little hairspray, some mascara and a lipstick. Ida sneaked behind the chimney pipe to spy on Marjukka and how she "got herself ready" for Christmas dinner.

Soon, Birgget bumped into Ida from behind. Her curiosity

won over, too, and she couldn't help but join Ida to find out about Marjukka's intentions. In secrecy, they watched how Marjukka dusted the tiredness off her face step by step, applied healthy colours on her cheeks and mysterious shadows around her eyes.

Once Marjukka finished her makeover, she opened a large carry bag beside her. She pulled out a pair of high heels and two dresses: a red and a black.

Amazed, Ida and Birgget thought they had seen enough. They didn't wanna get caught spying on Marjukka but returned beside the table to mind their own businesses.

As Marjukka revealed herself on a long black lace dress, a diamond bracelet with a matching necklace, two inch heels, which in those icy latitudes were considered as dangerously high, and her hair and face all made up, Ida and Birgget stopped and stared. Marjukka smiled shyly and asked everyone, 'What do you think?'

Birgget and Ida nodded approvingly.

Christian turned around and rubbed his eyes in wonder.

'You look... very nice,' Ida said, envious. She felt immediate pressure and insecurity about her own, unpolished looks.

'Very nice? She looks amazing!' Christian said excitedly.

'She does look great,' Birgget admitted while releasing a subtle, uncomfortable laughter. 'It's a shame I didn't bring my evening gown.'

'Ah, sorry,' Marjukka said and rushed back to her changing area. 'I might have something here for you two to wear.'

'Don't be silly,' Birgget said and waved the air.

However, Ida followed Marjukka. 'Really? That's nice. What do you have?' Ida asked curiously while grinning over her shoulder at Birgget.

'Well, I have the red dress I first thought about wearing,' Marjukka said.

'This is all the clothes you packed?' Ida asked, looking at Marjukka's selection.

'More or less.'

'They're all... party clothes,' Ida laughed. 'What were you thinking?'

'Well, you never know...'

'Who you gonna meet while trapped on the roof?'

'That's the life of a single. Have to be prepared, always. I thought it's Christmas time coming and...' Marjukka said, feeling a tad silly.

'Good thinking, I have to say,' Ida replied positively. 'Exactly what we need. A little makeover to cheer us all up.'

Finally, Birgget appeared behind them. 'Would you have anything... for an older lady?'

Marjukka raised her eyebrow and looked deeper inside the bag. 'The good thing is we're all about the same size,' she said and pulled out a dark brown satin dress and a set of white pearls.

'That looks lovely!' Birgget said with a youthful joy. 'May I try it on?'

Marjukka nodded and handed her the clothes.

And Ida settled for the long, red dress.

The backside of the chimney pipe suddenly turned into an open air fitting room. The women started giggling and chuckling like on a girls shopping trip or getting ready for a big night out.

Christian listened to the chattering of the women. He felt satisfied and powerful. *In the end, a Christmas that seemed to turn into a nightmare, is starting to look like one of the best celebrations ever. I am the only man here with three lovely women, all dressing up and making themselves pretty. First, we enjoy the roast and then... I rule the roost.*

Ida was the first one to step out into the moonlight. She posed for Christian and asked, 'What do you think?'

'Erm... You...' he started, but swallowed his words. 'You look... absolutely stunning. The most beautiful thing I've seen... well... ever.'

Ida responded with a smile Christian had never seen before. Her eyes sparkling, she disappeared again behind the chimney to help Birgget with her pearl necklace.

'What about me?' Christian said and stood up, yet still wrapping his body with blankets. 'Any tuxedos or dinner suits?'

Marjukka's head popped out. 'You look good as you are.'

'But you see... erm... I still haven't got any trousers on. Or anything.'

'Ah. That reminds me...' Marjukka said, her voice echoing behind the chimney pipe. 'I had a little accident. I hung your clothes to dry above the fireplace next to the ham, but then the trousers fell... into the fire.'

'You burned my trousers!?' Christian gasped. As a response, though, he could only hear more chuckling from the women.

'I'm sorry,' Marjukka said, still laughing a little. 'You can always borrow some of my clothes if you want?'

'Fine,' Christian sighed. 'What have you got left?'

'A couple of midi skirts,' Marjukka said, holding back her laughter, 'and tights.'

Christian chuckled uncomfortably. *It's harder to rule the roost in tights.*

Chapter 61

# LINKS THE ENGINEER

'All done,' Links said, dusting her paws together behind her laptop.

'Already?' Viljo said, surprised. 'That took only, what, twenty minutes?'

'Everything should be working again. The navigation system, the echo sounder. Let me know the co-ordinates and I can set them up for you. Where are we heading to?'

'Very impressive,' Viljo said, showing a rare, subtle smile.

'Number one in my class,' Links said and proudly flashed her graduation certificate from the side pocket of her briefcase.

Viljo switched the echo sounder on. Once the screen lit, the diagrams seemed distorted and colours blurry. He tilted his head to get a better understanding of the confusing graphics. 'You have installed the echo sounder... upside down!'

'Really!?' Links' eyes widened. Panicky, she started shuffling through her notes and papers.

'Yes! When the water's supposed to be deep, it's shallow and vice versa.'

'I'm sorry, but... I never said I am a marine engineer.'

'Can you see that?' Viljo pointed at the screen. 'Where the snowy island is supposed to be, the echo sounder says it's eighty metres deep!'

'Perhaps... it is that deep under the island?' Links said, hesitantly. 'It is after all a floating piece of ice.'

'Then, why does the echo sounder say we're supposed to be ten metres above the surface right now?' Viljo snorted. 'Have you actually dealt with echo sounders before?'

'I have... but really long time ago. It must be about year and a half ago.'

'That's not so long ago.'

'In cat years it is.'

Viljo sighed and shook his head. 'And you were the number one in your class? What did you study again?'

'CAT engineering in the University of Felinestad,' Links said proudly.

'Of course,' Viljo said sarcastically. 'Were you the only student?'

'There were about twenty of us.'

'All cats?'

'Cats?'

'CAT engineering?'

'Caterpillar engineering,' Links clarified.

'For cats?'

'Mainly for kids.'

'Kids don't go to university.'

'I'm not talking about students, but you know those small caterpillars you see at sand boxes.'

'They require engineering?'

'Lots. Kids are the worst at breaking things. Worse than grown-up builders with their adult size equipment.'

'Didn't know that,' Viljo rolled his eyes.

'There are so many things we don't know in this world.'

'Like... how to fix the echo sounder,' Viljo smirked.

'It still works. You just have to remember that shallow water is actually deep and vice versa. Think the opposite.'

'I'm too old for this,' Viljo sighed and turned away.

'We've heard that before,' Sven intervened, leaning to the door frame. 'Just take us to the centre of the town.'

Viljo switched on the navigation system that Links had supposedly fixed as well. He accessed the map of the town of Pihtamo. At the first glance, the map seemed to be at least right way around, but as he examined it in more detail, his face turned sour again. 'Something is not right here. For example, this street,' Viljo pressed his finger on the navigation screen, 'Tölkkikalankatu, doesn't exist anymore.'

'What's the problem now?' Links sighed, annoyed.

'And, what have you done to the navigation system?' Viljo asked.

'I fixed it.'

'But the street map is out of date.'

'Ah, yes. Glad you brought that up. I thought, perhaps, not many things has changed in the area within last thirty years.'

'You used a map from the nineteen-eighties!?' Viljo groaned.

'Late eighties.'

Viljo shook his head in awe.

'I'm sorry to say little fella, but lots of things have changed in thirty years,' Sven said from the doorway.

'Actually, that's not true,' Viljo pondered. 'In fact, most of the things have been there since the nineteen-fifties, like the bar and the building where the pie shop is today.'

'Well, you should remember. You have been around the longest,' Sven said.

'Thanks for the reminder,' Viljo snorted. 'There may be some roof tops that are not on this map. Supermarket is new. And the post office. Also, trees have obviously grown, the park has been created.'

'Links, why you couldn't use a map that was up-to-date?' Sven asked.

'It was too expensive to download the latest map. And besides, they don't give credit cards or Paypal accounts to feline. I got this one for free.'

'No kidding,' Viljo rolled his eyes.

'Hold on. You have the access to Internet? Here?' Sven asked.

'No. I downloaded these maps before we departed our flight with Yetilag.'

'No wonder you crash-landed,' Viljo said under his breath.

'We crash-landed, because we ran out of petrol! Because this lake is much bigger than on our map. It's like a vast ocean. It had nothing to do with how old our maps were,' Links raised her voice so that also everyone outside could hear her. 'What has happened? How can a thirty-year-old map be so inaccurate? This area is nothing like it used to be.'

'Well, you see...' Sven started.

'You're right. It's nothing like it used to be,' Viljo interrupted. 'Before everything was better, but that doesn't matter. Now, we have to decide what to do. You're asking me to navigate above a flooded town using a map that was created before this gentleman here was even born?' Viljo said, pointing at Sven, but still looking at Links.

'What other options we have?' Sven asked. 'We've nearly run out of petrol and food. We know at least from Squirr-El, there are survivors on the roof tops.'

'Or on the mountains,' Jaaku suggested from the top overhearing the conversation. 'And the mountains should be easier to approach.'

'The forest surrounding the mountains can be quite dense. There may be some tree tops lurking underwater,' Sven suggested.

'Tree tops are nothing compared to roof tops and pointy edges of buildings. Colliding on one of them could seriously damage the boat,' Viljo said.

'However, the people on the mountains, I would assume, can survive longer, whereas the people trapped on the roof tops have less time and chances to survive,' Sven said.

'We know exactly why you wanna head to town,' Viljo said.

'But it's true. People on the mountains are safe...r,' Sven argued. 'They have land, resources. They can start a new life if they want and can. But if there are people trapped on the roofs, they may have nothing. We must go and help them.'

'Fine. We should do that then,' Jaaku gave up.

Sven gave Viljo a pleading look. 'If we just approach the town slowly and wary of any obstacles.'

Links could only shrug her shoulders.

Viljo sighed and turned to face the front. Following the ancient map installed in the navigation system by a lynx, supported by an upside-down echo sounder and Viljo's vague memories of the lake, paved them the way towards the unknown - a town they all used to recognise. First and foremost, he had to rely on luck, which he wasn't sure he ever had. He was eighty-four years old and still alive. The only thing he considered himself lucky was the longevity of life. Those were all the tools they had left. Nothing else. The snowfall intensified.

Chapter 62

# CHRISTMAS DINNER

The set of candles stood flickering on the red cloth covering the dining table. Green napkins lay under each one's silver cutlery. The semi-circle shaped roasted ham sat on a golden tray, dominating the setting. Glamorously dressed women in Marjukka's best party wear had tucked under layers of woollen thermal undergarments and tights to keep warm. Only Christian seemed rugged, unshaven himself. Only his naturally straight blond hair received more volume and waves being unwashed and dirty for days. Surprisingly, the natural look made him even more attractive in the eyes of the adjoining females. Only his piece of clothing, Marjukka's red woolly tights, stripped some of that masculinity away. Even his longish leather coat reached barely below his hips. But the women were not really that bothered. They had other concerns.

Each one of the four around the table looked at one another. They acknowledged the fact that this may be their last fine meal together, ever. The hope of survival diminished hour by hour. The smiles never left their faces, though, but only faded. Yet, tonight there was no space for mourning. There was no discussion or mentioning about future anymore. There was nothing left to be said. They could only celebrate the little joys of life, savour the delicious food on the table and enjoy each other's company.

Potentially the ham, slightly shrunken whilst cooking though, would be enough to feed them for another day or two, who knew. The weather got colder by the hour. The wood or any other combustible items to be burned in the fireplace were running short, apart from the dining table and chairs they were sitting on. Marjukka had already planned to drop the dining set down the chimney once they had finished their meals.

Around the table, they formed a circle and held hands in unison. All eyes turned to Birgget as she started, 'I just want to say that... thank you for this time together. We have accomplished something unique together. We have survived up until today. The day we escaped on this roof, my first thought was that we won't make it 'til the next day. But here we are still after who knows for how long. It is amazing what a human spirit is able to achieve in times of pressure and stress. And look at us now, all around the same table, eating a delicious Christmas dinner. Even though, we don't even know exactly whether it's Christmas eve or not. But it sure feels like one. Thank you.' Birgget looked at each one of them. She let go of the palms holding hers, crossed her hands and sunk to whispering prayer. 'O Lord we thank you for the gifts of your bounty which we enjoy at this table...'

The others followed, closing their eyes and crossing their hands. Christian did so, too, but soon he separated his hands. His other hand wandered under the table on Ida's thigh next to him. First, he squeezed harder and then, gently caressed. Ida kept her hands crossed, but cleared her throat in confusion, before she sunk back into the prayer.

'Amen,' Birgget finished and they all opened their eyes.

Quickly, Christian pulled his hand away from Ida's lap.

'Well, I hope you enjoy your meals,' Marjukka said and began slicing the ham.

'And, thank you, Marjukka,' Ida said. 'You saved our lives. Without you, none of us would be here today.'

'True,' Birgget nodded and passed around the smoked salmon and swede casserole. 'How can we ever repay you? We have used all your supplies.'

Marjukka stopped slicing and put the knife on the table beside the ham. 'I think in these circumstances, anyone would have done the same. When facing a disaster like this, everything becomes community property. It's a humane instinct.'

'Amen to that!' Christian said and grabbed the knife. 'Shall we eat then?'

'Yes, please,' Marjukka said. 'Could you pass me the beetroot salad?'

'I wouldn't mind having some of that herring,' Birgget asked.

Once everyone had their favourite portions in front of them, they began eating as if they had never seen food before. In next few minutes, all their plates were empty.

Ida leaned back. She had eaten too fast on an empty stomach. She caressed her upper tummy, however, quickly straightening herself and not wanting the pregnancy to show.

But everyone was too distracted by the food on the table to pay any attention on Ida's belly or anything else. Marjukka served herself some more food and Christian followed.

'I thought we were supposed to leave some for tomorrow?' Ida said, worrying.

Christian stopped scooping the casserole, eyes widening of guilt.

'I would suggest,' Birgget said melancholically, 'we eat now as much as we feel like. It's Christmas time after all and this may be...'

'I agree,' Marjukka interrupted, licking her lips while looking at her second full plate. 'Let's eat.'

Christian nodded and looked at Ida.

Yet, Ida shrugged her shoulders, unsatisfied. 'So, do you think... anyone is ever gonna find us?' she asked, changing the mood. It was a question everyone was thinking, but tried to forget at least for a few celebrative minutes.

'I prefer we don't talk about it now,' Marjukka said firmly. 'At least, not tonight. Let's just enjoy. We deserve this one evening.'

Birgget nodded.

'But...' Ida said.

'There is one thing we could do,' Birgget interrupted. 'This may sound crazy to you, but... as lovely as our Christmas tree is, we should consider setting it on fire.'

Everyone rolled their eyes on Birgget's suggestion.

'Burning the Christmas tree? Are you crazy!?' Ida gasped. 'Christmas tree is... sacred!'

'Actually, they used to burn them in Germany in the middle ages. It was part of the Christmas ritual,' Birgget said.

'Well, it does sound very unusual,' Marjukka said, 'but she's got a point there. Eventually, we do need all the wood there is for the fireplace.'

'I was thinking about setting it on fire here on the roof as a sign for somebody, anybody out there,' Birgget added.

They all fell silent. Only Christian's cutlery clung against the plate as he dropped them accidentally.

'I mean, nobody knows we are here,' Birgget continued. 'We are surrounded by complete darkness, apart from these few candles burning on the table. But setting that tree on fire, would be like a flickering lighthouse guiding the way for anyone out there. There must be someone. We cannot be the only survivors. We just cannot.'

Ida turned to look in the dark horizon, the same direction as Birgget. Christian observed Ida beside her. However, he did not touch, intervene or disturb her. He knew what she was thinking. *Sven.* He got goose bumps. Christian's mind started racing. *Was there any way I could make her forget him? Would she be waiting for his return forever? Like Birgget waited for Roar for years. Or perhaps was still waiting today. Who knows? Some of us, never let go of the true love. Could that be Ida and Sven? True love.*

'I'd say we burn the tree,' Ida said, determined. 'Burn it now!'

Surprised, Birgget turned to Ida. Then, she looked at Marjukka. 'What do you think?'

'If that's what we have to do,' Marjukka spread her arms, 'as long as we don't end up burning the whole building underneath.'

'Well, one thing is for sure that we should have plenty of water around us to put down the fire, if it gets out of control,' Birgget said. Out of the corner of her eye, she saw Christian less satisfied. 'And you? What's on your mind, Mister?'

'Well... to be frank, I don't think it's such a good idea,' Christian said hesitantly.

'And why is that then?' Birgget crossed her arms.

'I agree with what Marjukka said first. We should rather

burn the tree in a fireplace to help us stay warm longer,' Christian explained. 'That's more important than randomly hoping someone would see the tree exactly when it's on fire. How long does that tree burn anyway? An hour? It would be a huge gamble.'

'It's also a huge gamble to have you and Ida share the mattress every night,' Birgget snorted.

'Please,' Ida said and looked away.

Christian sighed and fell silent.

'I would say we take a vote,' Marjukka intervened. 'Who wants to burn the tree in a fireplace?'

Only Christian raised his arm.

Birgget smiled victoriously, grabbed the knife and sliced some more ham for herself.

'Okay. So, we could lift the tree on top of the chimney pipe where it gets the best possible exposure,' Marjukka suggested. 'Once it's all burned up, we can just let the remains fall thru into the fireplace.'

'Shall we do it then?' Ida said.

'Now?' Marjukka asked.

'Yes! Let's use the candles to set it on fire,' Birgget said, stood up and grabbed two of the candles with her.

Ida stood up as well, yanking Christian's arm. But she felt resistance. 'What's wrong?'

'But I haven't finished my meal, yet,' Christian stammered.

'You can finish it later. We need you to lift the tree,' Ida ignored his cry, forcefully pulled him away from the table and walked him next to the tree. She held the tree from the middle of the trunk. 'Ready?'

Demotivated, Christian grabbed the tree and together with Ida he raised it up in the air. They hovered the tree above the chimney pipe.

'Don't!' Marjukka screamed. 'It may fall through the chimney.' She looked around for anything they could use to block the pipe. She went to pick up one of the dining chairs and rested it flat on top of the chimney pipe. 'I'm sorry. One of us has to eat standing up.'

Christian and Ida understood what Marjukka was after. They erected the Christmas tree on top of the backrest of the chair.

Then, Birgget tilted the flickering candles on the base of the tree. It took a few seconds, until the tree shot a few smaller sparks off its needles, and then the fire started to spread on the top branches and entire tree was burning. The light it shone almost blinded them. They haven't seen anything so bright for days.

Ida's skin reflected golden in the light of the fire. Christian turned to stare at her mesmerised. She pretended she didn't notice. But she did, yet she let him admire her. She was flattered.

Birgget clocked Christian eating Ida with his eyes again. 'So, what's next?' she interrupted the magical moment. 'Dancing around the tree?'

'Should we go and finish our meals?' Marjukka said.

All women nodded and went to the table. They took the three remaining seats. Christian followed looking displeased, not only because he had no chair left, but he had gotten used to the darkness that somewhat had helped him and Ida maintain their privacy from the observant eyes of Birgget. Now, though, they were fully exposed until the tree would stop burning.

Despite Christian's bad mood, the flickering tree created a bright, magical ambience. The heat generated by the fire brought a sensation amongst them they had forgotten exists. It felt like sitting next to a real fireplace. Or a bonfire. And most of all, the guiding flames restored their hope for survival. This was their last cry for help.

As much as the women appreciated the idea, Christian couldn't share the feeling of joy. He feared the burning tree would attract company he least desired. He came standing beside the table. His chair was taken away from him. He was moody and quiet. He sliced another thick piece of ham and savoured it in silence with his bare hands. He gulped a whole glass of red wine. He burped loudly. The women gave him a worried look.

Chapter 63

# A GLIMMER OF LIGHT

Viljo slammed the door of the kitchen cupboard shut and returned behind the wheel. The breeze blowing through the broken windscreen numbed his face. He could barely see anything past Sven sitting in front of him on Yetilag's suitcase and Yetilag itself. 'Nothing left, except a spoonful of sugar,' Viljo said.

No one replied. They all knew the end was near. From now on, they were only racing against hunger.

Sven tapped the side of the luggage and looked up pleading to Yetilag that only shook its head and spread its arms. *No food there either*, its body language indicated. Sven turned to Viljo. 'How about any ingredients? I could try and make those pies again. I promise I nail it this time.'

'No, thank you,' Viljo replied firmly.

Sven squinted his eyebrows and looked ahead.

As Jaaku looked down on the roof, he begun to hallucinate the weasels and rodents as roasts and skewers, rather than equal travelling companions. Drops of his saliva fell on Squirr-El's head. She wiped her wet face, looked up and saw Jaaku quickly turning his gaze away. Squirr-El gave him a suspicious glance while Jaaku felt the savage and primitive hunting instinct returning. *Is this what Börje and Kalle meant?* You have to reach the edge, push yourself to the limit, leave yourself with no other option than to eat another living thing. The only moral dilemma was that these animals talked, formed understandable words, spoke language familiar to them. Does that make it less acceptable to eat an animal, if the poor little thing is able to have a conversation and engage verbally with human beings? Is that what it takes for the weaker to survive alive: communication skills? That seemed to be the case until now. But when the worse comes to worst, the humans can feel superior to others. Jaaku was no different.

He saw out of the corner of his eye, Squirr-El examining the wet saliva on her paws. *If I just get my hands on Viljo's spear gun, we could all get some food. Raw food, though. Unless, we fry the meat on a hot engine. Or stuff it in the oven. The smallest of them could probably fit in. What if the others wouldn't mind my thought? We are all men after all. And we are hungry. What if the others feel and think the same, but are too afraid and embarrassed to admit that?*

His heart started beating faster like when confronted by moose and he had to pull the trigger for the first time. Back then he couldn't deliver, but now the situation was different. It was the matter of life and death. *If someone had to survive on this boat, it was the men first, then the animals. That was the pecking order. The men, not the animals, would eventually discover land, steer the boat to safety, begin again and continue to develop the civilisation. They had the power.*

Once he felt convinced enough and had justified his vicious plan to himself, he began climbing down the tree.

'Had enough on the top, ey?' Sven said.

'I thought I'd... try some of that... sugar,' Jaaku explained. He squashed himself between the sleeping polar bears and the entrance to the cabin. The sleep deprivation had taken its toll even on the bears. Their paws hung relaxed outside the railings.

'You know that sugar is just going to make you more thirsty,' Sven's voice came from behind the rodents and weasels on the roof.

'I must eat something,' Jaaku said and glanced at the little animals. 'Anything.'

'Shoot yourself.'

*Not myself, but someone else,* Jaaku smirked in his thoughts. He leaned forward over the roof. 'Aren't you hungry?'

Sven nodded. 'We are all starving. But I think I'll survive for another... few hours.'

'Few hours comes soon. I would start thinking ahead now how we can survive tomorrow, day after and so on. We can't keep drinking only that lake water.'

'What do you suggest? There's no point fishing either.'

'There has to be something we can eat on this boat,' Jaaku said. He looked straight at Sven while sensing the little animals becoming uneasy. Then, he peered inside the cabin.

Viljo turned his head and saw Jaaku's head prying inside. 'What do you want now?'

'I was wondering... if I could have some of that... erm... sugar,' Jaaku stammered.

'What are you sounding like that little stoat again?' Viljo smirked. 'Eating that sugar is not really a wise move. But help yourself if you can squeeze past and if you think it makes you feel better. It probably makes you feel only worse. The packet is in the cupboard behind Links' chair on the bottom shelf.'

'Thank you,' Jaaku said nervously. As he squashed himself inside, he spotted Viljo's spear gun upright next to the steering wheel. He froze there between the stool and the cupboard. The gun was still out of his reach. To get there, he had to push Links against her desk and Viljo against the wheel and the dashboard.

'It's just down there on the bottom,' Viljo turned to Jaaku and gave him a concerned look. He saw a few sweat drops on his forehead. 'Are you alright? Seasick?'

'No... I'm... to-totally fine.'

'You're stuttering again. What's going on?' Viljo did a full turn towards Jaaku.

Jaaku realised this was his moment to act, otherwise, Viljo would figure out and discover his plot. He elbowed Links at the back of her head throwing her against the desk. Her nose and whiskers slammed against the laptop screen. Next, Jaaku jumped on Viljo and pushed him to the steering wheel. The old man hit the back of his head against the window frame and collapsed on the floor. The little animals on the roof jumped. Sven stared in horror through the window frame as Jaaku reached out for the spear gun. He grabbed it and before Viljo had time to compose himself, the tip of an arrow already pointed at his chest.

'No, Jaaku!' Sven ran around the cabin.

'Not again,' Viljo panted while leaning against the dashboard. 'What has gone into your crazy mind now!?'

'It's nothing crazy,' Jaaku breathed heavily. 'You're all out of your minds. You're saying we have no food, even though we're surrounded by it. Just open your eyes!'

'I don't understand,' Viljo said, confused.

'We're not vegetarians are we? Are you?' Jaaku raged.

'No. I'm not. What's your point?' Viljo grunted.

'Drop the gun, please,' Sven pleaded from the doorway.

Jaaku flicked Viljo around and used his body as a shield between him and Sven.

'Are you thinking about... hunting again?' Sven asked.

Jaaku answered with a subtle nod.

'We are supposed to go and rescue people as quick as we can. And to save ourselves. Where do you think we'll find a forest now where you can hunt?' Sven asked.

'I wasn't thinking about hunting in the forest.'

'If not in the forest and the lake is empty of fish, where then?' Sven asked, but as he did ask the question, simultaneously, he understood. 'Don't say...'

As Sven cast his doubts, Jaaku glanced at Links and then looked up towards the ceiling. 'Yes. We are surrounded by food,' he said, determined.

'I despise you!' Sven gasped and shook his head. 'These creatures have saved our lives. Guided us. Given us hope. They are all... special!'

'But tell me something...' Jaaku started and moved closer to Sven while keeping Viljo at gunpoint between them. 'Who is more special in the end? Us or them? Who is more important in this world? If one has to survive, who that would be? The humans or the animals?'

'Please, as your best friend,' Sven pleaded, 'don't do this.'

'I'm doing this for you, for all of us. You will thank me later. Trust me,' Jaaku said. 'Now, move out of my way. I will start with the... bears. They should be easy targets now while asleep.'

Sven shook his head and looked down, but didn't move. He only grabbed the door frame from either sides and spread himself to block the exit.

'What do you think you're doing?'

'If you're going out there to hurt any of those animals, you have to... shoot me first,' Sven said firmly.

'How can you be so stupid? Don't you understand that I'm trying to help us all? Please, don't ruin this now.'

'We'll find another solution,' Sven said, unwavering.

'You know yourself there are no other solutions,' Jaaku said and lowered the spear gun. 'I'm sorry.' He fired a shot on Sven's thigh. Sven screamed in agony and pain as he dropped on the floor. 'I warned you,' Jaaku said and pushed Viljo against the dashboard.

'Yaaaawnnn!' a scream echoed as Yetilag followed the violent scene unfolding. Yetilag bang its fists on the roof and the sides of the cabin. The little animals bounced up and down.

Meanwhile, Links had shown signs of recovery. As Jaaku was stepping out of the cabin, she squeezed her laptop between her palms, jumped up on the chair and took a swing with her laptop on the back of his head. Jaaku went flying against the door frame. Immediately, Viljo got up and jumped from behind at Jaaku's back. He wrapped his arm around Jaaku's throat. Sven on the deck floor looked up and saw Jaaku's face turn red as Viljo strangled him, until he fell unconscious. Jaaku collapsed on the desk and Viljo fell against the throttle lever. His back made a loud cracking sound.

'The power of technology,' Links said and dropped the remaining pieces of the laptop on the desk. The laptop was split into two pieces.

'You just broke your laptop?' Viljo panted, concerned.

Links examined the pieces. 'I think I may have... but for a good cause.'

'Indeed and we're very thankful for that,' Sven said while holding his bleeding thigh.

'But what about the navigation system? Wasn't that controlled by the laptop?' Viljo said while breathing heavily and holding his chest.

'Unfortunately,' Links nodded.

Sven saw Viljo was in agony. The physical strain and age

had taken its toll. He had to sit down behind the wheel and take a rest. He was short of breath and sweaty. 'Are you alright, old man?'

'I'm just fine... and please stop calling me an old man!' Viljo grunted and grabbed the wheel. 'We have other things to worry about now... like for instance, where on earth are we heading next without navigation. We are back to square one.'

'Yaaaawnnn!' Yetilag said once the boat picked up speed.

'As you can hear, even Yetilag's concerned,' Viljo said.

'Is that what it said?' Sven asked.

'I have no idea. I guess.'

'Yaaaawnnn!' another, even louder roar followed.

Sven raised his gaze above the roof and asked Pole Vole, 'What is Yetilag on about?'

'It said there is apparently some flickering light in the distance,' Pole Vole translated.

'Yaaaawnnn!' Yetilag roared again even more passionately while pointing ahead.

Sven limped around the cabin to the front and hopped on Yetilag's luggage to get a better view. His path left a bloody trail behind.

'Yaaaawnnn!' Yetilag protested about Sven squashing his personal belongings or national treasures and dirtying his suitcases.

'I'm sorry,' Sven said and raised his palms. 'May I?' he said and attempted to climb on Yetilag's shoulders. Sven's hands running on its coarse fur tickled Yetilag. It shook and giggled a little, but Sven held on tight and kept on ascending, until he reached the top. He sat on Yetilag's wide shoulders, pulling its thick hair. He had always imagined this is what it would be like to ride an elephant.

Together, they stared at the dark vastness where a distant light shone. But in a blink of an eye, the light was gone. And then, suddenly, it returned for a little while to disappear again couple of times, until it remained lit permanently.

'I need to get a better view,' Sven said and looked at the abandoned viewing tower. He lowered himself from Yetilag's shoulders. He balanced around the cabin and dragged himself on the top of the tree. The view from the tower confirmed their earlier sight. *Another boat, a house or a town?* Anything was possible. A sign of life. 'Light! I can see light!' Sven rejoiced.

But no one joined his celebration. Polar bears were in a deep sleep. The little animals on the roof didn't seem too pleased either, since a glimmer of light or any sign of civilisation, as human beings call it, had a different meaning to them. They all came from the forest and the kind of light they were interested you find in the nature, like the sun, the moon and the stars, not the artificial light created by humans, like traffic lights, street lamps, car lights or even fire. All the latter ones were all threats to them and their existence, and disturbed their natural environment, habitat and biological rhythm. Nor did Sven hear any response from the others of his like either. The cabin remained all silent.

'Did you hear me? Viljo? Jaaku? We have found something!' Sven peered down, but since he was right above the cabin, he couldn't see inside. 'Go slightly left!' Sven tried to guide them towards the light. 'Viljo!? No. Don't stop! Why did you stop?'

Still no response. Only Links pushed her head out and said, 'I think you'd better come and have a look at this.'

'There's light out there! Can you see?' Sven kept pointing at the horizon.

'Yes, we all heard you,' Links said, yet not sharing Sven's enthusiasm. 'But I think you should come down here. The captain is not well.'

Chapter 64

# THE LAST SONG

After a glass of red wine, Birgget gained confidence to suggest they would sing Christmas carols. As a weekly participant of the church choir, she was prepared to lead. Once she opened her mouth and let the strong voice resonate, the others could only listen to her totally captivated. Eventually, Marjukka and Ida joined her with slightly weaker, yet beautiful voices, too.

Christian, however, remained silent. Some carols he had heard as a background music from the local supermarket loudspeakers usually starting to play every year around mid-October, yet even those handful of songs repeatedly echoing at the aisles hadn't helped him to memorise any of the lyrics. Despite his unwavering confidence in many other areas of life, he wasn't much of a singer. He was happy just to hum along with the ladies and join in only when the titles of the songs were being sung.

Once the first song finished, Ida noticed the fire on the remaining tree stump had nearly extinguished itself. She walked to the chimney pipe and sighed. The last resource had been used. The flaming tree had gone to waste and no rescuers at sight.

Christian grabbed the half-full bottle of red wine, two glasses and wobbled behind Ida. She felt his presence. He emptied what was left in the bottle in two glasses and served the other to her. They clinked glasses. 'To... us?' Christian said hesitantly.

'To all of us,' Ida corrected. 'Do you think we'll be trapped here forever? That no one will ever find us?'

'If so, then there's something I need you to know...' Christian said while Marjukka and Birgget started another, popular Christmas tune: Blue Christmas.

'What is it?' Ida raised her gaze, eyes glistening against the burning flames.

'I think, Ida, that I am...' Christian said and placed his hand on her shoulder, 'in love with you.'

But Christian's drunken confession only made her giggle. 'I... like you, too, Christian. I always have.'

'This is not really a laughing matter,' Christian said, confused.

'No. I'm sorry,' Ida covered her smile behind her palm, 'but your... pair of tights are.' She burst into laughter.

The response wasn't exactly what Christian had expected, but at least she didn't completely freak out. He moved closer to her and to his surprise, she didn't pull away, but instead she pressed her body against his. He put his wine glass on the edge of the chimney pipe, then took Ida's glass away and placed it next to his. Once his hands were free, he placed them on her hips and leaned over to kiss her. Ida tilted her head and puckered her lips. But as she did so, over his shoulder she saw movement in the distance. And a dot of light. She stopped moving forward, but instead tilted her head away from his approaching face and lips. Her head ended up resting on his shoulder as if they were only hugging. She wrapped her arms around him. They ended up in an embrace neck to neck, Ida peering at the horizon. Not quite the position again he had expected. He kissed her on the cheek, unpuckered his lips and sighed. Filled with disappointment, he let go of her.

But the glimmer in the darkness had vanished. *A mirage?* She blinked her eyes a few times, looked down and up again. The sight reappeared. Her eyes widened. This time, the moving, bright object remained visible. 'A boat!' Ida screamed and pushed herself away from Christian's weak embrace. 'Right there!'

Marjukka and Birgget stopped singing and in awe turned to look to the direction Ida was pointing.

'Isn't that just... another star?' Marjukka said, slightly

annoyed having been interrupted in the middle of her favourite song. 'Or maybe a satellite?' she added and elbowed Birgget. 'Where were we?'

But this time, Birgget ignored Marjukka. Birgget recognised the bright dot in the darkness, even though her eyesight wasn't the sharpest anymore. Or she desperately wanted to see something. So badly she wished this suffering to end.

Ida took a step closer to the edge. 'That's too low-lying to be a star or a satellite. The light is on the level of the horizon. Perhaps someone has seen the fire. The burning tree.'

Birgget nodded, whereas Marjukka only waited for them to continue singing. Somewhat sad expression on Marjukka's face showed, how she had thrown away hope of anyone ever finding them. Although if someone was to rescue them, she wished they could all remain friends also in the future. In some strange way, part of her had enjoyed the time on the roof with people she had only previously known by face, not by character. It took a natural disaster to make friends with strangers she had served for years. She hoped, if they were to survive, that this experience would be with them forever, as it probably will, and create a special bond between them. She didn't necessarily want the night of celebration to end, not just right now.

Neither did Christian want the night to end. He had been so close to Ida. He was certain she would have kissed him back, if that mysterious sighting didn't take her focus away from him. *Something always comes between us!*

'Aariak? Tomas? Can you see the light in the distance?' Ida called out to the men on the other roof.

No response.

She repeated louder, but only the howling wind responded.

Their peaceful Christmas celebration turned into a silent anticipation. The thought of seeing other human life paralysed their minds for different reasons. The snowflakes came down larger, starting to give the rooftop a thin, white cottony blanket. The remains of the burning tree were now just a size of a small bonfire. It was getting darker again. They still had two flickering candles on the table. And the dot of light in the distance.

As much as they all yearned back to safety and normal life,

this era of one peculiar kind was about to come to an end sooner or later. If the light was their rescue, the future frightened them almost as much as the current situation. How does Pihtamo ever recover from the disaster? What will each individual's life be like? No work. No home. Nothing. At least, on the roof, they had lived in an illusion they still had "something", their past, their life as they still remembered it like last week or month ago. But that previous life will cease to exist by the time someone will find them and take them to safety. Whatever that means: *safety?*

Chapter 65

# TAKING CHARGE

Sven appeared in the doorway to witness a disaster inside. Jaaku leaned unconscious against the desk. Links sat next to him on a chair examining her broken laptop. Viljo was curled over the steering wheel, his face turned blue. He was drooling on the dashboard, and his arms and legs were shaking. To create more space, Sven grabbed Jaaku by the collar and dragged his limp body outside. He left him in the arms of the sleeping polar bears. Then, he returned to the cabin and pushed past Links to help Viljo.

'Are you alright, old man?' he asked and lifted Viljo's head up from his chin.

Viljo's eyeballs rolled around uncontrollably. He didn't even react to Sven calling him 'an old man', which meant his condition must have been serious.

'We have to get him to the hospital,' Sven said and looked at Links gravely. 'Can you navigate us to the hospital?'

Links shook her head and waved at the halved laptop on her paws. 'I don't think so. All the electronic systems were controlled by this computer.'

'Can you fix it then?'

'I can try, but that can take hours. I may need to get some new parts too, which we obviously have none here on this boat.'

Sven took a deep breath and shifted Viljo on a seated position on the floor in the middle. Viljo panted heavily as Sven knelt beside him. 'Rest there. We're gonna get you some help.' Sven stoop up and saw the dim light again in the distance shining through the side window. 'I guess I should take over Viljo's job then,' he said hesitantly and looked at Links. 'Can you climb trees?'

'Links' don't climb, unless escaping from danger,' Links replied formally.

Sven sighed and saw the spear gun on the desk, left behind by Jaaku. He picked it up and caressed the trigger. 'I'm asking you again. Can you climb?'

'You're all just... crazy people!' Links snorted.

'Do you big cats climb trees or not!?' Sven ordered and pointed the gun at Links.

'Well, suddenly... I just remembered... I do!' Links swallowed, jumped out of the cabin and raced along the tree trunk up on the top branches.

'Thank you,' Sven said and put the spear gun down. 'Now, you stay there and guide us towards the light. Can you see the light?'

Since Links' eyesight had deteriorated after having spent unhealthy number of hours in front of computer screens, she had to rely on using Jaaku's telescope which she found clinging on one of the branches. She peered through it. 'I can see it. It's flickering.'

*Great*, Sven thought and began studying the dashboard and the cockpit. He had never sailed anything with engines before, only rowing boats. He didn't even have a driving licence for a car. He only knew how to steer kicksleds and wheelbarrows.

'Go leeward,' Links directed.

'Go lee...where? What are you talking about!? Some lynx language?'

'It's a nautical term,' Links said, rolling her eyes. She tried to think of a simpler expression. 'Go away from the wind.'

'And where is the wind blowing from?'

'Fine. Go three o'clock.'

'Three o'clock!?' Sven snorted. 'No. We go now!'

'Just follow the light,' Links snorted, frustrated. 'Can you see the light?'

'I saw it earlier, but I can't concentrate on that many things at the same time. I have to steer the boat, too.'

Links shook her head. She began missing Viljo's expertise. 'Just start turning the wheel right and I say "when", okay?'

Sven's confused eyes browsed through the dashboard. There were so many blinking lights, a speedometer, an oil gauge, a petrol gauge and a few unexplainable buttons of different colours. He pressed a button that said "start". The boat started. Then, he grabbed the wheel and looked for a gas pedal, but there was none. He pushed his head outside the window. 'You saw Viljo doing this many times. What should I do now the engine is running?'

'I think you have to pull... or push the lever or throttle on your right hand side.'

Sven pulled his head inside and located the one and the only lever in the corner next to the steering wheel. *Push or pull?* That is the question. He decided to push the lever down making the boat jump at fast speed.

'But carefully!' Links yelled, holding onto the branches.

The sudden acceleration threw the little animals from the roof in the arms of the polar bears. Yetilag fell backwards on its suitcase.

'Now turn around! We must go the opposite direction!' Links screamed at the top of her lungs. 'But slow down first!'

Sven grabbed the lever again and pulled it all the way up. The boat slowed down rapidly shooting all passengers in the opposite direction. 'Okay. I got it! It's just that one lever. This is simple.'

Finally, Sven managed to slow down and take the direction Links had instructed. Again, he pressed the lever down without a warning. 'Sorry, I forgot.' The passengers on board bounced back and forth. The boat started cracking and popping as they approached the dimming light.

'It looks like something is on fire,' Links observed. 'As if though, the light is getting smaller. Or further away.'

'Even though we're heading towards it?' Sven pondered.

'There are people... on the roof... and a tree is on fire. It's a... Christmas tree! Or what's left of it.'

'Sounds like some sort of... pagan ritual?' Sven yelled from the cockpit. 'That's what Germans did in the middle ages. I remember my mum told me. They burned Christmas trees.'

'The Germans!? Not again,' Viljo moaned quietly.

'Viljo! Are you okay?' Sven glanced over his shoulder.

'Don't trust them, the Germans,' Viljo hissed.

'I have never heard there were Germans in Pihtamo.'

'I hope not,' Viljo said and coughed, until his head collapsed back on the floor.

'We may be approaching the town. Slow down!' Links warned.

'What?' Sven asked.

'Good,' Links replied, thinking Sven had heard her warning, which he didn't. The engine roared too loudly.

Suddenly, the bottom touched something underwater, throwing the boat in an angle. But Sven stayed on his feet by squeezing the wheel. He looked at one of the monitors on the dashboard. 'How does the... echo system work?'

'Ecosystem?' Links heard while climbing back on the summit. 'That's quite a big question to ask right now! Not sure if I have time to answer that.'

'Not ecosystem, but echo sounder,' Viljo corrected, and fell unconscious on the floor again.

'Ah. Unfortunately, that was also controlled by my laptop, too. And besides, I only fixed it. I cannot read it. Viljo knows... or knew how to read it.'

'Viljo? Viljo!?'

No response, apart from his chest that was still pumping up and down. He was still breathing.

'If you slow down, I can try and observe the surface and warn you about any obstacles I see,' Links suggested.

'How's your eyesight? It's quite dark,' Sven said and nervously wiped his sweaty forehead.

'Decent. I can still spot a mouse from hundred metres away.'

*We should have got you up there earlier,* Sven thought.

'Take lee... left. Now!'

Sven turned the wheel left, but too late. A screeching noise came from the stern. The collision cracked the bottom open from the back corner. The bursting water wet the polar bears bottoms, waking them up from their winter sleep. They rotated

417

their arms and roared in tired anger and frustration. The boat tilted, dragging the sinking back.

'I cannot see the light anymore,' Links panicked.

'Doesn't matter. I can see the building... I think,' Sven said and sped up.

'You are heading straight towards it!' Links screamed. 'Slow down!'

Despite Links' cries, Sven increased a notch by pressing the lever all the way down, yet his enthusiasm broke the throttle. The lever came off. Sven had the metal stick in his hand. He grinned and chucked it over his shoulder on the floor.

The bottom of the boat took another touch on something. And another. It was pitch dark. And they were racing towards the unknown with no brakes and a fresh skipper on the wheel sailing on his virgin journey.

Chapter 66

# REUNION

All three women were lined up on the edge of the roof, once the boat engine became audible. They saw a dark shadow moving towards them alarmingly fast. Only Christian looked away to the opposite direction. He feared for the worst. He walked back to the table to finish off their cold dinners. He also started emptying the wine glasses left behind by the ladies.

Ida glanced over her shoulder wondering what was wrong with Christian. But her concern was short-lived. The main point of interest was now approaching them from the darkness.

'What is that?' asked Birgget.

'It's a... motor boat,' Ida said.

'There's smoke coming out of it... and it looks like it's partly sunken,' Marjukka said.

'And it's bouncing up and down,' Birgget said. 'It's hitting objects underwater.'

'Slow down!' Ida screamed.

'And it's full of passengers,' Marjukka said.

'Animals?' Ida rubbed her eyes and looked again. 'We are being saved by... mammals?'

'Is that... a cat in the tower?' Marjukka asked, squinting. 'No. It's not a tower. It's a spruce... growing in the middle of the boat?'

'And what's that white, hairy thing standing at front?' Birgget pondered.

'Christian?' Ida turned to the table.

But Christian didn't respond. Instead, he slammed the empty wine glass on the table and picked up another one. He took the ham from its bone and bit mouthfuls off it.

Ida walked beside him and said, 'I'm worried.'

'And so what?' he said unclearly, mouth full of shredded meat moistened with red wine. 'Now you need me, because you're worried?'

'Just take a look at the boat. It's packed with these weird... creatures.'

'Really? Look more closely,' Christian grunted. He finished the glass of wine and flushed it down with a big bite of ham. 'This is the best Christmas ever,' he said sarcastically, while pieces of soggy meat dripped down his chin. 'Maybe our last one before those predators on the boat will eat us alive. How about that kiss now?' He turned to face Ida and grinned. The gaps between his teeth were filled with shreds of ham and his gums were red from the wine. He puckered his wet lips.

'You're disgusting!' Ida slapped him on the cheek.

While holding the side of his face, he started laughing loudly. 'C'mon! It's Christmas time. We should be good to each other.' He chucked the remaining ham on the table and picked up the third glass of wine. 'Go and welcome our guests. I'll be here if you need me. Invite them to join the table... if there's anything left. Do as you wish. I don't care.'

Furiously, Ida walked away back to Birgget and Marjukka.

'Everything alright?' Birgget asked, worried, yet more pleased, after having witnessed the long-awaited quarrel between Ida and Christian.

'Never better!' Ida said ironically.

*I think that was the pie shop,* Sven remembered when the bottom hit a gutter.

'Slow down!' the women screamed.

'Yaaaawnnn!' Yetilag responded.

'Slow down!' shouted Links.

All the shouting brought Jaaku back to life. Face bleeding, he stepped away from the drowsy polar bears.

'I can't slow down!' Sven yelled. He tried to turn left and then to the right, but they kept going straight. They had lost the steering. And it was too late anyway.

The boat slammed on the corner of the post office. The shock of the collision threw the women against the roof tiles. Christian held onto the dining table and tried to rescue the leftovers. Sven shot against the dashboard. The polar bears hit the back wall of the cabin, squashing Jaaku under them. The rodents and weasels together with Links who fell from the viewing tower, landed in the arms of Yetilag whose body functioned as an airbag between the post office wall and the crash victims.

The boat had come to a halt, the bow crushed inside about a metre. The water started leaking through the holes. The boat began to sink.

The women helped each other back on their feet.

'Not sure if I wanna see what sort of a creature was driving this boat,' Birgget said and took steps back.

'That's not exactly the kind of rescue boat I was hoping to see,' Ida said, huddling beside her.

As the boat kept sinking from underneath, one by one, Links, Erm...ine, Pole Vole, Squirr-El, More Weasel and Less Weasel jumped on the rooftop of the post office.

The women stopped to examine the little visitors, until Yetilag's hairy hand slamming on the edge, made them all gasp.

'The big monster is coming this way!' Ida screamed.

The women backed off to the far corner behind Christian and the dining table.

Despite the pain and agony Sven was feeling, he was able to recognise some familiarity in the women's scream. He tasted his own blood in his mouth. He had broken parts of his body as he hit the dashboard. The cabin floor started filling up with water. 'We have to get out of here!'

Jaaku stood by the door, short of breath. The collision had taken the air out of him, yet brought him back to senses.

The polar bears started climbing over the roof of the boat.

'Yaaaawnnn!' Yetilag roared, once it reached the post office roof. It stood up straight, looking intimidating as a proper giant monster should.

'Ah, dear Lord, help us, God...' Birgget prayed as Yetilag towered in front of them all.

'Holy Mother of...' Christian said, dropping his jaw. 'Too much wine?'

'The polar bears are coming too!' Marjukka screamed and pointed at the edge where two pairs of white hairy paws slammed on the snowy tiles. The polar bears climbed up, and together with the other animals, took over a large part of the rooftop, squashing the original survivors in a tight corner. The three women and Christian couldn't back off any further, unless they would like to go for a swim.

Meanwhile, Sven held Viljo's head and Jaaku grabbed Viljo's legs. Together, they dragged the old man through the doorway and around the cabin to the front. 'He's heavier than he looks,' Jaaku said, as they brought Viljo's limp body upright against the post office wall. Jaaku climbed up on the roof first with the help of Sven pushing him from the bottom.

'Jaaku?' Ida recognised the seal skin costume appearing from behind the group of animals. Her heart nearly stopped.

Jaaku leaned over the edge and reached out his hands. He grabbed Viljo's arms as Sven assisted from below. Yetilag noticed the men struggling, hence it leaned over and offered its hand.

'Look! The monster is... helping?' Birgget said in awe, as Viljo was airlifted by Yetilag.

'It's Viljo, too!' Ida sighed passionately, while clapping her hands softly. 'Any more?'

Sven, the last person balancing on top of the sinking ark, waved desperately. Yetilag offered its long arm and a big hand for Sven to embrace. He was weakened and could barely hold on. But he did. He knew it was worth it. Something better was waiting.

Despite the threatening line-up of dangerous creatures in front of Ida, she defied them all and rushed past them. And they all let her. Once she reached the edge of the roof, clinging onto Yetilag's helping hand, Sven appeared in front of her. Ida burst into tears of joy as Sven landed on his feet opposite her. Simultaneously, *Aune* disappeared into the depths of the lake and onto the flooded streets of Pihtamo. And Ida drowned herself in the arms of Sven. A long-awaited embrace they both wished would last an eternity.

Chapter 67

# TOGETHER AGAIN

For a moment, Sven and Ida forgot themselves in each other's arms. It felt like their first embrace. Or better. They never wanted to let go.

Eventually, though, there was someone else who wanted a piece of him. 'Sven?' Birgget said, standing next to them, tears in her eyes.

'Will you excuse me?' Sven gently pulled himself away from Ida. She nodded approvingly and released him. 'Mother!' he smiled and spread his arms.

'I thought I'd never see you again,' Birgget fell in Sven's embrace. 'I cannot afford to lose another man in my life!'

'You haven't, mother,' Sven revealed, 'lost any of them.'

Instantly, Birgget pushed Sven away to arm length so that she could see his eyes. 'What's that supposed to mean? Have you hit your head or something? Obviously, you have.' She gently touched Sven's bruised chin.

'Are you okay?' Ida said and spotted Sven's bleeding leg. 'You're hurt.'

'You know, mum...' Sven started, holding back his tears. 'We found dad.'

'Your father? Roar!?' Birgget squealed.

'Yes,' Sven nodded, but then got serious. 'Or well... first we found him, but then...'

'You're confusing me,' Birgget said.

423

'When we found him, he was under some sort of weird spell fishing our lake empty and...'

'What!?' Birgget gasped. 'I cannot believe it!'

'Yes, it's true. Gladly, though, he got back to normal. And besides, he did it all for good cause. But then Mooses started the flood and...'

'Who?' Birgget interrupted.

'You don't make any sense now,' Ida said, concerned. 'Is he alright?' she asked and looked at Jaaku.

'He's just fine,' Jaaku nodded, 'and Roar is alive. Or was when...'

'I couldn't be better,' Sven interrupted and smiled subtly.

'Where is... he then?' Birgget asked while peering doubtfully behind Sven and Jaaku, yet only seeing an odd-looking group of animals.

'Well, we kinda... had to leave him behind,' Sven hesitated.

Birgget snorted in disbelief and turned to Jaaku to seek for reaffirmation.

Jaaku responded with another nod and all the animals nodded with him.

Birgget shook her head. 'It is true?'

'Yes, mum. We found him. Or he found us. I don't know. But once the flooding began and we started saving these weird... I mean... animals, our boat ended up filling up with survivors to the point that someone had to go.'

'And that someone had to be your father?' Birgget asked.

'He volunteered. He stayed behind on a sheet of floating ice.'

'Sounds like him.'

'Unbelievable,' Ida said and held Sven's arm. 'What a noble man, your father is.'

'I don't know what to say,' Birgget sighed. 'Unselfishness never seemed to have left him.'

'Now we can only pray for him,' Sven started, but was interrupted by Viljo groaning on the floor. 'And the old man here needs immediate help. Medical attention. Something. Anything.'

'I might have some medicine here we can try on him,' Marjukka said from the shadow.

'Great!' Sven replied.

'And we must wrap something on that bleeding leg of yours,' Marjukka added, pointing at Sven's bloody trouser hem.

'Who is she? A nurse?' Sven said, impressed.

'She's a real angel,' Ida said.

'You never keep surprising us, Marjukka,' Birgget smiled. 'What is it you don't have?'

'A boyfriend,' Marjukka said quietly and extended her arm for a handshake with Sven. 'I believe we haven't met. I am Marjukka. I've heard a lot about you.'

You have?' confused, Sven looked at Ida and Birgget

'Marjukka saved our lives,' Birgget explained. 'It was her idea to bring us all here on the roof. And take all these supplies with us. Without her, we all would have been doomed ages ago.'

'Team work,' Marjukka said modestly, and went behind the chimney pipe to fetch some medicine.

'And just for your information,' Sven explained, 'Yetilag here, our big white giant, and all the rest are totally harmless. There's nothing to be afraid of. Even the polar bears are fine as long they are being fed.'

'The polar bears seem to like pies,' Jaaku stepped out of the shadow. 'As long as they are not being made by Sven.'

'There are mince pies for dessert,' Birgget said and smiled. 'How lovely to see you, too.'

Birgget and Jaaku embraced.

Soon, Ida followed and hugged Jaaku as well. 'What happened to you? You look so bruised and battered?'

'That's... another long story,' Jaaku said and glanced at Sven.

As Marjukka returned with her first aid kit, she gave Jaaku an awkward glance, but said nothing. She pulled out a bandage from her small green briefcase and started wrapping it tightly over Sven's thigh. As she did, she looked up at Jaaku again. 'Have we met?'

Immediately, Jaaku remembered Marjukka's strong facial features and striking eyes from the dating app Pihinder. And the fact that she had stood him up. 'We may have,' he cleared his throat. 'It's a very small town.'

'It sure is!' Sven snorted, when he recognised Christian by

the dining table. 'And what is he doing here!?'

'Erm... that's one more story,' Birgget said.

'Well, I believe we all have time now as long as this building's not gonna sink,' Sven looked at Ida inquiringly, but she avoided the eye contact.

'I doubt it will sink,' Marjukka said confidently.

Suddenly, though, Sven ripped himself away from Marjukka's care and started limping towards the dining table, where Christian sat scraping the plates empty.

'Hey! I wasn't finished, yet!' Marjukka shrieked.

By the time Sven reached the table, the bandage from his leg had completely unfastened itself only leaving a trail behind him.

'So, you are here,' Christian snorted. 'A hero.'

'Why are you here?' Sven asked gravely.

'I came to deliver letters... with your missus,' Christian smiled and wiped his mouth on his sleeve.

'What is he talking about?' Sven turned to Ida. 'And why is he wearing... tights?'

'He's drunk,' Ida said and took a step closer. 'Don't listen to him. It was a coincidence. I came to the post office with your mother and he happened to be there at the same time. He was probably... following us!'

Christian jumped up and swung the bone of the ham in front of them. 'Ha! You think highly of yourself, little lady! Following you!? I don't need to follow... anyone!'

'Step back, Christian!' Sven ordered.

But Christian did the opposite and moved only centimetres away from Sven, so that Sven could smell the wine on his breath. 'Speaking about coincidences, do you think mine and Ida's kiss was a coincidence?'

'A kiss!?' Sven gasped and turned to Ida again.

Ida gave Christian a stare that could have killed him. 'You pressed your lips on mine! I had nothing to do with it!'

'What is going on here?' Pleading, Sven looked at Birgget, but she kept looking away. 'What has happened on this rooftop!? This is all crazy!'

'Crazy?' Christian laughed. 'A big word from a man who arrived here with a bunch of mythical entourage.'

'I believe you three can solve your issues once all this is over,' Marjukka intervened. 'We have more important things to worry about now.'

'I need to know!' Sven insisted.

'Please, Christian,' Ida said. 'Show some respect. Sven and his... friends came to rescue us.'

'Ha! What have they saved?' Christian snorted. 'Their boat sank. We're all trapped here. Nothing has changed, except that now there are even more mouths to feed. And a bloody zoo to be looked after.'

'And if you didn't eat half of our Christmas foods, we could feed even more mouths,' Birgget grunted. 'So, you keep your big mouth shut!'

A moment of uncomfortable silence fell upon them all, until it was broken by Erm...ine. 'Peop-le... a-a-are crazy.'

The three women's jaws dropped. Christian, however, was too drunk to care or pay attention.

'Who said that?' Ida asked, suspiciously.

Birgget and Marjukka peered around to figure out where the voice came from.

'Ah, sorry,' Sven said. 'We forgot to introduce our new friends. I want you to meet: Squirr-El, Pole Vole, Links, Erm...ine, More Weasel, Less Weasel, and of course, the polar bears.'

'Yaaaawnnn!'

'Sorry. And Yetilag.'

'You've given them all names?' Birgget asked, confused.

'They have names,' Jaaku added.

'T-t-three brave... f-f-fishermen saved... o-o-our lives,' Erm...ine said thankfully.

The women stared at Erm...ine in awe.

'We've been listening to that for quite a few days now,' Jaaku added.

'They all talk, except polar bears and Yetilag,' Sven explained. 'Yaaaawnnn!'

'Well, Yetilag does talk in its own way.'

'I don't know what to say,' Ida couldn't believe her ears.

'It took a while for us to get used to it,' Sven said. 'But once you do, it actually makes things more interesting.'

'Do you think... they'd be hungry?' Birgget asked.

'You can ask them, mum. They understand you.'

Birgget turned to them. 'Do you... eat meat?'

Even though in their natural habit not all of them were likely to eat meat, the hunger made them reconsider their dietary preferences. They all nodded.

'Not quite the Christmas that you would have expected, honey,' Sven smiled at Ida.

'Not exactly,' Christian snorted. 'So, where are you taking all these animals anyway? Have you become Noah now?'

'Please, Christian,' Ida pleaded. 'Stop it!'

'Enough of this cartoon! We were all just fine on the roof. Weren't we, Ida?' Christian stood up, walked to her and placed his hands on her shoulders. Then, he stared at Sven. 'Could you at least have stopped the boat before hitting the building? Now, we have no ways of escaping. We are all trapped here including yourself. There's only more of us and less supplies,' Christian said and caressed Ida's hair.

Ida only pulled away in disgust.

'You take your hands off her!' Sven stepped beside Christian and puffed his chest.

'It's not the first time I'd lay my hands on her while up here on this roof,' Christian smiled.

Ida cringed. 'How cay you say these things!?'

That was the final straw for Sven. He clenched his fist and threw the first straight right that Christian blocked. Next, an uppercut from Christian on Sven's chin that dropped him to the roof. Christian jumped on top of him. They began rolling around on the roof from side to side, throwing weakening punches at each other's bodies. The days without proper food and rest had taken the sharpest edge out of them both.

'Why are you dressed up like a woman, you wuss!?' Sven smirked.

'Because Ida likes it! Why do you fight like a woman?' Christian fired back.

Everyone else had gathered around them like spectators of a fight club.

'I... t-t-told you!!' Erm...ine snorted and jumped on the table to get a better view.

'Crazy, but entertaining,' Squirr-el said and raised herself above them all to see better.

'Stop it!' Ida screamed from the top of her lungs.

But her desperate pleads went onto deaf ears as the men scuffled. Not even a bright beam appearing on the sky and illuminating the entire roof top halted the two brawlers. The light blinded everyone else staring at it. They had to cover their vision behind their forearms and palms. Soon though, the gleam faded so that the least sensitive ones could open their eyes again. They saw an object travelling across the skies, leaving a white trail behind.

A familiar phrase echoed on the skies. 'Ho! Ho! Ho!'

Chapter 68

# CHRISTMAS MAGIC

Wavy patterns of green and red Aurora Borealis served as a backdrop for a sleigh of a white-bearded man and his single reindeer, when they began the descent on top of the post office. The group occupying the roof tucked away to different corners to create landing space. Only Sven and Christian remained tussling in the middle. Not until a big shadow covered them and they felt draft of the sleigh hovering above, the two brawlers stopped the fight and rolled to opposite sides.

'Aliens!?' Christian groaned while staring at heavens.

As the skis of the sleigh touched the roof, the entire structure beneath cracked and wobbled. The load had reached or exceeded the limits the building was designed to shoulder. They were soon to find out which one. The driver jumped on the roof and repeated, 'Ho! Ho! Ho!'

'Fa...fa...father C-C-Christmas?' Erm...ine stuttered.

'Indeed!' said the bearded man.

'The real Father Christmas?' Marjukka asked with a hint of suspicion.

'As real as it can be,' the man said convincingly, went to rummage through his backseat and picked a two big red sacks tied with Miller's Knots. He dropped the bags in front of everyone.

They all gasped.

Two scruffy looking men wearing elf's hats appeared in the backseat once the bags were gone.

'Aariak!' Jaaku jumped up joyfully as he recognised the men. 'And the bartender!'

'It's Tomas,' Marjukka said.

'How is this possible?' Jaaku asked and went to embrace Aariak. 'Have you become an elf?'

'No,' Aariak laughed. 'Santa here stopped along the way and picked us up. Since the tsunami hit, we've been trapped on the roof of the Arctic Bar.'

'Santa came at the eleventh hour,' Tomas said. 'We were on the brink of hypothermia.'

'And the only thing we could do was to drink Wodka,' Aariak added, 'which by the way, doesn't make you any warmer, despite what people think or say.'

Jaaku smiled and waved away the toxic fumes of alcohol. 'How good to see you, brother.'

'Ho! Ho! Ho!' the Santa intervened. 'It is again that time of the year. A Christmas Eve. Have we got any nice kids here?' He observed the diverse looking group surrounding him. 'Or childlike adults?'

Overwhelmed, the men and women stared at each other. Over the years, they all had seen so many versions of good and bad fake Santa's from house visiting social workers to failed actors in the shopping malls, trying to impersonate the most powerful man in the world for the sake of managing to pay their own rents. But this man was not an actor, or if he was, he did a darned good job and had the best props in the world. His costume was immaculate, the sleigh stylish and reindeer flightworthy.

'I believe we have many reasons to celebrate tonight,' Santa started. 'First of all, you have all fought for survival and helped each other's as well as strangers to you. Now we can only do our utmost to have a Merry Christmas together and give one another strength, joy and happiness, despite these difficult circumstances. We are all here for a reason tonight. I want to reward you all for your hard work, your great values and goodness you have all shown this year.'

'You really think... we've all been good this year?' Ida asked and glanced at Sven.

Santa raised his eyebrow. He noticed Sven's bruised lip and

Christian's blackened eye from their scuffle. 'That's something, of course, I have to check from...' he winked his eye and reached for one of his bags, 'my Good Book!'

Everyone gasped again.

'Is there anywhere I could sit down?' Santa asked politely.

Birgget pulled out one of the dining chairs and offered it to Santa.

'Thank you, Birgget,' Santa said.

*He knows my name,* Birgget smiled.

Santa sat down and pulled another dining chair next to him. He took the Good Book on his lap, opened it and began examining the first page. 'Who do we have here again?' He browsed the pages. 'Could you help me out a little bit... Ida?'

'Me?' Ida said in disbelief.

'Please. Come and join me. You can read the names.'

Hesitantly, Ida moved next to Santa. Santa gave her a red elf hat to wear and the Good Book to examine. But all the print and scribble was small and messy. The first open spread was filled with hundreds and thousands of names of people.

'What does that say?' Santa pointed at one of the scribbled names.

'It says... Pole Vault,' Ida squinted her eyes. 'That wouldn't make any sense.'

'Pole Vole,' Jaaku corrected.

In a matter of seconds, Pole Vole demonstrated his elasticity and jumped on the chair next to Santa.

'So, Pole Vault... my book says you have been a very good rodent this year. Is that true?'

Pole Vole looked at everyone and then, nodded.

'Good! What would you like for Christmas then?'

'Well, Father Christmas, during these recent days hassle and dazzle, I have lost my favourite pole. Since then, I've been a... poleless vole,' Pole Vole said with saddened eyes.

'Don't say no more. Let me guess,' Santa said and his hand wondered into the big red bag. 'Let's see what we have here for Pole Vault.' He stir his hand inside the bag, 'Yes. You have been a very good rodent this year. Here is a brand new pole for you.' Santa pulled out a half a metre long, light brown bamboo stick.

Pole Vole couldn't believe his eyes, neither did anyone else.

Ida could only shrug her shoulders and spread her arms.

'And who do we have next?' Santa asked and pointed at another name in the book.

'Squirr...' Ida tried to read.

'...El. Squirr-El,' Sven added.

Squirr-El took a big leap directly on Santa's knee.

'And what would you like for Christmas, little flying squirrel?'

'I would like a... bag of peanuts!' she said determined while puffing her chest.

Again, Santa reached into his magic sack. 'Since you have been a really good squirrel this year, I have some... superpeanuts that give you invincible superpowers throughout the year.'

Squirr-El's eyes lightened and biceps flexed. Suddenly, she felt energised, like on her heyday, even though she hadn't even tried any of the superpeanuts yet. She thanked Santa, grabbed the bag from him, flew in the corner of the roof and cracked open the first peanut shell with her tail. A glowing, dark brown superpeanut appeared full of goodness of proteins and energy, something dangerous for a normal squirrel and only to be consumed by supersquirrels like Squirr-El. She was the chosen one. *Bliss*, she felt, as she savoured one superpeanut after another, giving her the ultimate powers she felt she had lost long time ago. She was back.

Santa moved on giving More Weasel less but bigger presents than Less Weasel who got more but smaller.

Erm...ine asked and got lots of books. She loved to read and write rather than have conversations, understandably.

Links was given a combo pack: a new virus protection software and a rabies vaccination. The latter, just in case. And a new laptop, of course. Links was a very lucky lynx.

Yetilag asked for 'Yaaaawnnn!' and got it, too. Another Yetilag's wish, a chance to meet the real Father Christmas, had already come true. Together with Links, they had flown thousands of kilometres to meet him and suddenly here he was, Yetilag overshadowing him in size, yet Santa's presence, persona and authority made even Yetilag seem like a little child next to him. In fact, this one particular day of the year, they all felt like little children.

Next came Pie Polar Bears' turn. They received their own pie making machine.

Looking at the relatively small size of Santa's gift bags, it never stopped to amaze them how all these surprises fitted inside them. He was the man himself, there was no question about that. This Santa was truly enjoying his work and knew what he was doing. He gained even more confidence from seeing the happiness on the faces of the "children". The famous Christmas magic was utterly present. As if all this, everyone gathering, was part of a something pre-planned by more powerful forces.

There was nothing this Santa couldn't master. Like a dating coach he was, when he brought Marjukka and Jaaku closer together by asking them simultaneously, what they wanted?

Naturally, they both wanted to find someone.

'Hey, I remember you!' Marjukka said, looking at Jaaku beside her. 'We went on a...' she started, but awkwardly stopped the sentence.

'Yes,' Jaaku said bluntly.

'I'm sorry. I was really... I had to...'

'Don't worry. No need to explain. Maybe we can... try again once all this is over?' Jaaku asked shyly.

Marjukka looked away, but smiling, though.

'What about him? Viljo?' Sven intervened the awkward moment. He pointed at the mattress where Viljo was resting. 'Would you have something for the old man?'

'I already gave him some medicine, but not sure if it's working,' Marjukka said.

'I think I may have something stronger,' Santa said, stood up and took one of the sacks with him. He walked to Viljo and knelt next to him. 'Has he been a good man this year?' he asked and looked over his shoulder.

All eyes turned to Sven.

'He has been... a great man,' Sven said, lips trembling. 'The best of all. A true hero.'

Santa nodded and his hand went into the bag. He pulled out a bottle of ice cold Arctic Wodka. He uncorked the bottle and poured a few drops on Viljo's dry lips. Then, he opened Viljo's mouth and poured some more. And a bit more.

Impatiently, they all awaited, until Viljo's loud coughing broke the silence. Viljo opened his eyes and the first thing he saw after recovering was Santa's white-bearded face. His eyes widened. 'Am I in hell?' he gasped, grabbed the bottle and took a large gulp himself.

'It could be worse,' Santa smiled.

*Unbelievable,* Sven thought and shook his head.

Santa stood up, walked back to his designated chair and without even consulting Ida first, he asked, 'And, what would you like for Christmas, Birgget?'

Birgget stood in the shadow of Yetilag, sobbing quietly. 'I think I got it already. I got my son back.'

Touched by her lovely wish, Sven went to embrace her.

'Fair enough,' Santa said. 'But you know you can always change your mind.'

'I wouldn't change my mind about that,' Birgget laughed and cried at the same time.

Santa looked around if he had missed anyone. One by one, he had filled everyone's dreams and wishes like in the fairy tales or romantic comedies. 'Who do we have left?'

'I guess you never received our letters, Santa?' Sven said and looked at Ida.

She only shook her head and pointed below at the flooded post office.

'Do you remember what was written in those letters?' Santa asked. 'What is it you really want the most?'

Sven's face grew serious. He looked down to his feet. 'I don't think I deserve anything.'

'Don't talk nonsense,' Birgget said and tapped his back. 'You're a hero.'

'I'm not,' Sven shook his head. 'A true hero saves everyone. I should have made him stay with us and not on that freezing island. We could have fit one more person on the boat. We could have...'

'No,' Viljo's harsh voice interrupted his cry. Still lying on the mattress under the blanket with his gift bottle, he had remained conscious with the help of a few more mouthfuls. 'You did the right thing. The boat couldn't have hold a one single person more. I know. It is... or it was my boat and I know it better than any of you do. It would have sank with any extra load. Roar did the right thing. And so did you, Sven. If anyone here deserves presents, that is him. He saved us all. So many lives. Look at all these animals. Us here. He sailed the last stretch when everyone else was out of the game. We are all here, alive, because of Sven,' Viljo finished his speech and had another sip.

'It was...' Sven said shyly, 'a team effort.'

Santa nodded approvingly. 'Tell us then, Sven. What would you like for Christmas?'

Birgget rested her arm on Sven's shoulder and gave him an encouraging nod. 'Go on then. Make a wish.'

Sven looked at the others, looked at Ida. They all waited impatiently. 'I would like...' he tried to remember items they had written on the wish list with Ida months ago. There were fishing rods, tackle and nets. All fishing related. He tried to think outside the box. *A kicksled, a snow shovel, world peace.* There were so many things he wanted or had wanted, unlimited amount of stuff that would make him happy at least for a little while. But what could be more permanent and infinite? He had made an effort to write such a long list for Santa that was now wasted somewhere in the depths of the lake. Right below them in fact, sunken wet and unreadable. However, not even half of the list came to his mind, yet at this moment anything earthly or materialistic seemed unimportant. He wanted something that money can't buy.

Santa already had his hand inside the sack, as if he knew Sven's answer. As if he had every possible gift prepared inside. *What if I'd say a rabbit or a tractor, would he pull those out of the sack? One or the other. Does he really have... everything in that bag?*

Then, the idea of what he really wanted came to him. Something even the most filthy rich cannot buy. Something he had lost, twice, yet he doubted was in Santa's bag. 'I want to find my father again.'

Santa's hand froze inside the bag that second. He looked up

at Sven. 'Ah.'

'I want my father to be here with us. I know he is still out there somewhere. I can feel it.'

Everyone stared at Santa's reaction and waited for the hand to come out of the bag. Blushing, he pulled an empty hand out. There was no Roar sitting on Santa's palm or hiding inside his bag.

As much as Sven wanted Santa to make all of their dreams come true, he was old enough to understand that life was not perfect, not even the Christmas magic. 'But I know it won't happen,' he said, disappointed. 'So, may I have a new pair of oars... or something? Doesn't matter. Just anything... to do with fishing. Whatever. A new fishing rod?' he mumbled and walked away to the corner of the roof, angry and bitter at himself for leaving his father behind. Biting his teeth, he sat facing away from the others. He looked out on the lake, feeling Roar's presence.

Ida followed and sat next to him. 'I'm so sorry, dear. It must be hard. I wish there is something I could do.'

'I appreciate that, but there's nothing you or anybody can do. I just have to live with it. I thought I had him for a while. I had missed him so much for all these years. And knowing that he was still there, but I couldn't keep him, just breaks my heart... again.' Sven dropped his head down between his knees and cried like a little child, or someone who has lost a loved one forever.

Ida embraced him tighter. 'We can go and look for him. You know where you left him?' Ida asked and kissed the top of Sven's head.

'How?' Sven sobbed. 'We have no boat. We are all just stranded here on this tiny roof. By the time someone will come and rescue us, if ever, my dad will be somewhere frozen to the bone. The leftovers of the Christmas meal is all we have, unless that Christian in tights has finished everything by now. We will all be trapped here with all our stupid Christmas presents!'

'Please, don't say that. There's always hope. What if Santa would give you... a new boat? You know he can make every wish come true.'

'Well, he didn't pull Roar out of the bag. Do you think he could fit a boat in there?'

'I have a better idea,' Santa interrupted, standing behind Sven and Ida. 'Since I am the real Father Christmas, I can fulfil every wish and especially yours, since you have been an extraordinarily good boy this year, a hero, if I may quote. And you have a big heart. You have done such a great deed for the community of Pihtamo. Besides, not everything has to be written on the list. People are entitled to change their minds about their wishes last minute. And my job is to fulfill those requests. If that is what you want for Christmas, you shall have it and it is my responsibility to deliver it.'

'You're gonna give me a boat?' Sven snorted.

'Not a boat, but something better and faster. But I may need your help on this one. Both of you, Ida and Sven,' Santa said, grabbed his bags and walked to his sleigh. He jumped on the front seat. 'Get ready, Rhein Deer!'

'Where are you going?' Sven asked.

'What about... my present?' Christian appeared from the shadow.

'He wants leggings,' Jaaku witted.

They all laughed.

'I will sort you out later, naughty boy,' Santa pointed at Christian.

'What about a present for my brother?' Jaaku asked.

'Don't you worry. We got ours on our way here,' Aariak said and rolled a new set of metal hand cuffs around his finger.

'And I got a sample bottle of new Arctic Wodka that is not even in the market, yet,' Tomas said. 'I have no idea how Santa got a hold of it. It was supposed to be introduced next year.'

'Don't ask,' Santa smirked and made himself comfortable on the front seat of the sleigh. 'I believe you are all sorted now. It has been a pleasure meeting you all. We are going on a little journey now. Hop on my little helpers,' he said and looked at Sven and Ida.

Sven and Ida gave each other a confused look. 'Us?'

Santa nodded. 'And you, wear this one, too.' He threw Sven a red elf hat, similar to the one Ida was already wearing. 'You're not stepping on this sleigh without an elf's hat.'

'Of course not. That would be a disgrace,' Sven chuckled. He chucked his own hat away and replaced it with the red hat.

Sven and Ida hopped at the backseat of the sleigh, sat down tight next to each other and tucked beside the gift bags. They covered themselves under a thick, woollen blanket.

'I missed your embrace,' Ida said and put her head on Sven's shoulder.

'I missed you, too,' Sven replied and smiled.

Santa pulled the reins and the sleigh started moving.

'So, where are we going, Santa?' Sven asked.

'We are going to look for your father.'

Chapter 69

# SLEIGH RIDE

The flight path of the sleigh led above many snowy islands and ice bergs of different sizes and shapes. Some of them, looking down from the sky, seemed similar but not identical enough to the one Sven remembered them leaving Roar. The frost biting the lake surface connected some of the existing pieces of ice to one another further complicating the search. The increasing snowfall didn't help either.

'*Deutschland, Deutschland!*' the reindeer sung firmly, leading the sleigh over the lake.

'German reindeer?' Sven asked.

'Yes, indeed,' Santa said while pointing his eyes strictly ahead. 'The Germans came to Pihtamo during the war to breed reindeers. A special battalion from *Rheinland* wanted to create a master breed of reindeers to reinforce their troops. They called them, Rhein Force Deers, a super reindeer. The wartime generation reindeers were strong and fast. Everything they hit with their antlers, they destroyed. You can still recognise signs of those powerful genes in their descendants like Rhein Deer here with his outstanding physical capabilities.'

'He sure looks well build,' Sven observed. 'Glad we didn't bring Viljo with us, though.'

'Why is that?' Santa asked.

'Seems like he has some old score to settle with them, the Germans.'

'Don't we all?' Santa smirked.

Meanwhile, Ida leaned over the side. 'Have you got any recollection of where your father was left behind?'

Sven shook his head. 'It was just like any other floating piece of ice you see down there. Although there was a steep, snowy hill in the middle which is probably difficult to detect from above. And now everything below is turning white. Even Yetilag's plane wreckage sunk through the ice.'

'Maybe there's still a big hole in the ice where the plane went through?' Ida suggested.

'I doubt it. The weather has been getting colder. The hole's probably frozen shut,' Sven said worriedly.

'Your father is a capable man. He survived years and years alone in the wild,' Santa comforted.

'You knew him?' Sven asked.

'Of course I do. I know... everyone.'

Sven nodded, dazzled. He looked down to the ground. 'I often wondered what my dad really wanted for Christmas? He always said that he needs nothing. Or socks. But there must have been more. However, you must have taken some sort of vow of secrecy not to share such a classified information.'

'It's not rocket science, Sven. First and foremost, he wanted a happy family. He was a good man. He also thought about the community's best interest, always, and doing the best for people in Pihtamo whether before or after his disappearance. The best present for your father in this day and age is yours and your family's understanding and forgiveness.'

'I do forgive him. I understand now what happened. I'm just glad to know he is alive. Or I hope still is.'

'You are a good son. The awareness of that should give him strength to survive.'

Santa's attempt to lay hope on Sven somewhat succeeded, yet Sven didn't respond. He nodded and leaned further over the edge as the sleigh winded above the area. Most of the lake was now covered in ice with a thin layer of snow on the top. The entire scenery was turning white. There were no trails, contrasting colours or landmarks. It was supposed to be the lake he knew the best, yet it seemed like a place he had never seen before.

The highlands and the mountains became visible in the distance. Sven stood up amazed, but immediately Santa ordered, 'Sit down! Haven't you read the sign!? That's dangerous!'

'Ah, sorry.' Sven dropped down on his seat. 'It is just that I haven't seen land for so many days.'

'I never thought you would be so interested about land,' Ida smiled.

'I think I've learned to appreciate it. There's been enough water in my life for past days. A little too much I would say.'

Ida couldn't believe what she was hearing.

In the middle, the volcano rose. And flocks of people having escaped the floods scattered on the slopes, exactly as Squirr-El had described.

'That's where I'm heading next to give presents,' Santa pointed at the survivors. There were large groups having had set up camps and tents. Some huddled outside to keep warm. A few huts on the hillside had smoke coming out of their chimney pipes. The windows glowed light in the middle of all the darkness. As if the buildings were filled with a few extra visitors in need for a place to stay. Perhaps some who had lost their homes. From the distance, however, the atmosphere on the ground seemed somewhat warm and peaceful, despite the catastrophic conditions.

'A new life,' Ida said serenely.

'It's a good and fertile ground down there to resettle,' Santa said.

Sven and Ida gave each other a confused look. All his life Sven had lived by the coast and he couldn't think of anything else, especially, not resettlement inland and starting a new life. They both understood that nothing would be the same anymore. Everything old that they once knew was gone, destroyed, lying deep underwater. The lives of many effected would have to be restarted elsewhere. Or completely rebuild from the scratch. Would there be fishing industry anymore? What would their lives look like once all this is over? Change was inevitable, yet unimaginable. One thing in life Sven hated the most was *heading towards the unknown*. But now it seemed there was no other way. He had to start considering other career paths to secure their survival: farming animals, growing barley and rye, hunting game. But what if the animals he would be slaughtering have a voice like the ones they had rescued? It was too early to try and understand what that new life would look like.

He went through his trouser pocket and came across the map his father had given him before they separated, the map of the pond Roar claimed he had transported all rescued herrings. If he couldn't locate the pond and retrieve all that fish, Lake Pihtamo will be history. Only a large, dead sea would remain. All fish would have to be replanted and it would take ages for the lake to provide enough for every fisherman and their families. Nice for boating and water sports though, if not too cold, and an interesting reminder of the glorious past that everyone could only read in the history books and Wikipedia. But a graveyard, a ghost lake and a bitter memory for those real fishermen, herringmasters and the champions, like Roar, Viljo and Sven himself, who once felt pride of their career choices and got to enjoy the enormous success the bountiful lake gave them.

Sven leaned over the edge again. 'There was no land nearby where we left my father. There was absolutely nothing, except a few pieces of ice floating. He's not here. We can go away, back on the outer lake,' he hesitated. He began to lose trust whether they would ever find him. Already a large lake had doubled or tripled in size and they were looking for a small, malnourished older man. Like searching for a needle in the hay stack. From the aerial view, Lake Pihtamo seemed like the Arctic Ocean.

In addition, Santa Claus was under time pressure. He manoeuvred the sleigh back towards the middle of the lake. As they turned away from the mountainside, the people on the ground waved at them to come back, causing him even more stress. 'We really haven't got much time. I have lots of presents to deliver and it's getting late.'

'I understand. Just a few more minutes,' Sven sighed.

As they reached the open lake, Santa started circling eights around the area. 'Can you see anything?' he asked impatiently.

Sven saw no signs. He looked at Ida with saddened eyes.

Ida responded with an embrace. 'I'm sorry. So sorry.'

'How could I've been so stupid?' I had him. What kind of

idiot loses his father, twice?'

'Don't be too hard on yourself. He did what was best for you... as he has always done.'

'I'm sorry, Sven. Ida. I have to take you two back. I have the entire world to deliver. I hope you understand,' Santa said and turned the sleigh to the direction of the post office. 'We can only pray for your father.'

'I knew it!' Sven sobbed to Ida's ear. 'No difference to any other shopping mall Santa. Just all fake who cannot keep their promises. Even my late granddad was better Santa. I have been good this year, haven't I?'

Ida nodded and caressed Sven's neck as he slouched down on the seat.

Santa didn't need an elf to eavesdrop Sven's complaint. However, he tried to ignore it as painful as it may have sounded. He understood Sven's frustration. He wished he could help more. If Sven felt he had failed to stay with his father, Santa felt he had failed in his task, too. He couldn't keep his promise to deliver the present for Sven, the present he had specifically asked for.

All three sat in silence. The mood had dropped another notch. The sky was at its darkest. The stars laid across the black canvas. The shooting sleigh left a glittering trace behind. Any fancy special effect, however, didn't help restore the already ruined atmosphere. Father Christmas had let Sven down. *Or perhaps I wasn't that good boy after all,* Sven thought. *But it happens. It's life. You don't always get what you want. Get used to it.* And he was used to it. Again something he had learned from an early age having grown up without a father.

Melancholically, Sven stared at the full moon, the glimmering constellations and the fading Northern Lights. The brief moment spent with his father had given him some sort of peace of mind. If Roar was gone forever, at least they had spoken. No more uncertainty or big open questions. Roar learned that he is in love and he is married. He knows now why Roar left in the first place. And that Roar had forgiven Birgget's past mistakes. He had the answers they all were seeking for.

Sven tried to be positive. So many children were not even this lucky. He had a father who cared and wanted to be with his family, but was taken away, once, against his own will, and the second time, of his own choice to save the others.

As much as Sven tried to suppress the pain, still a few remaining tear drops began flowing from his emptying reserve. Ida took him in her arms and wiped the tears before they would freeze. Under enormous pressure, relatively introverted, Arctic man had surprised everyone including himself with an array of emotions he could portray in a short period of time from anger to sadness. But now there was nothing left to be said or done. *There's always hope, even when the hope is gone*, he remembered the last life lesson his father had taught him before his first disappearance, now seventeen years ago.

As he took a glance at the lake for the very last time, he noticed a flickering dot below them. He rubbed his dried-up eyes and looked again. This time, he saw a sharp, penetrating light shining straight up like a laser beam. He raised his head higher and hung his body over the edge to get a better look.

'What are you doing?' Ida said, concerned.

'I said, no standing!' Santa repeated.

'There's something down there,' Sven leaned farther over.

'Maybe it's the Northern Lights reflecting off the snow,' Santa said. 'Now, please sit down, will you.'

'Snow doesn't reflect light like that. You, if anyone should know that,' Sven said, his heart pumping faster. He lowered himself on the seat, but kept his eyes focused at the beam. Eventually, the light dimmed and vanished behind them. Sven snorted and sunk lower, but as he did, he remembered something long forgotten. A story from his childhood. He turned to Ida. 'You know... I had this funny thought. When I was a child, my father always carried this old mark coin with him that, apparently, saved his life once he was ice fishing in Greenland. He got trapped in the middle of a snow blizzard. So what he did to survive, he had left the mark outside a bear's den where he went to stay warm next to the sleeping polar bears, hoping someone would eventually find him. He thought the shiny mark coin outside the den could reflect light to the rescuers like a little lighthouse. And eventually he was discovered alive. Can you believe it?'

'Bear's Den Mark,' Santa said and glanced at Sven over his

shoulder. 'An old Danish urban legend.'

'My father told you the story, too?'

'I have heard it from many different sources. It's a classic. Everybody knows the story.'

'Really? I always thought it really happened to him.'

'Maybe he wanted to be your hero... like most fathers do in the eyes of their children,' Santa said and faced forward again.

Sven's jaw dropped. From all those made-up stories from Easter witches to tooth fairies his parents had used to brainwash him since he was a toddler, Bear's Den Mark was the only one he still believed in. Until now, when Santa revealed the truth. *Bear's Den mark was fake news!* He couldn't trust anyone or anything anymore. Not even his own father.

'I'm afraid we have to start heading back,' Santa said seriously. 'The others, the world is waiting. I'm sorry. So sorry.'

'But... you promised me my father! Typical! Sven snorted. 'No difference to any shopping mall Santa's.'

'Sven, please. Don't speak to Santa like that,' Ida said. 'He's only trying to do his job.'

Santa said nothing, but only kept looking ahead and hid his anger as well as his disappointment to himself for letting someone down. It was a common, negative emotion he had to deal with every single Christmas. There was always someone who didn't get what they wanted and they complained. It was part of the job, part of the impossible equation of having seven billion people in the world and only one man responsible of delivering all the presents. The stress and pressure he had to carry on his shoulders were enormous, something unbearable. No matter how hard he worked and always thought he did his best, yet he felt insufficient, as if he wasn't doing enough. Only Mother Christmas and the very few elves knew how hard he really worked. He genuinely wanted everyone to have a jolly and merry Christmas. Unfortunately, this one with Sven and Ida was turning into a disaster.

'Or... I have an idea,' Sven said, more calmly.

'We can't go back,' Santa said.

'You'll leave us the presents that belong to the people of Pihtamo and the surrounding areas. Me and Ida will be your little helpers and deliver the presents to everyone on the mountains. You can trust us the task.'

'Why are you doing this?' Santa asked.

'To give you more time to deliver the presents to the rest of the world... and so that we can go back and check that one stupid piece of floating ice where the light beam was shining. Otherwise, we've departed this journey for nothing, and instead, we could be enjoying a good Christmas meal with the others. Now, there's probably no ham left anyway, because that halfwit Christian has munched everything, so what's the point going back? All I asked was to have my father back for Christmas and you promised, Santa. You promised. You even said that I've been an extra special good this year. My name was in that book. You knew my name without even consulting Ida first. My name was in that book before you even arrived to the post office,' Sven said with great confidence. 'That's all I need. Only to check that source of light and we're done. Then, you can wipe my name off the Good Book forever, if you wish. Maybe, next year I get you into some trouble again, so better for you to take precaution now. I promise this will be my last wish from you ever... to ask you to do what you think is right.'

Santa didn't reply. He sighed and looked at his watch. 'What is... right?' under his breath, he asked himself.

Sven waited impatiently. Ida squeezed his trembling hand.

'Mother Christmas will... kill me for this!' Santa said, turned the sleigh around and back to the direction they had seen the light.

'Thank you, Santa. Thank you so much,' Sven composed himself. 'This will do as my Christmas present... whether we find something or not. I will ask you no more.'

'You better not ask,' Santa mumbled in his beard, *and you better not cry*. He picked up the reins and urged Rhein Deer at full speed.

A moment later the light appeared again. 'Can you see it now?' Sven pointed at the twinkle and stood up.

'I can see it,' Ida peered, extending her neck. 'It's coming from a snowy island.'

The sleigh begun its descent towards the light. Looking

from a bird's-eye view, the island seemed much smaller and the hill in the middle much flatter than Sven remembered. 'Slowly.'

'I know what I'm doing. I've been flying these things for hundreds of years.'

'Yes, but... we don't want to... disturb anyone,' Sven advised.

'Why are you standing again?' Santa glanced behind him, as they circled above the hill.

'There's something down there and...' Sven, before he finished the sentence, lost his balance and fell over the edge, yet clinging onto one of the runners like a stunt man of an action movie.

'Sven!' Ida screamed and tried to grab Sven's wrist.

'I told you!' Santa slowed down. 'I'm gonna bring the sleigh down, you hear me!? I'm trying to find a soft spot, in case you can't hold on much longer.'

'What did he say?' Sven asked Ida who was trying to pull him up.

'Santa's gonna land!' Ida yelled, feeling Sven's weight. He was too heavy for her. 'Hold on!'

'Hold it! Steady boy!' Santa gave orders to Rhein Deer. 'Slower!'

The beam was their only visual approach indicator. But their landing speed only grew, as Sven hanging in the ski only upset Rhein Deer's balance.

'Jump, Sven!' Santa shouted. 'Otherwise, we're gonna crash!'

'Jump, darling!' Ida screamed. 'I'm gonna let go.'

Sven gave Ida that last look, and then, let go of her wrist. His body somersaulted in the air before disappearing inside a thick pile of snow. Beside him, the sleigh crashed on top of another, thinner pile of snow. There was a complete silence. Sven couldn't breathe. He could only see white everywhere. He started fighting his way out. He kicked, punched and dug the moist walls around him. Eventually, he found freedom, fresh air. He rolled onto the ice and looked up. He was in front of an entrance to the cave. And the light source lay right in front of his nose. He shook his head and focused. It was a mark coin.

Chapter 70

# BEAR'S DEN

The coin was positioned exactly as in the bedtime story: neatly away from the snowfall under a protruding lid of ice built either naturally or purposefully on the edge of the cave entrance. The surface of the coin was flat facing the moon bridge and reflecting a beam of light back up in the skies.

Feeling like an old man with all his injuries, Sven slowly pushed himself upright. He clenched his teeth and tried to ignore the pain. As he got up, he picked up the coin with his mitt. He examined its authenticity. He bit the coin. He blew some cold air on it and rubbed it against his jacket. He tapped it on his shoe. It seemed like a real currency. The coin was dated on his birth year nearly thirty years back. He peered inside the cave and then back to the coin.

'Are you alright, honey?' Ida came and embraced him from behind.

'Never better,' Sven said thoughtfully, squeezing the coin inside his fist. 'How are you?'

'My bottom and neck are a little sore,' she said.

'And how's Santa?' he turned around.

'Santa is fixing the sleigh. I think Rhein Deer broke his leg,' Ida replied, but Sven wasn't listening. 'What's in your hand?'

Sven opened his palm.

'A coin?'

'A mark,' he said and looked at the cave entrance, 'Bear's

Den Mark.'

Her eyes widened. 'It is true? The story?'

'I don't know... but I'm soon to find out.'

'You're not going in there, are you?' she asked, concerned.

'Someone has to. I won't be long.'

'I'm coming with you,' she said.

'No. You're not, because... well... you know. You're carrying our child. But you can stay outside with Santa. If I'm not out in, let's say, five minutes, you go with Santa and...'

'I am not gonna leave you here!'

'Listen to me!' he squeezed her shoulders. 'We cannot risk you and the baby. You must stay safe. And Santa, too. You both have some delivering tasks coming up soon, if you know what I mean. You have already escaped the floods and spent days outside on the rooftop. No more danger for you!'

'You're as stubborn as your father. I don't wanna lose you twice like you didn't wanna lose him. You understand?'

'I must go and find out. Alone. It would be too dangerous and stupid to risk both of us. Our future child needs a parent. You will stay here and wait. If I'm not coming out, you will leave,' he said and gave the coin one last look. 'Don't worry. This mark will bring me luck.'

She looked down and frowned.

'Please forgive me,' he said and pocketed the coin.

'And this,' she looked up again and kissed him, but soon drew her lips away, 'should bring you luck, too.' She started walking backwards away from him while waving at the same time.

He blew her a kiss and turned around. Suddenly, his face turned grave, when he realised this might be the last time he will ever see her again. He looked over his shoulder once more, but she had already turned around towards the sleigh. He composed himself and pushed the negative thoughts aside. He disappeared through the dark entrance of the den. The wet slush mixed with frozen snow crackled under his boots. His clumsy effort to tiptoe made his footsteps even louder. Deeper inside he walked, the moon lit entrance behind him got smaller. Soon, it was pitch dark. 'Hello!' he called out, but only heard the echo responding. Like a blind man, he stretched his arms forward to feel any obstacle. The roof of the tunnel got lower and the walls nearer, forcing him to bend down. A sudden noise that resembled snoring echoed inside. He stopped to listen. Next, he heard growling, which got the ground trembling. Then, it got silent again. He took a few steps forward, until he felt softness under his boot. He took a step to the side and hit the soft spot again. He reached out his hands, and felt something furry and hairy. The growling repeated louder.

'Who is that!?' a familiar voice called out in the midst of all the roaring.

'Who is that?' Sven asked.

'Sven?'

'Dad?'

'Let's get outta here! Now!' Roar shouted. He rushed up clashing with Sven and stepping on his feet.

'I cannot believe it, dad!' Sven attempted to embrace him, but he pushed him away.

'Sorry. No time for this. This is bears' den and there are a couple of unhappy bears right next to us... or underneath us, literally. You have woken them up from their winter sleep. You woke me up, too.'

'Ah, sorry.'

'No. I'm very glad you did, but now we must run!' Roar pushed Sven from behind and off they went. Soon, the light shining through the entrance started to grow in the distance. The bears' heavy footsteps and roaring followed them closely. The layers of snow decorating the ceiling sprinkled on their heads and shoulders as they ploughed through the narrow tunnel. In an orderly queue, they raced towards the exit with two furious brown bears on their tail.

Sven came first flying out of the entrance. He slammed face down in the snow. 'Where are you? Dad!?' He stood up and looked inside the den.

Over the past days, Roar had weakened critically. He had fallen behind. The first bear was about to catch him and sink its claws on his back when Sven reached out his arm. In the last second before Roar was being mauled by the bear, Sven yanked him out of the den. Sven put his arm around Roar and together they trotted towards the sleigh.

'Run, Sven, run!' Ida cheered when she spotted Sven and Roar limping for life while being chased by the bears. She bounced nervously at the backseat.

Santa put away the half-eaten mince pie that he had started as a reward from fixing the sleigh. He picked up the fallen gift sacks, put them next to Ida and prepared for take off. Santa connected the trace and rein back on Rhein Deer. His only concern was Rhein Deer's current condition. He only had three out of four legs operational. Almost the same as one of the landing gears or engines were down.

'Have you got any more mince pies, Santa!?' Sven yelled, panting.

Santa checked his bag, pulled out another mince pie and chucked it on one of the bears' forehead. Distracted, both of the bears stopped running. As Sven and Roar reached the sleigh, the bears had already swallowed the pie. They threw the empty foil away and started gagging and spitting in disgust.

'Any more?' Sven hopped at the backseat next to Ida and helped Roar to the other side.

'That was my last pie, I'm afraid. It's been the worst Christmas ever so far. I'm sorry.'

'You should have saved them! I saw you eating one just now,' Sven said, frustrated.

'Don't be too hard on Santa, Sven,' Ida said. 'It's our job to leave them for Santa and he can eat them whenever he wants.'

'Fair enough. Those bears didn't seem too keen on pies anyway.'

Santa flicked the reins, but Rhein Deer didn't move. He flicked again, but Rhein Deer only apologetically looked over his shoulder. '*Geht nicht. Zu schwer.*'

'Ah, dear. We are too heavy,' Santa said. 'There's too many of us.'

'Not again,' Sven grunted. 'For such a skinny man, you weight a lot, dad. What have you been eating?'

'One of us have to leave behind,' Santa said.

'As if I've heard that before,' Sven snorted and looked

around. 'Well, no more, thank you! Enough is enough. There has to be another way to solve this.' He examined the inside of the sleigh while the bears approached threateningly, claws up and ready to attack. They were only some tens of metres away, when Sven came up with a suggestion. 'How about this sack here on our feet? We can get rid of that.'

'That's the Christmas presents to the children of...' Santa read the label tied to the ribbon, 'Canada.'

'Fine. That'll do,' Sven lifted the sack. 'Boy, it's heavy! Help me out, dad.'

Roar placed his hands underneath the sack beside Sven's and together they raised the Canadians' Christmas presents above their heads.

'Don't you dare!' Santa jumped up. 'Don't even think about it!'

'It weighs at least a ton! We must get rid of this. Otherwise, we'll all become bear food!' Sven insisted.

'If you do that, you will be in big trouble!' Santa panicked. 'I will be in trouble!'

Sven and Roar pulled the sack away from Santa's reach. Then, Sven looked at Ida, hoping she would justify their action. But she couldn't. She just sat there in silence unable to take sides. She spread her arms.

'I don't think we can be much more in trouble,' Sven said.

'Sven, Roar, give me the bag, please,' Santa demanded.

'I am so sorry, Santa... You have to give the Canadians something else instead... like...' Sven looked at Roar, he responded with a nod, and like father like son, together they threw the bag in front of the bears blocking their path, 'world peace!'

Aggressively, the bears tore the bag open revealing presents of different shapes and sizes. They began slicing the gift wrappings with their claws finding ice hockey sticks, pucks and gloves. One bear put a helmet on its head. The other, accidentally, slid its fingers open on the sharp blade of a skate. The bear growled in agonising pain, got furious, looked at Sven and thought they tried to harm them on purpose. Meanwhile, the other bear unwrapped a bottle of maple syrup, opened the bottle and started suckling it like a little cub.

'My days are over...' Santa covered his face under his palms.

'Don't worry. Canada is one of the richest nations in the world. They have everything. They should rather give away,' Sven tapped Santa on the shoulder.

'You think we can take off now... or should we get rid of more presents?' Roar examined another name tag. 'Here's one sack for people of... Sweden?'

'No more throwing away presents!' Santa ordered. He realised there was nothing they could do to save the Canadians' presents. They were all ruined. And the wounded bear was after them. 'I believe we can fly this thing now, don't you think, Rhein Deer?'

Rhein Deer gave Santa a tired nod and tried to change their direction, but the approaching bear kept blocking the runway. Rhein Deer shook his head, concerned.

'The runway is not long enough for a take off,' Santa said, looking ahead.

'How long does it have to be?' Sven asked, dumbfounded. 'You managed to land and take off from the post office roof!'

'That we can do when Rhein Deer is feeling hundred percent,' Santa clarified.

Sven sighed in his mind, *German engineering at its finest!*

They were clueless how to get rid of the bears. Seemingly, these bears didn't like pies. The presents they had thrown away didn't distract them enough either.

Sven was almost desperate enough to shoot an animal, if they had a gun. Luckily, they didn't. He studied the sleigh if there was anything useful left, when his eyes glued on the dashboard. 'How about a sat nav?'

'What about it?'

'Just give it to me. I got an idea.'

'Enough of your ideas. I cannot do that,' Santa explained. 'Without my sat nav, I'll be forever lost and cannot deliver any of the presents. The world would end up in chaos.'

They could smell the approaching bear's breath as Sven stood up on the backseat, reached for the dashboard and forcefully yanked the sat nav off. This time, though, Santa was fast enough to intervene. He twisted Sven's wrist, and together, they flew overboard and ended up rolling in the snow.

'Stop it, you two!' Ida screamed.

Roar stepped out and separated them. Although the sat nav remained in the hands of Sven.

'I have an idea too. Will you listen to me!' Ida raised her voice and stood up. 'We should have a complete world atlas book on the roof of the post office, if no one hasn't burned it yet. Perhaps, if you Santa let Sven do whatever he wants to do with the sat nav and we give you the world atlas, so you can navigate your way around the world.'

'A guide book? Like a map?' Santa pondered. 'I haven't used them for years.'

'But you sure know how to use one, right?' Ida asked.

'Of course,' Santa said.

Sven looked at the sat nav in his hands. In a matter of seconds, he programmed a destination a couple of kilometres away and threw the gadget between the two bears. Once the gentle female voice started announcing directions from the sat nav's speaker, the wounded bear stopped advancing. 'In one hundred metres, bear left...' The bear went to pick up the sat nav. 'Make a u-turn,' the female voice spoke. 'Bear right in fifty metres,' the sat nav continued as the other bear approached from the right, about fifty metres away. The bears were soon united, and shoulder to shoulder they walked away towards the moonlight constantly following the instructions given by the navigator. 'In twenty metres, bear left.' They took the direction accordingly, turned left and plummeted over the ice's edge into the water. Panicking, they came out of the trance and realised they had not found more bears what-so-ever, as much as the gadget had promised them. They began kicking and climbing back on the ice, whereas the sat nav submerged underwater and its female voice gurgled its last guidance before shutting down completely.

'Now, we go!' Sven hailed.

They all jumped in the sleigh while the bears struggled to get a hold of the slippery surface. Rhein Deer took his first step on a clear runway ahead. Santa's heart ached when they glided past the unwrapped and damaged winter sports equipment. The soaked bears managed to climb back on the ice, but too late, as the sleigh took off right in front of their wet muzzles. Beaten by

the technology, the bears crawled back towards the den whilst picking up some of the Canadians' gifts on the way.

'Sven, I'm glad you didn't wanna save those bears as well,' Roar smirked, looking down.

'Ah, good point,' Sven said. 'Should we go back?'

'Don't!' Santa raised his finger. 'The bears have plenty of maple syrup to enjoy. Whole year's supply.'

They all laughed.

Chapter 71

# FIRST PRIZE

'You came back to me.'

'I promised, didn't I?'

'You saw the coin.'

'Indeed. Thank you for all those bedtime stories you told me when I was a child. They live in me forever, and tonight the favourite tale of all saved your life.'

Roar smiled subtly and closed his tired eyes.

Sven leaned on the back rest, Roar on one side and Ida on the other. 'Dad. Are you still awake?'

'I'm not sure. I think so.'

'I know this is a question Santa should ask you, but...'

'Go ahead, Sven. You've earned it,' Santa said.

Sven smiled and nodded to Santa. 'What would you like for Christmas, dad?'

'Hmm... Haven't really had time to think about it. Something to eat would be nice.'

'Let's hope we have some food left for you,' Ida said.

As Sven threw his arm over Roar's shoulder, his dad felt so small next to him. The difficult, recent experiences had drained them all, but Roar in particular. He had had the toughest times, first as the Lord of Herrings, and then in the end being trapped inside the den. Sven, momentarily, felt as if he had become the parent, and his father, the little son. As if the roles had suddenly changed, even though he knew they never will. Perhaps only equalise. Nevertheless, he felt a sense of responsibility growing that he knew he would be needing in the future being a father himself. 'Ida. Are you awake?' Sven gently elbowed her to the side.

'Now I am,' Ida said, eyes closed.

'What do you want for Christmas?'

'Now, you're pushing it,' Santa smirked.

'You started,' Sven replied, smiling.

Santa replied with a smile and let Sven enjoy his moment.

'I want you to... be quiet for a while,' Ida witted. 'You speak too much for a fisherman from Pihtamo.'

'I guess these recent weeks have been so action-packed that it makes even the most reserved men open up. Seriously, what do you want for Christmas?'

Ida opened her eyes and looked deeply into Sven's. 'I want you to... stay with me and never go away. Be a good father to your son. Be a good husband to me,' she said and pressed her warm lips to his.

Santa cleared his throat and kept looking straight ahead.

Roar pretended to be asleep, but knew well what was going on. He leaned on the opposite side away from Sven and Ida.

Ida pulled her lips away. She looked down and went through her pockets. 'Actually, I have something for you too... from Santa.'

'Really?' Santa said, confused.

'I hope not a.... bearded kiss?' Sven joked.

Ida handed Sven a little wrapped gift. 'I knew you'd come back.'

'But I already got everything. I have my family around me. Whole family.'

'Open it, please.'

Slightly uncomfortable of all the attention, Sven accepted the gesture with a subtle smile. He started unwrapping the red gift paper around. 'I only gave you a kiss. I didn't have a chance to buy you anything.'

'I totally understand. You were busy saving Pihtamo. Let that be your excuse,' Ida laughed.

Sven revealed the inside. 'My ice fishing gold medal! You've kept it all this time!' He raised the medal up in the air, showed it to Roar, but he only responded with a humming snore. Sven left him alone and turned to Ida, his eyes full of light and joy. 'Where did you find it?'

'It's Christmas time. It's magic,' Ida said.

'Thank you so much. I love you.'

'I love you, too.'

Sven embraced Ida and as he did so, he placed the gold medal gently around his father's neck, who was asleep, and who he thought deserved it more than anyone else.

Chapter 72

# ONE LAST HERRING

Separated from the rest of the party, Sven stood in the corner of the roof waving at Santa flying past the full moon to complete his duties.

'What are you doing here all by yourself, son?' Roar stepped beside Sven and put a hand on his shoulder.

'Nothing. It's just...' Sven's voice trembled.

'I know. Everyone is here. What you always wanted, right?'

'Sure,' Sven said hesitantly.

'I'm not convinced. What's wrong?'

Sven stared in the distance. There was an unusual calmness on the surface of the lake, nothing like in the recent days. He looked up at the sky. Roar did so, too. The snowfall had ended and the clouds had given room for more visible constellations. A shooting star fired across, followed by another.

'Make a wish, son.'

'Dad...' Sven turned to his father, looking serious.

'You know you can tell me anything,' Roar said.

'It's still out there. Free.'

Roar faced away and looked at the waters. 'I know.'

'We don't know its powers, what it's capable of. What if there are more of them? You know how wolves are always in packs.'

'So do fish in schools.'

'Exactly. A perfect combination.'

'Dangerous combination. Lethal.'

'Lake Pihtamo will never be the same, until we stop this... Wolf Herring.'

'Wolferring.'

'We can do it together. You, me, Jaaku, Viljo. We are the best there is.'

'And perhaps some of those new friends of yours out there can help.'

'Yes! Let's do it. Finally, us together. The last fishing trip.'

'Or, perhaps, the new beginning.'

'So, what are we waiting for!? Let's go!' Sven grabbed the oars for the inflatable rescue boat, which was the last gift request along with a compass made by Christian before Santa went to deliver the presents to the rest of the world.

'Now?'

'Of course.'

'No. Tonight, we celebrate.'

'And?'

'Patience, son. It's Christmas time which means... I have one more thing I want to show you,' Roar took out a bundled newspaper hiding under his cloak and offered it to Sven. 'I want you to have this.'

'Didn't bother investing on the wrapping too much?' Sven smirked.

'It's about what is inside,' Roar said, remaining serious. He tapped the top of the wrapping.

'What is it? Fish and chips?' Sven said suspiciously and unwrapped the bundle, revealing a piece of a wooden stick. 'Your... I mean... The Lord's magic fishing rod?'

'The half what's left of it.'

'Thanks. What should I do with it?'

'The time will tell. It might come in handy.'

Sven examined the rod carefully inside the paper, but didn't dare to touch it.

'There's still some food left. Please come and join us, you two,' Birgget announced from the background.

'Come on. Let's eat,' Roar touched Sven's arm and stood up.

'Okay. Thanks, dad.'

Roar looked over his shoulder as he walked to the table. 'Merry Christmas, son.'

'Merry Christmas, dad,' Sven said, picked up the remains of the magic rod from inside the paper and used it to circle an eight in the air.